THE GIFT

BOOK 1 OF THE BLACK ANGEL TRILOGY

MIKE,
YOU INSPIRE ME! THANK
YOU FOR THE GREAT ADVICE.
ENJOY THE GIFT.
BLESSINGS W/ ALL OF
YOUR ENDEAVORS!

D. Lee Hatchett

AUTHOR @ BLACKANGELBOOKS.COM
EMAIL ME AFTER YOU MEET
THE CHARACTERS!

authorHOUSE™

1663 LIBERTY DRIVE, SUITE 200
BLOOMINGTON, INDIANA 47403
(800) 839-8640
WWW.AUTHORHOUSE.COM

First published by AuthorHouse 09/16/05

ISBN: 1-4208-7735-6 (sc)

Library of Congress Control Number: 2005907329

Printed in the United States of America
Bloomington, Indiana

This book is printed on acid-free paper.

DEDICATIONS

Thank you to my Lord and Savior Jesus Christ for "The Gift" of salvation.

My Past
This book is dedicated, in part, to the loving memories of my grandmother, Lucille Ricks Jones, and my father, Lee Allen Hatchett, Jr.

Thank you for your unconditional love and unceasing prayers.

My Future
This book is also dedicated to Olivia, Zachary, and Channing – continue to march onward and upward toward the light.

I offer you my unconditional love and unceasing prayers.

ACKNOWLEDGEMENTS

For providing "the look" – Thank you to Shannon Small, Dwayne Stephens, Ajene Jenkins, Quentin Odom, Anthony Johnson, Ken Meyer Jr., Ahad Pace, Joy Tyler, Ayesha Lakes, and Rameses.

For providing "the sound" – Thank you to Reco Griffin & Muson Artworx, Christopher Gaither, Aaron Arter, Johnell Easter, and Victoria Duruh.

For providing "the touch" – Thank you to Sheryl Chester.

And for taking "a taste" before it was completely prepared – Thank you Jodi Berry, Reginald Booker, Doris Hatchett, Talibah Mbonisi & New Moon Circle Book Club, Tia Jakes & Sistahs with Substance Book Club, and my personal angel, Lillie Hatchett.

PROLOGUE
STRANGE FRUIT

Cyrus was not like most young boys. He had never wanted to navigate his native bayou in search of her hidden treasures, or climb the old oak tree in his backyard to discover her ancient secrets. He could count the number of times that he had broken into a sweat, or run as fast as he could just because he could. His mother called him smart, while the old men said he was just a little *different*. Cyrus preferred activities of intellect, choosing to play in between complex words and conventional wisdom, yet today he found himself running, through the Georgia woods, faster than he ever had—running for his life.

His chest pounded in tandem with the trembling muscles in his legs, while hoof beats and thunder claps rounded out the percussive arrangement that resonated like a requiem. Rain and tears washed across his face and blurred his already failing vision.

"Cyrus! Cy-rus!"

A distant, fear-filled baritone penetrated the air like a tremor. Cyrus couldn't tell which one of his friends was calling, but was relieved to hear that at least one of them was still alive.

"Nathaniel? Oleander? Winston?" Cyrus cried between gasps for air. He listened hopefully for a response, but heard nothing between the hoof beats and thunder.

Cyrus' lungs and legs began to burn as he ducked and dodged, and twisted and turned through the wooded maze. Tripping over an exposed tree root, he fell forward into a muddy mixture of leaves and rocks. The barking of hound dogs added a scathing staccato to the sadistic symphony of human sport. He sprang up and glanced back into the faces of the wraithlike images—the ones that had been the subject of the elders' tall tales and night terrors. His left foot sunk

1

into a murky pool of mud. He pulled it free, stumbled, and then took a step with his right. Immediately he felt a sharp pain. Cyrus fell to the ground and cried out in shock when he realized that a broken branch had pierced his foot.

Cyrus clutched his foot, and felt the wetness of his blood seep through his shoe. He worked to free himself, but was abruptly interrupted. Before he could move, a rope was slipped around his neck, and tightened. In one quick movement his body was jerked upward, and then slammed back to the ground. He barely had time to react to the excruciating pain, before the rope jerked again, choking him. Suddenly his body was in motion, dragging across the cold, wet earth. Rocks and sticks dug into his flesh as the scenery above him blurred by.

In a brief moment of unselfish insanity, he wondered about his friends—and then his family. Images of pleasant faces and familiar places drifted before him like the June bug memories from his childhood. He danced dangerously close to the edge of unconsciousness. Then as suddenly as it had begun, the dragging stopped, and he found himself face up in a clearing of woods. The rain and thunder paused. The moon shone down and there was silence—as if Mother Nature was holding her breath between operatic choruses, anxiously waiting to see what would happen—what *could* happen next.

Cyrus felt the quivering of flesh against his flesh. He looked towards the source and realized that his hand was touching Oleander's bloody and bruised face. Both of Oleander's eyes were swollen shut—his nose was bloodied and grossly misshapen. Nathaniel and Winston were just a few feet away. Nathaniel was moaning softly, and writhing in pain, but thankfully still alive. Winston lay still and pale in the bitter, cold October night air. His dark eyes stared blankly like stagnant, yet reflective pools of nothingness.

"Where is it?" hissed a cold and jagged voice.

There was no response.

"Tell us where it is!"

The voice echoed off of Cyrus' soul, and sent a chill through his body.

"P-p-please let us go," Nathaniel begged. "We don't know—"

His pleas were interrupted by the crushing sound of rock against bone, and then there was blessed quietness. Fresh tears streamed down Cyrus' face as he mourned the death of his friend. And then he heard Oleander whisper faintly.

"Banjo—chur...ch"

Cyrus slowly covered Oleander's mouth, attempting to save their secret while most certainly ending Oleander's life. He couldn't help thinking how ironic it was that Oleander's last words, and his greatest loves, could be their undoing.

"I think this one said the church," another coarse voice yelled.

Almost immediately Cyrus felt Oleander being pulled away from him. He tried to reach for Oleander, or at least call out to him, but he couldn't get his faculties to work. He wasn't sure if he had actually managed to make a sound or only thought that he had.

"You got one more chance. Tell us where it is and we jus' might let you live. What about a church?"

"Why are you doing this?" Cyrus mumbled. As soon as he uttered the words, he felt the rope tighten around his neck.

"God, please just take me now," he prayed.

Then, Cyrus felt his body being jerked upward. The rope pulled tight and then slackened as hands touched him, almost in a caressing manner. For a brief instant he felt safe. But then the sensation of touch faded and his body began to swing, supported only by the rope around his neck. Cyrus felt his body rise and heave as his honey colored reality began to melt away. A vision of Winston, Nathaniel, and Oleander floating in midair like angels, awaiting the clarion call to heaven, flashed in front of him—ethereal, surreal, and then faint before fading to darkness. Cyrus welcomed death graciously as he bathed himself in the hereafter.

Black bodies swinging in the southern breeze.
Strange fruit hanging from the poplar trees.

- Billie Holiday

CHAPTER ONE

I love the soft wind's sighing.
Before the dawn's gray light.

My Loves – Langston Hughes

The short, fat, Latina nurse shuffled into the narrow, sterile, examination room. She shoved Matthew Meredith's file at the elderly doctor as if it had been an imposition for her to be asked to actually do her job. She huffed as she walked across the room. Her uniform was about a half-size too small, and the buttons seemed to beg for permission to relinquish the responsibility of holding in her bulk. There were folds and creases where her neck used to be, her stubby fingers looked like overstuffed sausages, and her ankles, which started where her calves left off, looked like thick stalks at the end of each leg. Whatever shape this woman might have had was long gone. And as if her appearance wasn't enough, she reeked of cigarette smoke and drugstore perfume.

"Here is the file you requested," she said, her voice thick with attitude. She never bothered to make eye contact with the doctor or his patients, as she backed out of the office.

Dr. Bryant shook his head, making a mental note to speak with her about her mannerisms—*again*. Then he looked down and reviewed the file for several minutes before commenting.

"Mrs. Meredith, we believe that your son might have—cancer."

The doctor's words were heavy, and stuck to the white walls and steel fixtures. Matthew felt light headed; his breath came to him in short gasps and his heart began to thunder in his chest. He could hear the doctor's words, but they didn't seem to register. Even still, he couldn't help but wonder why the white, wrinkled, gray-haired doctor was talking about him as if he weren't in the room. He swallowed hard, allowing things to sink in. Then surprisingly, Matthew's breathing leveled after a series of deep sighs, and an unsteady calm washed over him. His soul seemed to stutter and stop, the way the earth pauses before a devastating storm.

Matthew focused on the mirror across the room and examined his caramel colored skin—it looked fine. His sister, Olivia, had neatly and artistically cornrowed his six-inch Afro—it too, looked fine. He wondered if he would need chemotherapy and if it would make him lose his hair. He looked back in the mirror at his dark brown, slightly slanted eyes and long, angular features—*they* looked fine. More importantly, he *felt* fine—most of the time.

An abnormality found in his annual track physical exam was what had originally sent him and his mother to the doctor. Since then he had suffered the occasional loss of appetite, vomiting, and stabbing stomach pains. The doctors had recommended a series of tests over the last few months, but the Meredith's limited health benefits had slowed down testing progress. Eventually Matthew stopped mentioning the symptoms of his illness to his mother because she tended to overreact, and the cost of the doctor visits was starting to take a toll on the family.

"What do you mean these things can be complicated? I ain't crazy! You think I can't understand 'cause I ain't a doctor?" Isadora yelled, planting her hand on her hip. The high pitch of his mother's voice caused Matthew to reengage in the conversation that was taking place without him. "And why in the hell did it take you this long to find this out? I bet if your white son was in here you would have found out it was cancer a long damn time ago."

"Mrs. Meredith, you're overreacting," Dr. Bryant said, quietly, hoping to calm her.

"Overreacting? Overreacting?" Isadora Meredith's voice continued to get louder and louder. Her ratty Star Jones wig shifted slightly as she rolled her neck and waved her free hand in the air. The commotion caused the pudgy nurse to rush back into the room.

"Is there a problem, Dr. Bryant?" she asked, looking Isadora up and down.

"What you gonna do?" Isadora snapped.

Matthew looked over at his mother. Seeing her in that all too familiar battle stance was enough to warn him that things were coming close to crisis mode. Matthew quickly assessed his options and then sprung into action. At five-foot-ten, Matthew had at least five inches on his mother. Even with that and the fact that track kept him in excellent shape, dragging his nearly two hundred pound mother out of the office was no small feat. Their exit was less than graceful to say the least.

"Let's talk when you are calmer, Mrs. Meredith," the doctor called after them.

The ride home was void of conversation. Isadora was uncharacteristically quiet. The pained expression that was etched on her face had already taken residence in Matthew's memory. He remained extraordinarily introspective as Phyllis Hyman's melancholy voice flowed through the speakers, warning the world to be careful of how to treat her love. As the mini-van maneuvered Atlanta's peach-inspired streets, Matthew's fear and anxiety gave way to anger. He wasn't sure if he was mad because his mother had managed to figure out a way to embarrass the hell out of him on the worse day of his life, if it was because she had not stopped to think about how he was feeling, or if it was because he might not have a chance at a full life. As usual, she was more concerned about her own pain. It was all she ever thought about.

Isadora had been married to Roland, Matthew's father, for twenty-two years, but the marriage had lost its luster years ago. Even she wasn't sure if they were still together out of habit or fear. All she knew was that things had never really been the same after Matthew's twin brother fell from his crib and died while Isadora was supposed to be watching them. The couple had managed to have another child, Matthew's younger sister, Olivia; but even that had not brought back the joy between them. Since that day her husband remained aloof— someone Isadora no longer knew. It was as if he was punishing her for killing one of his sons, his twins—one of the only things that he had gotten right.

As a result, Isadora drowned herself in the drama of being a lower middle class housewife, and her husband drowned himself in cheap vodka. When he wasn't working the evening shift as a baggage handler at Atlanta's Hartsfield-Jackson International airport, he was doing carpentry work for various general contractors around town.

As they got closer to their small house on the southwest side of Atlanta, Isadora's silent tears turned to sobs. Matthew closed his eyes and laid his head back on the passenger's headrest of the blue Nissan minivan and listened to his mother's sighs and moans in between choruses from Phyllis Hyman. The ride seemed to last forever.

Finally the mini-van jolted to a halt in the driveway. They both exited the automobile without a word. Matthew rushed through the front door and headed straight to Olivia's room, the only person that kept him grounded. He entered without knocking, and found her on the phone with one of her girlfriends. The look on his face told her that something was wrong.

"What did the doctor say?" she asked, hanging up the phone in mid-conversation and giving him her full attention.

Matthew didn't speak at first. He looked at his sister, and he finally felt he could unload the stress of the day. Olivia was his best friend, his confidant, and his biggest supporter. She was a mirror image of him only smaller and more delicate. She had the same caramel-honey complexion, eyes, slim, yet triangular nose, full bottom lip, and large, straight, white teeth.

"He thinks it might be cancer," Matthew said blankly.

As Olivia stood awestricken before him, Matthew was reminded of how beautiful his mother must have been when she was Olivia's age. Pain, weight, and drama had taken as much of a toll on his mother as she had taken on the family. Isadora looked uncharacteristically old for a black woman of forty-something. He hoped that his sister never experienced anything that would cause her to age before her time.

"How do you feel?" she asked.

"I feel fine. This whole thing just has me a little twisted. What am I supposed to do with the rest of my life?"

"What else did Dr. Bryant say? What happens now?"

Matthew sighed heavily. "We really didn't get a chance to find out. Your mother got all ghetto and started yelling at the doctor. You know how she can be," he said, rolling his eyes.

"She was your mother first," Olivia joked, forcing a laugh in an attempt to lighten the mood. She wrapped her arms around her brother and hugged him tight.

Matthew broke away abruptly, his eyes brimming with emotion. He flopped down on Olivia's bed and began to cry, finally allowing himself to feel the impact of his situation.

Olivia wanted to go to him. She had always seen her brother as a pillar of strength, and seeing him cry was almost more than she could bear. Tears slid down her cheeks but she gave him space to experience his pain, and as usual Olivia poised herself for action.

Olivia dried her eyes, went straight to her computer, and began to research the various forms of cancer. She read off the symptoms to Matthew to see which he had experienced. She could tell from his frequent periods of silence that he had probably suffered more of them than he had told anyone. Olivia assumed that she knew just about everything about her brother, but lately, he had started to become a little more distant, even toward her. After downloading and printing thirty pages from the net, Olivia got on the phone and called Dr. Bryant's office. Pretending to be Isadora, she first apologized for her earlier behavior, and then asked probing question after probing question about the disease and Matthew's specific case. She scribbled notes furiously on the pad in front of her, pausing to reference the information she'd found on the Internet to make sure she understood everything he told her. She finally hung up the phone and turned to Matthew.

"The doctor says that he'll need to run some tests to see if the growth he found is malignant or benign. Then he can determine what the next steps will be. He said that if you come in this week, you could have the results before you leave for college orientation."

Olivia knew Matthew well enough to know how important going to college was to him. Sadly she was probably the only one in the house who knew how much her brother was celebrated at school for his academic achievement. Isadora and Roland Meredith had too much of their own baggage to be concerned about being good parents. They defined good parenting as having a daughter who was not pregnant and a son who was not on drugs. It was this lack of parental concern that taught Olivia and Matthew early in life to be there for each other. Their bond was a tight one because essentially, they were all they had. Matthew made it a point to be there every time Olivia cheered, and she never missed one of his track meets or debates.

Matthew was the first black valedictorian of his high school, and Ron Jackson, his guidance counselor, made sure that everyone knew it. The black faculty and staff tried not to show it, but they all took special pride in Matthew's perfect SAT scores, 4.0 GPA, and his local, regional and national academic awards. Matthew, however, was far from the typical scholar. He was a track athlete, president of the debate team, editor of the yearbook staff, and had been voted "Most Likely to Succeed" by his senior class. He was also a lover and wielder of the written word.

"Have you told Tessa yet?" Olivia asked, breaking the silence.

Matthew had been dating Tessa since sophomore year. Olivia didn't care much for her, mainly because she felt Tessa's upper middle class family looked down on them. Still she respected the fact that Tessa was a good girlfriend to Matthew, and was a part of his life.

"No. I don't know that I'll tell her until I know something for sure," he answered.

Olivia nodded silently in response. Matthew's need for privacy and secrecy didn't surprise her. She had noticed that over the past few weeks the two had been spending less time together. Since Matthew was planning to go to UNC-Chapel Hill and Tessa was going to Spelman, a break-up seemed inevitable.

"Is everything alright between you and Miss Spaulding?" she asked curiously.

"Yeah, it's cool, but I've been in a relationship for the last three years. I'm beginning to wonder what it's like to just chill—especially now with this cancer thing hanging over me." He paused. "And then the abortion—that made me wonder if I'm ready to settle down for the rest of my life."

The abortion was a secret that the three of them had kept from their families and friends. Olivia had covered for Tessa's absence at cheerleading practice, and she even gave the couple $100 from the money she had saved from her job at Lenox Mall, to help pay for the procedure.

Just then they heard the floorboard on the other side of the door squeak, a sure sign that their mother was on the other side eavesdropping *again*. They looked at each other and rolled their eyes the same way they had when they were younger.

"What ya'll talking about in there?" called Isadora. "I know ya'll talking about me."

Neither of them said a word, knowing that after listening for a few more minutes, she would go away. Once they heard her retreating footsteps, Olivia put on Aaliyah's last album, and they sang along to their favorite songs in between reading through the information that Olivia had collected from the Internet.

Eventually the two drifted off to sleep. They were awakened by a knock at the door. They were both shocked when their father sheepishly entered the room. Roland Meredith rarely journeyed beyond his recliner in the den or his bedroom, and never visited the children in their rooms. Olivia could not remember ever seeing him in her room.

"Your mother told me about your visit to Dr. Bryant," Roland said, as the stifling scent of vodka and Old Spice swirled around him, and filled the room.

Matthew and Olivia stared at their father as if they'd never heard him speak before. The quivering in his voice was uncharacteristic, and the way he continued to stand there made it seem as if he had something else to say.

Matthew wondered what fatherly words of wisdom Roland had to share concerning his diagnosis. He did not expect much since Roland didn't have much practice giving fatherly advice. What his father said next stunned them.

"I guess now is as good a time as any for me to share my news," he added, as he nervously adjusted his glasses. The puzzled look on his children's faces forced him to continue. "I may be moving out for a while."

Matthew felt as if he was reeling, the news sucking him back inside of the emotional hurricane that had kept him swept up most of the day. What else could happen to him today? Did he have the most selfish parents on Earth? It wasn't that he really cared about whether they were together, but here he was facing a life threatening illness and all his mother could think about was her pain, while all his father could think about was getting away from his mother.

"What do you mean you may be moving out for a while?" Olivia yelled.

Without warning, the scene unfolded like a bad remix of the day's earlier exchange between his mother and the doctor. Olivia stood up, her hand planted on her hip, glaring at their father. Before his eyes Olivia transformed, sounding as out of control and irate as their mother had. At that moment there was no question that she was definitely her mother's daughter. He knew the neck swivel was coming.

"Don't forget, I'm your father," Roland warned.

"Matthew just found out that he has cancer and you come in here with this shit? You are—"

Olivia never got to finish her sentence. The loud, popping sound of flesh against flesh was the next sound to fill the air. Both Roland and Matthew realized at the same time what had just happened. Roland had slapped his only daughter. What happened next was equally surprising.

Matthew and Olivia jumped on their father. The element of surprise and his alcoholic state put Roland at a distinct disadvantage despite his six-foot-two, two hundred pound frame. The three toppled to the ground in a heap of swinging arms and vicious clawing and biting. The scuffle lasted for several minutes before Isadora heard the noise and rushed into the room.

"What the hell is going on in here?" she yelled.

Isadora's yelling did not stop them, but by this time Roland had regained his composure, and was able to at least defend himself. Not knowing what else to do, Isadora quickly exited the room and came back with a pot of water, which she splashed on the three of them. The shock stopped them immediately.

No one said a word as they all sat on the floor of the disheveled room. Each of them was trying to catch their breath. Roland was also searching for his glasses.

"What in the hell is this all about?" Isadora demanded, breaking the silence.

"It's about him choosing today to tell us that you two are getting a divorce!" Olivia yelled.

"Divorce? What divorce?" Isadora asked, looking quizzically at her husband.

Before they knew what was happening, Isadora had jumped on Roland. This fight was more intense than the first one since the combatants had more years of pent up anxiety and frustration to release. Matthew was finally able to subdue his father. Olivia had a harder time with her mother, and wasn't able to stop her until she pulled her wig down over her face, threatening to suffocate her.

The room fell silent. Both of Matthew's parents left the room, each retreating to separate areas of the house to reflect on what this outburst of emotion meant.

In the days that followed, things were a little different. Though conversations were still a bit strained, the awkward silence of their dysfunction had been broken. The fight seemed to be a turning point in the Meredith household. Whether it was for the better or not was yet to be determined.

Matthew returned to the doctor at the end of the week for more tests, which again proved inconclusive. It was finally determined that he would need to return later during the month for a more complete examination.

The recent drama in his family, and his newfound illness changed Matthew's decision to go to UNC–Chapel Hill. Georgia Central's proximity to his doctor, his parents' pending divorce, his concern for his sister, and Ron Jackson's continued coaxing were enough to tip the scale toward Georgia Central University.

After two weeks of deliberating and a frantic call to Mr. Jackson to see if he thought Central would still take his acceptance at such a late date, Matthew was relieved to find out that Mr. Jackson had pulled some strings and gotten him in. Matthew's only stipulation was that he had to stay on campus. He had to get out of that house. He would be close enough to check on his sister, but far enough away to maintain his sanity. The winds of change had rearranged Matthew's life, and forced him to cling to the familiar. He decided to stay in Atlanta, and stay with Tessa, who would be going to Atlanta's Spelman College. After all, it might not be so bad to be in the same city with his family—as long as he didn't have to live with them.

Touch our bodies, wind.
Our bodies are separate, individual things.
Touch our bodies, wind.
But blow quickly

A House in Taos – Langston Hughes

CHAPTER 2

Black
As the gentle night
Black as the kind and quiet night
Black
As the deep productive earth
Body
Out of Africa
Strong and black
As iron
First smelted in
Africa

Me and My Song – Langston Hughes

Theodore Chauncey Walker was the eighty-four-year old patriarch of the most prominent black family in Nash County, North Carolina. He was respectfully known as T.C., 'Total Control' Walker, because he controlled his business, his family, and his emotions. Walker created a mini-empire in an era when colored men seemed to control very little, but he didn't let that fact stop him. He never allowed the racism from whites or lighter skinned blacks to be an excuse for his failure. Instead, he made living the life of a black man seem effortless, opting to take every negative thrown his way and turning it around. He exemplified and embraced the title of nigger, colored, Negro, black, and African-American with the authority and ease of someone who had lived life before. His uncanny wisdom and outlandish wit were deceptively cloaked behind sepia skin and southern slang.

As a young boy in the early 1920's, T.C. began working for the white-owned Hodge Funeral Parlor. It was then one of the largest funeral home chains in eastern North Carolina, with four parlors in two counties. By the time T.C. was seventeen, he knew the funeral home business inside and out. By eighteen, he convinced Nolan Hodge, the owner, to let him rent an old parlor and some obsolete equipment. His plan was to use this as a means to service the growing number of Negro clients who could not afford to pay. Hodge agreed, on the condition that T.C. pay him a small percentage of the proceeds.

T.C. worked hard at his new business, often putting in an additional four to six hours after working nearly ten hours for Mr. Hodge. After nearly a year of saving, T.C. finally saved up enough money to go out on his own. He was only eighteen, and though he lacked formal training in mortuary science, his clients did not complain because his work was top notch. Besides, he was the only black funeral home within three counties.

Nolan Hodge admired T.C.'s enthusiasm, initiative, and entrepreneurial spirit. He longed to see even a modicum of that same drive in any of his three sons. While none of them seemed interested in dealing with the dead, they were all more than willing to squander the parlor proceeds on cheap alcohol and even cheaper women.

By the time Nolan Hodge died, T.C. had stopped renting and bought the old parlor outright. Out of respect, T.C. handled all of the details for Mr. Nolan Hodge's funeral and while it was one of the best funerals that the white community of Nash County had ever witnessed, they still refused to patronize a black owned business.

In contrast, Nolan's sons had managed to retain very little about the funeral business, and even less about handling the finances. As a result, the next white funeral after Nolan's passing was a complete disaster. The body was still unprepared by the time of the scheduled viewing, and was already discolored and slightly decomposed by the time Nolan's sons found a white funeral home owner in the next county to come clean things up. After that the Hodge Funeral Parlor empire crumbled quickly and gave way to an up and coming chain out of Raleigh.

Over the years, the Hodge Family came to resent T.C. They blamed him for stealing the Hodge business, and ruining the family, most of whom were now residents of the local trailer park due to the mismanagement of Nolan's hard-earned money.

In a sad moment of desperation, they even started rumors that T.C. had poisoned Nolan Hodge as a final plot in a master scheme to ruin the Hodge family and steal their money.

Nothing could have been further from the truth. T.C. had a healthy respect for Nolan Hodge, and had earned everything that had been given him. By watching Mr. Hodge he had learned the psychology of dealing with the family of the deceased, the exacting science of preparing the body, and the organization required to manage all of the pre and post funeral details—from obituaries, to payment arrangements, to grave site preparation.

T.C. never had delusions of catering to the white community. He saw the opportunity to service the blacks of Nash County, and he took it. He felt that they deserved greater respect and caring than a white home was able or willing to give them during their moments of grief. He had seen far too many white funeral homes overcharge poor black families for the necessities of a service, and then skimp on the niceties that were freely given to white families.

While Hodge had taught him everything about handling a funeral, T.C. had to learn the subtle difference between a mortuary service and a *Homegoing* on his own. Habits steeped in black tradition dictated that things be handled differently when the dearly departed was of a darker hue. Black funerals, unlike those of whites, were not typically held within two days. The bodies did not discolor as quickly, and family members from the North often needed time to get money together to travel back down South for the funeral. It wasn't unusual for a Homegoing service to be conducted four to five days after the death. The emotional energy expended at white viewings and funerals paled in comparison to Negro events. A funeral wasn't truly over until three spirituals had been sung, Big Mama had flung herself across the casket, and several chickens and hogs had been sacrificed.

Though his business was going very well, T.C. was smart enough to know that he could not go it alone. He knew that behind every great man there was a great woman, so at nineteen, he started courting and eventually married Maytrude Ricks.

Maytrude was a rare jewel in Nash County. She was the sassy talking, strikingly beautiful, mahogany complexioned, only daughter of Paul Ricks, the owner of Rick's Family Barbecue, and granddaughter of Robert Ricks, the pastor of Rick's Baptist Church, the largest black church in Nash County.

Given her family background, and his growing success, T.C. and Maytrude's wedding was a major event. It was as if they were local royalty. Shortly after the wedding, the funeral parlor business took off at a rapid pace. T.C. and Maytrude renovated the building far beyond the expectations of any of the locals. Bereaved families saw T.C. as a trusted face, and Maytrude, an angel of mercy, capable of giving the most eloquent and touching eulogies.

T.C. and Maytrude had four sons—Chauncey Jr., Earl, Carl, and Seymour. Chauncey Jr. went away to mortuary school, and then came back home to marry his high school sweetheart. As the oldest and most responsible, he helped infuse the family business with the latest techniques of embalming.

Earl, the ladies' man, went off to the military, under the impression that it would require less work than helping with the family business. Being in the Vietnam War however was enough to disprove that theory, and he ended his tour early with a dishonorable discharge. He returned home with fabled stories of heroism, and several women expecting child support for the children he fathered. Shortly after he returned, he married his high school sweetheart, and secured a job as a foreman at the local mill. Since Earl was never one for taking orders that, like the military, was a short-lived experience. He believed that being his own boss was something he was better suited for, and so he ultimately opened Walker's Barber Shop in the center of downtown.

Carl found contentment in taking over his mother's family's barbecue business, while Seymour, the youngest, heard the calling and became the pastor of his great, great grandfather's church.

The Walker-Ricks family was well connected and wealthy by all local standards, so any family outings were grand and well put together. Maytrude Walker always made sure of that. However she took special care in coordinating the family gathering, for T.C.'s grandson, Torrin Chance Walker, who was on his way to college.

Although T.C. didn't think anyone noticed, it was obvious that Torrin was the favorite of his eighteen grandchildren. Torrin knew it too. He didn't know if it was because he looked so much like his grandfather or because his grandfather appreciated the fact that he, like his grandfather, seemed to make a success of anything he touched. They had been practically inseparable since Torrin's birth. Maytrude often said that they were peas in a pod and that they took to each other from the moment that Torrin was born.

At 6'0", with the type of physique that only youth, great genes and regular exercise could provide, Torrin was striking. Like most of his immediate family members, and just like his grandfather, T.C., Torrin had a rich, dark chocolate complexion. In Nash County, he was known as another one of those dark-skinned Walkers. The Walker genes were as strong as their constitution. In New York, Paris, or Milan, he could have easily been a male super model. Torrin was a good student, graduating in the top 10 percent of his class, but he was best known for his athleticism and leadership on the field. By graduation, Torrin had lettered in three sports, made All State in two, and was president of his high school graduating class.

Torrin's older brother, Chauncey III, was a complete contrast. Chauncey III sought the attention and respect of his elders but always seemed to pale in comparison to Torrin's athleticism and leadership. Mediocre grades and a fear of being left out of the family forced Chauncey III to stay near home and attend the local community college. Torrin's younger twin brothers, Cobyn and Jacoby, on the other hand, were just entering the eleventh grade, and were as athletic and popular as Torrin.

The smell of freshly cut grass mingled with southern fried cooking, the sounds of the Canton Spirituals, and children's laughter were all familiar smells and sounds at a Walker-Ricks' family gathering.

Several of the Walker Funeral Home tents adorned the Walker's spacious, two-acre backyard. The largest was set up about twenty feet from the house. Folding chairs had been lined up in perfectly even rows, with an aisle in between, facing a small wooden podium and microphone. A sound system and speakers had been set up on a table behind the podium, and was playing gospel quartet music—the preferred choice of both T.C. and Maytrude. There was also some Smokie Norful, Fred Hammond, and Tonex thrown in occasionally for the younger listeners.

Torrin sat in a folding chair under one of the tents and surveyed the scene that was unfolding in front of him. His family, high school friends, and neighbors had all come to give him a send-off like no other. Everyone was talking and seemed to be having a good time. The Walkers never really needed a reason to throw a bash. They used any occasion—weddings, funerals, family reunions, or births. It didn't matter. They loved to laugh, eat and fellowship. This was, however, the first time that the entire family had held a cookout in Torrin's honor.

Torrin took a moment and reflected on the fact that this would probably be the last family event that he would attend while he still lived under his father's roof. Torrin looked past the podium and saw his father and uncles. Each of the men was the color of dark earth, with strong, square shoulders, full lips, ample noses, and big hands. His Uncle Carl was directing his employees where to put the food and how to prepare it, as if they hadn't done it a hundred times before. His Uncle Seymour was surrounded by a group of guests, and undoubtedly entertaining them with another humorous story. His father was mingling in the midst of another group of guests, a serious expression plastered on his face. Torrin watched him for a moment and sighed. His father always seemed too busy to laugh or have fun. It was as if he felt he always had to shoulder the full weight of the Walker family name by himself.

Torrin continued to scan the yard, and found his Uncle Earl, standing alone off to the side of the grill. He was preoccupied with eyeing the bevy of scantily clad young women, grinning and glancing at them on the sly, being careful to make sure that his wife wasn't watching. Torrin frowned, pulled out his inhaler, and took a couple of quick puffs. He couldn't be sure if the reason his asthma had flared up was because of the smell of grass in the air, or his complete disdain for his Uncle Earl, who was by far his least favorite relative. He surmised it was the latter.

Torrin's mother and aunts stood in a small circle just beyond their husbands, as if it was their place to remain dutifully within earshot of their men. Their conversation was much more superficial—limited to clothing styles and home décor items they had each seen during their last shopping trip to Raleigh. They were all local women related through marriage, yet secretly competing. They each knew that part of being a Walker wife was maintaining the façade of close family ties. Maytrude wouldn't have it any other way. They all vied to see who could get closest to Maytrude, lose the most weight, find the nicest dresses, or decorate the best home. Individually, they kept each other at the top of their game— collectively they set a standard that the other women of Nash County struggled to achieve.

Torrin's grandmother sat at a picnic table just behind the house with the other members of the church Mother's Board. The older women seemed content fanning themselves, and looking over the crowd in amazement at how much all of the children had grown and matured. Occasionally they would lean in really close to each other and whisper secrets that only old souls could tell.

At the far end of the yard, the most popular of Torrin's classmates were sitting under a large oak tree, making false promises to each other about how they would stay in contact after graduation. Cheerleaders, athletes, and honor students, all came to celebrate Torrin. Torrin's white classmates, with the exception of the Hodges, were the only white people at the event. Older white citizens were respectful of the Walker family, but thought T.C.'s money had gone to his head, and that he had long forgotten his place. While the white parents weren't excited about having their children at a Walker-Ricks function, they all wanted to get details on what the family was really like. Torrin, being a part of generation X, was slightly more oblivious to the undertones of racism that still existed in the small southern town.

Sharon, his high school sweetheart, caught his glance and gave him a wink. She was undoubtedly one of the prettiest, and most well developed young ladies in Torrin's class. Sharon, a honey-dipped southern belle, with large, dark brown eyes, and a bouncing bob haircut, was the typical cheerleader. But for all of her beauty, Torrin found her aspirations of going to cosmetology school and remaining in Nash County disappointing. He knew that she would be perfectly content being a Walker wife, but he had no intent of becoming another predictable piece in the Walker family puzzle.

Just then T.C. stepped up to the microphone and asked all the guests to take their seats. Torrin walked over to the tent, and took his seat. Sharon immediately took her place next to him on the front row. His mother and father sat directly behind him, and his friends, family, and neighbors also took their seats. His father reached forward and patted him on the shoulder, and his mother kissed him on the cheek.

As the crowd took their seats, Torrin couldn't help but reminisce about the times he'd spent with his grandfather, many of those times outdoors at burial sites as the big machines moved the earth away to create a final resting place for the deceased. Torrin would never forget the smell of raw earth, the feel of Carolina clay between his toes, or his grandfather habitually checking his pocket watch. Torrin thought about his grandfather's numerous words of wisdom.

"They can kill you, but they can't eat you," he'd often said when referring to doing business with white men. "Pigs get fat and hogs get slaughtered," was what he'd said when warning him about the risks of being gluttonous or greedy. To say that Torrin had learned a lot from his grandfather was an understatement. T.C. had been the ultimate mentor.

"Let's begin with a prayer from Seymour," T.C. said, quieting the crowd.

Torrin's uncle, Pastor Seymour Walker, stepped to the front of the tent with all the dignity of a southern Baptist minister, and addressed the group in a strong clear voice.

"Let us bow our heads," he said when he took the podium. "Lord, we come before You humbly and meekly this day, thanking You for all of the blessings that You have bestowed upon us. We thank You for family and friends and the opportunity to celebrate the gifts that You have given one of our own. As the earth brings forth fruit to nourish Your children, so may You bless Torrin to bring forth gifts to bless Your people. In Jesus name we pray, Amen." Pastor Walker concluded and walked quietly back to his seat. As he sat down, T.C. stepped back toward the microphone.

"I will not be befo' you long this afternoon, 'cause I know you are ready to get to some of that good barbecue we got there in the back. It is with great pride that I stand here today. One of our very own is going away to the Georgia State—umm—Georgia Central University in Atlanta, Georgia. Whilst we know that he will not be gone fo'evah, we do know that he will be missed. He has made us proud over these last few years and we know that he will continue to do so over the years to come. He had an opportunity to go to several dif'rent schools on athletic scholarships, but he chose the road less traveled—the road of a scholar and a gentleman. He is going away to study the law. Our family and our community would do well to have a lawyer. As a token of my pride and joy, I would like to give my grandson a going away gift."

T.C. held up a small gift wrapped box and a check for Torrin. His cousins and brothers tried not to appear jealous.

Torrin rose with a mechanical-type ease as if each muscle engaged before moving, and made his way to the podium to accept his gift. His completely muscular frame was apparent even through his clothes. He had begun to perspire under the sultry summer sun and the white cotton Calvin Klein tank top drew a striking contrast to his dark skin. He made it to the stage, hugged his grandfather and grandmother and took the gift. His grandfather had always given the grandchildren a check for $100 and a watch when they graduated from high school so Torrin poised himself to act surprised.

He accepted the gifts and gave an eloquent acceptance speech thanking friends, family and neighbors for everything that they had done for him over the years. Like most of the Walker clan, he was used to making speeches at reunions, funerals and weddings.

"He is such a good speaker," his Aunt Sarah whispered as he made his way back to his seat. "Sounds just like white folk. I jus' know he gone be a good lawyer one day. Maybe even a preacher."

While Torrin was aware of his privileged upbringing, he often found resentment in the ritualistic, assumptive and monotonous rural way of life. He hated the way people drew out his name as if they were never going to stop saying it, *Tor-rin*. He hated the fact that his high school girlfriend's greatest ambition was marrying him. He hated the way his family kept calling it Georgia State University, an all-white institution, despite his continued correction that it was Georgia Central University, one of the nation's premier all-male, black institutions. He hated the fact that they all assumed that he would ever be coming back to Nash County when he graduated. He didn't really know what else was out there, but he knew that there had to be more.

When he got back to his seat, he looked at the check and realized that it was a check for $5000. He opened the gift box and saw that his grandfather had given him his pocket watch. A smile crept across his face. After all, he did love his family.

> *Its an earth song-*
> *And I've been waiting long*
> *An earth song!*
> *A body song!*
> *A spring song!*
> *And I've been waiting long*
> *For an earth song.*

Earth Song – Langston Hughes

CHAPTER 3

Sing me a song of the Revolution
Marching like fire over the world

Song of the Revolution – Langston Hughes

Mrs. Vines recognized the rhythm the first time she happened into the Ethos vintage music store on the south side of Chicago. The thirty-two year old, preacher's wife had come in to find an anniversary gift for her husband.

Jo'sha noticed the petite, brown-skinned woman, with the shapely figure immediately, and had been more than willing to assist her. He licked his lips and moved in dangerously close while they perused the popular fusion section. When he brushed against her she felt the full extent of his young manhood, and smelled the lust that seemed to emanate from his every pore. By the time they reached the classics section, the desire in his voice was thick and obvious. At Jo'sha's recommendation, she special ordered an Etta James collection, and asked him to deliver it to her at her home in west Chicago.

On the Friday afternoon that he arrived she opened the door wearing a black lace Victoria's Secret robe. The Reverend Vines had just left for a minister's conference and was not expected back until Monday afternoon. The two chatted for a while, exchanging nervous glances and superficial pleasantries until the erogenous energy grew stronger than the desire for decorum.

Jo'sha dropped the package in the foyer, grabbed Mrs. Vines, and pressed her against his hard young body. He began kissing her neck hungrily while his hands grabbed her ample ass and squeezed. The soft moan that escaped her lips fueled him. It was a familiar sound—

like music to his ears. He felt her nipples hardened against his chest, and imagined the moistness that was stirring between her thighs. He swept her size six frame up into his arms and carried her upstairs to the first available bedroom. It was sparsely furnished and appeared to Jo'sha to have been a guest room—not that it mattered.

He laid her down, parted her legs gently, and then hungrily buried his tongue into her folds. Her screams and moans filled the air as the scent of passion entered the room like a long awaited visitor. Jo'sha waited until he felt the familiar tremors of climax before mounting her. When he entered her he filled her up completely, and she quivered beneath him. The two lovers became consumed with the fervor of their lust, and were oblivious to anything else. It was when Jo'sha turned her over that they heard the front door unlock. Jo'sha began to stroke harder. They heard footsteps in the foyer, and Jo'sha began to stroke deeper. She froze in terror momentarily, not knowing what to do or what to say, but Jo'sha's steady rhythm commanded her body to respond. By the time the footsteps were at the stairwell downstairs, both of them were deep in the throes of orgasm. It was her third.

They dressed quickly and quietly, and then she whispered to Jo'sha to wait in the closet until she returned and all was clear. He would make his escape through the bedroom window and climb down the trellis. She quickly unlocked and opened the window before scurrying out of the room.

Jo'sha sat in the closet in silence, listening to muffled voices and infrequent footsteps for twenty minutes. Finally, he heard the doorknob turn and his heart stopped. It opened quickly, revealing a completely nude Mrs. Vines, wanting and needing more of him.

"He just forgot his wallet," she purred. She dropped to her knees directly in front of him, untied his pants, and began licking his inner thighs.

Jo'sha threw his head back, enjoying the sounds and sensations, while grinding to the rhythm of his heartbeat and her passion. The cadence began to take a life of its own and seemed to grow louder. Suddenly Jo'sha realized that the beating was not his heart—that the pounding was not her passion, but the returning footsteps of Reverend Vines. The good reverend came charging into the guest bedroom hurling the collected works of Etta James at Jo'sha, missing him and hitting his wife square in the face. Jo'sha pulled up his pants and dove toward the window, scrambling out just before Mr. Vines could step over his unconscious wife and get to him. Jo'sha landed on the roof, climbed down the trellis, and ran toward the train station—back home to the south side where it was safe.

∞

Jo'sha blazed carelessly down the old wooden basement staircase, ignoring the rickety rail, consumed by thoughts of his future and afterthoughts of his afternoon rendezvous. Each stair creaked a little louder than the last; heralding his descent into what had become his haven. Each step reminded him that this would be one of his last times in this space. The smell of damp earth and spring fresh laundry detergent created an inorganic bouquet that Jo'sha had come to associate with peace and solitude. Once he reached the bottom of the stairs, Jo'sha instinctively snatched the dangling string to the ceiling light fixture—and then there was light.

Just to the left of the stairs was an old Kenmore washing machine and dryer. The washing machine rocked violently alongside the seemingly uninterested dryer, which was an indication that Foster wasn't too far away. At the end of the room was an old bar that always reminded Jo'sha of an altar at the front of a church. It was one of those 1970's creations, made of thin, faded imitation wood, and accented with brown padded plastic. Atop the bar were several bottles of unopened gin and vodka, scented candles, and an old AM/FM radio. A cloth, tie-dyed picture of Bob Marley was nailed to the wall behind the bar like a faded Jesus waiting to be worshipped.

Between the stairs and the bar was a weight bench surrounded by several neatly stacked iron weights. To the side sat an old orange and yellow plaid recliner in front of a floor model black and white television. The opposite wall was fully covered by mirrored glass that was chipped in the upper right corner.

Jo'sha turned on the radio and was immediately blessed by Common's rap tribute to Assata Shakur. He pulled a joint from his pocket and reached behind the bar for a match. He lit the joint, along with one of the patchouli scented candles on the bar, and tossed the dead match on the cold concrete floor. He took a long, slow drag and held his head back, inviting in the smell of raw earth, the feel of good weed, and the sounds of Common's sense. When he heard Foster's footsteps upstairs, he instinctively put out the joint and stuck it back in his pocket.

"Jo'sha, you down there?" Foster yelled, as he sauntered down the stairs.

In his late-thirties, Foster had the physique of a man ten years his junior, and the temperament and didactic inclination of a man many years his senior. He moved with a confident, Jim Brown— Richard Roundtree old school gait that most black men settled into after adolescence and before their first divorce.

"Yeah, old man, you ready for a good work out?" Jo'sha taunted.

"I see you, young brother," Foster said, greeting Jo'sha in the same way as he always had from the day they met. "Can't stay long today, soldier," he continued. "I have business to handle, but we can recap the day while we do a few reps."

Jo'sha frowned with disappointment. He had hoped that he would have a chance to spend more time with Foster before heading off to college.

"Not a lot happened today. I just delivered a record collection to a customer on the west side," Jo'sha said, in a matter of fact tone.

Foster looked around suspiciously as his presence filled the room. The mixed scent of marijuana and patchouli was a dead give away.

"Are you trying to find something or hide from something within those flames and that temporary state of delusion? Pure creativity does not require hallucinogens. You should let life be your muse. The body, young brother, is a temple. You should be careful with your gift," Foster preached, as he had many times before. He intentionally bumped Jo'sha on his way to change the radio station, and then the two headed over to the weight bench.

Jo'sha knew that Foster did not approve of anything that wasn't good for the body, mind, spirit or soul. Foster's pedagogy did not end in the classroom. Dogmatic in his delivery, he saw every moment in life as an opportunity for a lesson.

Jo'sha Jabari Imarah was a seed blown far afield—a late blooming flower of the black power revolution. Conceived in a fiery passion by two teenage runaways from the south side, Jo'sha was left as a ward of the Chicago foster care system after his parents, Akili and Ishwa Imarah, were killed in an automobile accident when he was still a small toddler.

His parents died on a late summer day, in a deceptively innocent August rain. Akili, his father, had been more focused on his young family and the radio than the increasingly hazardous driving conditions. He had just turned his attention back to the highway after tightening Jo'sha's car seat when he ran into a puddle of rain. After skidding for twenty feet, Akili attempted to turn in the direction of the skid and pump the brakes, but they did not work. The car spun several times before barreling into a tree. Akili and Ishwa died that summer day in the explosion of the car crash. Their friends all said that the accident had been an act of sabotage by Akili's detractors. They believed that his radical views on race, and his involvement in civil rights activities had angered the local powers that be, and that their deaths had been an intentional hit.

Jo'sha survived his parents. The impact of the crash had thrown Jo'sha and his father's briefcase a few feet into a wooded area. It was several hours before rescue workers found Jo'sha turned upside down in his child safety seat, crying in the pouring rain. The briefcase was propped beneath the car seat allowing young Jo'sha just enough space to breath. An "L" shaped burn mark on his left forearm and haunting nightmares, served as his constant reminder of that day.

At eighteen his nightmares were no less intense or frequent and they always began with thunderous sheets of water followed by azure explosions, scarlet screams, and cold sweats. Like random sparks from an unattended flame, memories of his parents were vague and scattered, fueled only by a Polaroid from their union ceremony, a collection of his father's handwritten speeches on the power and responsibility of people of color, and his father's research on religions of the world.

Jo'sha stood a modest five-foot-ten, with a buttery milk chocolate complexion, full lips, and a strong, shapely, broad nose. His deep, dark penetrating eyes could look into the souls of black folk, and past the ways of white folk. His shoulder-length locks framed his face like a mane and somehow seemed to make his confident, lion-like prowl make sense. He carried the L-shaped burn mark on his left forearm as a reminder of what a bitch fate had been.

Despite the absence of a father's guiding hand or a mother's loving touch, Jo'sha had the confidence of ten young men his age.

Jo'sha was known among the young women in the neighborhood for his sexual prowess and extraordinary endowment. His passion and intensity always proved too much for just one sister, so he had never had a steady girlfriend. The young ladies didn't seem to mind as long as Jo'sha didn't neglect to come by periodically to give them each a little bit of attention. Of course Jo'sha was more than willing to oblige. He spent his entire last week in Chicago giving his female friends *something to remember him by.*

The brothers on the south side wouldn't miss Jo'sha as much as they would his steady supply of 'smoke'. Though he was careful never to reveal his sources, Jo'sha could always be counted on for good, clean, seedless weed. He considered any other drugs to be too heavy, and kept a steady and reliable clientele.

As an honor student, ladies' man and dependable supplier, Jo'sha was an indispensable commodity in the neighborhood. He was not, however completely understood. He never forged strong relationships with any of his high school classmates or any of his four foster families. He found little in common with his peers beyond the sex and the drugs. Instead, he immersed himself in his passion for creation, and his father's works on various religions.

His high school music instructor, David Foster, was the first person to realize that he possessed extraordinary creative gifts. With a voice reminiscent of Donnie Hathaway, an ability to wield the written word as craftily as a young James Baldwin, and an eye for color and design like a budding Gordon Parks, Jo'sha was a pure Renaissance man.

Jo'sha's first day in Dr. Foster's sophomore music class climaxed with Foster and Jo'sha dueling on opposing pianos to excerpts from Joe Sample's 1994, *Did You Feel That?* album. The class watched in amazement and confusion as the two went back and forth playing snippets of Sample combined with innovative improvisations. From that day Jo'sha had found a mentor in Foster, and in Jo'sha, Foster had found a reason to keep teaching. Jo'sha spent that evening in Foster's music room telling him about his love of theology, close calls with drug dealers, aspirations of musical success, nightmares of his parents' death, and subsequent foster families.

David Foster took him to his first spoken word event, where he listened to poets spit powerful works of literary perfection. Foster taught Jo'sha how to play the harp, and educated him on the history of just about every instrument known to man. He also coached him on controlling his breathing while singing, introduced him to The Last Poets, unraveled the mysteries of the great Eastern religions, and ultimately became his legal guardian when his fourth and final foster family kicked him out.

Devout Church of God in Christ church members, the Henderson family found Jo'sha's polemic prose and ponderings about the practicality and purpose in their practices to be offensive and disrespectful, so it was no surprise that they asked him to leave when they found he had brought marijuana into their home.

Along with cultivating Jo'sha's mind, Foster sought to teach Jo'sha to treat his body well. Jo'sha's naturally toned frame was becoming more defined as a result of the daily workouts with Foster, a six-foot-two vegetarian and all around health enthusiast. At 38 years old, Foster's short Afro was just beginning to gray at the temples. The two worked out under the cover of smooth jazz for close to forty minutes before either of them said anything. Foster was high off of the music and Jo'sha was just high.

"You know I am proud of you don't you?" Foster said.

Jo'sha simply smiled and nodded his head—words escaped him. Even after three years with Foster he wasn't used to the positive feedback.

"I also think you made a fine choice in Georgia Central. It takes a man to raise a man—especially a *black* man. Some people think that all male schools should be a thing of the past, but I think the time for them is here and now. As a matter of fact, we should start our young boys out in all male training schools from kindergarten."

Jo'sha braced himself for another of Foster's lectures, but much to his surprise, Foster stopped as quickly as he started. For the next few minutes the only sound that could be heard coming from the basement were the grunts of man versus weight.

"One of my Morehouse brothers is an English teacher at Georgia Central," Foster commented, breaking the silence. "I'm planning on calling him—ask him to look out for you."

"And what makes you think I need that?" Jo'sha responded as he lay back on the weight bench to begin his next set.

"Jo'sha, I know you feel like you can take care of yourself because you have for most of your life, but you are entering a new phase of your life. You won't necessarily breeze through college the way you did high school. Georgia Central University is a tough school," Foster stated. "You can't afford to be so flippant. Eventually you are going to have to slow down and really care about something. Life calls for that. Sexual conquests and casual drug use can't lead to happiness." Foster spotted Jo'sha as he continued his first set.

"So what about you, Foster?" Jo'sha challenged. "You went to Morehouse and then on to GCU to get your doctorate in music. Now you're stuck teaching a bunch of untalented kids on the south side of Chicago? Are you happy?"

"This is not about me. I did what I had to do. Teaching is what I enjoy. I created my own reality and I revel in it. Besides, what's wrong with teaching?" Foster asked.

"Nothing if you like being underpaid and unappreciated," Jo'sha responded.

"The gratification of mass appreciation pales in comparison to the joy of self-acceptance," Foster answered.

"I'm going to school," Jo'sha said with conviction. "And don't worry, I'll graduate—but I'm going to have a good time while I'm doing it."

"Well before you head off, you need to clean up those dirty dishes upstairs in the kitchen and all these matches that you keep throwing on my basement floor."

"Aight, aight," Jo'sha blasted.

He sat up and admired his growing biceps in the basement wall mirror, and then laid back down to finish his last set. Just as he finished his ninth rep, Foster's cell phone rang. Jo'sha had anticipated Foster's help on the last rep, and frowned when he saw the older man rush to the corner to answer his phone instead. Unexplained phone calls followed by mysterious disappearances weren't unusual for Foster. While Jo'sha appreciated the fact that Foster had taken him in, he was annoyed by Foster's frequent comings and goings, and his infrequent explanations about his actions.

"Jo'sha, got some business to handle, son. I've gotta run," Foster blurted as he headed for the stairs.

As Jo'sha struggled to lift his final set, he saw Foster hurry up the stairs out of the corner of his eye. He battled with the weight unsuccessfully until he finally had to shift it off of his chest onto the floor. He called for Foster, but there was no answer. He hoped that Foster would be back to see him off in the morning.

Jo'sha went to his small 8 x 10 bedroom on the second floor. He lit two scented candles on the nightstand and turned on the small lamp. The absence of windows and the burgundy walls gave the room a hard yin edge. *Cooley High, Carmen,* and *Cabin in the Sky* movie posters covered the wall just above his small single bed. An old wooden rocking chair and a matching wooden nightstand were the only other pieces of furniture he had. It was the only space that he ever felt he could call his own and he loved it. He could only wonder how his accommodations at Georgia Central would compare.

Of limited material possessions, Jo'sha took great care with the few things that he had. He had one large traveling suitcase, an old guitar that Foster had given him, and a used leather saddlebag that he had gotten from his third foster family. He carried the bag with him everywhere. He had packed earlier in the day, and though he did not have very many things to take, rechecking his bag was a way to release his nervous energy. His few clothes barely filled the suitcase. He had two pair of oversized faded jeans, a few pair of cotton drawstring pants, several long sleeved linen shirts, five pair of socks and boxers, a pair of black boots, brown leather sandals, and one pair of running shoes. Oddly stylish, most of his clothes were prizes from the local thrift shop.

In his saddlebag, he had his parents' picture, his father's bound book of handwritten speeches, his sketchpad and pencils, and a notebook of music that he had written. He had also packed his portable CD player along with a few compact discs, and a copy of Octavia Butler's *Parable of the Talents*, which he was planning to read on the bus. Also tucked away in his bag were his last one hundred forty-two dollars and a 10" by 12" by 6" metal box containing his Dunbar scholarship award materials.

Harland Dunbar was an early Georgia Central University alumnus, and the first graduate of Georgia Central University to become a millionaire. He was also the first student to graduate with both a bachelor's of art and bachelor's of science degree, which he used to start one of the country's most profitable hair care companies. With the success of his first million, the Dunbar foundation was created. The foundation granted two scholarships annually to the most deserving incoming freshmen, who lacked the financial means to attend Georgia Central University—one in art and one in science.

Jo'sha opened the box and pulled out the certificate and smiled. He looked at the letter detailing his award for housing, tuition, books, and a university meal plan. And then he pulled out the box containing the coveted Dunbar medallion. He had only glanced at it once or twice, but never very closely for fear of becoming too emotional. He opened the small box and pulled out the circular medallion and wondered why anyone even went to the trouble. He turned it over and noticed that his initials, J.I., were engraved in the back. Another nice, but unnecessary touch he thought. He was about to place it back in the box when he noticed that there was another medallion in the bottom of the box. He picked it up and examined it as well. Like the first, it was engraved, but with the initials, J.L. Jo'sha wondered why he had received two medallions and planned to let someone know when he arrived on campus.

After checking his luggage for the fourth time that evening, he checked the alarm clock, tied his shoulder-length dreadlocks back, and got ready for bed. It was only 8:42 p.m. However, the anticipation of his new life made him anxious and sleep evaded him. He got up, and paced through the house waiting for Foster to return, but grew tired and went back to his room to play his guitar. Melodious and original tunes filled the duplex. Jo'sha found the blue note and played with it like an experienced lover tickling the g-spot until the flatted third collapsed in a mellow, sweet, and quivering crescendo.

Thoroughly spent, Jo'sha threw himself back on the bed, lit the joint from his pocket and inhaled. His nerves began to settle, and the world around him felt heavy with color until he finally drifted off to sleep.

The first day of the rest of Jo'sha's life began at 6:00 a.m. with Tom Joyner and the Morning Show blasting from the radio alarm. Jo'sha shut off the alarm and stretched vigorously as he did every morning. His morning routine began with a randomly selected reading from the Qu'ran, Bible, Kabalah or other religious work. He finished his morning ritual by meditating on the text and communing with the Creator. Jo'sha didn't subscribe to any particular religion, but counted himself a spiritual being who needed and deserved a quiet moment at the break of day. His morning conversations with God had begun as the simple and earnest pleas of a lonely and loveless child, but had progressed into powerful prayers and communion with the higher power.

He ran over to Foster's room to see if he had returned, but he was nowhere to be found. Jo'sha was disappointed, but didn't let that slow him down. Disappointment had become a way of life for Jo'sha and he knew how to handle it.

He showered, shaved, and brushed his teeth in less than thirty minutes. Then he splashed on a few drops of frankincense oil. He went back into his bedroom to dress and discovered that a second suitcase had been left beside his bag. He immediately opened the suitcase, assuming that it must have come from Foster. Inside he found several shirts and pants, a black Kenneth Cole suit, black Todd Welsh dress shoes, a matching tie, a briefcase, an envelope with $1000, and a note from Foster. The note read,

"Jo'sha,

— Know that you have been uniquely and fiercely made. You are a creative force. I am sorry that I cannot travel with you to orientation, but know that I travel with you in spirit always. Unfortunately, I have a lot going on right now and there are other things that I must handle. Call me when you arrive in Atlanta. Be strong, young soldier. — Foster.

Jo'sha felt a lump in his throat as he realized that none of this would have been possible were it not for Foster. Before Foster, he had not planned to go to college, incorrectly assuming that college was out of the question for someone without a *real* family. Foster had been adamant about planning Jo'sha's academic future, and highly recommended Georgia Central.

Jo'sha dressed quickly in boots, oversized jeans, and an Indian-influenced red tunic. He grabbed his luggage and coat, locked up the house, and headed to the bus station. Jo'sha appreciated the gifts, but would have preferred seeing Foster before he left. After all, he was the only real family that Jo'sha had ever known.

All night in bed
Waiting for sleep
He lay,
Feeling death creep-
Creeping like fire

Creeping like fire from a slow spark
Choking his breath
And burning the dark.

The Consumptive — Langston Hughes

CHAPTER 4

I've known rivers:
I've known rivers ancient as the world and older than the
flow of human blood in human veins.

I've known rivers:
Ancient, dusky rivers.

My soul has grown deep like the rivers.

The Negro Speaks of Rivers – Langston Hughes

Wade's heart raced as he entered the recreation center on the south side of Baltimore. This would be the last time that he would see Tony, Kenny, Raphi, and the other young boys who frequented the center. He shifted his backpack on his left shoulder as he hurried down the hallway to the game room.

When he entered the room the seven young boys looked up from their activity. Seven-year-old Tony ran up to hug him, almost knocking his glasses off, a ritual that had started almost two years ago when they met.

"You are late today," Tony signed after breaking the embrace.

"I know," Wade signed back. "I had to stop and do a few things first."

Wade had begun working at the recreation center when he was sixteen because his family required him to do something charitable. The Grahams always gave back to the less fortunate. Reluctant at first, Wade had come to enjoy his work at the center. He had developed a bond with several of the boys that came there, though his was probably closest to Tony.

Tony was a bright little boy who had begun to suffer from progressive hearing loss at the age of four. When Wade learned of the his condition he took a class in American Sign Language and taught it to Tony and some of the other boys in the center so that Tony wouldn't always be left out of every conversation. With a single mother who had not really taken an interest in his special educational needs, Tony also learned to substitute lip reading for failed hearing.

In the two years since Wade had begun working at the recreation center, he coordinated several fundraisers and public relations events in the local community. Through those events he raised enough money to repaint the building and get new locks and latches for the doors and windows. He also convinced his father to donate additional money to buy video games, computers, lockers, and a pool table. In an effort to help Tony improve his communication skills, Wade also found an American Sign Language tutor to work with him— absorbing the cost since he knew Tony's mother could not. Wade's family did not have a problem giving to charity. They applauded Wade's philanthropic activities as a positive way to give back. However Wade's motivation was much deeper.

Wade glanced across the room and reflected, remembering the ego that had long drowned in the ocean that separated him and his young companions. He had been born in privilege—they in poverty. He had been exposed to debutantes, cotillions, and balls—they to drugs, cops and ballers. When he'd first arrived many of the boys had been leery of him. Wade didn't seem like one of them, and they noticed that immediately. His cinnamon brown eyes, vanilla colored complexion, and wavy, loosely curled hair contrasted their own, and they commented on it often. Even though Wade attempted to dress down when he came to the center, his twelve years of private school training made him stand out. Had it not been for the inner similarities that they all shared, the boys would have surely rejected him. His frequent visits to the center over the last few years had made him a part of each of the young boys' lives. He had become a big brother, and even father figure to some.

"Is it true?" Tony signed.

"Is what true?"

"That you will be leaving," he asked, his fingers moving quickly.

All of the young boys looked at Wade intently, waiting for his answer. For the first time in a long time, Wade felt uncomfortable around them. He knew that his answer would not be well received. He wasn't necessarily happy about having to leave them either.

"Yes, I am going to be leaving. I have to go to college," he answered.

Raphi, who was normally very reserved, began to tear up immediately. Tony began to cry.

"Who is going to take us to baseball games, and teach us, and help us with homework?" he asked, tears streaming down his face.

Wade had anticipated these questions, but he could not answer them. Volunteers at the center seemed to come and go unexpectedly, none of them ever staying long enough to develop any sort of continuity. With that in mind, Wade wondered if these young boys would fall victim to the streets like so many of their fathers, brothers, and uncles before them. The thought concerned him, something he had not considered when he began volunteering at the recreation center several years ago.

"Do you have to go?" Tony asked, his eyes pleading.

"Yes, I do have to leave, but I want each of you to remember everything that I have tried to teach you—and remember that I love you," Wade answered, speaking and signing at the same time.

"My big brother says boys shouldn't love boys," Kenny said matter-of-factly.

Wade was used to Kenny's brother's comments and had learned to ignore them. He asked the boys to gather around him.

"What are some of the things that you should never forget?" he asked.

"Remember to do our homework because knowledge can never be taken away from you," Tony signed.

"Always remember your goals," Kenny added.

"Believe in yourself, and you can do anything," Raphi said, his eyes full of sadness.

"My brother said that all that is easy for you to say because you have ends," Kenny responded.

Wade pretended to choke Kenny, and they all laughed.

"All that is exactly what I want you to remember," he continued. "And even though I'll be at college in Atlanta, I won't ever forget you. As a matter of fact, I have something for each of you to remember me by."

With that, Wade reached into his bag and pulled out seven copies of a small black book by Kahlil Gibran entitled *The Prophet*. He had read from the book for them many times before. He knew that they didn't understand some of it, but thought it would come in handy one day when they were older. It was one of his favorites. He had personally signed each one of them, leaving them with his forwarding college address. Inside each book was a mall gift certificate for $100.

Each of the boys started to talk excitedly about what they were going to buy with their gift certificate—all except Tony, who grabbed Wade around the neck and hugged him again.

"Thank you. I'll write you a letter every week."

Tears welled up in Wade's eyes as he thought about how much he would miss the young boys. When the boys looked at him and saw that Wade would miss them as much as they would miss him they responded by giving him a group hug, which ended in a pile on wrestling match. Wade spent the remainder of the afternoon playing everything from dominoes to video games, and even helped several of the boys read from their new books.

When the center closed at five o'clock the boys grabbed their belongings and filed out as they had every other Saturday for the last two years. It was almost as if they had forgotten that Wade would not be back next Saturday. Wade liked it best that way and tried to make everything seem as normal as possible. When the last boy was gone, Wade pulled his Rolex watch from the pocket of his jeans and calculated that he had a few hours to kill before his graduation celebration party at eight. It would be tight, but he figured he could sneak off to D.C. and be back if he hurried.

On the way back from D.C., Wade adjusted his glasses, looked down at his Rolex watch, and realized that he only had thirty-two minutes before his graduation party started. His black BMW SUV was going 80 miles per hour, speeding up 695, from D.C. to Baltimore. There was no way he could be late. His mother would have a fit.

When Wade left home early that morning he'd told his mother that he was only going by the recreation center for a few hours. That had been many hours ago, and it was now 7:30 p.m. Wade glanced at his cell phone and sure enough, his mother had left five messages already. He pressed down on the gas—90 miles an hour. He had thirty minutes—his mother would not be happy.

Wade looked in the rear view mirror to see if any police cars had spotted him. All was clear. He looked back into the mirror into his light brown eyes, and guilt and confusion stared back at him. His wavy, black hair was damp and matted to his head. As soon as he got there he would have to take a shower before going into the party.

Wade was only minutes from his family's estate when he saw the blue lights flashing in his rear view mirror. He pulled over slowly and laid his head back on the headrest. The portly white officer approached the SUV slowly and cautiously.

"You seem to be in a big hurry young man," he said as he peered into the car with his flashlight. "Let me see your license and registration."

Wade obliged and waited patiently. His parents were going to kill him! The officer took Wade's license and looked at it with the flashlight.

"Oh, Mr. Graham, I didn't realize that was you. Good to see you this evening. I saw that you were in a hurry and I just wanted to make sure that everything was okay this evening. I'll let you get on your way. Please give Judge Graham my best."

Wade took his license back and thanked the officer. He knew that there was absolutely no way that he would be mentioning this meeting to his father. Wade drove 55 the rest of the way home. When he got there he drove to the back of the estate, rushed to the back of the house, and climbed up the trellis to his third story bedroom window. He opened the window quietly and crept into his room. Once inside, he could faintly hear the partygoers downstairs. He undressed quickly and rushed for the shower.

Victoria, Josephine, and Grace Wallington were the daughters of Courtland Wallington II, one of Washington D.C.'s most prominent doctors. Victoria, the oldest and fairest, had rightfully married Wade Graham III of the Baltimore Grahams, in what had been one of Baltimore and Washington's most elaborate weddings. Wade Graham IV was their only child, and their pride and joy. Victoria did not know what she would do now that he was going away to college.

"I am so glad that Wade finally decided to go to Georgia Central. For a while there, I thought he was surely going to Morehouse. Our men have always gone to Central. I am glad he realized his obligation to the family and its traditions," Victoria Graham stated proudly from her position at the head table.

"Morehouse is a great school, but it's no Central." Josephine responded. "What finally changed his mind, Victoria?"

"I don't know, Josephine, but I'm glad," Victoria answered.

"Well I think it's wonderful that you're giving him such a beautiful going away party," said Grace. "I know it's going to be hard to see your only child go so far away."

Josephine nodded. "Where is Wade anyway? I'm sure he knows that it is in very poor taste to be late to one's own party."

"He'll be here," Victoria answered with more certainty than she felt. Wade's recent disappearances had started to concern her, and even she didn't believe that he was spending all of his time at the recreation center.

"Ah, there he is now." Grace answered.

Victoria looked at her Baume & Mercier watch. It was 8:15. She was slightly irritated, but definitely relieved that Wade had finally shown up.

The three sisters watched with pride as Wade, moved from table to table, greeting well-wishers, and working the room with the sophistication and grace of the well-bred.

"Look at him. He is so handsome. Those glasses set off his stunning light brown eyes—just like father," Victoria beamed.

"He has mother's soft features," Josephine added.

"You know mother often said that he bears a striking resemblance to Langston Hughes," said Grace, smiling as she watched her handsome nephew.

"Is he dating anyone?" Josephine asked coyly.

"Can't seem to find anyone quite good enough," Victoria sighed. "I won't allow him to see just anyone. You remember how terrible it was when your William started dating that dark-skinned girl from Columbia," Victoria said haughtily. "Just as soon as she found out that he came from money, she tried to claim she was pregnant. I have always told Wade that his future is far too important," Victoria said.

Grace chuckled.

"Yes, dear, you are right about that," Josephine said, slightly embarrassed that Victoria had brought up the incident.

"Victoria, call him over here so we can get a good look at him," Grace urged.

Victoria lifted her left hand up as if she were a queen and waved gently. Wade had seen this royal gesture before and knew that his mother wanted him.

As he made his way over, he realized how much his mother and aunts looked alike, each of them had a complexion the color of warm cinnamon, with dark brown hair, and light brown eyes. Laced in Mikimoto pearls and Tiffany diamonds, they all sat perched like old birds on a wire. When Wade reached the table, he pushed his glasses up on his face, kissed each of them on the cheek, and pulled up a chair. This promised to be unbearable.

"We just wanted to tell you how utterly proud we are of you, Wade," Grace said once he was seated in front of them.

"Did you say hello to Chandler Young?" Josephine asked, cutting right to the chase. "She's such a beautiful young girl, and I've seen her watching you."

"Yes, she comes from a very good family. Boule, Jack and Jill—all of the right associations—they are definitely top shelf," Grace added.

"And I hear she is going to Spelman in Atlanta," Victoria chimed in.

Wade was only half listening. He had already heard that Chandler was going to college in Atlanta. As his aunts rattled on about who was old guard and who was new money, Wade glanced across the room. The sight was the same as it had been all his life. The family dining room was filled with Maryland's upper class African-American elite. He couldn't help think about what a contrast all this was from his day at the recreation center and his clandestine trip to Washington.

"Wade! Wade? Are you listening to me?"

His Aunt Josephine's shriek, finally caught his attention.

"Who are you dating?" she repeated.

"Uh, I'm not dating now. I want to focus all of my attention on my studies for my first two years." Wade answered.

Grace and Victoria gave Josephine a smug look.

"Oh? Well where were you all day today? We came over early to spend time with you." Josephine continued to pry.

"Uh, excuse me, Aunt Josie. I had better go spend some time with Chandler before someone snatches her up," Wade lied, dashing off to escape further questioning.

"Make sure you are front and center when your father makes his toast," his mother called after him.

Wade rushed straight for the front door and went outside onto the huge porch to get a breath of fresh air. He stood out there for several minutes glad to be away from all the festivities for a moment. Just as he was about to turn and go back into the house, his cell phone rang.

"Hello." He paused and listened to the voice on the other end.

"No, I can't leave now," he said. "My parents would kill me," he explained. "I know, but I'm leaving tomorrow—I just can't."

After several more exchanges, he hung up and looked back into the house through the expansive front window. He could see his father gathering all of the guests.

Inside, Judge Graham was tapping his wine glass with a fork, quieting his guests for the toast. "I'll go ahead and begin. It's getting late, and I am sure that several of you would like to eat," Judge Graham announced. "Where is the guest of honor?"

Wade tiptoed around the house toward his SUV with every intention of leaving. As he rounded the back of his SUV and took his keys out of his pocket, a familiar falsetto stopped him.

"Wade Graham IV!"

He recognized the voice instantly as his Aunt Grace.

"Yes, Ma'am," he said instinctively.

"Now you know you can't leave now. It would simply crush your mother," she scolded.

"That's the problem," Wade responded. "This party isn't for me. It's for her and father. I didn't even ask for it."

"But you did ask for this big truck, and all those fancy clothes," Grace lectured. "Your mother has always made sure that you were exposed to the finest things that money could buy. Surely you can suffer her this one small favor. You're going away, and that's a lot for her to handle. This small sacrifice isn't too much for your mother now is it? Besides, you wouldn't want to give your old Aunt Josie the satisfaction of rubbing this in your mother's face now would you?"

Wade smiled. He put his keys back in his pocket, took his Aunt Grace's arm, and walked back into the house to a large round of applause. When he saw his mother and father beaming at him with pride he put everything else out of his mind. After all, it was just one more evening with the family.

How still,
How strangely still
The water is today.
It is not good
For water
To be so still that way.

Sea Calm – Langston Hughes

CHAPTER 5

*I am the first son of Rhyme and Reason. Patience stood as
midwife at my birth as Perseverance made a place for my crown.
First. Fearsome. Fanatical. Fiery. Forbidden. Forceful. For-no-
other-reason-than-because-I-can.
I am the quintessential being.
Capable of instantaneous intellectual erections, and sustained
emotional orgasms, I fathered Peace and nurtured it until it
became Purpose.
Last. Lethal. Limitless. Livid. Luminous. Liberal. Let-me-show-
you-the-way-I-have-been-there-before.
I am the quintessential being.
Bearing the weight of your world only made me stronger, but
even truth does not live forever. My dying breath blew out the
flames of ignorance and intolerance.
Real. Rare. Receptive. Resonant. Right. Revolutionary.
Remember-that-I-was-the-one-who-brought-you-balance.
I am the quintessential being.*

Rhyme and Reason – Matthew Meredith

Georgia Central University was quickly becoming the nation's
leading historically black university—replete with ivory-colored
buildings, dormitories and a history of producing some of the
country's most prominent African-American leaders. Recent
advancements made by the university's School of Medicine on the
use of mitochondrial DNA to accurately identify the genealogy of
African-Americans, had catapulted the university into the forefront
of the national media.

Championship football and basketball teams fueled the buzz, as did the emergence of famous alumni. Anthony Goins—a.k.a. *Agonize*, was on the rise of the neo-soul music scene, and Mr. Thursday Brownleigh, one of the few African-American CEO's of a Fortune 100 company, further served to highlight Georgia Central's presence on the urban contemporary landscape. And if that weren't enough, Chancellor Weatherspoon had retained the nation's leading African-American public relations firm, Brandfire, to publicize the university's upcoming 100th anniversary.

The result of all this was an overwhelming influx of applications by the nation's youth. And from the looks of the applications, this year's crop of students was undoubtedly the best and brightest.

Winfrey-Combs Hall was the newest dorm on the campus of Georgia Central University. Built to house the recent flood of freshmen, the dorm was designed by two of the nation's top African-American architects. Each suite had two rooms. Each room accommodated two students and was joined by a common bathroom and study area.

"Wade, wake up! We're going to be late."

Wade didn't respond to the booming baritone.

"Wade! Wake up, pahtnah! We're going to be late for our first day of class!"

Wade groaned, rolled over, and pulled the cover over his head, as if that would somehow create a barrier between him and his roommate. Before Wade could quench the embers of slumber and stoke them into coals of consciousness, he felt the cover being yanked from him. A rush of cold air swept over him, and then he felt his body being lifted and tossed toward the ceiling.

"Chaaaannceee!" Wade yelled as his slim frame fell back on the dormitory mattress with a thud. "Must you play all of the time?" he reprimanded.

Having grown up an over-privileged only child, Wade wasn't used to sharing or living with others in such close proximity. He certainly wasn't used to the type of pranks and horseplay that his roommate constantly bombarded him with. Chance, on the other hand, grew up with three brothers, where horseplay was the norm.

"No, I *must* not, but you should be getting dressed."

Chance knew that his wrestling was unsettling for his new roommate, Wade, and Wade had already warned him several times that his fair skin bruised easily, but it was just too much fun. For Wade it was less like wrestling and more like Chance practicing the latest wrestling moves with him begging to be set free. Once back in the safety of his bed and completely awake, Wade glared at Chance.

"See, that's what you get for laying over there whispering on the phone late last night," Chance lectured as he continued to get dressed.

"I have told you about that shit!" Wade yelled as he reached over toward his desk for his glasses.

"I have told you about that shit," Chance said, mocking him. He reached into his closet to get a throwback sports jersey to put over his wife beater. "Are you sure you aren't white?" he teased, looking at him sideways. "I have never heard a black person say 'shit' quite the way you do."

"Well I am sorry I can't be down like you, Tor-rin," Wade shot back knowing that his roommate hated his first name.

Torrin Chance Walker had decided to shed his country veneer when he got to college. A name change from Torrin to Chance and a conscious effort to eliminate his southern drawl were just the beginning of his transformation. His family wasn't quite privy to his transformation though, and still asked for Torrin when they called to make sure that he was carrying his asthma inhaler. Wade noticed how his roommate cringed whenever they asked for him.

Chance ignored the shot. "Yeah, well, I keep it real. Now hurry up and let's go." Chance continued to admire himself in the full-length mirror, making sure that his gear looked just right. He was a walking advertisement in throwback jersey, Timberland boots, and a pair of Ryan Kenny urban designer jeans.

"It is just an introductory freshman course about university history. It's not even worth a class credit, and they're not going to tell me anything I don't already know. My family has been a part of this university since its inception. I know the Georgia Central history like I know my family history," Wade boasted.

"So what if your bourgeoisie, uptight family has been here since 1904?" Chance responded.

"For your information, my 'bourgeoisie, uptight family' is one of the most prominent African-American families in Maryland. The Graham-Wallington family is known up and down the entire east coast. As a matter of fact, my family built the new Graham law library wing. And you don't seem to mind watching that big color television that my family brought in here," Wade charged.

Thanks to Wade's family 400-A Dubois Hall was probably the most well equipped dorm room on the campus of Georgia Central University. Victoria Graham would suffer nothing less for her only son. However the Walker family was not about to be outdone by some uppity Baltimore judge's family, and had provided Chance with quite a few luxuries as well. Original artwork, the latest in computer equipment, media and video technology, and designer clothes were all organized by color coordinated high end storage solutions.

"You, and that television, and all your *things*," Chance said, shaking his head. "You are probably one of the most superficial brothers that I have ever met. My family has more than enough money to buy me a television—and don't forget, that stereo system you're always listening to came from *my* peeps."

"Don't know why I had to live on campus anyway," Wade mumbled, disregarding Chance's comment about the stereo.

"Anyway, you don't have much time to get dressed, and there are four of us to a bathroom, so you need to hurry. I *will* leave you," Chance lied.

It was an idle threat. Wade's family was very popular on campus among both students and faculty. Chance enjoyed the special attention that he received when he was with Wade. It was the first time that being a Walker didn't make a difference. There were many important families in the Georgia Central College community and Walker was not yet one of them.

"And who is this Dr. Smith anyway?" Wade asked as he shuffled over to his closet and pulled out a pair of slacks and the matching shirt—both from Banana Republic.

It was customary for Chancellor Weatherspoon to teach each freshman orientation class on the history of Georgia Central University, and African-American education in America. This year was going to be different. With the recent growth of the University, and the influx of a few prominent new professors, Chancellor Weatherspoon had agreed that having a few of the new professors teach freshman orientation would be a good way to ease his growing workload, and introduce the new faculty to the university community.

"Why does it matter to you if we don't get to take our introductory course with Chancellor Weatherspoon?" Chance asked in an irritated tone.

"My mother's family is very close to the Weatherspoon family. They have been with the university for years too. If I have to take this stupid class then it should be from someone who really understands the history. I have half a mind to call my father."

Chance didn't say anything at first. He found Wade's constant ranking and sorting of everyone and everything interesting, but also a bit humbling.

"Dr. Smith comes highly recommended, with experience from some of the nation's best Ivy League colleges. Maybe having a top white professor at Georgia Central will give the school more national recognition," Chance said.

Wade frowned at his roommate's comment. It displayed typical southern thinking. It was as if the only way for a black establishment to have any credibility, it had to have some sort of white endorsement.

"I don't know that we need him," he stated. "Georgia Central has done quite well all of these years on its own. It is one of the country's top African-American institutions of higher learning. It has turned out some of the country's most prominent African-American leaders."

"And you won't be one of them if you don't get dressed," Chance reminded him.

"Alright, alright," Wade responded. He grabbed his shower caddy and towel, and headed for the adjoining bathroom and shower between 400-A and 400-B.

Meanwhile in 400-B, a much more modest dorm room, Matthew Meredith was putting on his favorite t-shirt and his Wal-Mart *Faded Glory* jeans. With the exception of a few personal items, 400-B looked very much like it had before either Matthew or Jo'sha had moved in.

"How long have you had those damn jeans? Olivia asked. "You're a college man now. You should look the part," she chided her big brother.

"My scholarship only pays for tuition, housing and books—and you *know* Isadora and Roland don't have any spare coins for a brother."

"Well that's why I came by," Olivia said. She got up from Matthew's bed and stuffed some money in the back pocket of his jeans. "That should help you pay for your meal plan. Don't say I never gave you anything," she joked.

"Thanks, Sis. I completely forgot that the money was due today—had a few other things on my mind." He was referring to the cancer tests that he had been undergoing recently. He kissed Olivia on the forehead to show his gratitude. "How are Isadora and Roland doing?" he asked, reaching into his closet for the only pair of athletic shoes he owned.

"Well, he hasn't moved out yet, and I've noticed them acting differently. It's almost like they're starting to talk *to* each other instead of *at* each other," Olivia said, commenting on her parents.

"You know, O, sometimes I think it's more convenient for them to stay together. They're both set in their ways, and no one else could deal with either one of them. Dad wouldn't have anyone to clean up after him, and Mom has never had a full time job outside of the home. It's symbiotic," Matthew stated.

"Well, whatever you call it, I'll be glad to get the hell out," Olivia said.

She stretched, got up, and then walked across the room to look at Jo'sha's textbooks on art and music history. Matthew looked her over, certain that his sister had attracted quite a bit of attention on her way to his dorm. Her tight half tank revealed ample breasts, and her flat, mocha mid-drift, while her shapely hips were packed into a pair of form-fitting, low-rise designer jeans.

Olivia stopped at a copy of *A Candle In The Dark* by Edward A. Jones. She thumbed through the book and stopped on page 197 at a book marked passage that read, 'They were considered, as some teachers still regard them today, luxuries which Negro students could ill afford, either financially or ideologically.'

"What are you doing? Put his stuff down," Matthew instructed, as he stuffed his foot into his three-year-old gym shoes.

"This is a pretty interesting passage on fraternities that Jo'sha has highlighted. Is he thinking about pledging already?" Olivia asked.

"Jo'sha will do anything that puts him in the spotlight. He's a natural born performer."

"So how are you feeling?" she asked, placing the book back on the shelf. She knew that Matthew wasn't always comfortable talking about his health. Even with her.

"Fine. The cancer thing seems to weigh heavier on my mind than my body. Waiting on these results has been torture. "

"Have you told Jo'sha yet?"

"No, I don't want anyone feeling sorry for me."

At that moment, Jo'sha entered the room partially dry, with a towel wrapped around his waist, and his locks tied back by a single piece of string.

"Sorry for what?" he asked.

"Nothing—and put on some clothes—disrespecting my sister like that!" Matthew snapped.

"What am I supposed to do? Shower in my clothes? She's in *my* room at 7:00 a.m.! How did she get in the dorm this early anyway?" he asked, jokingly.

Matthew didn't find it funny.

"I'll just go wait in the hall," Olivia volunteered. She could tell that Jo'sha was playing around, and besides that he *did* have a point. But she also knew that Matthew took his role as big brother and protector very seriously. On her way out to the hallway, Olivia couldn't help but notice the bulge under Jo'sha's towel—no doubt a direct response to her tight, low-rise pants—the kind that accentuated a behind that only a "sistah" could carry.

"So what is it that you are not telling me, roommate?" Jo'sha asked once Olivia was gone.

"Nothing, just hurry up and get dressed so that we can go."

Jo'sha kept quiet. He had noticed that Matthew had become increasingly moody over the past few days, but so far he had been unsuccessful in getting him to talk about it. It was something that bothered Jo'sha particularly since he was making such an effort to get Matthew to open up. He did not take the prospect of Matthew's friendship lightly since he would be the first real friend that Jo'sha had ever had. He found Matthew's intellect fascinating, and they both shared a deep love for reading and writing. In the few days since they had arrived at the university, Matthew had already gone with him to the music room several times, where he would just sit and listen. It was Matthew who had given him the idea to call the music critic for Atlanta's *Rolling Out* magazine to get additional publicity for his music.

Jo'sha respected Matthew's creativity. Matthew had allowed him to read some of the poetry he had written, and Jo'sha had been front row when Matthew recited some of his work at Yin Yang Café in Atlanta. Matthew had even given Jo'sha several of his poems to use for lyrics in some of his new songs. Jo'sha's favorite was entitled, *Rhyme and Reason*. Jo'sha had taken excerpts from the poem and mixed them into an up-tempo, neo soul tune that promised to gain tremendous popularity in the local area.

"Can I come back in yet?" Olivia yelled through the door.

Jo'sha slipped on black cotton slacks with no underwear, a pair of patterned leather Prada sandals that he had found at a local thrift shop, and a vintage, striped shirt.

"Look, man, sorry that I've been grouchy. I'm normally not like this. It has nothing to do with you," Matthew said apologetically, as he offered Jo'sha his hand.

Jo'sha smiled, relieved slightly that his chance at friendship was still intact. He gave Matthew a quick handshake before opening the door for Olivia.

"You can come on in—"

Jo'sha stopped mid-sentence when he saw a tall, young brother propped up against the wall—in the midst of delivering his tightest rap to Olivia. Neither Matthew nor Jo'sha recognized him. They both looked at the brother with the ruddy brown skin, freckles and brownish-red hair, and then over at Olivia, waiting for some sort of explanation.

"This is my brother, Matthew, and his roommate, Jo'sha," Olivia said.

The three young men exchanged a quick, obligatory head nod.

"Sundiata," said the tall brother, giving them another nod. Neither Matthew nor Jo'sha responded, sending Sundiata the message that he was not completely welcome.

Sundiata read between the lines. He gave Olivia a sweeping head to toe gaze. "Hollah at you later, baby girl." He gave her a wink, slung his knapsack over his shoulder, and strolled off down the hallway.

Olivia smiled shyly before walking back into the room, which was heavy with the suffocating protection that only a big brother could give.

"You two on your way to class now?" Olivia asked, attempting to change the subject.

"Yeah, we have university orientation with that new white professor, Dr. Smith. It kinda defeats the purpose of being at a historically black university," Jo'sha said, throwing his saddlebag over his shoulder.

"You and that saddlebag," Matthew said, chuckling and looking at Jo'sha.

"You mean my *book bag*?" Jo'sha questioned. "Might not hurt *you* to invest in a real book bag, instead of carrying around that joint you've had since the sixth grade," he said referring to Matthew's tattered canvas backpack.

Matthew smirked, while Olivia made a mental note to go shopping for her big brother. "Well, let's go. I don't want to be late," he said.

Olivia kissed Matthew on the cheek. Jo'sha leaned forward as if Olivia were going to kiss him too. Olivia glanced at Matthew, waved politely at Jo'sha, and then took off down the hallway.

Jo'sha went over to the adjoining door for 400-A and rapped repeatedly and methodically. Seconds later Chance came to the door looking like an urban street wear ad, matching all the way down to his backpack. Wade followed in sharp contrast with slacks, a dress shirt, Kenneth Cole loafers, and a briefcase.

"Good morning," Chance said, with a bright smile.

"I see you," Jo'sha asked.

"What?" Wade asked.

"Just an African greeting," Jo'sha said.

"Oh. Well, hello," Wade answered. He looked from Jo'sha to Matthew, making note of the fact that Matthew had been in the same jeans and gym shoes since they arrived on the campus of Georgia Central over a week ago.

"Are we all ready?" asked Chance, looking at the other three for confirmation.

Everyone nodded. They closed the doors to their respective rooms, and the four of them walked across campus on their way to Dr. Smith's freshman orientation class—the first class of their college careers.

CHAPTER 6

The four young men took the scenic route towards Hughes Hall on their way to their freshman orientation class with Dr. Smith. They passed through the campus courtyard—affectionately referred to as the Brickyard by the students. It was a long-standing tradition for Black Greeks from all of Atlanta's surrounding colleges to post up on the university on the first day of class. Black Greeks held court in different sections of the Brickyard creating a kaleidoscope of collegiate contact and communication. Greek calls filled the air as members publicly reunited after summer break and competed for the attention of anxious onlookers.

"Have any of you ever thought about pledging?" Chance asked as they passed by the brothers of Omega Psi Phi, who were decked out in their colors of purple and gold.

"Well my entire family is Greek," Wade bragged.

"So what does *that* mean?" Jo'sha challenged.

"It means that I am a legacy. All of the men in my family are in the same fraternity and all of the women are sisters of the same sorority. It's a tradition; my family expects me to pledge to the same frat as well." Wade concluded.

No one seemed particularly impressed.

"I think I might pledge," Chance offered, glancing back at the Omegas.

"Some of us have more important things to think about," Matthew said, thinking specifically about the fact that he needed to go pay for his campus meal plan. He made a mental note to leave early enough to go do so before heading to his work-study job at the campus library that evening.

"Whichever organization I pledge is going to be bringing the hotness," Jo'sha bragged as he exchanged seductive glances with an eye-catching member of the Sigma Gamma Rho sorority adorned in blue and gold.

"Give it up, Jo'sha. There is no way that a Greek upperclassman is gonna give you the time of day. Besides, she's looking at *me*," Chance said.

"You trippin'. She's not thinking about your big collard-green eating, cow-throwing, country ass." Jo'sha said, still looking at the young lady, who had turned to continue her conversation with her sorors.

"Yeah, but what's the purpose? What good do they do?" Matthew asked, returning to the original conversation.

"What do you mean?" Wade responded. "Black Greek letter organizations have birthed some of this nation's most famous African-American leaders—Dr. Martin Luther King, Jesse Jackson, Andrew Young, Dr. Louis Sullivan, and our own Dr. Weatherspoon."

"They're all old school. What kind of impact are they making now?" Chance asked with genuine interest.

"They all do great service projects. They each serve special charities," Wade responded.

"Well, why can't you just do service projects without being in a fraternity or sorority," Matthew challenged. "You almost have to wonder if the concept of Black Greek Letter organizations is as antiquated as that of Black leadership. What about affirmative action, a cure for sickle cell, the disproportionate number of brothers in jail, or even the recent rash of Black male killings right here in Atlanta? Why aren't they using their influence to make a difference in those things?"

"Yeah, what's up with that?" Jo'sha asked distractedly. He was licking his lips, still gazing at the same young lady.

"I was listening to the radio this morning while I was waiting for Wade and it seems that the local authorities have already found the bodies of six young black men. All of them were between the ages of fifteen and twenty-one. Most have little or no family, and were found shot or strangled to death in areas just outside the city. One of them was even dragged to death like that dude in Jasper, Texas. Folks say they haven't seen anything of this magnitude since Wayne Williams and the Atlanta child murders," Chance informed.

The news seemed to send a pall over the conversation. They walked past the brothers of Phi Beta Sigma in their blue and white, and continued toward the underground tunnel leading to the academic side of campus.

"Homecoming is going to be off the chain this year. It's the 100th anniversary of the university. Agonize is performing, and Chancellor Weatherspoon says that they've got a few special surprises for the students and alumni," Jo'sha said, attempting to lighten the mood. However the seriousness of the news and thoughts of entering their first college class proved far too heavy, and they walked the rest of the way in silence. Jo'sha, Wade, Matthew and Chance reached Hughes Hall and entered with anxious anticipation.

"Our class is on the fourth floor in room 4377," Matthew advised, as he led the way toward the staircase.

They entered the room and found twelve chairs arranged in a semicircle facing an ornate, wooden, oak podium, in a small rectangular room that looked more like a meeting room than a classroom. Seven of the seats were already filled with freshmen that Jo'sha, Wade, Matthew, and Chance recognized from orientation week. The four took available seats, looked around the room and exchanged greetings with their fellow classmates.

"Where's the professor?" Chance asked the group, looking at his Nike sports watch.

"It's only 7:52," Wade answered.

No sooner than he said that, a tall and striking, but weathered gentleman entered the room. He locked the door behind him, strode to the podium, and placed his briefcase deliberately on top. He had a build that suggested that he might have been very fit when he was in his prime. His gentle blue eyes sparkled, and seemed out of place against his leathered skin and graying blonde hair. Everything about him was precise—his manner, his carriage and his dress. From his button down shirt and sweater vest, to his wing tip shoes, he exuded academia.

All of the students sat attentively as he carefully opened his briefcase and took out his materials as if he were a doctor preparing for surgery. After exactly three minutes of preparation he began speaking in a pronounced, yet controlled southern accent. His voice was rough, jagged and alarming—difficult for the students from up north to understand, but familiar to those from down south.

"Gentlemen, good morning, and welcome to your first class as undergraduates. Let me first introduce myself. My name is Dr. Cornelius Smith. I will be teaching this section of freshman orientation where we will be focusing on the history of Georgia Central University and the Neg—umm—African-American in higher education."

Jo'sha glanced at Matthew out of the corner of his eye to see if he had caught Dr. Smith's seemingly inadvertent use of the antiquated term. Neither Matthew nor the rest of the class seemed to notice.

"I am here to head the newly formed history department, but Dr. Weatherspoon has asked me to take advantage of this opportunity to meet a few of the students. In addition to assuming responsibility for the African-American studies program, I will also be adding a European history component. You may notice that these orientation classes have only a few students. That was designed so that that we faculty members can really get to know each of you. Our distinguished psychology department has taken it upon themselves to organize each orientation class into groups of twelve based on Myers-Briggs personality results so this should be very interesting. In some cases, we instructors were able to make a few recommendations based on our personal interests."

Just then the class was startled by a knock at the door. Dr. Smith continued as if he hadn't noticed the interruption, expounding on his academic and professional credentials. The knocking continued.

"Excuse me," Dr. Smith said as he made his way to the door and opened it slowly.

On the other side of the door stood a short, skinny, dark complexioned young man with a haircut that he had obviously given himself. His brand new, baggy, knock-off urban designer clothing dwarfed his slight frame. In addition to his oversized clothes he wore a large gold cross that hung midway to his torso.

"Is this Dr. Smith's class?" he asked, with a pronounced southern drawl.

"Yes, and you are?"

"My name is James Lynch, sir. Sorry I am a little bit late. This campus is so big—I guess I just got turned around," he explained.

He squeezed in through the small opening that Dr. Smith had left in the door, and hurried toward the last available seat. Jo'sha chuckled to himself as he noticed that James' large gold cross had gotten tangled up in his book bag.

"Well, Mr. Lynch, might I remind you that this class begins promptly at 8:00 a.m. I am not sure what you are used to where you come from, but in this class we begin on time."

Jo'sha glanced around the room to see if anyone else was even mildly offended.

"You have been on campus for over a week now. Surely, you have had ample opportunity to find your classes," Dr. Smith continued. "Let us not let it happen again. Am I clear?"

James nodded his head and edged uncomfortably into his seat. He made it a point to avoid eye contact with Dr. Smith and his new classmates.

"Now if I may continue, I would like for each of you to introduce yourselves, giving your name, your hometown, and one interesting fact about yourselves. Let us start with you Mr. Lynch."

The nervous Mr. Lynch was shifting uncomfortably, having gotten his college career off on the wrong foot.

"M-m-my name is James Lynch and I plan to major in engineering," he said nervously, fidgeting with his cross.

The class sat quietly waiting for Dr. Smith's response. "Again, you seem unprepared, Mr. Lynch. From which state does your family come?" Dr. Smith asked in a slightly irritated tone.

"I don't have much family to speak of, sir. My only relative, Aunt Francis, was sent to a nursing home when I got the Dunbar Scholarship to come to Georgia Central on account of the fact that she couldn't see that well and was always wandering out the house."

Dr. Smith seemed less than interested with the young man's ramblings. He glanced at Wade, who was sitting next to James. Wade smiled confidently.

Jo'sha listened intently. He felt a connection to James since he was the other Dunbar Scholarship recipient. And then it dawned on Jo'sha that the second medallion that he had received with the initials J.L. must have been intended for James Lynch. He made a mental note to bring it to class and surprise James. He had forgotten all about it since he arrived on campus. He doubted that James even knew that he was supposed to receive it.

Finally it was Wade's turn.

"My name is Wade Graham IV of the Baltimore Grahams, and I was recently recognized in the Black College Journal for having founded the Wallington-Graham Youth Outreach Center for the Deaf in Baltimore, Maryland. It benefits and supports inner city youths with hearing disorders," Wade boasted.

Jo'sha rolled his eyes. He was more than mildly disgusted by Wade's condescending attitude.

Dr. Smith however nodded approvingly. "You are too modest, Mr. Graham. You should also mention that the Graham family is the benefactor of the new law library wing."

Wade gave a practiced nod, pleased that someone else was singing the praises of the Graham family. The dog and pony show forced Jo'sha to huff loudly.

"Mr. Imarah, perhaps your deep sigh is an indication that you are ready to share with the group," Dr. Smith offered.

"My name is Jo'sha Imarah of the Chicago Imarahs," Jo'sha mocked, sounding surprisingly like Wade.

Jo'sha's comment drew snickers from more than a few members of the class. Dr. Smith and Wade were the only ones not amused.

"But for real do'—my name is Jo'sha and I am from Chicago—the sexy south side, where the playas play. I am a musician. I play eight different instruments and I'm going to be Georgia Central's next Grammy award winning artist," Jo'sha stated proudly.

Dr. Smith gestured to Matthew once Jo'sha finished.

"My name is Matthew Meredith and I am from Atlanta," he began.

"Ah, Mr. Meredith, the recipient of *the* prestigious GCU Founder's Scholarship," interrupted Dr. Smith. "If my memory serves me correctly, you come to us with a 4.0 grade point average, a perfect S.A.T. score, and an impressive I.Q. You have quite the academic resume. We are glad to have you with us," he concluded.

"Yes, sir," Matthew responded.

Dr. Smith seemed satisfied and nodded to the young man seated next to Matthew.

"My name is Robert Black, from New Orleans, Louisiana, and I am on the Georgia Central University Lions football team," Robert said proudly. Chance recognized him immediately as Robert "Blaze" Black, Georgia Central University's standout freshman athlete.

"Next," Dr. Smith instructed.

"My name is Alexander Onahu, from Porto Novo in Benin, Africa. I plan to finish medical school, return to my country, and open my own medical practice—perhaps even a hospital," Alexander said.

"Is that the dude that's an African prince?" Jo'sha whispered to Matthew. Matthew shrugged.

"Mr. Onahu, I am particularly pleased to have you in my class. I find the stories of the mines of Porto Novo to be quite interesting. Perhaps you can spend some time later sharing more about life in the Gulf of Guinea, Prince Onahu," Dr. Smith added. "And there will be no whispering in my classroom gentlemen."

Dr. Smith shot a look in Jo'sha and Matthew's direction. Jo'sha huffed again, and Matthew returned his attention to the professor as his classmates continued.

"Well, my name is Maxwell Carmichael-Wright of the Richmond Carmichael-Wright's," Maxwell said nodding politely at Wade. "My family has attended Georgia Central for years. My great, great grandfather founded Richmond's first Black bank. I plan to major in finance, return to Richmond, and take over the family business," Maxwell finished.

Dr. Smith smiled and nodded to his next pupil.

"My name is Sundiata Bazemore. I am from Nashville, Tennessee, and I am a psychology major," Sundiata mumbled.

Jo'sha and Matthew exchanged glances, recognizing Sundiata as the young brother that had been talking to Olivia earlier. Sundiata looked over at them with an expressionless stare, and then looked back at the instructor.

"My name is Peyton Latrell Anderson, and I am from Miami, Florida. I plan to major in design," he said. He crossed and then uncrossed his legs, suddenly feeling very self-conscious about the slacks and shirt that he had designed for his first day of class.

Dr. Smith nodded for the introductions to continue.

The next young man was strikingly handsome with a golden bronze complexion, curly black hair, and piercing black eyes.

"My name is Roman Riley, and I am from Hollywood, California," he said.

The entire class recognized Roman as the son of Conrad Riley, the African-American Oscar nominee. Roman leaned back balancing out the room with his intense west coast vibe. Chance was next in line.

Normally eloquent, but uncharacteristically nervous in the presence of his peers, Chance muttered. "My name is Chance Walker, and I am a pre-law major. I am from North Carolina, and I can bench press 285 pounds," he said, trying not to sound too southern.

The class laughed and though Chance wasn't sure exactly why that was all he had to share, he laughed along with the class as if he had meant to be humorous.

The last young man sat next to the wall and was 6'6". His long legs seem to go halfway across the room.

"My name is Amir Regan, I am from Brooklyn, New York, and I plan to major in English and become a writer," he said, in a thick New York accent that was a sharp contrast to Chance's drawl.

"Gentleman, thank you for sharing," said Dr. Smith. "Some more eloquently than others, but thank you none the less," Dr. Smith said glancing at Wade and Maxwell Carmichael.

"Before we begin our first lecture, I would like to take a few moments to share some information with the class. You'll hear about this via your student email and formal campus postings, but I would like to give you a personal preview. In recognition of the university's 100th anniversary and this year's homecoming we are inviting student groups to compete to present the university history at the Founder's Day celebration. The presentations are particularly important this year because they will be televised on BET. Desmond Tutu and Coretta Scott King will be in attendance." Dr. Smith paused and looked around the room, making sure he had their attention. "Homecoming is the second weekend in November so you don't have much time. The deadline for registering is August 28th. That will give you September and October to prepare your presentations. The Chancellor and his executive staff will privately judge presentations during the first week in November. The top three groups will present at the homecoming coronation, where the winning group will be announced."

Chance, Jo'sha and Wade looked at each other. Matthew listened intently, waiting for Dr. Smith to continue.

"The presentation groups cannot be larger than four students. Presentations should be no more than twenty minutes, innovative, informative, creative, and original. The winners will not only get to present at the coronation, but will also be given a page in the 100th anniversary edition of the student yearbook, box seats at the homecoming game, four free tickets to all of the homecoming events, special introductions to the university's homecoming special guests and alumni, and a $20,000 student expense scholarship. Copies of the winning presentation will also be archived in the Chancellor's office and in the university time capsule to be opened in the year 2104."

The class seemed to brighten up most at the possibility of winning money. And like most Georgia Central men, they each thought that they could come up with an idea to win.

Dr. Smith continued, "Now, let us begin. Please pull out your books entitled, *Heart of a Lion: A History of Georgia Central University* by Gordon Hall. Who can tell me how Georgia Central University was founded?"

Wade and Maxwell's hands shot up immediately. Jo'sha slumped down in his seat. It promised to be a long class.

CHAPTER 7

"Matthew, I don't think I have seen anyone catch on as quickly as you have here at the library. It's only been two weeks and you have mastered all of our filing systems, and the improvements that you made in the computer lab are phenomenal," said Miss Vaughn. "You seem to love coming to work," she added.

"Thank you, Miss Vaughn."

Though Matthew appreciated the praise, the elderly Miss Vaughn wasn't aware that he had an ulterior motive. Matthew, Jo'sha, Wade and Chance had decided to enter the university's 100th Anniversary History Presentation competition. Matthew was motivated by the money, while Jo'sha, Wade and Chance were equally motivated by the recognition. Matthew's job at the library had proven to be very useful for gathering information on the university's history.

Miss Vaughn was also very helpful. She had been with the university for over thirty years, serving as executive assistant to the Chancellor, university historian, and head librarian. She had given up the thought of marriage as a young woman when her fiancé was killed in a train wreck just two weeks before their wedding. The university had become her life.

All of the students at Georgia Central were required to purchase a copy of *Heart of a Lion: A History of Georgia Central University* by Gordon Hall, and most were using the text to prepare their speeches, skits, and presentations on the university's history. Matthew however had found a lot of additional information on the university and its founders in the library and from Miss Vaughn. Miss Vaughn had even introduced him to Gordon Hall Jr.

Gordon Hall Jr. had followed in his father's footsteps and was a journalist. He had been commissioned to update the history and author the 100th anniversary edition of *Heart of a Lion*. Matthew was sure that the introduction would allow them to obtain more detailed information than any other group. The only other thing they had to do next was come up with an awesome presentation.

∞

It was late Saturday afternoon and the library was practically empty. Miss Vaughn and Matthew were the only staff members still around since the library closed at 6:00 p.m. on Saturday.

"Matthew, I need you to take my keys, go down to the copy room, and bring up those new copies of the campus map. The homecoming planning committee says that they are not to proper scale, and I need to take a look at them," Miss Vaughn urged. "God knows they are worrying the pure devil out of me! First the time capsule, and now the maps," she said, shaking her head.

"What time capsule?" Matthew asked curiously.

"Well, I'm really not supposed to mention it, but everyone will know soon anyway. It seems that one of our founders, Mr. Hines, had the foresight to create a time capsule to be opened at the university's 100th anniversary. It's being kept in my office. That public relations firm wants to come and get it for safekeeping, but I told them that I've had it for thirty years, and it's been just fine. I don't trust them. They just want more money. They're destroying all of the things that matter here at Georgia Central. They're making things too commercial. I for one am not going to help them mess up several decades worth of history. They'll get that time capsule the week before homecoming as planned."

"What do you think is in it?" Matthew asked.

"I don't know, but that public relations firm has got the media all whipped up. I get three or four phone calls a day about it. Now take my keys and go down to the copy room to get me those maps. I need to take a look at them. They're by the globe," she said.

"No problem, Miss Vaughn."

Matthew didn't mind going the extra mile for Miss Vaughn since she favored him in the assignment of work hours—allowing him to make money that he desperately needed. Matthew also had other business down in the copy room. Matthew went downstairs in the library basement, unlocked the door to the copy room, flipped on the lights, and closed the door behind him. Miss Vaughn's office was in the far corner of the copy room. Matthew had not seen her use it since he'd been working in the library. Due to the seclusion, he felt comfortable hiding a gathered box of letters, books, and copies under a large university flag that lay between the water fountain and a lopsided bookcase.

Matthew went to the box and quickly rifled through it to make sure that he had everything he needed. He had secured a copy of Gordon Hall's original notes, the first draft of the 100th anniversary revision written by the junior Gordon Hall, copies of personal letters from the original founders, and several books on the history of Black colleges and universities. Matthew pulled his box out first and slid it by the door. He looked around a few seconds before he found the globe and the campus maps that Miss Vaughn requested. He took a quick look at them and decided to take four copies for himself and his friends. He loaded a small dolly with his contraband and Miss Vaughn's maps, before picking up the phone. The phone rang in 400-B, but when Jo'sha didn't answer, he called his suitemates in 400-A.

"Hello," Wade answered.

"What's up?" Matthew responded.

"Nothing much, I'm just hanging out watching television and waiting for you guys to come back so that we can work on our project. I finished my French homework hours ago."

"The life of leisure," Matthew teased.

"Not exactly, I'm sitting here watching the local news and the authorities just found the body of another young Black man. That takes the toll up to seven. This is starting to get national attention." Wade said.

"This *is* getting serious," Matthew agreed.

"More serious than you know. The last victim was a student from Emory. Police have put out a warning that all local college students should be very careful," Wade warned.

"Where's Jo'sha? He should be back from the music room by now. Have you seen him?"

"Umm yeah, he came back about an hour ago. He has company."

"Who is it?"

"I don't know her name. *He* probably doesn't even know her name," Wade joked.

"You're probably right. I shouldn't have even asked," Matthew said, laughing.

"Chance went to the gym. You know how he is about working out. He's been gone almost two hours. He should be back any minute," Wade offered.

"Well, I will be back at 6:30 p.m. like we planned, so tell Jo'sha and Chance to be ready," Matthew ordered.

Wade looked at his watch. It was 5:15 p.m. He was sure that Chance would be back, and he could only hope that Jo'sha would be finished by then. Before he could answer, his phone clicked. "Matthew, I have a call coming in. I have to go."

"Oh, a-ight, see you at six-thirty."

Wade clicked over. "Hello," he said with a smile.

∞

"Whew, I'm exhausted!" Jo'sha exclaimed as he walked into 400-A. He immediately walked over and plopped down onto Wade's expertly made bed.

"Can you please not sit on my bed?" Wade complained.

Jo'sha laughed, thinking it was a joke, but then quickly realized that Wade was all too serious after he offered him a chair. Jo'sha looked at Matthew with a smirk of disbelief. Once they were all settled, the four began to thumb through the reams of notebooks that they had just received from Matthew. In each one Matthew had given them an exhaustive summary of the histories of the existing black Greek letter organizations, and excerpts from *The Divine Nine* by Lawrence Ross, and *Black Greek 101* by Dr. Kimbrough. He also inserted an article entitled *Why Blacks Call Themselves Greek* by Tony Brown, Miss Vaughn's maps of the university, and letters and notes from both the junior and senior Gordon Hall. There were some other university archives mixed in as well.

Chance offered his new friends food and drink, serving Jo'sha first as a peace offering for Wade's less than polite behavior.

"What's up with all of the fraternity information, Matthew?" Jo'sha asked.

"Well, since we've talked about pledging, I thought it couldn't hurt to get just a little bit more information. I'm sure that there's information here that even Wade doesn't know."

Although they had planned to spend the early evening preparing their presentation, the events of the afternoon had taken more out of them than they realized. None of them felt mentally alert

63

enough for the task at hand. Instead they spent the remainder of the evening debating the merits of Black Greek fraternities, talking about the recent string of Atlanta murders, and discussing the need for strong leadership in the African-American community. When the conversation got too heavy, they lightened the mood by talking about females, playing video games, and watching sports. Somewhere into the evening they also wound up discussing their career aspirations.

"I plan to become a lawyer," Chance said, as he maneuvered the controller on the Playstation. "My family thinks that I'm coming back home to North Carolina, but I don't think that will happen."

"Shit, you should be glad that you got a family to go back to," Jo'sha commented. He paused for a moment. He hadn't meant to voice his thoughts aloud. He quickly changed the subject. "You know I am all about my music career."

"I'm the first person on either side of my family to go to college," Matthew interjected.

"Really?" Wade asked, in a tone of complete disbelief. "I'm a fourth-generation college student," he added smugly.

Jo'sha cut his eye at Wade.

"So are you really going to be a journalist?" Chance asked, looking at Matthew.

"Yes. Tavis Smiley and Ed Gordon-type joint for real," Matthew answered.

"Well, you have a perfect voice for radio. You could be a nationally syndicated disc jockey," Chance suggested.

"He's got a face for radio too," Jo'sha teased. They all laughed.

"I hear they make good money, but that's just not me. I don't know why, but I don't really consider shock radio to be journalism. Feels more like entertainment," Matthew replied.

"And what's wrong with entertainment?" Jo'sha asked defensively.

"How about you, Wade?" Matthew asked, ignoring Jo'sha's question. "What are you going to be when you grow up?"

"A white man," Jo'sha said, before Wade could answer.

Matthew and Chance burst out in laughter, but of course Wade didn't find it funny.

"No," Wade said, attempting to ignore Jo'sha, "I really like publicity and fundraising."

The group seemed somewhat unimpressed with his choice, so Wade felt the need to explain further, but before he could speak,

Chance interrupted. "My grandfather says that every Black man should have the four T's."

"The four T's?"

All of them looked at him, waiting for him to elaborate.

"Yeah, the four T's—a trade, training, talent, and theology," Chance said. He was proud to share his grandfather's wisdom with his friends.

"What's the difference?" Jo'sha questioned.

"A trade is something that you learn how to do and usually involves your hands. My trade was learning to cut hair. I learned in my uncle's barbershop. Training is more like formal education. Like me getting my law degree. You use your mind and that is where you make the big bucks, but you still have your trade to fall back on in case something goes wrong. Your talent is that special gift that God gave you. For me, it's my athleticism. For you, Jo'sha, I guess it's your musical ability. Granddaddy T.C. says that you have to identify it and cultivate it. Last but not least, you have got to have theology—your own relationship with God."

The group took note. Even Wade and Jo'sha, who were typically very critical, simply nodded in agreement. The rest of the evening was filled with more conversation ranging from the transformation of Minister Conrad Mohammed to Robert H. deCoy's book entitled *The Nigger Bible,* to their views on religion. It was the conversation of youth, where every word seems to bring forth new life and educates the speaker as much as the listener.

"Isn't it interesting that we don't have a rite of passage?" Chance asked.

"What do you mean?" Wade asked.

"Well, Jewish boys have Bah Mitzvah, but what do we have to mark our passage into manhood?" Chance asked.

"Our first sexual experience," Jo'sha said.

"Opening our first bank account," Wade guessed.

"In Africa, young boys used to leave the village with the elders for manhood training," Matthew informed them.

"Sounds like a good idea," Chance said. "I wonder what happened to that."

With each topic, they continued to learn more about each other. Everyone was amazed at how many minor facts, figures and details that Matthew knew. Wade and Chance were amazed at how many young women Jo'sha had managed to sleep with in just a short time at college. They all took measure of themselves as Chance demonstrated his dedication to the maintenance of his physique through his conversation, spontaneous exercising, and weight lifting. Being a Graham had always made Wade feel special, but in this time and place, it didn't seem to matter.

Before they knew it, they had eaten themselves full, talked themselves out, and drifted off to sleep. It was well after midnight before Jo'sha woke up from the pallet he had made on the floor. He began thumbing through the materials that Matthew had collected. "Hey, wake up," he yelled.

Chance woke up immediately, followed by Matthew and Wade.

"What is it?" Matthew asked.

"Look!" Jo'sha yelled, getting their full attention. "Take a look at this information. There's a letter from one of the founders of the university in here."

"What?" Matthew asked.

"It's a letter from one of the benefactors of the university, written to one of our founders." Jo'sha started to read,

October 12, 1904

Dear Mr. Hines,

> *It has come to my attention that four of the students of our beloved Georgia Central School have gone missing. My sources inform me that Masters Oleander Vaughn, Winston Wright, Cyrus Wilkes, and Nathaniel Charles have not been heard from since the beginning of the month. As you might imagine, their families are quite distraught. Of particular note is the fact that all of these young men come from families that are prominent in their local communities. I don't have to tell you that a situation of this nature could most certainly undermine the formation of a Negro training school. Your prompt attention to this matter would be greatly appreciated. I anxiously await your post.*

Sincerely,

Mr. Coppedge.

"Wow, the university history book doesn't say anything about this," Wade said.

"And listen," Jo'sha continued. "This the response."

October 17, 1904

Dear Mr. Coppedge,

> *I regret to inform you that Misters Vaughn, Wright, Wilkes, and Charles have been located. Their bodies were found swinging from a poplar tree in a clearing some forty miles south of the city of Atlanta, Georgia. While we have reported it to local authorities, we fear that we do not have their complete cooperation.*
> *I am most assuredly prepared to meet with the families of each of these*
> *noble young men to express our deepest sympathies. It is my hope that*
> *this single unfortunate incident does not deter you from continuing to*
> *extend your financial and spiritual support toward the formation of the Georgia Central School for Colored Men.*
> *As is customary, we will be sending their personal belongings home to their families. But with special permission, a few of each of their personal effects will be maintained by the Georgia Central School to erect some type of memorial in their honor.*

Sincerely,

Mr. Hines

"Damn!" Chance exclaimed, speaking what they all were surely thinking.

"I wonder why none of this is in the university's history book. They must have come across it," Matthew reasoned.

"Well, if they haven't they certainly will with all of the attention on the 100th anniversary," Wade answered.

"Uh, that may not be possible," Matthew answered.

"Why?" the three asked in unison.

"Well, I made copies of most of the information from the archives, but I got tired. I just took this pack of old letters. I planned to return them when we were finished," Matthew admitted.

"What?" Wade yelled. "You mean you *stole* the letters?"

Matthew sighed. Jo'sha smiled. "Hey, wait!" he exclaimed, an idea suddenly coming to him.

"What now?" Chance asked.

"Miss Vaughn was telling me about a time capsule that a Mr. Hines left. The university is planning to open it for homecoming. That must be one of the surprises the university has planned," Matthew said.

"So what are you suggesting?" Chance asked.

"Well, maybe we should take a look at some of the artifacts. That would certainly give us an edge in the presentation competition," Matthew said.

"You mean you didn't steal the time capsule while you were stealing all of the other precious university artifacts?" Wade remarked snidely.

"I didn't steal. I *borrowed*," Matthew emphasized. "I can always take it back."

"So where is this time capsule and how do we get to it?" Jo'sha prodded.

"You can't be serious," Wade admonished.

"Let's hear him out, Wade. It can't hurt to take a peek," Chance said, becoming more interested.

"Well, the time capsule is in Miss Vaughn's office. Her office is in the back corner of the copy room," Matthew added.

"I don't know," Wade said skeptically.

"You do want to win that presentation competition don't you, Wade?" Chance asked. "No one is expecting freshmen to bring it. This could put us on the map. Fraternities will be knocking down our doors."

"Not to mention the females," Jo'sha added, licking his lips.

"Alright," Wade conceded, telling himself there wouldn't be any harm in just looking.

"I'm scheduled to work at the library on Monday from nine to noon, after Dr. Smith's class, and then again in the evening from nine to eleven. I can scope things out in the morning. Nia and I are the only ones scheduled to close on Monday night. That will give us a chance to get back in there and see what we can find. So you three meet me at the library at ten-thirty on the second floor," Matthew said.

"I didn't know female students could work in our library," Chance mentioned.

"There are several GCU jobs that are open to anyone in the Atlanta University system," Wade answered.

"Does this really require all four of us?" Wade asked, looking for a way out.

"You mean fine ass Nia Baptiste from Spelman?" Jo'sha asked.

"Yeah, you might have known that she worked there if you ever bothered to come to the library," Matthew answered, completely ignoring Wade.

"We're in this together and we need to keep this between us. We have a lot to gain," Chance said, primarily addressing Wade.

And a lot to lose, thought Wade.

"All in agreement?" Chance asked, looking around for a vote.

"Agreed," Matthew and Jo'sha answered instantly.

Chance looked at Wade.

"Agreed," Wade said reluctantly.

"Hey, you guys wanna go to that mega church on the south side of Atlanta tomorrow morning," Jo'sha asked.

"Not really," Wade said quickly.

"Come on," Chance urged. "It can't hurt."

"I don't want to go either. I don't really like dressing up," Matthew said, ashamed of the one hand-me-down suit that he owned.

"That's the beauty of it. You don't have to dress up," Jo'sha answered, eliminating Matthew's excuse.

Neither Matthew nor Chance could imagine going to church in casual dress.

"But we probably *should* wear suits," Wade instructed.

"Hey, then maybe we can shoot by your crib and have dinner. Your mom shouldn't mind cooking for you and a few of your friends," Chance said to Matthew, assuming that everyone understood southern hospitality.

"Well it's too late to call her now, and I'm sure that she needs some advanced notice to cook for four extra people," Matthew hedged.

"We can call her first thing in the morning," Jo'sha suggested.

"How are we going to get there? The church is all the way on the south side of the city," Matthew asked.

"Oh don't worry. My car is parked in a lot just off campus," Wade answered, proud that he alone among his freshman friends had a car at college.

"Then it's settled. We'll meet tomorrow morning at 8:30 a.m. I'll make sure that everyone gets up," Chance said, as he demonstrated a wrestling choke hold on Wade.

CHAPTER 8

Wade and Chance were waiting in the dorm lobby at exactly 8:30 a.m. Both were impeccably dressed in new, tailored, Etro and Karl Kani suits with matching accessories. Matthew and Jo'sha arrived minutes later. Matthew looked uncomfortable, and felt extremely self-conscious. He was sure that his friends would notice that he was wearing the same four-year old, pinstriped, double-breasted suit that he had worn to freshman orientation. Jo'sha on the other hand, looked comfortable and relaxed. He was dressed very casually in distressed denim jeans and a basic white cotton shirt. His locks were covered in a red, blue, and green yarn woven cap, with a row of cowry shells around his neck.

"Right on time," Chance announced.

"My truck is parked in the secured parking deck on the north end of campus," Wade said, eyeing the wide lapels on Matthew's shiny old suit.

With the exception of Chance, all of them were very tired, having gotten less than six hours of sleep. Chance however, seemed as alert as ever, and welcomed the opportunity to go to church. Since starting school he had not managed to make it to church. Having spent every Sunday in his uncle's church back home, he was looking forward to getting back into that familiar setting.

Wade and Matthew were less spiritual than the other two. Matthew couldn't remember the last time that anyone in his family had gone to church. His mother said that it always reminded her of his twin brother's funeral, and so she hadn't stepped foot in a church since. Wade's family attended First Presbyterian in Baltimore about once a month—typically on religious holidays, or when a member of Baltimore's social elite was speaking or being honored.

After a brisk twenty minute walk, they made it to Wade's SUV. Chance jumped in the front passenger's seat, and Matthew and Jo'sha climbed in the back.

"Must be nice to have a car at college," Jo'sha said, communicating exactly what Matthew was thinking.

"Matthew, what's your mother cooking for dinner?" Chance asked.

"I didn't get a chance to call her this morning, so maybe we should take a rain check," Matthew said, relieved that they wouldn't be able to go to his house.

"No problem," Wade said, pulling his new cell phone from his coat pocket, and passing it back to Matthew. "You can call her now before it gets too late."

"Yeah, call her now," said Jo'sha, who was looking forward to seeing Olivia again.

Matthew dialed slowly, praying that no one would answer. After three rings, he began to feel hopeful that his prayer would be answered, but that hope deflated quickly when his mother answered the phone on the fifth ring.   "Hello."

"Hey, Ma, it's me. I was calling to let you know that—ummm—I may be home this afternoon," he said cautiously.

"Where are you calling me from?" she asked suspiciously. "I don't recognize this number. You ain't in no trouble are you?"

"No, Ma, I'm calling from a friend's cell phone. I was calling to tell you that we might stop by for dinner. There are four of us." Matthew sucked in a breath and waited for his mother's inevitable response. He wished he'd lied and told his friends that today wasn't a good time to drop by. The truth of the matter was that his family wasn't normal. Inviting people over wasn't something he ever did. It had the potential of being far too embarrassing.

"And what do you expect them to eat? You know we ain't got no whole bunch of food here. You done gone to college and lost your memory and your mind?" Isadora questioned.

"Okay, then maybe later," Matthew said, feeling both embarrassed and relieved at the same time.

"Naww, go ahead and bring them over. It'll give us something to do. I'll scrounge something up, but tell them don't be coming over here trying to eat us out of house and home," she warned.

Matthew stifled a sigh. He'd almost been home free. "Okay, Ma, see you after church," he said.

"Church? You going to church? You ain't in no cult are you?"

Matthew winced. He was sure that his friends could hear Isadora's shrill soprano coming through the cell phone. To avoid further conversation he faked a quick and pleasant goodbye and then hung up the phone. "Thanks," he said, handing the phone to Wade. Then he leaned back in his seat and remained quiet for the rest of the ride to church.

"I'm surprised you were actually serious about going to church this morning," Wade said, looking at Jo'sha in the rearview mirror. "You seem like the least likely person to attend church."

"What's that supposed to mean?" Jo'sha asked defensively.

Chance and Matthew looked at each other, preparing themselves for another argument between their respective roommates.

"You just don't seem like the religious type," Wade clarified.

"You have a point," Jo'sha conceded. "I wouldn't call myself religious. I would say that my journey is spiritual. I start every day with a reading and prayer. I also like to attend different religious services to see how different people worship. I think denominations are man's feeble attempt to define and commercialize God. I like to spend time searching for the common strands between the different religions and not the differences. I think the real truth is in there somewhere," Jo'sha ended.

"What about smoking marijuana, womanizing, and cursing?" Wade questioned.

"Who says those things are wrong? Man or God?" Jo'sha challenged.

The car fell silent. Wade wasn't versed enough in any of the particulars of the Bible to respond to Jo'sha's comment, and therefore felt it best to abandon the argument. Chance was about to interject a quote from the many scriptures that he had learned in his uncle's church, but Wade popped in a CD and the silence was filled by a husky, melancholy voice.

"Is that Stephen Simmonds?" Jo'sha asked.

"Yes," Wade said, amazed that Jo'sha had even heard of the artist. "I picked it up a couple of summers ago when my family was vacationing in Europe. I even had a chance to hear him live."

"For real?" Jo'sha asked, with the enthusiasm of a child at Christmas. "I *love* his work. It's deep. I think my favorite cut is *Alone*"

"That one's good, but the best song on the album is definitely *Judgment Day*," Wade responded.

To Matthew and Chance's surprise, Wade and Jo'sha spent the remainder of the ride bonding over their mutual appreciation for Stephen Simmonds' music.

Greater Faith Ministries was huge, and one of the biggest and most well known churches in Atlanta. Being from Atlanta, Matthew had heard the rumors about the extravagant ministry, and the pastor's financial reign over his parishioners. As he surveyed the sprawling church campus, Matthew was further convinced that the rumors about the pastor fleecing his flock were true. Because of the throngs of early arrivers, the group was forced to park several blocks away from the church. They got out, and joined the procession of worshippers that were marching obediently toward the dome. Matthew, watched them, sure that each was prepared to give his or her last dime. He secretly clutched the last four dollars that he had in his pocket. He had no intention of parting with his money. He needed it and wasn't about to give it to a preacher who already had everything.

The church and its large congregation appropriately impressed Chance. His uncle's Baptist church paled in comparison to this structure. While it was the largest African American church within a fifty-mile radius of Nash County, Chance was sure that his uncle's church wasn't even a tenth the size of the church in front of him. He would be glad, however, to report back to his family that he had actually made it to church. He could hear his Grandmother Maytrude quoting her favorite Bible verse, *"Raise up a child in the way he should go and when he is old he will not depart from it."* It was a verse she used every time she had an opportunity, and Chance knew that she was talking to each of her grandchildren.

Wade tried not to act as impressed with the size of the church as his friends. He was sure that no matter how big this church was, there was more old money in First Presbyterian.

A jolly, mocha complexioned brother with braids and glasses startled them. "Welcome," he exclaimed, as he rushed to open the door.

As they entered the expansive red sanctuary, ushers offered blessings, programs, and tissues. None of them were quite sure what the tissue would be needed for, but they accepted it just to be polite. Chance moved to the side and leaned on one of the big white columns to tie his shoe.

"Excuse me, sir, we ask that you not lean on the columns."

At the sound of the soft, feminine voice Chance looked up immediately, and found himself looking into the eyes of Aspen Walker, the Sigma Gamma Rho that he'd seen on campus on the first day of class.

"Huh?" he asked.

"We ask that you not lean on the columns," she repeated, giving him her Harlem girl smile.

"Sure," Chance responded, captivated by her smile and mesmerized by her accent. He shifted his weight off of the pillar to comply with her request.

"Welcome to church," she said.

Chance looked around nervously. His friends took that as a cue for privacy, and stepped off to the side of the entryway.

"It is my first time," Chance responded.

Aspen giggled.

"At church I mean," Chance said, instantly embarrassed by his unnecessary clarification.

"Well, if you have any questions, please don't hesitate to ask," she said.

Just that quick Aspen turned and walked to the back toward the church's bookstore. Chance stood there, searching for the words to regain her attention, but nothing came to mind. When he turned to face his friends, he was met with a chorus of laughter.

"That's the girlie from campus, huh? She's kinda hot, Bruh," Jo'sha teased. "But your game is too slow. That's a New York shortie. You gotta be quick on your feet cornbread."

"Whatever, I was just speaking to her," Chance muttered. Before they could tease him further he marched off toward the sanctuary. His friends chuckled and followed behind him. They hadn't gone more than a few steps when they heard someone call Wade.

"Mr. Graham."

Wade turned and saw Dr. Weatherspoon, a robust, dark-skinned man with a short, well-formed, salt and pepper Afro, and a tailored suit.

"You're Victoria Graham's boy aren't you? William is it?" he asked.

"Wade, sir," he responded.

"Oh—yes," the Chancellor said absently. "I was wondering when I was going to run into you. Your mother called me and told me that you were here. I thought I would have seen you on campus by now.

Please tell her that I did check up on you. How is Victoria—and uh your father?"

"They're fine, sir," Wade beamed. He was glad to have his friends see him talking to the Chancellor. "I didn't realize that you attended this church," Wade said, trying hard not to sound judgmental.

"Yes. The pastor is a huge financial supporter of the university's campus ministry," Dr. Weatherspoon responded, sounding more like a publicist than a parishioner. He looked past Wade, waving to the affluent as they entered the church, and conveniently looking past the afflicted.

Just then a young man rushed up to Dr. Weatherspoon. He looked at Wade, but didn't bother to excuse himself. "The mayor just arrived," he said in a loud whisper. "If we hurry we can get a seat close to her."

Dr. Weatherspoon nodded enthusiastically, welcoming the opportunity to rub elbows with someone important. "It was very nice seeing you again. Please give your family my best, William— uh—Wade. Tell them that I will see them at homecoming!" Dr. Weatherspoon hurried off without waiting for Wade to respond.

Wade turned confidently and looked at his friends.

"Why didn't you introduce us?" Chance asked.

"He was in a hurry," Wade said defensively.

"He was preoccupied," Matthew said, correcting him.

"He's a very busy man," Wade said, still defending the Chancellor.

"He would have made time if you asked. He seems to know your family real well," Chance continued.

"Yeah, he seems to know your *moms* real well. Are you sure he ain't your daddy?" Jo'sha joked.

"Shut up," Wade snapped.

"But, I guess if he was your daddy he would have at least known your name," Jo'sha continued, jokingly.

Matthew and Chance laughed, inviting correcting stares from other more seasoned churchgoers. They quieted down quickly, remembering where they were. Then the four of them made their way into the sanctuary.

The size and layout of the sanctuary was amazing, and unlike anything any of them had ever seen. A short, dark-skinned sister with a press and curl hairdo, directed them to seats in the middle of the church. They crowded into the middle row of the middle section of the huge sanctuary. Once they were settled, the church lights went down, and an articulate, young, caramel complexioned sister came up on the screen of two large video monitors located on either side of the church. The announcements were clear and concise, and lasted for exactly six minutes.

As if on cue, the choir rose as soon as the announcements were over. When the music started they started to rock, their scarlet and gold robes swaying from side to side. They performed two selections. The first was slow and reverent. The second selection was an upbeat John P. Kee song that lifted Jo'sha immediately out of his seat. He started rocking to the beat.

Wade looked around as member after member popped up from their seats and joined in, clapping and rocking with the choir. Some got caught up in the spirit, while others were simply caught up in the music. The scene was definitely not something that Wade had seen before in his reserved, Presbyterian upbringing. He found the entire experience somewhat sacrilegious and unsettling.

Matthew and a confused Wade sat still in their seats and watched as Jo'sha rocked and bobbed his head as if he were auditioning for *Soul Train*. Chance was happy to be in the house of the Lord, but felt a little overwhelmed by the intensity and grandeur of the large church. Several minutes later when the song ended, the pastor emerged from a small room behind the main stage, and was escorted to the pulpit. The congregation greeted him with a rousing standing ovation.

"Open your Bibles to—"

The pastor's voice was clear and commanding. He paused, waiting for everyone to get to the scripture he'd selected. Several members surrounding the group asked if they had brought their Bibles. Jo'sha was the only one who had, so they all leaned over and tried to look at Jo'sha's tattered old King James Bible so as not to have to deal with any of the members. Chance craned his neck to see the scriptures, and made a mental note to pick up the Bible that his Grandfather T.C. had given him when he went home again.

The minister delivered an insightful, yet surprisingly humorous sermon, which lasted for only thirty minutes. Parishioners were engaged during the entire message, often laughing in response to the minister's anecdotes. Matthew and Wade continued to look around in amazement at the way the service was conducted.

"Can I get an Amen?" the pastor said, as he closed his Bible.

The music started, and the choir stood again, this time swaying very slowly. The pastor looked out into the congregation. "The doors of the church are open right now. Won't you come and give your life to the Lord?" He continued to extend the invitation of salvation to those sitting in the congregation. None of the four young men had been to a church that took the altar call quite so seriously, and they each found this portion of the service overwhelming.

Wade was seated directly beside a very devout member of the church. Sister Hosannah Murphy was a twenty something, unmarried, pumpkin colored woman, with full cheeks and long orange braids. She had been eyeing Wade during the entire service, and had asked him more than once if he would like to share her Bible. She saw the alter call as her opportunity to really communicate. She grabbed his hand and looked into his eyes.

"Have you dedicated your life to Christ?" she asked intensely.

Having come from a more reserved church, these practices and terminology were strange to Wade. When he hesitated to answer, the well meaning Hosannah grabbed his arm and began to pull him out to the aisle, and up toward the front of the church. Wade looked back helplessly at his friends, but they had no idea what to do. Wade was halfway to the front of the church before he broke free. He ran back down the aisle and out the door. The others followed close behind. Chance was embarrassed, Matthew was confused, and Jo'sha was laughing hysterically.

On the way back to the truck Wade continued to press the wrinkles from his sleeve as if Sister Hosannah had somehow damaged his designer suit. Matthew's nerves reminded him that they were still going to his house. All of the activity at church had taken his mind off of introducing his friends to his family. He had not even called Olivia to see if she would be home. She knew Jo'sha, but had not yet met Chance or Wade. He knew her being there would make things more bearable.

"Where's your house?" Wade asked, as he started the truck. He was still feeling a little shocked from the tussle that he had gotten into at church. Something like that would never have happened at his church in Baltimore.

"On the southwest side not too far from campus," Matthew answered nervously.

"I didn't know that," Jo'sha said. "You live right here in Atlanta, and I've never even been to your house."

Jo'sha, Wade, and Stephen Simmonds, were the only sounds in the automobile. Chance was thinking about the beautiful young sister that he had let get away, and wondering where his composure and confidence had gone. Matthew was thinking about all of the embarrassing things that were sure to happen when they got to his house.

Matthew directed Wade to his small home. His heart sank deeper and deeper as they got closer. He wondered just how much Wade and Chance would look down on him because of his meager dwelling.

"Why are you so quiet?" Jo'sha asked.

"No reason. Just tired from staying up so late and then getting up early to go to church," Matthew answered.

Wade pulled his new SUV in behind Matthew's parents' old minivan. As they got out, Matthew's head began to pound. When they reached the front step, Isadora came out, dressed in a very tasteful, purple cotton dress. For the first time in a long time, she wasn't wearing a wig, her hair was cut into a short neat afro, and she had on make-up and earrings. She grabbed Matthew and gave him a firm hug when he got to the front door, and for the first time in an even longer time, she gave him a kiss. Her display of warmth nearly brought a tear to his eye.

"And who do we have here?" Isadora asked.

"Ma, these are my suitemates Chance Walker, Wade Graham IV, and my roommate Jo'sha Imarah," Matthew answered.

"Such handsome young men," Isadora responded. "Well come on in. I cooked a little something for you. I hope you're hungry."

Matthew and his friends followed Isadora into the house and were greeted by the aroma of fried chicken, turnip greens, cornbread and apple pie. As Matthew took it all in, he couldn't help but wonder where his real mother was, and who had kidnapped her. He was even further surprised when he walked into their small living room and saw his father sitting in his favorite chair—sober.

"Son, are these your young college friends?" Roland asked.

Matthew didn't answer right away. He hadn't been sure what to expect from his father since their last interaction had been that physical confrontation a few weeks ago. His cordial attitude was hard for Matthew to grasp. And the fact that he had cleaned up and was sober was even harder to believe.

Chance stepped up quickly to shake Mr. Meredith's hand and introduced himself. Wade followed suit. When it was Jo'sha's turn, he made it clear to Mr. Meredith that he was Matthew's roommate and best friend.

"Come sit and watch the game with me for a few minutes while Issy finishes up dinner," he suggested.

It was all Matthew could do to keep his mouth from dropping open. He could not remember the last time that he had heard his father use his mother's nickname, Issy.

All four of them sat in the living room with Matthew's father and watched the Atlanta Falcons football game. Chance and Mr. Meredith clicked immediately, and talked endlessly. Matthew was shocked to find out that his father had actually spent some time in North Carolina while he was in the military and knew some of Chance's distant relatives. Wade sat quietly since he didn't know a lot about sports. Instead he studied his surroundings. He couldn't believe that an entire family actually lived in such a small house. Jo'sha got up and walked into the kitchen to join Isadora, while the others continued watching television.

"Mama Meredith, do you need any help?" Jo'sha asked, flashing a smile. He knew that his charm worked on women of any age.

"No, baby, I'm fine," Isadora responded. "How are you and Matthew getting along over there at Central?"

"Mad cool. Mad cool. I never had a family or anything like that and Matthew is a good roommate. He's like the brother I never had," Jo'sha answered, smiling.

Isadora nodded, a sad smile on her face.

"Yeah, you know Matthew had a twin brother that died when they were very young."

The news came as a complete surprise to Jo'sha, and left him at a loss for words.

Isadora continued rambling. "I wouldn't be surprised if he hasn't told you. We never talk about a lot of things around here, but life is too short. Be there for him, Jo'sha. He mentions you to me every time he calls so I know he likes you. He doesn't take to just anybody. He tells me about all your great singing. My daughter talks about you too." Jo'sha smiled as Isadora continued. "My son is very private and proud—he holds things in. That isn't good for him and it is my fault that he hasn't learned how to do better, but I couldn't teach him what I didn't know myself. We're going for counseling—me and my husband. Just like Dr. Phil and Oprah and them. Whoever thought black folk could see a psychologist? But I still worry about my boy. He is as bright as a whip, but it is hard for him to share. You know my baby has cancer."

For the second time in the short and impromptu conversation, Isadora exposed another of Matthew's secrets, again leaving Jo'sha speechless.

Isadora continued, "Now I know that he won't want me telling you any of this, but he needs to learn how to open up. It ain't healthy to keep it all inside," Isadora said.

"What are you two in here talking about?" Matthew asked as he entered the kitchen. He quickly searched Jo'sha's face, afraid that his mother might be embarrassing him.

"Oh nothing," the two answered in unison, sharing a smile between them. "Go get everyone for dinner," Isadora instructed.

Matthew looked at his mother curiously, and wondered where she had been hiding her maternal and homemaking instincts all this time. He also wondered why she thought he needed to go get anyone since the living room was right next to the kitchen and everyone was within earshot.

"Food is ready," he called into the living room.

The words were barely out of his mouth before they all stormed into the kitchen.

"Where do we wash our hands?" Wade asked, wondering why no one else was looking for the restroom.

"Our bathroom sink is broke, so you can wash your hands at the kitchen sink," Isadora said, handing him the dishwashing liquid.

Wade had never washed his hands with dishwashing liquid and could not believe that Mrs. Meredith would recommend such, but he didn't want to offend anyone, so he went over to the deep, aged white sink and rubbed his hands into a lemony fresh lather. The others washed their hands at the sink, only because Wade had highlighted the need to clean up before dinner.

Isadora set the table with fried chicken, turnip greens, corn on the cob, corn bread, mashed sweet potatoes, and ham.

"This looks great, Mrs. Meredith," Chance complimented. "Not like cafeteria food, and just like back home."

"We have to say grace," Jo'sha challenged, before Mr. Meredith and Matthew could dive into the food. Jo'sha grabbed Mrs. Meredith and Wade's hands, since they were beside him. The rest at the table followed suit.

"Creator, we thank you for the opportunity to share and fellowship with friends and family. Bless the hands that prepared the food and the head of house that welcomed us," Jo'sha ended, giving Isadora's hand a special squeeze as thanks for welcoming him into her home and her heart. Everyone smiled and plowed into a very good meal. Jo'sha, a vegetarian, careful not to offend Matthew's mother, continually commented on how good the vegetables were.

"Why don't you eat meat?" Roland asked Jo'sha right in the middle of the meal. "You ain't one of them Muslims are you?"

"No disrespect, sir, but I have been a vegetarian for several years now and I believe it is just a healthier way to live. The Bible says in Genesis 1:29 that God gave us every herb bearing seed which is upon the face of all the Earth, and every tree in which is the fruit of a tree yielding seed; to you it shall be for food," Jo'sha said.

Wade rolled his eyes and prepared himself for another one of Jo'sha's back-to-Africa lectures.

"Besides, all the facts point to the notion that God designed us to eat off of the land. Flesh eating animals have a short bowel to enable them to rapidly expel putrefactive flesh, while man has a long and complicated alimentary tract to enable plant nutrients to be slowly absorbed. Flesh eaters have long, sharp teeth, while man's teeth are like grain eaters. Men, horses, cows, antelopes all sweat through their skins. All flesh eaters sweat through their tongues. Man sucks his liquids and flesh eaters all lap. Besides, I feel better eating true." Jo'sha smiled politely and continued, "As for religion, I don't prescribe to any particular religion. I just try to find the Creator where I can."

After the few seconds of awkward silence required for everyone to digest Jo'sha's food for thought and regain their appetites, the conversation resumed. Roland and Isadora were careful not to ask Jo'sha any more questions about his diet. The rest of the conversation was lively and engaging and Matthew only counted two other times when his mother or father said something that embarrassed him.

Dinner ended and Isadora went to the stove for the apple pie and then to the freezer for a box of store brand vanilla ice cream.

"Where's Olivia?" Matthew asked, realizing that he had not spoken to his sister since yesterday morning. Jo'sha perked up immediately to hear the response.

"She's at work. She should be home any minute. She just had to go in for a few hours for inventory," Mr. Meredith said.

Matthew was surprised that his father knew or cared where his sister was. When dinner ended, they all agreed to help clear the kitchen, but Isadora insisted that she could handle it herself.

"You don't need to help me clean to thank me, but there is one thing you can do," Isadora said, cautiously.

"What is that, Mrs. Meredith," Jo'sha asked.

"You can entertain us with a song," Isadora answered.

"Hold on. Hold on just one second," Roland Meredith exclaimed as he disappeared down the short hallway and came back with an old guitar case. Matthew knew things had been going entirely too well and was preparing himself for the ultimate embarrassment. They all went into the living room and Roland began to pick out a Sam Cooke tune.

"You don't know nothing 'bout this," Roland teased Jo'sha.

Jo'sha joined in immediately with a velvety voice, never missing a beat or a note. Everyone was amazed at his voice. Matthew had heard Jo'sha sing before, but had never heard him sing with such passion and intensity, nor was he aware that his father could play the guitar. They were still applauding and cheering when Olivia burst through the door.

"All this for me?" she asked with a laugh.

Jo'sha smiled and adjusted his clothes and his locs as Matthew rose to greet her.

"Oh! Matt," she said as she gave her brother a playful embrace. "Whose car is that outside?"

Matthew introduced her to Wade and Chance, who were each impressed by Matthew's fine younger sister. Olivia was impressed by them as well. Jo'sha waited until Olivia had spoken to everyone else and made his way over to her and surprised her and her family by giving her a big hug. Roland and Isadora noticed the extended glance between the two of them. After a few more songs and many more laughs, Matthew decided that they needed to leave. Things had gone too well and he didn't want to press his luck.

"We should be getting back now," Matthew chimed in after thanking his mother and father for one of the best gifts that they had ever given him—the semblance of normalcy.

The ride back to campus was a thoughtful one. Matthew was thinking about how cool his parents had been; Chance was still thinking about the young sister at church, Aspen Walker; Jo'sha was thinking about Matthew's sister, Olivia; and Wade was thinking about how different the little house on the southwest side of Atlanta was from his own.

Halfway back to campus, Wade grew tired of listening to Stephen Simmond's and turned on the radio. The on air personality was reporting.

This is a special announcement. Local Atlanta authorities have just identified an eighth victim in the recent string of Atlanta male murders. The latest victim was found in an abandoned field in

Union City, Georgia, just outside Atlanta. The victim's name has not been released as family members have not yet been notified.

The news melted the introspective mood, leaving depression and disbelief in its wake. Wade turned off the radio and the ride back to campus was perfectly quiet.

CHAPTER 9

In that not quite so familiar space between life and death, where indigo passions sear the souls of unrequited lovers, and shock white fears freeze time and space, Jo'sha found himself on fire—and he screamed.

"What's wrong?" Matthew asked, jumping up from a less than restful sleep. Before he was fully awake, Chance was pounding on the common door between the two rooms.

"Hey, what's wrong?" Chance yelled from the other side of the door.

Matthew turned on the room light, unlocked the common door, and went to Jo'sha's bed. Chance rushed in right behind him. Jo'sha was sitting up in the bed rubbing the scar on his left forearm. He looked disoriented.

"What's wrong?" Matthew repeated. Chance went back to his room and quickly returned with a bottle of water for Jo'sha.

"That light is too bright," Jo'sha mumbled. Chance switched the light off and turned on Jo'sha's small lamp. There was a knock on the door leading into the dorm hallway.

"You gentlemen alright in there?" asked Ronnie Chisholm, their resident advisor. Although Winfrey-Combs was a freshman dorm, each floor had an upperclassman that served as its resident advisor, responsible for disseminating critical student information, handling administrative matters, and addressing general student issues. The job involved much more however, and the resident advisors often became surrogate big brothers to their charges, helping them with everything from homework problems to sexually transmitted diseases. Ronnie had a key to every suite and room in the building and was authorized to enter any room if there were legitimate signs of trouble.

"Are you gentlemen alright? Jo'sha? Matthew?" he called out again.

"It's all good, Ronnie. Just a little accident," Matthew responded, looking at Jo'sha for confirmation. Jo'sha remained silent.

"Okay. Well, call me if you need me."

"Okay," Matthew responded.

A few seconds later they heard him shuffling back to his suite. Once he was gone the trio sat there, waiting for Jo'sha to tell them what happened. Matthew stifled a yawn. He hadn't slept much lately, worrying about his upcoming final series of cancer tests. He had tried to bury himself in his schoolwork, the presentation preparation, and his job at the library, but it was becoming increasingly difficult. When he glanced over at the clock and he saw that it was 5:00 a.m. he sighed heavily.

"Now *what* is up?" Chance asked, seeing that Matthew was getting frustrated with Jo'sha's unresponsiveness.

"I have nightmares," Jo'sha finally said. "Well, they're actually night terrors. You know Foster isn't my dad. He's just my legal guardian," Jo'sha said.

"I wondered why you always referred to him as Foster. I would never call my daddy by his first name," Chance interrupted. "What does that have to do with your nightmares?"

"Foster is his last name," Jo'sha answered. "He's a real cool dude. He was there for me when no one else was. Anyway, when I was a baby my parents and I were in a car accident. They didn't survive. They died in a fire from the car crash. I've had nightmares about the accident ever since. I normally only have them if I've really been thinking about my parents and stuff. I am not sure what triggered it this time," Jo'sha said, fighting back tears and embarrassment.

Matthew and Chance sat in silence for several seconds not sure how or if they should respond.

"The doctors think I might have cancer," Matthew blurted.

"Whoa!" Chance exclaimed.

Jo'sha was thankful that the lights were dim and the mood was already heavy so that he didn't have to pretend to be surprised.

Sometimes in the bearing of souls and sharing of secrets there is no comfort in mere words, only in acknowledging—and so secrets were shared as men often share secrets—with limited information and even less emotion—dancing delicately back and forth from the related to the unrelated until the pain subsides. Chance sat looking up at the ceiling. He felt humbled that Matthew and Jo'sha had shared personal secrets, and slightly guilt stricken that he lacked the courage to share his own. His discomfort caused him to change the subject again.

"All this commotion and Wade is still asleep," he commented.

"I guess it is easy to rest when your life is perfect," Matthew responded.

Jo'sha's silence sounded like assent to Chance, who wondered if they also saw him as a part of the pious, peaceful privileged.

They spent the next hour talking about the fragility of life and frailty of the human spirit until natural light crept in and replaced the counterfeit offered by Jo'sha's lamp.

"Since we're all awake, come and go to breakfast with me," Chance offered. He was the only one of the four who routinely made it to the dining hall for breakfast. Chance missed very few opportunities to eat breakfast, lunch or dinner.

Wade just wasn't a morning person. Matthew often skipped meals to save money, and Jo'sha wasn't fond of the smell of cooked bacon and sausage that permeated the dining hall.

"I can put it all on my meal card, and Jo'sha, they have a great fruit bar," Chance said, trying to convince them.

"I really shouldn't," Jo'sha said. "I have an English paper to reprint this morning. Remember I have English right after Dr. Smith's class.

"If we hurry we can run down and be back in no time. And if we get back early enough I can show you how I wake up Wade," Chance joked.

Matthew, Jo'sha, and Chance got dressed and headed to the dining hall, agreeing to return quickly. When they got back, Chance motioned for them to be quiet outside the hallway door for 400-A, hoping to sneak in and surprise Wade. Instead they were the ones to be surprised. Not only was Wade already up, but he was in the middle of a phone conversation.

"This is not a good time. I have to get ready for class. We can talk about it later, but I just don't think it's a good idea if I tell my parents about us just yet. They won't understand," Wade warned, in hushed tones.

The three friends listened for a few more seconds, each drawing their own conclusions about the nature of the conversation. Chance realized what they were doing, and shook the doorknob as he entered the room.

"Wade, time to get up—oh you're already awake," Chance said, feigning surprise.

"Uh, yeah," Wade responded after quickly and quietly ending his phone conversation.

Jo'sha and Matthew followed Chance into the room. Matthew finally broke the uncomfortable silence. "You all remember what happens today, right?"

"My English paper is due for one. Chance, can I use your computer to print my English paper?" Jo'sha asked. "I don't want to go downstairs to the computer lab."

"Sure," Chance said.

"Is anyone listening to me?" Matthew asked.

"Not really," Jo'sha said, walking over to his room to get his computer jump drive.

Wade jumped up without making eye contact and headed for the shower. Matthew looked at Chance's open closet, which was filled with urban designer clothing. The bottom of the closet was covered with several types of athletic shoes, and several pair of Timberland boots in colors that Matthew didn't even know they made. He even had all of the newest Nikes and Adidas. Matthew couldn't help but notice how sharp a contrast it was to his own closet.

"You like those?" Chance asked, noticing that Matthew was looking in his closet.

"What do you mean?" Matthew asked.

"Those new Nikes," Chance answered.

"Oh—yeah, they are nice," Matthew commented.

"You can wear 'em. I got them a couple of weeks ago and hardly ever wear them," Chance offered.

"Naw, I am cool," Matthew said.

"Quit tripping," Chance said. He took the shoes from his closet and threw them at Matthew.

"I'll just wear them today," Matthew said, grinning slightly.

By the time Wade returned from the shower, Matthew had on Chance's new shoes.

Jo'sha ran back in the room as if he were going to dive onto Wade's unmade bed. Wade tensed up, dropped his towel and shower caddy. The three of them laughed as Wade fumbled around naked trying to pick up his toiletries and towel.

"You really need to relax," Jo'sha mocked.

"Quit playing, Wade, and get dressed. We're going to be late," Chance said.

"Yeah, quit playing," Jo'sha continued teasing.

Wade dried off and hurriedly got dressed in a pair of Kenneth Cole slacks and a matching Donna Karen sweater.

"Do you guys remember what happens today?" Matthew asked again.

"What?" Chance asked, deciding to indulge Matthew.

"We go take a look at that time capsule," Matthew stressed.

"Now why are we doing this again?" Wade asked.

'There may be something in there that will give us an edge in the competition," Matthew answered.

"Well don't you think they'll know that we broke into the time capsule if we have information that no one else has?" Wade asked.

"We'll make sure our tracks are covered. We can always say that it was just good research," Matthew answered.

"Yeah, research that no one else has," Wade argued.

"Aren't you the least bit curious about what happened to Cyrus and them, and why it was left out of the history books?" Chance asked.

"Miss Vaughn told me that the university's homecoming committee and the public relations firm are going to open the time capsule shortly before homecoming. We'll just have the advantage of having the information early enough to include in our presentation. Besides, who's to say that someone from the committee won't let it leak out anyway?" Matthew ended.

"Excellent point!" Jo'sha yelled, as his English paper began to print.

"Now this is the plan again," Matthew instructed. "I have to go to work this morning after Dr. Smith's class. I'll make sure that everything is straight for tonight. Miss Vaughn is normally at the library for closing, but she has a meeting with the homecoming committee tonight. It'll just be me and Nia."

"Yeah, Nia with the big round booty," Jo'sha said, organizing his English paper. Chance laughed.

"Be at the library at 10:30 p.m. on the second floor by the periodicals," Matthew continued. "I'll come up and get you. Chance and Wade, bring your cell phones and have them on vibrate. Wade, you'll keep an eye on Nia to make sure that she doesn't come downstairs near the copy room. If she does I want you to call Chance's phone immediately, and then keep her busy."

"Why Wade?" Jo'sha asked.

Chance and Matthew wondered if Jo'sha had made the same conclusion based on the phone conversation that they had overheard.

"Yeah, why me?" Wade asked.

"Well, for one you don't have a cell phone, *and* she isn't hardly interested in you," Matthew said to Jo'sha.

"How do you know that?" Jo'sha asked.

"She saw me with Wade on campus the other day and asked me about him. Said something about his light brown eyes blah, blah, blah," Matthew added.

"Look at my roommate. You got the females on notice!" Chance said, punching Wade in the arm.

"Ouch!" Wade said, rubbing his arm.

"Her father is Byron Baptiste, Chief of Staff at the local hospital, and she never stops talking about Jack & Jill so you two should have a lot of bourgeoisie, superficial things to talk about."

Wade rolled his eyes and continued getting dressed.

"Bring your books with you so it will look like you came to study," Matthew instructed.

"That's what we should probably be doing anyway," Wade mumbled under his breath.

"Except you, Jo'sha. Empty your saddlebag before you come—just in case we need to *borrow* something. Oh, and bring a flashlight," Matthew ordered.

"You mean *steal* something," Wade corrected.

"Alright, we got it for the nine hundredth time. Now let's go. We damn sure don't want to be late for Dr. Smith's class," Chance said.

Matthew, Jo'sha and Wade gathered their things and exited the suite. Chance left last, picking up his inhaler and Matthew's old shoes. He tossed them in the trashcan, threw his inhaler in his pocket, and locked the door behind him.

CHAPTER 10

Matthew looked at his watch and it was 10:27 p.m. "Nia, I'll be back in a second. I gotta run and return these books to the stacks before we close," Matthew said.

"Okay," Nia said, not bothering to look up from filing her nails and reading the latest edition of *Essence* magazine.

A high school track athlete, Matthew was upstairs in no time. Chance, Jo'sha and Wade were seated at a table in a far corner by the periodicals.

"What are you doing?" Matthew asked, looking at Wade.

"Studying. This *is* a library," Wade said.

"Well stop it. We don't have much time."

"Everything okay over here gentlemen?" asked a security guard who had rounded the corner and walked up behind them.

Matthew recognized the smell of cheap vodka on his breath. "Yes, everything is fine. Just helping these students with periodicals," Matthew said with a smile. He waited for the security guard to move outside earshot.

The security guard staggered away, clearly under the influence of a few drinks, having asked his question more out of habit and a desire to appear sober than concern for the security of the building.

"You didn't tell us security guards would be here," Wade hissed.

"You didn't ask. Besides, as you can see, he's usually as drunk as hell. He probably won't even remember seeing us," Matthew said. "Now let's go. Here are two keys. One is to the copy room in the basement. The other key is to Miss Vaughn's office. It's in the back corner of the copy center."

"How did you get her keys?" Jo'sha asked, smiling.

"Do you have to ask?" Wade said.

"I borrowed her keys this morning, jetted across the street to the shoe repair shop, and had another set made," Matthew said.

"Wasn't that a little dangerous?" Wade asked.

"Naww, she's always misplacing her keys, and she gives them to just about everyone that works here so that they can run down to the copy room for her," Matthew answered.

"Why do you lock a copy room anyway?" Chance asked.

"They keep a lot of other university artifacts and stuff down there. Not to mention access to the university's copy machines."

"How do we get there?" Jo'sha asked, anxious to get started.

"Go down the stairwell to the first floor and then take the service elevator to the basement level. The copy room will be directly across from you when you exit the elevator. Do you have your phones on vibrate?" Matthew asked, looking at Chance and Wade.

"Yes," they both responded.

"Okay, then let's go."

"We don't have to synchronize our watches?" Wade mocked.

"Good one," Jo'sha laughed. Wade was starting to relax and Jo'sha liked it.

"You two go down and see if you can find the time capsule. I'll go back and check on Nia. I'll stay there for a few seconds and then make another excuse to leave. I'll be down there in a minute," Matthew said, ignoring Wade's wisecrack.

"What the hell does a time capsule look like?" Jo'sha asked.

"How should I know?" Matthew said, shrugging his shoulders.

"Oh, God!" Wade said.

"Just go look for something that might hold old stuff—something that looks 100 years old."

"Oh, like your book bag?" Jo'sha joked.

"Wade, you go down to the first floor and sit at the guest table across from the front desk and keep an eye on Nia. If she moves you keep her busy," Matthew instructed, ignoring Chance.

Jo'sha unbuttoned Wade's top button further revealing his skinny, smooth chest. "Maybe not," Jo'sha laughed, buttoning it back up.

Chance gave his one book to Wade, who placed it in his briefcase and took off to the first floor. Jo'sha grabbed his saddlebag. By 10:45 p.m., Jo'sha, Matthew, and Chance were all inside Miss Vaughn's office.

"We've gotta make this quick. We only have fifteen minutes before Nia and I have to meet the security guard for shut down," Matthew advised.

"Fifteen minutes!" Chance exclaimed.

Jo'sha pulled an industrial flashlight from his saddlebag.

"Where did you get this big ass flashlight?" Chance asked.

"I borrowed it from Ronnie," Jo'sha said, in a matter of fact tone.

"You borrowed a flashlight from our resident advisor to break into someone's office? Why didn't you just ask the campus police to come help us?" Chance asked, his voice laced with sarcasm.

"Who are you? Wade Jr.?" Jo'sha shot back.

"Alright, dammit, we don't have much time," Matthew spewed.

"Hey, what is that?" Jo'sha asked, pointing the flashlight toward a large, antique chest in the corner by Miss Vaughn's desk.

Matthew rushed over to inspect the ornate, antique chest. The latch was facing the wall. Matthew attempted to turn it around, but couldn't move it. The chest measured a full four feet by three feet by three feet. It was made of rosewood, and fortified by detailed metal fixtures. A small engraved metal plate on the top read:

To be opened in the Year of our Lord Two Thousand and Four.

"Move. This is man's work," Chance said, planting his feet firmly and then turning the huge chest. The latch was sealed with a rusty old lock. "Now what do we do?" he asked, wondering if he should have listened to Wade.

"I got this," Jo'sha said. He pulled a small metal pick from his saddlebag. "I thought this might come in handy."

Five minutes later Jo'sha had picked the lock. Chance lifted the heavy wood and metal lid releasing a dank and musty odor.

The articles in the chest were expertly organized. It was filled with reams of neatly stacked papers, photographs, and numerous types of paraphernalia marked with the university's first shield.

"These photographs are great," Jo'sha said.

"Hey, look at this picture. This must be the first class of students," Matthew commented.

"Is that VanDerZee written in the lower left corner," Jo'sha asked, squinting to see the signature under the flashlight.

"Who is VanDerZee?" Chance asked.

"VandDerZee was one of the first African-American photographers. He was really famous for photographing the Harlem

Renaissance, but this must have been early in his career," Jo'sha stated.

"Born June 29, 1886 and died May 15, 1983. He would have been about 18," Matthew muttered, still rifling through the chest.

Chance and Jo'sha just looked at each other, still amazed by Matthew's retention of random facts and figures.

"Most of these papers are about the university's incorporation," Matthew said, as Jo'sha stood beside him with the flashlight.

"Anything interesting?" Chance asked, still holding the lid.

"A few things," he answered distractedly. Here, take this stack of papers and pictures and start to make copies," Matthew said, handing Chance a stack of papers.

Chance opened the lid completely and rushed over to the nearest copy machine while Jo'sha and Matthew kept exploring the contents of the chest.

In the corner of the great chest lay a large leather satchel with the initials N.C. branded on the bottom. Matthew lifted the satchel out carefully and laid it on the floor beside the chest, pulling out the contents one by one. The first item that he pulled from the satchel was a large piece of parchment that read:

October 12, 1904

To Whom It May Concern,

> *These items are of a most personal nature. And like all of the articles in this chest, they are meant to illuminate the Negro learning experience in the year 1904. This satchel is of particular interest as it and its contents are the personal effects of four of our students who have, much to our dismay, tragically lost their lives in an unexplained circumstance.*

> *We pay tribute to them and all of the Negro male students who have taken up the plow of education in times such as these. May they be forever blessed.*

Sincerely,

Hiram L. Hines, President

"What's in it?" Jo'sha urged.

The first item was a sweater from a student who must have been at least as large as Chance. The initials N.C. were hand stitched in the collar. The other was a bound leather diary. The first page on the inside read Cyrus Wilkes. The address on the inside cover read 235 North Peters Avenue, New Orleans. The third item was a gold money clip with the initials W.W. engraved in it. The final item was a banjo case.

"Wow!" Jo'sha exclaimed, admiring the banjo case.

"What?" Matthew asked.

"Damn," Chance exclaimed.

"What?" Matthew asked again.

"I don't know what Jo'sha is yelling about, but my phone just vibrated. It's Wade and the text message reads, 'Get out now!'"

CHAPTER 11

"Put this in your saddlebag," Matthew instructed, handing Jo'sha a pile of papers and photographs. Chance grabbed his pile of copies along with the originals, and stuffed them into Jo'sha's saddlebag as well.

Matthew stuffed the sweater, money clip, banjo case, and the leather bound diary back into the satchel. He picked it up to place it back in the chest when an alarm sounded.

"Oh shit!" Chance yelled.

"Shut up!" Matthew whispered, placing the satchel back on the floor.

The alarm blared, getting louder and louder by the second.

"Turn off that flashlight, Jo'sha," Matthew whispered, attempting to remain calm. Chance felt his cell phone vibrate again.

"My cell phone is vibrating," he whispered.

"Answer it. Maybe Wade can tell us what the hell is happening."

They all waited, sitting on the floor of Miss Vaughn's office in complete darkness amidst the unorganized contents of the old chest, and under the oppressive sound of the siren-like alarm.

"Hello," Chance whispered.

"Where are you?" Wade asked.

"Still in the basement."

"Where are you?"

"Just outside the library. Get out now! Didn't you get my text message?"

"Yeah, but the alarm went off. What's going on?" Chance asked.

"That was me," Wade answered.

"Huh? What are you talking about?"

"I had to. Nia got a phone call at the front desk. She got up to head toward the elevator to go downstairs and I tried to stop her. She said that Miss Vaughn called and told her that she needed something from her office for a late meeting that she was in. Evidently she left her keys with Nia. She asked that drunk security guard to go with her downstairs. I pulled the fire alarm when they got in the elevator. It was all that I could think to do. They're stuck in the elevator now, the campus police will be here any minute. I can hear the sirens from here."

"Meet us back in the room and keep your phone on," Chance advised. Chance got off the phone and told Jo'sha and Matthew what Wade said.

"Alright, alright, let me think," Matthew said.

"We're going to get kicked out of school. I can hear my parents now," Chance moaned.

"They're in the elevator, right?" Jo'sha asked.

"Yeah," Chance answered.

"Then we can go out of the emergency exit that leads up to the street. The alarm is already on so it won't matter," Jo'sha explained.

"Good thinking, Jo'sha. I should go back upstairs and out of the front exit since I am supposed to be at work. The campus police will be looking for everyone on duty. I'll stall them as long as I can. You and Chance will have to put things back like we found them. I'll meet you back in the room. Be sure to lock the door behind you." Matthew said.

Matthew rushed out of the office and toward the emergency exit so that he could be back upstairs when the campus police arrived. He planned to explain that he'd been up in the stacks putting away books when he heard alarms go off.

Chance busied himself with closing the chest, returning the latch, and shoving it back in the corner. In the darkness and confusion, Jo'sha managed to secure his saddlebag *and* the leather satchel with its contents.

"Alright, let's get out of here," Chance said.

They were out of the library and halfway back to Winfrey-Combs when Chance noticed that Jo'sha had his saddlebag and the satchel.

"What the hell is that?" Chance asked, pointing to the leather satchel.

"Come on. We have to get back to the room," Jo'sha said, looking over his shoulder.

"That was not a part of the plan. We went to see what was in the time capsule, make a few copies, maybe borrow a few items and return them, but not to steal everything," Chance lectured.

Jo'sha was silent all the way back to the room.

Ronnie was at Wade's door when Chance and Jo'sha got back to Suite 400. Jo'sha instinctively handed the satchel to Chance.

"Hey, guys. Up studying late?" Ronnie asked.

"Uh, yeah," Jo'sha responded.

"You know we want to win that suite scholarship award," Chance added.

He was referring to the Winfrey-Combs academic award for the suite with the highest collective grade point average at the end of the year. Ronnie was particularly pleased to hear that since the scholarship competition was his own pet project.

"That shouldn't be hard for you four. You're probably one of the smartest suites in this dorm, but you do have some competition from 209. I've already gotten several local Atlanta companies to donate some really nice prizes for the winners. I wouldn't be surprised if other dorms tried to do this next year," Ronnie said, proudly.

Wade was turning a bright shade of red and mouthing, *flashlight*, from behind Ronnie.

"I was just asking Wade if he had seen you. I need that flashlight. I have to change a bulb in the stairwell on the ninth floor," Ronnie said to Jo'sha.

"Oh, the flashlight," Jo'sha stuttered, hoping that he hadn't forgotten to stuff it into his saddlebag.

"Is everything alright?" Ronnie asked, noticing Jo'sha's stuttering and Chances unusual silence.

"Oh! Here it is," Chance exclaimed as he handed Ronnie the flashlight, guessing that Jo'sha might have inadvertently stuffed it into the satchel in all of the confusion.

"Nice leather bag. Kinda big for books though," Ronnie said to Chance.

"Thanks," Jo'sha said, relieved that they hadn't left it in Miss Vaughn's office.

"What did you need the flashlight for anyway?" Ronnie asked.

"Umm, well, I, umm—we had to—" Jo'sha stammered, trying to come up with an answer. "We were, uh, using it for a presentation," he said finally.

"What kind of presentation?" Ronnie pressed.

"What a night at work," Matthew interrupted, rushing into the suite.

"What happened?" Wade asked, trying to mask his anxiety.

"It was almost closing and I was up in the stacks replacing books, when all of the sudden the alarms went off," Matthew said, delivering the barely rehearsed story with ease.

"What caused it?" Ronnie asked curiously.

"Not sure. The campus police came and everything. They asked me, Nia, and the security guard on duty if we had seen or heard anything," Matthew said.

"Is everyone alright?" Ronnie asked, getting into Matthew's story.

"Yeah, poor Nia got trapped in the elevator for a few minutes with that old security guard. Other than that everything is okay," Matthew said.

"Well, stuff like that happens all of the time. Probably just an electrical malfunction or something," Ronnie surmised.

"Yeah, probably," Matthew agreed.

Jo'sha and Chance went into their respective rooms in an effort to avoid Ronnie's continued barrage of questions.

"Well, I have to go replace that bulb before someone else falls in the stairwell. Let me know if you guys need anything," Ronnie said. He gave them a final nod, and then rushed out of the suite and down the hallway.

Once Ronnie was gone Wade and Chance rushed back into Matthew and Jo'sha's room with the satchel.

"What in the hell is that?" Wade asked, referring to the leather satchel.

Chance locked Matthew and Jo'sha's door behind him. "Don't ask," he said.

Matthew shook his head in disapproval. "Why didn't you leave it in the chest?" he asked.

"There was just too much going on. Things got confusing and we had to get out as quickly as possible. Besides the banjo case in this bag is priceless," Jo'sha added.

"I knew it!" Wade exploded. "Don't you idiots know that we could get expelled for this?"

"No we won't because no one will ever know," Matthew said, confidently. "Now let's spread everything out on the floor."

"Are you serious?" Wade asked, looking at Matthew incredulously. "This is not what we went in there for!" he said angrily.

"Calm down," Jo'sha said. "No, we didn't go there for this, but it's happened now and we can't change that. We may as well take a look at everything and then figure out how we can put it all back tomorrow."

"He's right," Chance reasoned. "No sense in arguing about something that's already done."

Wade hesitated for a few seconds longer and then finally nodded his agreement. They sat in the floor and gathered all of the items that they had collected from the library—items from the satchel and Jo'sha's saddlebag. Wade began rifling through the photographs on the off chance that he might find a picture of one of his own ancestors.

"This banjo and case are beautiful," Jo'sha said admiringly.

"Why? What makes them so special?" Chance asked.

"See this leather brand on the side of the case—T & H Conti. That stands for Turner and Hall Conti. They were two brothers, slaves famous for making banjos and leather cases. African slaves introduced skin-over-gourd stringed instruments called banjars or banshaws to America. Well anyway, Leonardo Conti, the descendant of wealthy violin manufacturers from Italy, owned Turner and Hall. Turner made the best banjoes. Hall made these fine leather cases for the banjoes." Jo'sha turned the case over admiringly. "Foster has been looking for one of these for years. There are only a few around that are still in mint condition. This is a collector's dream—a banjo *and* a case. But there is something else about this banjo. What is it?" Jo'sha wondered aloud.

"Look at this diary, it belonged to Cyrus Wilkes. He must have been from New Orleans. The address is 235 North Peters Avenue, New Orleans, Louisiana. It only has three entries in it." Matthew said excitedly.

Chance grabbed the satchel and the sweater. "These must have belonged to the same dude. They both have the same initials on them," Chance said.

"What were those names again?" Wade asked, handling the money clip.

"Cyrus Wilkes, Nathaniel Charles, Oleander Vaughn, and Winston Wright," Matthew said.

"Nathaniel Charles," Chance repeated as he tried on the sweater.

"Hey, that belongs to a dead guy," Wade said.

"And? Remember my family is in the mortuary business. Death doesn't scare me. Besides, it fits me perfectly." Chance ended. "Listen to this. It is the first entry from Cyrus' diary."

August 28, 1904

Dear Diary,

> *This first entry marks my first day at what is now known as the Georgia Central School for Colored Men. I am particularly proud to be in such auspicious company. Dr. Hines and the rest of the faculty are quite impressive. They have placed every male student here into groups of four that they refer to as quads. We are charged with looking after each other and helping one another with studies.*
>
> *My quad consists of three rather interesting individuals: Winston Wright from Richmond, whose family is in the banking business. Oleander Vaughn, who is quite the musician. And Nathaniel Charles, who is as large in spirit as he is in stature. I trust that we will be fast friends until our dying day.*

Wade and Chance continued to listen as Matthew flipped the page and read the second entry. Jo'sha opened the banjo case and began inspecting the instrument.

September 6, 1904

Dear Diary,

> *I had intended to be more regular in my entries, but the volume of coursework is overwhelming for us all. Classes, however, are coming along nicely. As one might imagine, our pursuit of higher education thrusts us in the middle of the great debate between W.E.B DuBois and Booker T. Washington. Even our own instructors are split on this issue. In light of all of the other things that are going on around us, several of the male students here are talking about starting a fraternity just like the*

white schools. My good friends Oleander, Nathaniel, and Winston are most keen on the idea. I must admit that it would be quite an honor to be the founders of the first black Greek letter organization.

On a more personal note, it appears that I have relatives in this very area. One cousin in particular, Samuel Wilkes, visits me here at the school often and has even helped in designing some of our learning buildings. He is an interesting fellow. This decision to attend Georgia Central School for Colored Men has brought me nothing but joy.

Matthew flipped the page and continued reading. They all listened intently as Jo'sha gently plucked the strings on the banjo in cadence with Matthew's reading.

September 29, 1904

My dear cousin visited me this morning and was in quite a way. He would not tell me why. It appears that he has items that he would like for me to put away for safekeeping. My fear is that these items are of great value and that someone is after him.

My dearest friend, Oleander, says that it feels like nothing but trouble and advises me to distance myself from my cousin. While I certainly see his point, there is no one who values the concept of family more than me. I will do what I must and trust that my friends will support me or at least understand.

"Wow!" Jo'sha said.

"Hey, does that first letter say Winston Wright is from Richmond?" Wade asked.

"Yeah, why?" Chance asked.

"Do you think that he is any relation to Maxwell Carmichael-Wright from Dr. Smith's class?" Wade asked, adept at remembering and valuing lineage.

"Could be," Matthew remarked.

"Why does it matter?" Chance asked.

"Well for one thing, this money clip could actually belong to one of his ancestors," Wade said forcefully.

"That's it!" Jo'sha exclaimed.

"What?" Wade asked.

"The T&H Conti banjoes were made famous because of the cases and not the banjoes. Foster told me all about it. Hall Conti built a secret compartment inside each case. Slaves used them to hide small books, expensive items, and other things that they didn't want their masters to find. Legend has it that Turner and Hall were literate slaves who would forge freedom papers and hide them inside each case. When the slave owner would purchase a T&H banjo and give it to the slave, he would be giving him more than the gift of music. That was until Leonardo Conti found out what they were doing and had them hanged." Jo'sha began to inspect the banjo case. "Look! Right here in the curve of the case. It's a secret compartment."

Jo'sha pulled back a small leather tab revealing a leather tray housed inside the banjo case. Inside the compartment was a cloth sack bag secured with twine. Jo'sha pulled it out and opened it slowly. The pouch contained five smaller cloth sack bags, each also closed by twine. Four were filled and one was obviously empty. Jo'sha threw a bag to each of his friends, kept one, and threw the fifth, empty bag back into the banjo case.

The air in the room stood still as they each opened their small leather bags. Simultaneously, they pulled small stone ankh charms from the bags. Each ankh looked nearly identical, a brilliant opal tinted with its own distinct hue. Jo'sha's was red, Wade's was blue, and Matthew's was yellow. Chance's was green, but appeared to be exactly half the width of the others.

They marveled at the relics' craftsmanship and wondered for whom they had been made. They seemed to have an otherworldly quality.

"Hey, do you smell that?" Matthew asked.

"Now that you mention it, I do," Wade stated.

"Smell what?" Jo'sha asked.

"Well, it's the faint scent of mint or eucalyptus," Matthew answered as he sniffed his bag.

They all instinctively sniffed their bags.

"My bag smells like cinnamon and frankincense," Jo'sha said.

"This one smells like one of the oils you use, Jo'sha," said Wade. Jo'sha took a sniff of Wade's pouch. "That's chamomile and myrrh," he said.

"I don't know what this smell is," Chance said, sounding helpless.

They each took turns attempting to identify the smell, but couldn't identify the storax and benzoin odor.

"We can't keep these," Wade said.

"Well, we can't exactly go give them back," Jo'sha said. He went to his desk drawer, pulled out a roll of leather string, and began making seamless leather loops for their new charms.

"This stone feels strange. It almost seems alive," Chance stated.

"They're not like anything I've ever seen before," Jo'sha responded.

Matthew noticed that his bag also had a piece of paper in it. The thick corner of parchment had an illustration and a few lines of script,

$$\Omega$$

$$T$$

> *My colleagues and I opened the chest. We found the contents intriguing. The Crux Ansata, an inspiration for the formation of our fraternity. But the situation has grown grave. I have not heard from Samuel as promised and the local rumor is that he is on the run for stealing.*
>
> *Under the advisement of my associates, I am separating the contents. My dear queen, Nina, will know what to make of this.*

"Now what in the world is that?" Chance asked, checking his bag for a note and finding it empty.

"That symbol on top is the Greek letter Omega and if both are Greek letters, then that symbol underneath that looks like a T is a Tau. That must have been the name for their fraternity, Omega Tau." Wade informed the group as he looked over Matthew's shoulder.

Chance and Jo'sha moved closer to Matthew, Wade and the parchment.

"Do you see that?" Jo'sha asked.

"No, what?" they asked in unison.

"Those two letters form an ankh when they are placed together. Just like the ankh's we have. The Crux Ansata," Jo'sha concluded. He completed a leather necklace and handed it to Chance for his ankh.

"What?" Wade asked.

"The Ankh—the original cross," Jo'sha explained. "I know a lot about it because it shows up constantly in the study of ancient religions. It is also called the 'Crux Ansata,' and is of Egyptian origin. It can be traced to the Early Dynastic Period. It appears frequently in ancient religious artwork. The circle or loop at the top symbolizes eternal life and the cross below it represents the material plane. The ankh signifies life in the language of Ancient Kemet. Kemet was renamed Egypt by the Greeks and was a rich land filled with people of color. The ankh is also a symbol for the power to give and sustain life. It is usually associated with material things like water or air. Egyptian kings were often depicted holding them. The ankh was also supposed to symbolize eternal life and bestowed immortality on anyone who possessed it. It is believed that life energy emanating from the ankh can be absorbed by anyone within a given proximity. The ankh also resembles a key and is considered the key to eternal life after death. It serves as an antenna or conduit for the divine power of life that permeates the universe. The amulet is a powerful talisman that provides the wearer with great protection."

"Well, I think this ankh looks good on me," Chance said, admiring the mysterious opal-like stone against his ebony skin. Jo'sha completed three more loop leather necklaces for himself, Matthew and Wade.

"Did we get any information that will help us with the presentation?" Wade asked, hesitantly placing Jo'sha's homemade necklace over his head.

"Not exactly," Matthew said. "There are still some unanswered questions. We need to do some more research. We need to find out what 235 North Peters Avenue is all about."

"In New Orleans?" Jo'sha asked.

"Yeah, and then we need to find out a little bit more about Samuel Wilkes—find out what else he might have given Cyrus. It might have been these ankhs, and if it was then we need to find out why they were so important. And last but not least, we need to see what else Miss Vaughn knows without tipping her off. She's been around the university community for a long time. She might be able to shed some extra light on all of this."

CHAPTER 12

It was shortly after 6:00 p.m. when Matthew walked into the student center consumed with his impending medical exam and the fallout from the episode in Miss Vaughn's office two nights prior. Wednesdays were his light class and work days, and Tessa had been insistent about coming over from Spelman to see him. The cool yellow ankh rested flush against his chest, under his t-shirt, reminding him of Monday night's adventure.

Having grown up in Atlanta, Matthew knew quite a few people who attended Central so he had spoken to at least a dozen classmates, associates and friends before making it through the student commons area. He had agreed to meet Tessa by the phone bank. He had only been there for a few minutes when he heard someone else call his name.

"Matthew!"

He turned to see Jo'sha and Wade coming his way.

"You don't have to yell. He can see you," said Wade.

Even though he had complained about taking it, Wade was wearing the blue ankh underneath a matching blue Calvin Klein sweater. Jo'sha on the other hand, had decided to wear his red ankh on the outside of his shirt. As soon as they reached him, Matthew tucked Jo'sha's ankh inside his shirt and gave him a disapproving look.

"Is Tessa here yet?" Jo'sha asked, growing accustomed to Matthew's cautiousness.

"Can't wait to meet your girlfriend," Wade interjected, suspecting that Tessa was what his mother and aunts might refer to as bottom shelf.

"She'll probably be late," Matthew said without much enthusiasm.

"What's wrong with you?" Jo'sha asked.

"Miss Vaughn got suspended," Matthew whispered, with an air of finality.

"What?" Wade exclaimed, immediately realizing the potential gravity of Matthew's statement.

"Why?" Jo'sha asked.

"It seems that after the alarms went off on Monday night, the homecoming committee became concerned about the security in the library. The public relations firm had been pressuring Miss Vaughn to give up the time capsule in her office. After they investigated, they had reason to believe that someone had been tampering with the contents. Not only did Miss Vaughn have to relinquish the time capsule, but she got suspended. And because Nia was found with Miss Vaughn's keys she got suspended," Matthew explained.

"So do they think Nia and Miss Vaughn tampered with the time capsule?" Wade asked.

"They don't really know what happened, but it was enough to get Miss Vaughn suspended. I overheard one of the investigators say something about papers sticking out of the chest," Matthew answered.

Jo'sha cringed.

"Does Miss Vaughn think you had anything to do with it?" Wade pressed.

"Not as far as I can tell. As far as she or anyone else knows I was up in the library stacks returning books when everything happened," Matthew answered.

"Whoa," Jo'sha sighed, thinking back to how quickly and carelessly he and Chance closed the chest.

"What about the security guard. Did he say anything about seeing us?" Wade questioned, trying to cover all bases.

"Not a credible witness. He was drunk as hell," Matthew responded, having asked himself all of the same questions. "Is Chance still working on that internet research for us?" Matthew asked Wade.

"Yes. He's in the room right now. He's been at it for a while."

"Are we still on for the trip to New Orleans on Saturday?" Matthew asked, looking at them both for confirmation. His tone suggested that he was really telling them rather than asking.

Wade and Jo'sha each nodded in the affirmative, but were both growing tired of Matthew's bossiness and growing obsession.

"Have you spoken to Miss Vaughn since she got suspended?" Wade asked.

"No, but I need to. I'm really concerned about her, and I would love to know what she knows about Cyrus and his friends. She gave me her address, and I'm planning to go by her house tomorrow."

"Matthew!" cooed Tessa as she glided up to the trio.

Matthew gave Tessa a hug and a kiss on the cheek. He quickly looked over his long-time girlfriend.

Tessa would have been average looking if not for LASIK eye surgery, four years of braces, monthly dermatologist visits and weekly trips to the beauty salon. Tessa was charming if nothing else. She could hold her own with the best of the sisters, but was always one biscuit away from shopping at Lane Bryant, and one bad hair day away from an insecurity complex.

"These are my boys, Wade Graham IV, and Jo'sha Imarah."

"Tessa Spaulding, very nice to meet you both," Tessa said with all the charm of a Georgia peach.

Jo'sha and Wade both smiled politely.

Tessa gazed at Wade for a moment, as if she'd seen him before. "Are you related to the Baltimore Grahams?"

"Why, yes I am," Wade said proudly.

"My father is a lawyer, he knows Judge Graham," she bragged.

"Oh really?" Wade asked with interest.

"Yes, I was introduced to your father at the grand opening of the law library last year," Tessa continued.

"Uh, let's go get a table," Matthew said, interrupting the conversation.

After getting their plates the group found a table in the corner of the student commons eating area. Wade and Tessa continued talking about mutual acquaintances for the next fifteen minutes, while Jo'sha and Matthew exchanged small talk. Matthew noticed that there was a member of the football team staring at them from the other side of the room.

"Jo'sha, do you see that guy over there? The football player," Matthew said, tapping Jo'sha on the arm.

"Where?" Jo'sha asked, noticing that something seemed different about his arm.

"Over in the corner by the condiments. He's staring at us," Matthew said.

"He isn't paying attention to us," Jo'sha said, returning his attention to his fruit bowl.

"Matthew, I would like some salt," Tessa said, more out of a desire to be waited on than a desire for salt.

"I'll get it for you," Wade said quickly. He was glad to be in the company of someone that appreciated his company so much. Wade rushed over to the condiment stand. On his way back to the table, the large football player bumped into him. "Excuse me," Wade said instinctively.

"You damn right, excuse you," the stranger responded.

"Is there something wrong?" Wade asked.

"I think you know what's wrong. Watch yourself," the football player responded, pushing Wade against a nearby table and onto the floor. Wade's glasses and the saltshaker scattered under the overturned table.

By the time Jo'sha and Matthew noticed what had happened, the football player had charged out of the eating area. Jo'sha and Matthew rushed over to Wade, who was still on the floor.

"Are you alright?" Matthew asked.

Tessa knelt down under the table to pick up his glasses and the saltshaker.

"What happened? Who was that?" Jo'sha asked.

"I don't know," Wade responded breathlessly. He grew silent and reached for his glasses. He looked at his friends, shook his head, and put on his glasses. A second later he pulled them back off. Was this really happening? Though his vision was a little blurry, it was becoming increasingly clear. In moments, Matthew and Jo'sha came into clear view—without his glasses on!

"What's wrong with you?" Matthew asked when he saw the strange look on Wade's face.

"I can see now!" he exclaimed excitedly.

His friends remained quiet for several seconds. Neither of them knew what to say. Jo'sha, who had a habit of rubbing the scar on his arm, reached to touch it but only felt smooth skin.

"Jo'sha, look at your arm!" Matthew exclaimed.

Jo'sha looked down and noticed that the burn mark on his left forearm was completely gone.

"I gotta go!" Matthew exclaimed suddenly, leaving Tessa and Jo'sha standing over Wade. Matthew rushed out of the commons and toward the train station. Both Jo'sha and Wade were still in complete shock.

"What is going on?" Tessa yelled after Matthew.

Wade and Jo'sha just shrugged their shoulders.

∞

It was late Thursday night before any of them saw Matthew again. Jo'sha was sitting near the window, delicately plucking on the banjo. Chance was sprawled out on Jo'sha's bed, and Wade was doing homework at the desk when Matthew came bursting into the room.

"Where have you been?" Jo'sha scolded.

"I don't have cancer!" Matthew exclaimed. He was more emotional and excited than any of them had ever seen him.

"What are you talking about?" asked Wade, sounding confused. He had no idea what Matthew was talking about since he had not been there when Matthew revealed his medical secret.

"I don't have cancer!" he repeated more forcefully. "I left last night because I had to find out as soon as possible."

"Well, it was very rude of you to leave Tessa like that," Wade responded, sounding miffed.

"Don't you get it?" Matthew asked incredulously.

"Get what?" Chance asked.

"We've been healed, and it must be because of the ankhs!" Matthew exclaimed. "The doctor's examined me yesterday and all day today. There is no sign of cancer. Wade, you said yourself that you can see now. And, Jo'sha, the scar is gone from your arm."

Neither Wade nor Jo'sha spoke. Both of them had spent the last twenty-four hours enjoying their physical improvements, wondering how they had come about, and extremely excited by the occurrence.

"Wait a minute," Chance said, looking at Wade. "You mean you can see now? I was wondering why you weren't wearing your glasses."

"Jo'sha and I wanted to wait until we were all together to tell you," Wade said.

Chance didn't know what to make of what he'd just heard. He went over to the alarm clock in the far corner of the room by the desk. "Can you read this?" he asked Wade.

"It's 11:06 p.m.," Wade said proudly.

"Let me see your arm, Jo'sha," Chance said.

110

Jo'sha pulled his sleeve up proudly revealing a scar-free arm.

"Well, I'll be damned," Chance said in amazement.

"What did the doctors say to you?" Jo'sha asked.

"They thought I was crazy when I rushed into the hospital demanding to be tested last night. They kept me for observation and finished the testing this morning. They were all skeptics, but I knew just as soon as Wade said he could see that something was different. I just felt it. This is bigger than all of us. We've found something special," Matthew said.

"If these ankhs are so special, don't you think someone will come looking for them?" Wade asked.

"I don't think anyone knows about them but us," Matthew said.

"Yeah, us and whomever is at 235 North Peters in New Orleans," Jo'sha said.

Matthew nodded slowly, considering the possibility that what Jo'sha said was true. "So what are you guys doing?" he asked, changing the subject and settling down on his bed.

"Your timing is great. I was just about to explain some of the things I found on the Internet," Chance said. "My research comes from a piece by Ida B. Wells entitled *Lynch Law in Georgia*. A Black man by the name of Samuel *allegedly* killed a white landowner by the name of Alfred Cranford, and accosted his wife on September 27, 1904. It is rumored that the original disagreement was over wages Alfred Cranford owed Samuel. Samuel fled the scene, fearing for his life, and wasn't caught until October 3, 1904."

Chance flipped his page of notes. "Samuel was stripped naked and burned at a stake in a place called Newnan, Georgia, at 2:30 p.m. on October 5, 1904. It's about forty minutes from here. Two thousand white citizens stood around and watched as the flames ate away at his flesh—onlookers practically fought over his remains as souvenirs of the event."

"What does that have to do with anything?" Wade asked, failing to see the point in Chance's history lesson.

"I'm getting to that, here is the link. Samuel's full name was Samuel Wilkes. He had a younger cousin by the name of Cyrus Wilkes who had come to Georgia from New Orleans to go to college. I found this out by looking through the registration records of the first class of Georgia Central University. Cyrus had identified Samuel as local next of kin. This explains the letters. It's still not clear what's in New Orleans, but based on everything that I have been able to find it must be pretty important. Anyway, the article went on to say that speculation was that the confrontation was not really about money, but about the fact that Alfred Cranford had stolen something from Samuel Wilkes. Samuel went to Cranford's house and evidently got into an argument, killed Alfred Cranford, took his belongings back, and fled. In the days after the murder and before Samuel was caught, he must have somehow given these ankhs to his cousin Cyrus and his friends."

"Do you think that Cyrus, Nathaniel, Winston, and Oleander knew about the healing power of the ankhs?" Jo'sha asked.

"I don't think so. Don't you think that the ankhs would have protected them?" Chance asked.

"There is a big difference between protection and healing," Wade stated.

"Maybe the healing comes from wearing them and not just having them," Matthew concluded.

"Whatever the deal I am not taking mine off," Jo'sha stated. "And if you keep getting into fights you may need to keep yours on too," Jo'sha said, joking with Wade.

"What fight?" Chance asked.

Wade had been too embarrassed to tell Chance.

"Wade didn't tell you? Some football player tried to pick a fight with him in the student center the other day," Jo'sha continued.

"Well who was he?" Chance asked, unafraid to defend a friend.

Wade was flattered that Chance seemed to be genuinely interested in his safety.

"It was probably just a case of mistaken identity or test stress," Matthew advised.

"Well he better not try it if I am around," Chance warned.

"Do you know how much people would pay for something like this?" Jo'sha asked, changing the subject back to the ankhs.

"Yeah, I just wonder if this is permanent. Like what would happen if we took them off," Matthew asked, thinking about his cancer.

"Well which one of us is willing to sacrifice to find out?" Wade asked.

"You know it seems as though we have completely lost sight of preparing for the homecoming presentation," Jo'sha said.

"I think being healed from poor vision, cancer, and a burn mark is just a little bit more important than making a presentation," Wade said.

"We just have to make sure that we don't tell anyone. At least not until we understand it," Matthew warned again.

"Speaking of understanding it all, I think *we* need to come to an understanding," Chance said.

"What do you mean?" Matthew asked.

"You have been making all of the decisions and calling all of the shots, but we're all intelligent men," Chance said, voicing what the others had been thinking.

Matthew was quiet, but obviously stunned.

Chance continued, "We don't *all* have to go to New Orleans together, and you don't need to go see Miss Vaughn by yourself. Jo'sha and Wade get out of class early on Friday. They can make the trip to New Orleans. You and I can go talk to Miss Vaughn."

"I was planning to go see Miss Vaughn by myself," Matthew protested.

"Is it that you don't trust us?" Chance challenged. "What are you going to say to Miss Vaughn that I can't hear?"

"Well, nothing. I just thought she might be more comfortable talking to me since she doesn't know you guys," Matthew said.

"I'm sure she'll just be glad to get some company," Chance responded.

"And it is a pretty long drive to New Orleans," Matthew continued.

"Jo'sha can help Wade drive. It's only six hours. They'll tell us if they find anything in New Orleans," Chance said.

Jo'sha thought it interesting that while Chance was reprimanding Matthew for being bossy and taking them for granted, he seemed to be doing the exact same thing.

"What he's saying does make sense," Wade added, attempting to keep the peace. "Splitting up means that we will get more information sooner and we *are* all in this together."

Chance stood square and strong using his stature and stance to enforce his point more than even he realized. Matthew conceded reluctantly, not feeling completely comfortable sharing his role as self-appointed leader.

Wade interrupted the awkward waves of silence by grabbing four glasses and pouring each of them a half glass of Voss. "What about a toast to new beginnings?" Wade saluted, sounding like his father.

"To health," Jo'sha said, raising his glass.

"To healing," Matthew said, still a little put off by Chance's challenge, but happier about his latest prognosis.

"To new sight," Wade added, raising his glass.

"To friendship," Chance responded, privately wondering if the ankh had healed him of his asthma.

CHAPTER 13

Miss Vaughn lived just off of Auburn Avenue, a historic area of Atlanta, famous for the birthplace of Dr. Martin Luther King, Jr. The previous evening's friction between Matthew and Chance had subsided. Chance was not one to hold on to grudges, and Matthew realized that for once in his life he did not have to try to manage everything by himself.

Another Friday evening and Atlanta's MARTA train was packed with pedestrians eager to get home and start their weekends. Matthew and Chance exchanged casual conversation as they exited the city train and made their way toward Auburn Avenue.

Able bodied men lay strewn across the concrete in the middle of the day, where purpose or principle should have propped them up, and angled old women crept silently from block to block, burdened with bags of their penny's last breath. Chance surveyed his surroundings and exhaled heavily.

"It bothers you doesn't it?" Matthew asked.

"What?" Chance asked.

"The homelessness," Matthew answered.

"I'm just not used to it," Chance responded.

Having grown up in the rural south, this scenario seemed strange to him. Young people walked about with so much pride that there was none left for any of creation. They thought it all right to yell out loud and leave debris and refuse in their wake. Chance hurt for them and their ignorance. He longed for the simple purity of home.

"What's the address?" Chance asked, ready to get to their destination.

"120 Channing Avenue. It's just off of Auburn Avenue."

A few blocks later they found the house. They made their way up to the two-story wooden home and knocked on the screen door. They stood on the concrete porch several minutes before hearing anything.

"Is this the right address?" Chance asked.

"Yes."

"Did she know you were coming?"

"Yes," Matthew answered again, slightly annoyed.

Then they heard someone on the other side of the door. The normally proper and prim Miss Vaughn came to the door in a pink nightgown covered by a thin white cotton robe, house slippers, and curlers. She wasn't wearing her glasses and barely recognized Matthew.

"Miss Vaughn, it is me. Matthew. Matthew Meredith," he said.

"Oh, Matthew," she said with a smile. "Son, how are you doing? Come on in."

The young men walked into Miss Vaughn's home. The window shades were drawn and the house was dark and dank. It reminded Chance of his grandmother's house, filled with antique furniture covered in plastic. China and porcelain baubles and knick-knacks adorned every shelf, celebrating European romance.

"I'm fine. My friend Chance and I came to see how you were doing since that thing at the library," Matthew said, when they reached the front parlor.

Miss Vaughn sat down in her reading chair and turned on a standing lamp that stood nearby. "You children and these names— Chance is it?" she asked.

"Yes, ma'am, Chance Walker," he responded politely.

"At least you were raised properly," she said, nodding her approval.

"So how are you, Miss Vaughn?" Matthew asked.

"Child, it's a terrible thing what they did to me. I've been with that university all of my life. I remember when Clarence Weatherspoon first stepped foot on that campus, and now that he's some big shot he's forgotten where he came from. Just because they believe that someone might have tampered with that old chest, they suspended me until they finish their little investigation. I do believe I was set up. That public relations firm has had it out for me from the beginning. They've got all up in Clarence's head. All they want is money. I wouldn't be surprised if they wanted to sell the time capsule. I have history with that school," she vented.

"Is there anything that we can get for you? Do you need something from the drug or grocery store, Miss Vaughn?" Chance asked.

"Son, you are so kind. I'm not particular about store bought food, but I sure could use some tea and pound cake," she said. "I just haven't been to the grocery store lately."

"I'll be right back," Chance said, having seen a small corner store a half block up. "I'll get your trash for you too if you don't mind," he said, heading for the trashcan in the adjoining kitchen, which was running over.

"Here child, let me get you some money," Miss Vaughn said, attempting to get up to go get her purse.

"It's not a problem. I have the money, Miss Vaughn," Chance answered. He tied the trash bag and was out the door in a matter of seconds.

"Such a nice boy," Miss Vaughn said, sitting back down with Matthew.

"He's a good friend," Matthew agreed.

Miss Vaughn and Matthew spent the next fifteen minutes discussing the particulars of her suspension. Matthew asked question after question until he was absolutely sure that he and his friends were free and clear. The only reason that they would launch a full-scale investigation is if they had reason to believe that someone had taken something from the chest. Matthew also reasoned that it wouldn't make sense to take fingerprints since so many people had probably handled the chest.

"That public relations firm has the time capsule now," Miss Vaughn said with tears in her eyes. "I've been with that school for years. They wouldn't have known about the chest if not for me. I deserve to see what's in it. I don't deserve to be treated this way."

Matthew was at a loss for what to say. Though he felt relieved that there didn't seem to be anything that linked him or his friends to what happened, he felt bad seeing Miss Vaughn so sad. Just then Chance knocked on the door, and Matthew rushed to let him in. Chance gave the tea and pound cake to Miss Vaughn. She shuffled off to the kitchen to prepare the tea and cake, while thanking Chance profusely.

"Well?" Chance whispered to Matthew.

"Everything seems cool. I don't think they can trace anything back to us," Matthew said.

"What about her last name? Any association to Oleander Vaughn?" Chance continued.

"We haven't gotten to that yet. I didn't want to seem too obvious," Matthew said. "Good touch going to the grocery store and taking out her trash. I never would have thought of that. I'm sure that we have her complete trust now."

Chance didn't answer. He wasn't being manipulative when he offered to do those things. He was just being kind.

Miss Vaughn came back into the parlor a few minutes later with three cups of tea and three small slices of pound cake, all on her finest china. She carried it in on a decorative silver platter.

"Here you go," she said, setting it down on the table between them.

Chance helped himself and had eaten his piece of cake before Matthew or Miss Vaughn even got started.

"Miss Vaughn, we entered the presentation competition for homecoming," Matthew said.

"Oh, that is a fine contest. Our university has a proud history. We used to hold the same competition many years ago. Georgia Central men have always been fine public speakers. I was the one who reminded Clarence about those contests. I'm sure you will do just fine."

"We've been doing some research on the first class of students and came across the name of one young man named Oleander Vaughn. Is he any relation to you?" Matthew asked tentatively.

Miss Vaughn grew silent and then a faint smile crept across her face. "Oleander Vaughn was my great uncle. As a matter of fact, he was my great grandfather's twin brother. Oleander and Othello—they say they were like two peas in a pod until Oleander went to Georgia Central. They grew up not thirty miles from here in Fayette County on six acres of my family homestead. Sad as it is to say, I am the sole heir. After high school, Othello decided to follow his father into the ministry. Oleander came to Atlanta to Georgia Central where he met three other young men, Cyrus Wilkes, Nathaniel Charles, and Winston Wright. Then it was called Georgia Central School for Colored Men" she explained, pointing to a picture on her mantle for reference.

Matthew and his friends had seen the four young gentlemen in the pictures that they had stolen from the library. Now thanks to Miss Vaughn, they could put names with faces.

"They became fast friends. They had only been at Georgia Central for a short time when they all went missing. Funny, my daddy always believed that the nightriders killed them," Miss Vaughn explained.

"Nightriders?" Matthew asked.

"Yes," said Chance. "Nightriders were groups who went around and tormented blacks, burning their houses and churches, as well as lynching them." Having grown up in the rural south, Chance had heard his grandfather speak of nightriders and the Ku Klux Klan.

"That's right," Miss Vaughn echoed.

"Why would they have killed four young college students?" Chance asked.

"Who knows? Negro education wasn't very popular back then. There were a lot of people who thought that training the Negro was a waste of time. Some of the family rumors say that Oleander and his friends were thinking about starting a fraternity, and rival students accidentally killed them while at horseplay. But my grandfather Othello was sure that it had something to do with some old trinkets and a slave diary."

Matthew instinctively clutched the ankh under his shirt. "What slave diary?"

"It seems that Cyrus, one of Oleander's friends, had stolen something from one of the most notorious nightriders. Uncle Oleander and granddaddy Othello warned him. Cyrus came from New Orleans—them Creole voodoo people, and he wouldn't listen. Well they all got tied up in it."

"Where is the slave diary now?" Chance asked.

"I don't know. I haven't thought about that in years. It could have been taken by the nightriders. It may have never even existed. My grandfather rambled about it often in his old age. My great uncle Oleander was a great musician you know—famous for his banjo playing."

Chance saw the gleam in Matthew's eye and knew that he was on to something.

"Miss Vaughn, it was good seeing you again," Matthew said, abruptly bringing the visit to an end.

"You boys don't have to go now do you?" she asked, sounding disappointed.

"We better get going. We have some studying to do, but we'll be back to visit," Chance said.

Their visit seemed to have released Miss Vaughn from her depression and she smiled as she walked them to the door.

"I am sure that you will be back in the library in no time. Things just aren't the same without you," Matthew said.

"Who knows what the good Lord has in store," she answered.

Matthew and Chance walked briskly back up the street and were at the city train station before Matthew spoke.

"It must be that slave diary," he said.

"What do you mean?" Chance asked.

"Remember the note from Cyrus? That might just be what's in New Orleans."

∞

Jo'sha fell for what seemed like an eternity until he found himself lying in a clearing. Then he was lifted, bound, and tied to a stake, surrounded by hundreds of chanting translucent faces. The rope dug into his wrists and seemed to get tighter and tighter as the chanting got louder and louder. Then as quickly as it had begun, the tightening and the chanting stopped, and in the distance there was a spark. The spark turned into a flame, the flame turned into a blaze, and it came closer and closer heating his flesh, engulfing his memories. The flame started at his feet and grew until it consumed him. He screamed out in pain, begging to be set free. His screams fed the flames and he felt his flesh beginning to separate from his body until a slim dark figure came through the fire and placed his hand on Jo'sha's left forearm where his burn mark had been. The figure's cool, transforming touch sent chills up Jo'sha's arm. The figure raised his hands and the flames miraculously froze. The two resided there inside the pyre safe from the screaming faces, and there they communed, and Jo'sha found peace. Then as suddenly as he had come, the figure vanished and Jo'sha was alone.

Wade was startled by Jo'sha's screaming. It only took him a couple of seconds to get off of the phone and rush over to Jo'sha's door.

After several seconds of banging, Jo'sha woke up and opened the door.

"Are you alright?" Wade asked as he walked into the room.

"Yeah, just a nightmare," Jo'sha said.

"But it's one in the afternoon," Wade said, thoroughly confused.

Jo'sha had decided to take a quick nap while waiting for Wade to return from class before their drive to New Orleans.

"I know, but this one was different. I feel—at ease now."

"What do you mean?" Wade asked. "I don't know if you would understand. Hell, I am not even sure if I understand," Jo'sha said.

"Well, try me. I am a pretty good listener."

"I have reoccurring nightmares about the car wreck that killed my parents. They died in a fire caused by the explosion and I guess all of that talk about Samuel Wilkes got my mind going. Well, my dream felt like I was the one being burned at a stake. It was so real I could feel the fire. It wasn't like a regular dream or even a nightmare. I could literally feel the rope around my wrist and I could hear people calling me names, and then if that wasn't weird enough, there was a real presence in my dream. I think it was Samuel Wilkes," Jo'sha said.

"Then what happened?" Wade asked apparently very interested in Jo'sha's story.

"Well, he touched me. Here on my arm," Jo'sha said as he pointed to his left forearm where his burn mark had been. "A cold sharp pain shot up my arm when he touched me."

"And then what happened?" Wade asked.

"Then the fire died down and he vanished," Jo'sha ended.

"Wow!" Wade responded, not knowing what to say. "Are you still up for the trip?" he asked, tentatively. They had all agreed that he and Jo'sha would leave on Friday afternoon as soon as they got out of class, but now he wasn't sure.

Jo'sha sat in silence for a few seconds and then a smile crept across his face. "Let's get the hell out of here!"

It was 11:00 p.m. and Wade and Jo'sha were less than an hour from New Orleans. Jo'sha had insisted that they stop for fruit and alcohol for the trip to New Orleans, and had spent a majority of the trip drinking coconut rum and pineapple juice, while Wade drove. Jo'sha had a high tolerance for alcohol, while Wade on the other hand, had only been exposed to wine and was starting to feel real good under the influence of just one shot of Malibu rum.

"Well, if you can't eat meat, then why is it okay to drink alcohol?" Wade asked.

"There is no meat in alcohol." His answer caused them both to laugh uncontrollably as they sped toward New Orleans.

"Jo'sha, man, I'm glad we came to New Orleans together," Wade said.

Jo'sha reached into his saddlebag, pulled out his case of CDs, and popped in Stevie Wonder's *Songs in the Key of Life*. When he began to sing along, Wade joined in, and surprised Jo'sha by being in near perfect pitch. They laughed and sang loudly all the way to New Orleans.

∞

"This is a damn club," Jo'sha exclaimed as he and Wade rode past what they thought was 235 North Peters Street.

"No. You're looking at 236. The building right beside it is 235 North Peters," Wade said.

"Oh," Jo'sha responded. "That sign says *LeBeau Family Museum.*"

"Well it is 11:30 p.m. Let's go get a hotel room and come back and check it out in the morning," Wade suggested.

"Are you serious? This is New Orleans. This city never sleeps! Let's go check out the club. The night is young. We can have some fun," Jo'sha urged.

Wade was tired from the drive, but agreed to go anyway. As they entered the packed club, Wade was self-conscious, having had on the same clothes since he left Atlanta. Jo'sha on the other hand, was only interested in getting a drink, looking at females, and having a good time.

The pulse of the music woke Wade up and he began to look around, taking in the extraordinary sights of New Orleans nightlife. He was also looking for anything that might connect the varied bits of information that they had collected. He assumed that Jo'sha was doing the same, but when he turned to ask Jo'sha if he thought the voodoo dolls on the wall in the foyer had any special significance, he realized that Jo'sha had disappeared. Before Wade could get angry, he realized that he had the car keys and that Jo'sha was hundreds of miles from Atlanta. That meant he would have to wander back eventually.

The décor in the club was extremely eclectic. From the writing on the walls, Wade could see that the club was called Nina's. Stuffed alligators, shrunken heads, and antique mirrors decorated the burgundy and gold walls. The crowd was primarily African-

American, and the music was straight R&B and hip-hop. Kid Capri had spun the crowd into a fevered pitch and brothers and sisters alike were sweating profusely.

Several young ladies looked Wade up and down as if he were a snack, mistaking him for a New Orleans Creole instead of a member of Baltimore's social elite. Wade stood in the corner for several songs, trying to blend in. One shapely, young, dark-skinned sister with burgundy shoulder length twists approached him from the back, grabbed his waist, and asked him if he wanted to dance. Wade politely declined, as he looked past her at a portrait of what appeared to have been a Caucasian woman.

"Would you like to go up to the VIP lounge? I have two passes," she persisted.

Wade looked at the chocolate complexioned sister and wondered what his mother and aunties would think of such a forward young lady. That thought alone was enough to cause Wade to look at her wide brown eyes, smile, and accept the invitation.

The young lady introduced herself as Charlotte and shook Wade's hand as they made their way upstairs. Wade found her pleasant and mildly attractive, except for the fact that her breath smelled like warm cheese and vodka. When they arrived in the VIP area, Wade was not surprised to see Jo'sha sitting at the piano at the front of the room, playing and singing a Curtis Mayfield song over the microphone. The crowd was mesmerized by his voice. One of Charlotte's friends ran up to them as they found a table.

"Isn't he cute?" her friend asked, referring to Jo'sha.

"Yeah, he is alright if you like that look," Charlotte replied in a half interested tone, not wanting to offend Wade.

Jo'sha finished singing and gave Wade a special introduction. Charlotte and her friend looked at each other with raised eyebrows. Jo'sha got up from the piano, walked over to the club manager and thanked him for letting him play. Although they were several feet away, Wade could tell that the manager was trying to get Jo'sha to stay. Jo'sha respectfully declined and then made his way over to Wade and his two new friends. Jo'sha licked his lips seductively as he extended his hand and introduced himself to Charlotte and her friend.

While Jo'sha began talking with Charlotte and her friend, Wade looked around the room and noticed that the walls were the same shade of burgundy as downstairs, with accented gold molding and thick gold velvet curtains. The upstairs was much less ornate than the first floor. There were no wall hangings. Skeleton keys hanging from the ceiling by fishing twine were the only decorations. The lounge was just as crowded as downstairs. R&B bled through from the floor beneath, but the lounge crowd seemed more interested in talking and connecting mentally, than dancing and connecting physically.

Wade was snapped back into reality by a pat on the back from Jo'sha.

"Are you ready to go get that hotel room now?" Jo'sha asked, having already invited Charlotte and her friend over for a visit.

Wade gave him a blank stare when he noticed that Charlotte and her friend were heading back downstairs.

"Where are they going?" Wade asked.

"With us," Jo'sha responded, his eyes fixated on the behinds of the young ladies in front of them.

"Are you for real?" Wade asked.

"Am I for real? I couldn't be more for real," Jo'sha answered, grabbing himself and smiling.

"What are you planning on doing?"

"Me? How about 'what are we planning on doing?'"

Jo'sha and Wade drove down the street a couple of blocks to a Ritz-Carlton. Jo'sha would have been comfortable staying in the Motel 6 just off the interstate, but Wade could not even imagine it. The girls followed them to the hotel in a small blue Volkswagen, and waited while Wade got a room.

Once they entered the room Charlotte sat on one bed and her friend sat on the other as if they had done this type of thing before, or at least discussed it. When Wade turned on the television and then walked to the other side of the oversized room to sit on a chaise lounge, they all gave him a disapproving look.

Completely unaffected, Jo'sha immediately began to take off his clothes revealing his chiseled body and a full erection. Charlotte's friend took his cue and removed her clothes too, revealing a slim, but shapely, vanilla frame. As Jo'sha and his new friend got acquainted, Charlotte looked over at Wade, who was somewhere between feigning sleep and actually falling asleep.

The first time he woke up, it was 3:00 a.m. Charlotte and her friend were both in bed with Jo'sha grunting and sweating as if this was the last piece of sex that any of them were ever going to have. Wade wondered if her breath would still smell like warm cheese and cheap alcohol after she finished giving Jo'sha oral sex. Wade rolled over, covered his ears, and went back to sleep. When he woke up again the small alarm clock on the dresser read 9:05 a.m. The girls were gone.

Jo'sha was standing in the center of the room completely naked, drying his damp body with the thick cotton towel.

"Don't you have any issues with having indiscriminate sex with women that you just met?" Wade lectured as soon as he saw him.

"Not if they don't have any issues with having indiscriminate sex with me. And by the way, my sex ain't indiscriminate. It's indescribable! Just ask around." Jo'sha laughed. "Besides, I always travel with my heavy duty super sized condoms!"

Jo'sha's explanation didn't satisfy Wade and he lectured on sexual responsibility the entire time they got dressed and until room service arrived.

Eventually, the conversation turned to their reason for being there. Wade realized that the message light on his cell phone was blinking. Jo'sha flipped the television channels while Wade retrieved his message. The local New Orleans news anchor was delivering a bulletin about the recent rash of male murders in Atlanta, Georgia.

"Who was it?" Jo'sha asked, turning his attention away from the news story.

"It was Chance. He called several times. We must have been out of range when he left the message. He said that we should be looking for a diary of some sort."

Wade stared at Jo'sha blankly for a moment and then rushed to get dressed, remembering that they still hadn't investigated the museum at 235 North Peters. By the time they ate, checked out, and got back to the address on North Peters, it was just before noon.

They entered what was the parlor of an old home. A short, buxom, Creole woman in her early thirties greeted them as they entered.

"Hello, Gentlemen. My name is Pera. Welcome to the LeBeau Family Museum," she said.

Pera seemed to know everything about New Orleans past and present. Wade listened intently. Jo'sha however, kept getting distracted as Pera's sizable breasts heaved under her tight, white body shirt—her cleavage seeming about ready to explode from the v-neck. After listening to several minutes of rambling about New Orleans, Wade steered the conversation to the present address.

"I am so glad that you asked," she said.

"It is such a beautiful home," Wade added quickly.

Jo'sha leaned in close to her and licked his lips. She had certainly noticed his advances and smiled as she began to share the history of the building.

"This home used to be the estate of the LeBeau family—my family. My great grandmother Nina Wilkes used to be a feared and powerful priestess. Much to the dismay of her family, she had two bastard children by a young white aristocrat named Simon LeBeau. Their first born, a young son named Cyrus, was sent to college in Georgia for his protection, but was mysteriously murdered shortly after arriving at the school. Cyrus was my great, great uncle. Although we never found out why he was killed, Nina believed that it was the work of the LeBeau family. You see, Nina and her two children were a constant reminder of Simon's infidelity and Simon's wife's barren womb. After Cyrus, her oldest son died, she fell into a deep state of depression. The loss drove her mad and she promised to make the LeBeau family pay. Over the next few months the entire LeBeau family died, each from various and sundry reasons. Although no one was willing to say it aloud, everyone knew that Nina had cursed them. To add insult to injury, Nina purchased their house shortly after they all died—this house. The locals were appalled. Obviously a strong believer in the occult and hereafter, Nina turned all of the locks on the building upside down so that the ghosts of the LeBeau family couldn't enter and haunt her. She also hung several keys in the attic to confuse the spirits should they ever return."

Pera paused to make sure that she still had their attention. "The house has been in my family ever since. I give museum tours during the day. The story is always interesting to out of town guests. I restored a lot of the old furniture and restored a lot of Nina's personal items as if she were still here. If you are really quiet you can hear Nina Wilkes moaning for her lost son."

"We would love to see the museum. How much are tickets?" Wade interjected.

"Just four dollars each," Pera said, in her thick Creole accent.

Wade gave her ten dollars and told her to keep the change. She smiled.

Jo'sha yawned and stretched, raising his shirt, revealing his six pack abs. Intrigued, Pera smiled again. She took them through every room of the house explaining fact after fact about Nina Wilkes and her son, Cyrus.

It was as if they had stepped back into history. It was when they got to Nina's bedroom that they thought they had found what they were looking for. In the corner by a window was an old desk. Inside the desk were several letters from Cyrus to his mother along with an old, old diary.

"What is this?" Wade asked casually of the letters, not wanting to seem too interested.

"Those are old letters from Cyrus to his mother. I keep them there for effect. He sent them to her shortly after he got to school in Georgia. Most of them don't make sense—probably just the idle ramblings of a loving mother and her devoted son. He lovingly referred to her as Queen Nina and spoke of relatives that he had met after arriving in Georgia. The rest is really unclear. It has been ages since I've even read them. I have more upstairs in the attic," Pera said.

"Do you mind if we look at them?" Jo'sha asked.

"Stay right here. I'll be back in a moment," Pera said.

She rushed up to the attic. When she returned Jo'sha and Wade were looking through the items on the desk.

"Is any of this stuff for sale?" Wade asked.

"Oh, no." she said, shaking her head. "It's priceless. These are precious family heirlooms," she responded, half convincingly while still looking at Jo'sha.

Jo'sha rubbed his pectoral muscles and feigned another stretch, keeping Pera's attention. He motioned for Wade to leave when she wasn't looking, but it took several seconds before Wade got the hint.

"I guess I'll go check out a few more sights in the city," Wade said. He wasn't completely comfortable leaving Jo'sha but went back to the truck and waited anyway. An hour later Jo'sha came running up to the truck.

"Did you get it?" Wade asked.

Jo'sha smiled.

Wade rolled his eyes.

"I guess I should clarify that. Did you get the diary and the letters?"

Jo'sha reached into his pants pocket and pulled out the letters and the diary. Wade laughed and started the truck. They hit the road toward Atlanta leaving New Orleans and a very satisfied Pera behind.

CHAPTER 14

Jo'sha, Matthew, Wade, and Chance sat in the empty lobby of Winfrey-Combs dorm, not unusual for a Sunday night. With the exception of Ronnie, who was once again on duty in the resident advisor's office across the room, they were the only ones in sight. Still they whispered so that Ronnie couldn't hear.

"It was like we had traveled back in time," Jo'sha said, explaining the tour of the LeBeau Family museum.

"Now what did you find out again?" Chance asked fascinated with the few tidbits that Wade had shared.

"It's an actual slave journal. It seems that the ankhs had been kept with the diary up until Cyrus decided to separate them. But there are two entries that are particularly interesting. One appears to have been written by Nat Turner himself. He says that it was a gift from God, but when he wore them he was given unto mystic visions," Jo'sha said.

"That would have been between 1800 and 1831," Matthew said.

"Do you think that had anything to do with the vision that you had the other day?" Wade asked.

"What vision?" Matthew asked.

"I'll tell you later. This is more important. The other entry was from Harriet Tubman—the conductor herself!" Jo'sha said excitedly. "She says that when she wore them she was able to traverse many miles of terrain undetected, wielding the very tools of angels—earth, air, water, and fire, but was left prone to seizures and spells," he concluded.

"That would have been between 1820 and 1913. Her birth name was Araminta Ross. That means that the ankhs were somehow delivered from Nat Turner to Harriet Tubman to Samuel Wilkes,"

Matthew remarked again, the only one in the room interested in that level of detail.

"Do you think we should be wearing these things?" Chance asked.

"Don't know," Wade responded.

"What can it hurt?" Jo'sha said.

"Nothing has happened to us so far," Matthew said, trying to reassure himself as much as his peers.

"Yeah, if you call being healed from blindness and cancer nothing," Chance said.

"Can you imagine what happens if you wear all four?" Jo'sha said.

"Didn't Nat Turner get killed in a slave revolt?" Chance asked.

"Yeah," Matthew said, "But we don't know if it had anything to do with the ankhs."

"There are several more entries in here, but none from names that I recognize," Jo'sha explained.

"I hear you gentleman are entering the presentation competition," Ronnie interrupted. He had walked up on them without any of them noticing.

"Uh, yeah," Matthew responded.

"We were just working on that now," Jo'sha added.

"No wonder you're down here on a Sunday night," Ronnie said.

"Gotta get a jump on the competition," Chance chimed.

"Good luck," Ronnie said. He waved and headed over to the soda machine.

"We haven't done anything on that presentation," Wade commented, wondering how the others were feeling.

"I was thinking about that," Matthew said, hesitantly. He didn't want to seem overbearing. "It may be in our best interest not to draw too much attention to ourselves."

"I agree," Chance said.

"What about the money?" Jo'sha asked. "Unlike some of us, I ain't rolling in money."

Neither Wade nor Chance had a response.

"Well the risk of getting caught for stealing and breaking and entering far outweighs the possible benefit of winning the money," Matthew reasoned. When none of them responded he assumed that their silence was assent.

"What if we started our own fraternity," Chance asked the group, changing the subject.

"What do you mean?" Jo'sha asked, liking the sound of it.

"Omega Tau. What if we picked up where Cyrus and 'em left off?" Chance responded. "It's our chance to make a difference. To do it right. And you've got to admit that the ankh Omega Tau concept is nice. It's a connection to the Black Greek letter organizations, but ties us to our culture and heritage."

"Aren't there already enough Greeks?" Matthew asked.

"Yeah, but they aren't making a difference," Jo'sha added.

"Hey, wait a minute. My father is in a fraternity and they make a big difference in the local community," Wade defended.

"Would you rather be a member of an organization or a founder of one?" Chance challenged.

They spent the next hour discussing the potential of starting a fraternity until they were all at least partially sold on the idea.

"First things first, though," Matthew said. Let's lay low for a while and make sure that no one is on to us. After a while if it seems cool, then we can talk about starting a fraternity, okay?" When they all nodded Matthew smiled. He had become a lot more relaxed since he found out that didn't have cancer and they were all enjoying the difference.

"How long is a while?" Jo'sha asked.

"Let's chill until homecoming. If no one has made a big deal about any missing contents of the time capsule then we can consider it. But even then it won't be a simple task." Matthew said.

"In the meantime, we can make sure that we are all on point academically," Jo'sha said.

"Yeah, it will look good if all the founders of our fraternity have perfect grade point averages," Wade said.

"It also wouldn't hurt you three to join me in the gym. Have you seen the Omegas?" Chance added.

"What have they got on me?" Wade asked. He made a muscle with his puny yellow arm. They all laughed.

"We can also spend some time studying those books that Matthew got for us," Jo'sha added.

"Which ones?" Wade asked.

"*The Divine Nine* by Lawrence Ross, *Black Greek 101* by Dr. Kimbrough, and that article entitled *Why Blacks Call Themselves Greek* by Tony Brown," Jo'sha said.

Matthew smiled, impressed that Jo'sha remembered. It was nice to know that they didn't completely disregard the things he said. He'd be even happier if they agreed with him to keep things quiet.

"In the meantime, this is our secret, right?" he asked, looking at each of them.

"Our secret," they affirmed.

The next morning they all got up early and hit the gym with Chance. Then they dropped by the cafeteria for a quick breakfast. By 7:30 a.m. they were all dressed and on their way to Dr. Smith's Monday morning class—a full thirty minutes before class started. Wade, who wasn't usually a morning person, was impressed with his new burst of energy.

"Do you think it would be a problem if I entered the homecoming talent competition?" Jo'sha asked. "I really need the money."

Wade contemplated asking him how much he needed, but decided against it. He didn't want to say anything that might be offensive.

"Maybe not," Matthew said, surprising them all. "A lot of people are expecting you to enter and we can't completely disappear off of campus. As a matter of fact, we can say that we lost a member of our presentation team to the talent competition just in case someone asks us why we are withdrawing from the presentation competition."

"Works for me," Chance said.

"What are you planning to do?" Wade asked.

"I may do an original piece inspired by a poem that I got from Matthew, or a piece from Donnie Hathaway," Jo'sha said proudly.

Wade jetted over to a nearby mailbox and dropped in a dozen letters.

"That's a lot of mail," Matthew said.

"He has kids back home," Chance responded.

"Huh?"

"I was really involved in a community center back home in Baltimore. I still write to the kids so that they know that I haven't forgotten them," Wade said humbly.

Jo'sha nodded approvingly. It was the first time that he had seen Wade exercise humility, and he was impressed.

When they got to 4377, Peyton was the only one in the room. He smiled coyly at them as they took their seats, but only Matthew seemed to notice.

The class filled up slowly, but by 7:55 a.m. just about everyone was present and accounted for. Jo'sha, Matthew, Wade, and Chance exchanged greetings with their classmates as they entered the room. Roman came in bragging about his father's latest movie with Vivica Fox, Sanaa Lathan, Gabriel Union, and Angela Bassett. Jo'sha perked up when Sundiata had the nerve to ask Matthew about his younger sister, and Amir complimented Chance on his Roc-A-Wear jacket. Robert Blaze, the phenomenal freshman football player, seemed uncharacteristically interested in Wade.

"Wade, I was in your dorm the other day. You stay in Winfrey-Combs, right?" Robert said.

"Yes," Wade remarked.

"Which room?"

"400-A," he said, flattered that a star athlete had decided to befriend him.

"Oh, I thought you stayed in 400-B," Robert responded.

"No, Jo'sha and Matthew stay in the B room."

Robert seemed satisfied with the information and ended the conversation as abruptly as it had begun.

"Hey, where's James?" Alexander Onahu asked, in his pronounced African accent.

Everyone looked around and noticed that James was not present. After the episode on the first day of class, James was always the first one in his seat in every class. While he was the constant target of jokes and jibes, they had all begun to view him as the hapless little brother, needing to be monitored.

Dr. Smith came in with his usual stoic and stern demeanor. "Today, Gentlemen, in an effort to more intimately understand the African-American experience in higher education, we are going to discuss current events in the form of a debate," he said. They each sat up attentively. "The first two participants are Mr. Imarah and Mr. Carmichael-Wright. Mr. Imarah you will stand in favor. Mr. Carmichael-Wright you will stand in opposition," Dr. Smith said, as he motioned for them to come to the front of the room. "The topic is affirmative action in higher education."

Matthew discreetly motioned for Jo'sha to tuck his ankh inside his shirt as he moved to take his place alongside Dr. Smith's podium opposite Alexander. Jo'sha reluctantly conformed although he didn't see the harm in showing it off.

Once the two were in place the class readied itself for a lively debate. But Jo'sha was the only one who recognized that the meticulous Dr. Smith had not bothered to notice that James Lynch was not present.

CHAPTER 15

Wade walked out of his Philosophy class Tuesday evening with a broad smile, having aced another one of Ms. Bartlett's exams. He was on his way to meet Jo'sha, who was at the library with one of his many female friends. On his way into the library, he noticed that five football players had gathered at the entrance. When he got closer, he recognized two of them. One was Robert Black. The other one was the young man that had knocked him down in the student center. As he passed through the crowd, he heard them talking.

"Is that him?"

"Naw, I had the wrong one. It's his suitemate."

"Excuse me," Wade said, keeping his head down when he walked through them. He hoped that he could pass through without any trouble. They kept talking, seeming to ignore him.

"So are you sure her roommate told you that she was going to be at the library with this dude at six?" asked one of the beefy athletes.

Wade kept walking, wanting to distance himself from the group. He pushed into the library, and exhaled relief when he realized that no one was following him.

The library was fairly crowded for a Wednesday evening. He walked past the reference desk where Matthew worked and stopped by to ask Nia if he was there. She seemed glad to see him, and was more than willing to talk to him. After several seconds of idle conversation, he found out that Matthew wasn't scheduled to show up until seven. Wade politely excused himself, and headed toward the elevators to the second floor where he and his friends usually studied. As he rounded the corner and headed toward the library, he remembered that Jo'sha was coming to the library with a female friend. That's when the conversation he'd just heard made sense.

The football player had said something about his girlfriend and a guy coming to the library at 6:00 p.m. It was too coincidental. Wade spun around immediately, and headed back out of the library to go catch Jo'sha before he made it to the entrance.

When he got to the entrance and looked outside the glass, he saw that he was too late. The football players were crowding around someone that looked like Jo'sha. One of them was dragging a young female away and the other four moved in closer to the lone male figure. Wade took a deep breath, said a prayer and rushed outside to see if the person at the center of the circle was Jo'sha. As soon as he stepped out, he heard Jo'sha's voice.

"She ain't tell me she was your girl."

Wade knew immediately that his friend was in trouble. "Security, Security," he yelled. Unfortunately, the nearest security guard was drunk and asleep on the sixth floor.

The entire group turned and looked at him, wondering if he was serious. At that moment, Jo'sha took off to the left. Three of them immediately followed him. One of them stayed behind to deal with Wade.

"I guess you got your boy's back, huh?" he asked sarcastically.

"I don't want any trouble," Wade said, trying to mask his nervousness.

"So what's up?" he continued, balling his fist and charging toward Wade.

Wade looked around trying to figure out what to do next. At that instant, Jo'sha came out of nowhere and hit Wade's would-be attacker in the back of the head knocking him down. Wade was shocked, and stood frozen in place.

"Come on, dammit," Jo'sha said with a sense of urgency and a smile.

Wade got the odd impression that Jo'sha was somehow enjoying all of this. Jo'sha took off running again, with Wade right behind him, book bag in tow and struggling to keep up. After running off campus and into the surrounding city area, Jo'sha and Wade stopped by a barrel of burning trash in a nearly empty lot, both heaving and panting heavily. Jo'sha started laughing because he could not believe that Wade had run the entire way with his book bag on his shoulder.

"Why didn't you throw that shit down?"

Wade gasped to catch his breath.

Jo'sha turned to face the flame, waiting for Wade to start breathing normally.

"I need my books—that's why. And where did you come from back there? I was sure that they had caught you and were beating the hell out of you," Wade answered.

"See, son, I know this campus like that back of my hand. Just for situations like this. I shook them off no problem. They're probably somewhere in the center of campus looking for me."

"That gets you out of trouble for now, but what about tomorrow, and the next day, and next week? They aren't going anywhere, and they certainly aren't going to forget. What were you doing dating one of their girlfriends anyway? Is she the one that's been coming by your room during the day?"

"I didn't know that she had a boyfriend," Jo'sha answered slyly.

Wade continued to lecture. "That's why that football player attacked me in the student center. He must have thought she was coming to our suite to see me." Wade broke from his tirade noticing that Jo'sha wasn't paying attention. Instead he seemed captivated by the flame in front of them. "What is it, Jo'sha?" he asked.

Jo'sha didn't respond. His gaze seemed focused on the flame, and the fire responded, almost dancing for him. Wade watched in amazement as the blaze grew with Jo'sha's interest. The two stood there motionless. Jo'sha watched the flame, and Wade watched Jo'sha. They were so engrossed that they didn't notice the three football players that came barreling from behind a nearby building. Two of them took Jo'sha down immediately. The other began to pummel Wade, who had never been in a fight in his entire life. He could only scream and attempt to block the blows. Jo'sha, on the other hand, enjoyed a good fight and was holding his own with the two others until one of them connected a right hook that hit him in the jaw. Jo'sha went reeling back into the barrel of fire turning it over. The two young men looked over at Jo'sha, who had tumbled into the barrel, catching his shirt on fire. They ran, leaving Jo'sha and their third member who was still fighting Wade, behind. Jo'sha screamed out instantly as he flashed back to the explosion he had been in as a small child.

Everything seemed to freeze when Jo'sha realized that the fire was burning his clothes, but not his flesh. His fear diminished. He began to command the fire, and wield it so that it formed a cloak around him. He rose and the energy from the fire fed his spirit. What had been a fear of fire was now a fascination. Jo'sha looked around for the two brothers that he had been fighting and didn't see them. He then turned his attention and anger to the young man beating Wade. The crackling sound in the air caused Wade and the young man to look up. What they saw was Jo'sha enshrouded in a cloak of fire and seemingly floating in the air.

Jo'sha reached out toward the young man who had been punching Wade and a ball of fire shot toward him, singeing his collar and missing Wade by only a few inches. The young man jumped to his feet and darted off toward the adjoining street.

Wade looked over at Jo'sha who had collapsed in a cold sweat. Wade rushed over to him and put his head in his lap. He noticed that Jo'sha was sweating profusely, and that his skin was very warm. He reached in his pocket for his cell to call Chance when suddenly he heard tires screeching. There was the bloodcurdling scream of a young man milliseconds from mortality, then a fatal thud. Suddenly there was silence, and there they stood in the valley of the shadow of death, where the childish things must be put away and the things of men are regarded. It was one of those moments where Jo'sha and Wade were the only two people in the whole world.

"What do we do?" Wade asked.

Jo'sha rose slowly without speaking. He rounded the corner and headed toward the street. Wade gathered his things and followed in silence. The young man's body lay limp in the middle of the street with an expression of shock and fear still torn into his face.

They stood over him for several seconds before dogs began barking and yard lights began shining from houses in the neighborhood. Jo'sha instinctively knelt over the body checking for money and jewelry. Wade looked on in horror while Jo'sha lifted Victor Greene's wallet, his Rolex watch, and his personalized championship football ring.

"C'mon! We gotta get out of here," Wade yelled.

The two turned and dashed back down the street towards campus.

∞

None of them went to class on Wednesday, thinking that Wade's black eye would invite too many questions. Matthew didn't even go to work. They sat up in Chance and Wade's room processing everything that had happened to them. Chance milled about the room lifting dumbbells, while the others sat inside a disturbed silence, talking then napping, and then talking some more. By the time Monica Kaufman came on the evening news they were all emotionally and physically oppressed under the pressure of it all.

Monica Kaufman's hair was platinum blonde this evening. She was known for changing the color of her cropped Afro several times a month. She delivered the evening news with her normal grace and precision, but the four young men paid minimal attention.

—And now the latest on what is being called the Atlanta Male Murders—

It was that announcement that caused Matthew, Chance, Wade and Jo'sha to become instantly glued to the television set.

Local authorities have determined that there is a connection between the nine recent homicides, and are referring to them as the Atlanta Male Murders. Authorities have now released the names and identities of the last three victims. Of particular interest is the fact that the last three are all college students. The seventh victim is Omar Holland, a sophomore from Emory University. The eighth victim, James Lynch, was a freshman from Georgia Central University. The most recent victim was Victor Greene, also from Georgia Central University and a member of the Georgia Central football team. All three gentlemen were African-American. The bodies of Holland and Lynch were found shot in the back of the head and abandoned near Cascade's Niskey Lake. Victor Greene, like the second victim appears to have been the victim of vehicular homicide. His body was found just behind the university campus. —Now in other news, local police and fire officials are investigating the latest rash of church burnings—

Chance got up and turned off the television.

"Well this means they don't have any idea that you two had anything to do with Victor Greene's death," Matthew said.

"We *didn't* kill Victor Greene!" Wade yelled.

"I didn't mean to—" Matthew was about to apologize for the implication of his statement, but Chance motioned for him to be quiet.

"Those bastards didn't even tell the police that they were out there. And whoever hit Victor Greene kept going. They're all willing to let someone else take the blame," Wade said angrily.

"So are we," Matthew said forcefully, ignoring Chance's motion to keep quiet.

"How many people might have any idea that you were—involved?" Chance asked calmly.

"There was the girl that Jo'sha was messing with," Wade started.

"Her name is Celeste," Jo'sha inserted.

"—her boyfriend, the one that bumped me in the student center, Robert Black, and two other members from the football team that we didn't know," Wade finished.

"Wade, I'm sorry. You never should have been involved in this. They were after me," Jo'sha apologized, for what was the third or fourth time.

"Never mind it. We're in this together," Wade said, surprising everyone in the room. He shot a steely glance at Jo'sha, reminding him that he had not shared his secret about the stolen wallet, watch and ring.

"They probably don't want to get in trouble either," Chance said, speaking of the football team.

"So what's this about you throwing fire, Jo'sha?" Matthew asked, curious about the details of the incident.

Chance poured some bottled water into glasses for each of them.

"It just happened. I didn't do it on purpose. My adrenaline was rushing. Wade was in trouble and it just—happened," Jo'sha said.

Wade relived the moments in his mind as Jo'sha was talking, and suddenly he felt himself getting swept away, caught up in the events once again. No one noticed that the glass of water beside him was starting to swirl.

"You've gotta go back and do it again," Matthew urged.

"Huh?"

"We need to go back," Matthew repeated. "You said yourself that the lot was abandoned. If we can control fire, then we need to know that."

"I don't know about that," Wade said, sounding skeptical. The fact that someone could still possibly discover that they'd been there when Victor Greene died was enough to keep him far away from that vacant lot.

"I agree with Wade," Chance said. "Besides, weren't you the one who said we should lay low? How's it going to look if we go back to the umm—scene of the crime?" he asked.

Matthew looked around the room. Even Jo'sha, who was usually the adventurous one, seemed to have doubts about his suggestion. "Well, of course we'd have to be really careful, and go when it's late and no one else is around," he said. "But think about it—how are we going to understand these things if we don't test what they can do?"

When he looked at his friends again he could tell that they were considering his argument. After a few more minutes of urging and coaxing they agreed with Matthew, and decided to go back to the lot to *experiment*.

Several hours later the four friends headed back to the old abandoned lot where Jo'sha had controlled the flame. Matthew and Chance brought several old Atlanta Journal & Constitution newspapers, a book of matches, a lighter, a stolen dorm extinguisher, and a bucket of water.

Jo'sha brought a small bottle of vodka, and Wade carried a heart full of guilt. The two of them stopped at the spot where the young man had been hit by the car. The chalk outline was still visible on the pavement. Jo'sha stood there for a moment, silent and motionless. Then he pulled out the bottle and poured some vodka out on the asphalt. "May this soul rest in peace," he said solemnly.

Wade was struggling with his emotions, feeling somehow responsible for the fact that a young man died in the place where he was standing. Matthew saw that Wade was fighting back tears, and he put his arm around his shoulder for support. They all stood there for another quiet moment.

After a few minutes they marched slowly and solemnly from the curb to the lot, re-tracing Victor Greene's steps. When they got back to the barrel, Jo'sha threw the newspapers inside and set it on fire.

"Now—how'd you do it?" Matthew asked anxiously. "How did you control the fire?"

"Shhhh," Jo'sha said. "I need to concentrate. I really don't know how I did it. I was just in the moment—kinda like when I'm singing." They all gathered around the flame. "Now just focus on the flame," Jo'sha instructed. "See it moving in your mind—creating shapes—feel it move." The fire seemed to come to life with Jo'sha's words, which amazed even him.

"Let me try," Matthew begged. He stood in front of the barrel and focused on the flame. While he was concentrating, a subtle gust of wind came and blew the fire out. Disappointed, Matthew stepped back to let Wade try. Chance relit the fire as Wade readied himself.

Wade stepped up to the barrel of fire and began to concentrate on controlling it and shaping it as Jo'sha had instructed. The fire did not seem to respond, but he felt an unnatural surge of power so he continued to try.

"Hey look at the bucket of water!" Jo'sha screamed. "He's making the water rise!"

They all looked at the bucket directly beside Wade in amazement. When Wade saw that he was in fact manipulating the water, he began to focus even harder. The water took shape and made a solid column reaching up twelve feet into the air.

"That's it! That's it!" Matthew yelled.

"What's it?" Chance asked.

Just then Wade collapsed, completely exhausted.

"We've got to go back to the suite and get the diary. It's just like the book said! Let's go!"

No one knew what Matthew was talking about, but they quickly gathered their belongings and hurried back to the dorm. When they got inside the room, Matthew rushed into Chance's closet, and pulled out Nathaniel Charles' satchel where they kept all the items from the time capsule. The others watched intently as Matthew pulled out the slave diary and opened it. He flipped through quickly until he found Harriett Tubman's section, and immediately began reading aloud.

"'When I wear them I am able to traverse many miles of terrain undetected, wielding the very tools of angels—earth, air, water, and fire, but I am left prone to seizures and spells alike—'"

When he looked up, Matthew noticed that all of his friends appeared puzzled. None of them were completely clear about why he was so excited. "That's exactly what I thought. Don't you get it?" Matthew asked.

"Get what?" Chance asked.

"It says it right here—earth, wind, water, and fire. They are the four basic elements. Jo'sha must be able to control fire. Wade must be able to control water, and when the wind blew the fire out that must have been me. Don't you see it? I can control wind—so Chance that means that you must be able to control earth."

"What does *that* mean?" Chance asked, still confused.

"I don't know, but we have to find out," Matthew answered. He picked up a half full glass of water. "Jo'sha, give me a match." Matthew took the match, lit it, and held it up to Jo'sha's face. "Okay, let's try it again."

Jo'sha began to concentrate on the flame in front of him. This time he managed to turn it into a small ankh, which he continued to manipulate and reshape. Chance and Wade hollered in excitement.

"Okay, Wade, now your turn!" Matthew instructed as he set the glass of water in front of Wade.

Wade began to concentrate and focus on the water and then on Jo'sha and the fire ankh that he had created. Suddenly the water rose from the glass and doused the flames, splashing Jo'sha in the face. They all fell out in laughter.

"Okay so maybe we do have to work on controlling this, but it's awesome!" Matthew yelled.

"Shhhh," Chance said. "We don't want anyone to hear us. Ronnie will get suspicious if he has to keep coming down here to check on us."

"Well what about you two?" Jo'sha asked. "Let's see what you can do."

"We can't do it in here. There's no earth here," Chance said, disappointed that everyone but him had discovered their new abilities.

"Alright, alright," Matthew conceded. "Let's go out, but we have to find a private spot. In fact I know just the place. It's in midtown Atlanta, but it should be secluded at this time of night," he said.

The four young men rushed to Wade's truck, and drove out to Piedmont Park. When they got to the park, Matthew directed them to a spot by a man made lake in the center of the park. A love-struck young couple walked by, barely noticing the four. When the couple was out of earshot, the friends began talking again, speaking barely above a whisper.

"Okay you two, it's your turn," Jo'sha said, talking to Matthew and Chance.

Matthew stepped into a clearing and focused his attention on a small tree. After a few moments the wind began to grow, twirling and swirling, until a small hurricane whipped all of the leaves off of the tiny tree. Matthew yelped in a moment of excitement. Jo'sha and Wade both gave him a high five.

"Okay. I'll go now," Chance said nervously. He stood in front of the bare tree and stared at the mound of earth beneath it. After several minutes of concentrating, nothing happened.

"Try it again," Jo'sha suggested. He walked up to Chance and placed the ankh on the inside of Chance's skintight, long sleeved thermal shirt. Then he grabbed his shoulders. "Concentrate."

Chance felt a rush of energy and then they felt the ground rumble and then shake. The earth ripped open exposing the roots of the small tree, leaving a gapping hole. Both Wade and Matthew were knocked to the ground. Jo'sha maintained his footing and managed to shake Chance out of his trance before he could do more damage.

"Whew, that felt great!" Chance yelled.

"Are you crazy? You damn near caused an earthquake!" Matthew yelled.

"We have to get out of here," Wade warned. "That is sure to draw some attention."

Jo'sha stared at Chance who was still high from the rush that he had received. They laughed all the way back to the car, unable to contain their excitement over the amazing powers they'd uncovered.

"Doesn't it feel great?" Matthew asked.

"It's awesome!" Chance answered.

"Yeah, it does," Jo'sha agreed. "But I wonder why you two don't feel spent after you use your powers?"

"I don't know. It felt great to me," Chance responded.

"And did you see how powerful Chance is?" Jo'sha asked, his voice full of admiration.

"Maybe it has something to do with his physical condition," Wade commented.

"It can't," Jo'sha said, shaking his head. "I'm in just as good shape as Chance."

"I wonder what would happen if we changed necklaces," Matthew said.

"Well, I'm completely happy with mine," Jo'sha said.

"I am too," Matthew added, "I just wondered what would happen."

"I think we should take some time to learn how to manage the powers that we already have," Wade added.

"I think so too," said Jo'sha.

"Well, now that we've settled that—I'm hungry," Chance said.

"What a surprise," Wade said, rolling his eyes.

Wade drove over to the *Varsity,* a popular Atlanta drive-in. Once they placed their order they started talking about all the things that had happened over the last few days.

"I'm talking about some *big* breasts," said Jo'sha, spacing his hands apart to illustrate for his friends. "This girl had to be packing some double D's—ask Wade."

They all laughed at Jo'sha who was looking to Wade to back up his story. When Wade didn't respond an uncomfortable silence fell over the table. Chance was the first to finally speak up. "I know this may be awkward, Wade, but there's something that we need to talk about."

"What is it?" Wade asked, turning down the radio.

Chance hesitated for a moment, looking to the others before continuing.

"We've heard your little secret phone calls—and Jo'sha told us how you didn't want anything to do with the girls in New Orleans—and well—we just need to know if—" Chance faltered.

"Know what?" Wade shouted. He swerved off of the road a little and nearly hit a parked car.

"If you're gay," Jo'sha blurted.

"I am *not* gay!" Wade yelled.

"Are you sure?" Chance asked. "You don't have to lie to us."

Wade laughed out loud, unable to believe that his friends had made such an assumption.

"Then what about the girls in New Orleans?" Jo'sha asked.

"I wasn't attracted to them," Wade answered.

"What about the secret phone calls?" Chance asked.

"What has that got to do with anything?" Wade hedged.

"What about the way you dress?" Jo'sha joked.

"Shut up! *One* of my shoes costs more than all of the clothes in your closet," Wade spouted.

"Oh no, he didn't!" Jo'sha mocked.

"Well what about the secret phone calls and 'your family not being ready for it'?" Chance asked again.

"You were eavesdropping?" Wade asked incredulously.

No one answered. The reality of Wade's claims embarrassed them slightly. They *had* been eavesdropping—invading Wade's privacy. Wade finally broke the silence.

"If you must know, I have a girlfriend back home. Well, actually she's in D.C., and she's not exactly someone that my family would approve of," Wade said finally.

"What, you dating a hood rat?" Jo'sha asked.

Matthew jabbed Jo'sha in the side.

"She's not a—hood rat. Her name is Quay and—she's pregnant," Wade shared.

"And your family doesn't know?" Chance asked.

"No," Wade said.

"What are you going to do? When are you going to tell them?" Jo'sha asked, suddenly realizing the reason for Wade's lectures on safe sex.

"I have no idea," Wade said, sighing heavily. "I have no idea."

Matthew, who had been silent the entire time and listening intently, felt bad that Jo'sha and Chance had interrogated Wade to the point of revealing something he'd wanted to keep secret. He hated to admit that he'd been just as interested in the answer as the others.

CHAPTER 16

Jo'sha, Chance and Wade rushed to the student center after another of their recent workout sessions. Wade's black eye had healed quickly, and the boys resumed their normal routines. Though they'd made some changes in their schedules, they were intent on heeding Matthew's advice to draw as little attention to themselves as possible.

"That was intense," Jo'sha said, tying his locks back to let the cool September air brush his neck.

"Yeah, didn't it feel good?" Chance asked, poking Wade.

"Yeah," Wade responded sarcastically, massaging his still trembling biceps.

"You were unbelievable," Jo'sha said to Chance.

"I guess all of my working out is really starting to pay off."

"Yeah, but bench pressing 325 pounds? That's your record," Jo'sha said.

"Thanks," Chance said, equally impressed with his personal best.

"Hey, is that Robert Black and the rest of those jocks over there?" Jo'sha asked angrily, as they got closer to the crowd.

"Yeah, but this isn't the time for that. Let's go this way," Chance directed.

There was complete silence as the men of Georgia Central University gathered to mourn the loss of two of their own. It was the kind of cool September evening that called for reflection and required retribution. Poster sized pictures of James Lynch and Victor Greene sat on easels on either side of the small podium at the top of the student center stairs. Dozens of colorful floral arrangements surrounded the podium. Each of the assembled students and faculty members held burning candles signifying the form and frailty of human life. Chancellor Weatherspoon, under the advisement of his public relations agency, had invited select city officials and top local television and radio stations to the memorial service for the two slain students.

"Where's Matthew?" Chance asked. "He was supposed to meet us at the gym."

"He's probably still in the room studying that diary. He's consumed with you-know-what," Jo'sha said, referring to their ankhs.

"What is he consumed with?" Wade asked.

"Where they come from? Who had them before us? What do we do with them? You name it and he wants to know," Jo'sha answered.

"Is he still planning to go to Piedmont Park with us later this evening?"

"Yes, I'm sure he is. He says he has some new theory that he wants to try out."

"Just remember that we can't stay out all night. It's Sunday and we have class tomorrow," Chance stated.

After pushing their way through several students, they found a space at the front of the crowd, near the base of the stairs. Chance stopped a fellow classmate who was passing through the audience carrying a box of candles, and grabbed one for each of them. He handed one to Wade and one to Jo'sha, and then tilted his candle toward his nearest neighbor to get a light. Once his candle was lit, he reached over and lit Wade's candle. Jo'sha waved him off when he attempted to light his candle. Instead, Jo'sha took a half step back and focused on Chance's flame until it arched up and over to his own candle. The fire danced on his wick as delicately as a street fairy.

"What in hell are you doing?" Chance whispered.

"No one's looking at us," Jo'sha whispered back, pleased at his accomplishment.

"Ugh," Wade moaned.

"What's wrong, Wade?" Jo'sha asked.

"Can't you feel it?"

"Quiet. Dr. Weatherspoon is starting to speak." Chance nudged his friends and directed their attention to the podium.

"Good evening to all of you. First and foremost I want you all to know that the safety of our students remains a priority here at Georgia Central University. We are not just an institution of higher learning. We are a family and we grieve this great loss. I will personally see to it that our campus security is reinforced with additional officers. Effective immediately, we will also institute sundown curfews for the unsecured sections of the university, install ten additional public safety call boxes across campus, and conduct safety awareness seminars in each dorm. Grief counselors will also be on hand in the student infirmary for any of you who may need them." Dr. Weatherspoon paused. His empathetic tone made it seem as though he really meant the words he'd said. It was his posturing for the camera, and quick glance at his public relations agent however, that obliterated what was perceived to be sincerity on his part. "We will now open the podium to any of the friends or family members of these two young men who would like to share this evening."

After reflections of precious childhood memories from Victor Greene's father, several of the GCU football players stepped up to memorialize their friend and teammate. Jo'sha and Wade exchanged guilt-filled glances since they knew that Victor was not a victim of the Atlanta Male Murderer. Once all of Victor's loved ones had paid their respects, Dr. Weatherspoon asked if anyone else wanted to come forward. There was silence. No one in the large crowd seemed to know James Lynch well enough to speak on his behalf.

"Somebody's gotta say something. Be ready," Chance whispered in Jo'sha's ear before speaking up. "Dr. Weatherspoon, I have a few words," Chance said, making his way up to the podium.

Dr. Weatherspoon shook Chance's hand and stepped back, allowing him access to the microphone.

"James Lynch was my classmate and a fine example of a Georgia Central University man. Although small in stature, he had the heart of a lion and the intellect that we are known for worldwide. Most people don't know this, but James was the recipient of the Dunbar Scholarship for Science. Those of us who knew James knew that he was also conscientious, with a thirst for knowledge. He was always the first one to arrive in class," Chance exchanged smiles with a few of his classmates from Dr. Smith's class. "Now we will have a song in honor of James Lynch performed by another of James' classmates, Jo'sha Imarah," Chance announced.

Jo'sha didn't miss a beat, though the request for his performance was completely impromptu. He stepped up to the podium, took the microphone from the stand, and gazed out into the audience. The flickering lights caught his attention and he was momentarily mesmerized, by the sea of fire.

Jo'sha cleared his throat, closed his eyes, and began singing the score from the funeral scene of the movie *Cooley High*. The flames seem to shine brighter with each note. As the flames danced higher,

Wade's mood became heavier, and the collective mourned. A pall settled over Wade and he wept uncontrollably, drawing the attention of those standing closest to him. Clouds crept in overhead. By the time Jo'sha was nearing the end of the song, several of the mourners had blown out their candles because the flames had consumed them. When Jo'sha finished singing and opened his eyes, the heavens opened up and it rained. The media crews, mourners, and event organizers all hurried inside the student center for cover.

The shower seemed to end as quickly as it had begun, but by the time Dr. Weatherspoon was prepared to make closing remarks most of the mourners had gone their separate ways. Having missed the opportunity for a ceremonious ending, Dr. Weatherspoon mingled with remaining friends and family. It was important that he not let these unfortunate events put a damper on the upcoming homecoming and centennial events. Dr. Weatherspoon knew how important this year's celebration was for Georgia Central's financial future and his career. Not only an opportunity to celebrate the institution's one hundredth anniversary, but a chance to garner significant financial support when other historically black colleges and universities were simply struggling to keep the doors open. The Atlanta Male Murders could not have come at a worse time for Dr. Weatherspoon.

"Are you alright?" Chance asked, noticing that Wade was still somewhat emotional.

"Yes. I am now. It was as if I could feel what everyone in the crowd was feeling."

Jo'sha and Chance exchanged glances. "Do you think it has something to do with—"

"You have a beautiful voice young man," Dr. Weatherspoon boomed walking up to Jo'sha.

"Hello, Dr. Weatherspoon," Wade interjected, as he continued to collect himself.

"William?" he asked, raising his eyebrows as if trying hard to remember.   "No, sir. It's Wade,"

"Yes, Wade it is. Your friend here has an incredible voice. I see that you were as moved as I by his great voice. I trust that you will be encouraging him to enter the homecoming talent show," Dr. Weatherspoon said, turning back toward Jo'sha.

"I'm considering it," Jo'sha said.

"And your name again?"

"Jo'sha Imarah."

"That sounds very familiar," Dr. Weatherspoon said thoughtfully.

"I was the other Dunbar Scholarship recipient. I received the Dunbar Scholarship for Art. Maybe that's it," Jo'sha said.

"Yes. Perhaps it is. Another fine member of our music department then?" he asked.

"Yes."

"Well, I look forward to seeing you perform again at the homecoming talent show," Dr. Weatherspoon encouraged, before rushing off to visit with Victor's family.

Jo'sha smiled at Wade.

"Hmph," Wade replied.

"Why didn't you introduce me?" Chance whined.

"That again?" Jo'sha mocked.

"Please don't start that arguing again," Wade warned. "It's been giving me a headache."

Chance's cell phone rang. It was Matthew. "Hello."

"Is the memorial service still going on?" Matthew asked.

"No, it just ended. You missed the whole thing. I thought you were going to join us at the gym. "

"Sorry about that. I got caught up. I'll make it next time. I promise," Matthew answered.

"You still up for the trip to the park?"

"Yes, I'm still ready for the trip, but there are some things that I want to show you guys before we go. Are the others with you?"

"Yes. We should be back to the dorm in a minute."

Matthew had cleaned the room, put away his and Jo'sha's personal items, and emptied the room of anything that was not absolutely necessary. The room looked more bare than normal with the exception of a map of the slave states that he had tacked on the back of the door, and a timeline that he had drawn in black marker, around the entire perimeter of the room just above the door.

The timeline started January 1, 1600, and ended on the day they found the ankhs. Most dates were written in blue marker, but a select few had been written and circled in red. The letters from Cyrus and the numerous papers they had collected from the library and the time capsule were neatly organized on Matthew's desk. Matthew had begun a diary of his own where he was keeping facts, figures, and points of reference.

"Wow. What is this?" Chance asked, referring to the timeline.

"Damn! Thanks for cleaning up the room," Jo'sha said.

"It's about time," Wade joked.

But Matthew's countenance was far from light.

"What's wrong, Matt? And what's up with the writing on the wall?" Jo'sha asked.

"Brothers, I think this is more serious than we imagined," Matthew said solemnly. "We know that there were entries about Nat Turner and Harriet Tubman in the diary, but they weren't the only significant entries. There are entries in this diary dating back to right after the first slave trades. Most of them were written by revolutionaries or those closest to them," Matthew lectured.

"So what are you saying?" Wade asked.

"That we're dealing with something special here. I have read and reread every entry in this diary and I'm still amazed. This isn't just a slave diary. It's an instruction manual for these ankhs," Matthew answered.

"Any idea where they came from?" Jo'sha asked, suddenly sensing the gravity of Matthew's comments.

"I have some theories and they have to do with the small markings on the underside of the ankhs, but we can get to that later," Matthew answered.

They each examined their pendants more closely.

"I noticed that mine is exactly half the thickness of the rest of them," Chance said somehow feeling cheated.

"Almost as if it had been broken or cut in half," Wade added.

"They do have markings on them. I hadn't noticed that," Jo'sha said.

"What is that anyway?" Wade asked.

"Later," Matthew responded.

"You haven't really told us *anything*," Chance said, growing annoyed with the lack of clarity.

"There's so much to tell. There are several different entries in this diary, and just about each entry has something to do with a slave revolt. The first one that I can actually verify through research happened in Gloucester, Virginia, in 1663," Matthew explained.

"So we've found a diary kept by slave revolutionaries," Chance concluded.

"In 1800, a slave by the name of Gabriel led a revolt in Henrico County, Virginia. In his own words he says that he planned to lead a revolt in August of that year, but on the designated day a torrential rain began and he described it as the most terrible thunderstorm that he had ever witnessed in the state. Gabriel was betrayed by two of his co-conspirators before he could launch the revolt. He was eventually caught and killed," Matthew answered.

Chance, Jo'sha, and Wade exchanged inquisitive glances as Matthew continued.

"And then there was Denmark Vesey. His story is practically the same. Denmark gained his freedom in Charleston, South Carolina in about 1800 and attempted to lead a revolt in 1822, but he too, was betrayed. Don't you get it? They decided to rebel and fight the system because they had access to power—the power of these ankhs. Some were more successful than others, but they each had them. Each time someone used them, they wrote down their findings in this journal. Nat Turner talks about spiritual visions. In an entry marked May 12, 1828, Nat Turner says, 'I heard a loud noise in the heavens, and the Spirit instantly appeared to me and said the Serpent was loosed, and that Christ had laid down the yoke he had borne for the sins of men, and that I should take it on and fight against the Serpent, for the time was fast approaching when the first should be the last and the last should be first.'"

Matthew paused for a moment, hoping to get a reaction from his friends about the information he'd just shared. "In February, 1831, Nat Turner mentions an eclipse of the sun. On August 13, of that same year, he talks about an atmospheric disturbance in which the sun appears bluish-green. He was eventually caught and hanged, but there is no doubt that he was dealing with something that was very powerful," Matthew added.

"Jo'sha had a vision the other day, remember?" Wade interjected, looking at Jo'sha.

Jo'sha nodded in the affirmative, but before he could explain the vision, Matthew continued with his story.

"Probably the most successful person to carry these things was Harriet Tubman, but even she suffered from seizures and blackouts."

"Well at least the timeline makes sense now," Chance said, looking at the detailed markings, which went around the entire room.

"But we still don't know where they came from," Jo'sha argued.

"More on that later," Matthew promised again.

"So what's the punch line?" Chance asked.

"This is it. I think there is at least one important thing that they didn't figure out. They all attempted to wield this power alone. It looks like they each tried to carry all four ankhs. We accidentally got that part right. When Jo'sha handed each of us an ankh, it kept any one us from having to carry the complete burden," Matthew explained.

"Burden?" Chance asked.

"More than one of them is too much for one person. The torrential rains, seizures, blackouts, eclipses are proof that one person can't control this power. The one thing that they were successful in was keeping their slave masters from finding them. They kept relocating them. If you look at this map on the back of the door, you'll see everywhere that we know that the ankhs were used," Matthew answered.

The map was marked with pins, numbers, and dotted lines from New York to South Carolina.

"We already know that we can control the elements. My guess is that they weren't really sure which ankhs controlled which elements. And I guarantee you they didn't take the time to practice using them like we will," Matthew said.

"They probably didn't have that much free time," Jo'sha joked.

"True, but there's more. Based on all of the entries, I think that there are other powers. Chance, how much are you bench pressing now?" Matthew asked.

"About 350—I feel like I am getting stronger every day."

Matthew nodded, as if making a mental note of Chance's comment.

"Wade, have you noticed that every time there's an argument that you get a headache, or if we are around someone that is experiencing intense emotion that you feel it?" Matthew asked.

"Yeah. Like at the memorial service. I could feel what everyone was feeling. The depression and sadness was heavy," Wade answered.

"Jo'sha, haven't you been having visions?" Matthew asked.

"Yeah, it was like—"

"It's been pretty crazy for me too," said Matthew, interrupting Jo'sha again. "It's like—well—like I can't stop thinking. My mind is always racing. I've already finished reading all of my textbooks for this semester. Haven't you guys figured it out? The ankhs have given us extraordinary physical, emotional, spiritual, and mental abilities as well."

"Yeah," Chance said, looking at his biceps in the mirror. "But there are other perfectly good explanations. I'm just in good shape. I eat right and I work out. Matthew, you're smart as hell and the freshman curriculum just isn't challenging you. Wade cries whenever he sees *The Color Purple* so it's no wonder that he is always emotionally wound up. And Jo'sha sees visions 'cause he smokes weed. It's as simple as that," Chance challenged.

"Even if you are right that doesn't explain our ability to control the elements, and it doesn't end there. I have another theory that's just a little bit more troubling. Chance have you had to use your inhaler lately?" Matthew asked.

"Not that I can remember?" Chance said.

"Too risky," Matthew pondered out loud.

"What are you thinking?" Wade asked.

"It's just a thought. I'm not really sure, but I'm concerned about our attachment to these ankhs. I am wondering what happens if we take them off." Matthew said, not wanting to alarm his friends.

"Well let's just find out. It can't be that bad," Wade reasoned. He removed the ankh from his neck and tossed it on the bed. Only a few seconds passed before the base of his neck began to ache and his pupils began to water and burn.

"Auuuuuurrrrrggggghhhhh! I can't see! I can't see!" he yelled.

Chance held Wade down while Jo'sha slipped the blue ankh back around Wade's neck. It was a full forty minutes before the dark spots disappeared from Wade's eyes, and he could see again.

After they were sure that Wade's vision was restored and he had calmed down, they formed a small circle, on the floor, in the center of the room.

"That was my worst fear. We are linked to these things now. In one of the earlier entries, it goes on to mention the blessing and the curse," Matthew said.

"But we aren't the first ones to wear them. What about the others?" Chance asked.

"My guess is that most of them were killed or hanged shortly after using them so it didn't matter. They must have trusted someone close to them to keep them moving—to keep them away from the slave masters."

"So now what do we do?" Wade asked, looking to Matthew for answers.

"We figure out how to live with them."

CHAPTER 17

In other news, local scientists are still baffled by a seismic jolt recorded near the heart of downtown Atlanta a few days ago. The minor quake was recorded at a 1.5 on the—"

Wade flipped off the radio. "Did you hear that?" he asked.

"Yeah, 1.5 on the Richter scale. Man, you're something else!" Jo'sha commented.

"It's a good thing we got out of there," Matthew said.

"How high can you go?" Jo'sha asked.

Chance shrugged his shoulders. He was still amazed by the fact that he had been able to do it at all.

Wade pulled into a parallel parking space directly across the street from an abandoned junkyard on the east side of town. It was well after 11:00 p.m. by the time they got to a junkyard not far from the park where they'd first experimented.

"We can't stay out here all night," Chance reminded them when they got out of the truck.

The early afternoon rainstorm had left some parts of the yard muddy. Wade was careful to avoid the mud puddles in his designer loafers. Matthew followed in his footsteps since he still had on Chance's shoes and didn't want to mess them up. Jo'sha on the other hand, had removed his sandals and made it a point to find every mud puddle, enjoying the feel of the mud squishing between his toes. Chance brought up the rear in a pair of his old boots. They stopped when they reached a clearing behind stacks of twisted metal.

"Now what?" Chance asked.

"I want to test a theory," Matthew answered. He cleared a small section of dry earth and started a fire with matches, leaves and paper. "Jo'sha, I want you to concentrate. Close your eyes and really concentrate. I want you to contain this fire. We can't afford to let it

154

spread. We don't need any extra attention. Shape it into whatever form you choose, but I want you to do it with your eyes closed."

Matthew removed a blindfold from his pocket and covered Jo'sha's eyes. Jo'sha concentrated on the small blaze, seeing the flames in his mind. He shaped it until it became a ball of fire swirling and twirling four feet in the air. Matthew stood next to him and watched in silence. When he finally spoke his voice was soft yet deliberate.

"Good job, Jo'sha. Now tell me what you feel." Matthew motioned for Chance to stand directly behind Jo'sha while he and Wade stepped several feet away.

"What do you mean? I don't feel anything different. I can still sense the fire. It's suspended in the air like a ball."

After several minutes Matthew motioned for Wade to change places with Chance. "What do you feel now?" he asked.

"I feel—a drain. It's harder to control the fire, and my head is starting to ache. Why? What are you doing?" Jo'sha's face creased as if concentrating on the fire was requiring more effort. The once perfect ball of fire fluctuated between an oblong and oval shape, and was hovering just a few inches above the ground despite Jo'sha's best efforts to control it.

"You're doing great. Just keep concentrating," Matthew said, exchanging places with Wade, and motioning for Wade to step several feet away. "Now what do you feel?" he asked.

Jo'sha was silent for a few seconds. The ball of fire had resumed its original round shape and grew steadily in circumference and intensity.

"Stronger," Jo'sha answered confidently.

Slowly but surely Wade and Jo'sha began to see what Matthew had surmised. The series of experiments proved Matthew's theory that each of them was connected and interdependent on each other. The four of them continued experimenting until well after midnight.

"What does this all mean?" Chance asked as he removed the blindfold after what was Matthew's final test.

"It means that these things are connected and that we are connected—that we fortify and temper each other. Assume that each one of us represents an element. I am air. Chance is earth. Wade is water, and Jo'sha is fire. Air feeds fire so when I am in close proximity to Jo'sha it makes him stronger. Water opposes fire so Wade's presence actually puts a damper on Jo'sha's power," Matthew explained.

"Figures," Jo'sha said, looking at Wade.

"No. That is a good thing. You see there is a delicate balance here. One that we need to understand and respect," Matthew added.

"How did you figure this out?" Chance asked.

"Some from the Internet and some of it is just logic. Some of it reading, rereading and deciphering the diaries," Matthew explained with feigned modesty.

"Any other interesting facts?" asked Jo'sha.

"Yes. I think if we practice, concentrate and focus, we should even be able to use these things to sense and locate each other," Matthew added.

"Wow! Now that's deep." Chance exclaimed.

"I have a question. Why can't I start a fire by myself?" Jo'sha asked.

"Good question. I am not sure that you can't. Basic science says that a fire requires heat, oxygen and a source of fuel. We know you can generate heat. We all feel it before you move fire. Oxygen is present in the air all around us. My guess is that if you can focus on an appropriate source of fuel then you can start a fire. That's something for us to practice later."

"What about me?" Wade asked.

"It's still basic chemistry. Water is two parts hydrogen and one part oxygen. It's all around us in the air. If you concentrate I think you may be able to literally pull water from the air. But that is something we'll have to test out carefully. Remember humans are also made up of water too. This is nothing to take lightly," Matthew warned.

"Shouldn't we be getting back? It's getting late," Chance said, yawning

"Yeah, it is after midnight," Matthew said a little reluctantly.

They were gathering their belongings and taking steps to erase their tracks when Jo'sha noticed the silhouette of a large figure on the hill near the entrance of the junkyard. "Do you see that?" he asked.

"See what?" Matthew asked, straining to look into the darkness.

Seconds later they heard a thud followed by tires screeching.

"Damn! Let's get out of here," Chance warned.

They all broke into a swift run toward Wade's car.

CHAPTER 18

James' seat was conspicuously empty and everyone in Dr. Smith's Monday orientation class seemed to be at a loss for words. Raw emotion colored Wade's thoughts, louder and more vivid than anything else in the room.

Robert Black gave Wade and Jo'sha threatening looks as he took his seat between Matthew and Alexander Onahu. His anger was tangible to Wade—like tiny, hot knives piercing through his skull. All of their other classmates were grieving for James on some level, with the exception of Roman Riley who never thought about anyone except himself. The entire cluster of emotions was as heavy and real to Wade as Robert's anger and the beads of perspiration that were forming on his brow.

"You got a damn problem?" Jo'sha asked, looking across Matthew and directly at Robert.

"You know what the damn problem is!" Robert responded, jumping up from his seat.

Jo'sha hopped up as well. Matthew got up quickly and attempted to keep the two apart, but Robert easily pushed him aside. Before Matthew could regain his balance, Jo'sha and Robert were locked up and wrestling around the room. Peyton screamed. Amir and Chance moved quickly to break them up, while most of the others left their seats to get a better view of the fight.

The tempers and temperature in the room rose quickly. Wade's head began to swim, and his breath grew shallow. By the time Chance and Amir had broken up the fight, most of the desks in the room were overturned.

"What the hell is up with you dudes?" Amir asked, leading Robert back to his seat.

"We can get expelled for fighting," Chance warned, pushing Jo'sha in the opposite direction.

Everyone else rushed to restore the classroom before Dr. Smith arrived. When Dr. Smith entered, the classroom was unusually quiet. Judging from his expression, it was obvious that he could sense that something was different besides the elevated temperature, but he didn't say a word. Instead he went about his meticulous routine of preparing for his lecture. Just as he was about to begin speaking, Wade fainted, sliding out of his seat and onto the floor. His blue ankh fell outside his shirt.

Matthew rushed over to him, and discreetly tucked the ankh back inside Wade's shirt. "He hasn't been feeling well," he explained quickly.

Wade regained consciousness moments later, but was still slightly disoriented. Jo'sha and Chance watched the scene nervously, but Matthew signaled to them that he had it under control.

"Mr. Meredith, Perhaps you should escort Mr. Graham to the infirmary," Dr. Smith suggested, looking at them skeptically.

"Yes, sir," Matthew replied, gathering their books.

"Punk asses," muttered Robert under his breath as they exited the classroom.

"If there are no more interruptions, I would like to begin today's discussion. We are going to be comparing and contrasting the learning experiences, graduation rates, and professional contributions of historically black college alumnae versus some of the country's other institutions of higher learning," Dr. Smith began, appearing more interested in hearing himself talk than in the subject matter or the students.

Jo'sha and Robert were still seething from their earlier confrontation, and with Matthew gone there was nothing standing between them. Robert glared over at Jo'sha each time Dr. Smith turned his back. Even though the class seemed to drag on and on as Dr. Smith quoted statistic after statistic, neither Jo'sha nor Robert's anger subsided. Thirty minutes into the class, Jo'sha was still fuming and the air in the room grew warm and thin. The more Jo'sha concentrated, the warmer Robert became. Robert began to perspire profusely, and then suddenly he started to hyperventilate.

"Dr. Smith!" Alexander interrupted.

"Yes, Mr. Onahu," Dr. Smith answered, looking up disinterestedly.

"I don't think Robert is feeling well either."

Just then everyone in class noticed that Robert was drenched in sweat and taking deep and hurried breaths.

Chance looked over at Jo'sha who was still glaring at Robert. "Jo'sha! Jo'sha!" Chance yelled instinctively.

Then Robert began to convulse. Several members of the class rushed to his side.

"Does anyone have a cellular phone?" Dr. Smith asked. Several members of the class responded affirmatively. "Call the student infirmary," Dr. Smith ordered.

Maxwell pulled out his cell phone and began dialing.

Chance rushed past the crowd that was forming around Robert and grabbed Jo'sha, who seemed to be in a trance. He shook Jo'sha hard. "What the hell are you doing?" he whispered.

Jo'sha buried his head in his hands and shook his head back and forth.

"He's not breathing!" Alexander yelled.

"Oh God!" agonized Peyton.

Robert Black was motionless on the floor when the campus paramedics arrived. They placed him on a gurney and rushed him to the student infirmary.

"Gentlemen, today's class is dismissed. Misters Imarah and Walker, can you please follow me to my office?" Dr. Smith said, gathering his belongings.

Chance looked at Jo'sha, who seemed to be regaining his composure.

Dr. Smith's office was just around the corner. With the exception of a pair of muddy boots by the door everything was in complete and perfect order.

"Now I don't have to tell you that the series of events that transpired in the classroom today were unusual—two students passing out—everyone unusually quiet—and you two seem to be at the epicenter. I have been in the university setting for quite some time. Far be it from me to surmise, but I am aware of the prevalence of drug distribution and use amongst young men like you. I have to tell you that it is not tolerated on this campus and most certainly not in my classroom!"

Dr. Smith paused, and was about to continue with his lecture when Alexander rushed into the office.

"Dr. Smith, the campus paramedics are downstairs and they need to see you. It's about Robert," Alexander huffed, half out of breath.

Without a word Dr. Smith rushed out behind Alexander.

"See what you did!" Chance whispered.

"What I did?" Jo'sha shot back.

"What were you thinking?"

"It just happened. I was thinking about the fight and the night Victor got killed and before I knew it Robert was on the ground," Jo'sha said apologetically.

"We could be in big trouble. Even if Dr. Smith doesn't know what's really going on, we don't need any of our professors thinking we're drug dealers!"

"I'm wondering why that was his first conclusion," Jo'sha said, indignantly. He stood up and walked over to Dr. Smith's desk. He opened a drawer and began rifling through his things.

"It doesn't matter. He'll probably send us to the campus infirmary for drug tests *and* call our parents," Chance sighed.

Jo'sha didn't seem nearly as concerned as Chance. He was more interested in the contents of the desk drawer. "Look, he's just speculating. He has nothing on us. We're *not* drug dealers, right? Hey—look at this," Jo'sha said, holding up a small object that he pulled from Dr. Smith's desk drawer.

"What is it?"

"A gold cross. Just like the one James was wearing the first day of class," Jo'sha said.

"That could belong to anyone," Chance responded.

"But it looks like the one James was wearing." Jo'sha said.

"Let's get out of here before you get us into anymore trouble!" Chance snapped.

Jo'sha stuffed the cross in his pocket while Chance wasn't looking, and followed him out of the office.

∞

Jo'sha, Wade, and Chance were on the second floor of the library near the periodicals when Matthew came bounding up the stairs. It was 10:05 p.m. and there had been no other activity on the floor with the exception of a few random security guard patrols. The inebriated security guard had been replaced with two off duty Atlanta policemen. Jo'sha and Chance were still talking about the morning's events in Dr. Smith's class, and Wade was on his cell phone with his girlfriend, Quay.

"Who's he talking to?" Matthew asked, nodding in Wade's direction.

"Quay," answered Chance. "He's thinking about having her come up to visit so we can meet her. She's just in her first trimester so an airplane ride shouldn't be a problem. Plus I don't think things are going well for her at home," he explained.

Matthew joined Chance and Jo'sha in the discussion about the day's events not having seen them since he and Wade left Dr. Smith's class.

Wade remained on the phone for several more minutes before sharing hushed I-love-you's with Quay. By the time he joined the conversation Matthew was trying hard not to yell.

"What in the hell were you thinking, Jo'sha?"

"You weren't there. I didn't plan it. It just happened," Jo'sha said, defensively.

"Can you keep your damn voice down? This is the library," Chance scolded

Wade grabbed his temples. The arguing was starting to affect him.

"Do you know that everyone is talking about what happened this morning? It's all I heard about all day long."

"Which part, Wade passing out, Jo'sha nearly burning Robert alive from the inside out, or Dr. Smith accusing us of selling and using drugs?" Chance asked sarcastically.

"What?" Matthew barked.

"Oh, that's right. You didn't know about that part. Dr. Smith called Jo'sha and me in his office after class. He said that we were acting strange and confronted us about drugs. Fortunately, Alexander came and got him out of his office to see about Robert. We waited for him for a while, but he never came back."

"Any word on Robert?" Wade asked.

"Yeah, I had gym with Amir this afternoon. He told me that they released Robert early this afternoon. He said Robert seemed fine. Just a little dehydrated and disoriented. They aren't sure what happened to him. They said that it might have something to do with football practice, but they are still examining the building. He said that he heard that Hughes Hall will be shut down for a few days to test for carbon monoxide poisoning. They seem to think that Wade and Robert's fainting spells may have been be caused by carbon gas," Chance said.

"Damn!" Matthew said.

"Well how did the whole university find out about my fainting spell?" Wade asked. "We never went to the infirmary."

"Thought it might have been too risky," Matthew interjected.

"Dr. Smith must have told them," Jo'sha answered.

"Well if anyone asks, tell them that you started feeling better just as soon as we got outside and you got some fresh air," Matthew instructed.

Wade nodded his head in agreement.

"What happened to you anyway?" Chance asked.

"It just became too much. The anger was stabbing at my temples, and the grief just began to suffocate me like a hot wet blanket. I got a little dizzy and the next thing I knew I was on the ground," Wade said, recalling the experience.

"Well you've got to learn how to control that or block it out or something 'cause there's no way that you're going to be able to avoid people with emotions!" Matthew snapped.

"Easy for you to say," Wade retorted.

"There is one other thing," Jo'sha said tentatively. He glanced uncertainly at Chance.

"What now?" Matthew huffed.

"While we were in Dr. Smith's office we saw something," Jo'sha began.

"It was nothing. Jo'sha shouldn't have been snooping," Chance interrupted.

"We found James' cross in Dr. Smith's office," Jo'sha said.

"What cross?" Matthew asked.

Just as Jo'sha was about to explain, two security guards came off of the elevator, one a six foot six inch, light complexioned man, and the other a slightly shorter, more robust, older chocolate gentleman.

"Just patrolling the university buildings this evening," said the taller of the two. "You boys should be getting back to your dorms. Make sure you travel in groups and be careful. Just in case you hadn't heard, a tenth victim was just found at a junkyard on the east side of town."

"What?" They asked in unison.

"Yeah. Good news is that the police may finally have a lead."

"What do you mean?" asked Matthew cautiously.

"I'm a full time police officer during the day. I just do this at night for a little bit of extra change," he bragged. "Anyway, I was down at the precinct earlier and they were saying that they found some footprints and a pair of sandals at the junkyard where the body was found. They may be able to finally pull together some decent clues. I guess that guy finally got careless."

The security officers left to finish their rounds. Matthew remained silent, wondering if any of these clues would lead police to the ankhs. Chance and Wade weren't sure what to think, and Jo'sha shuttered not wanting to tell them that he had left his sandals behind that night in the confusion.

CHAPTER 19

Chance, Jo'sha and Wade adhered to strict schedules for the next two weeks, only going out of the suite when necessary. Matthew had made a strong case for staying on the down low. Beyond their trips to the gym, class, and the library, they maintained limited visibility on campus. Matthew managed to go to work and to visit Miss Vaughn. Jo'sha went to the campus music room for practice, but Matthew insisted that either Chance or Wade go with him. The self-imposed confinement was starting to get to each of them.

"Matthew, we can't hide out in this damn suite forever! Besides, no one is looking for us. The officer said that they were just gathering clues. Do you know how many footprints are probably around that junkyard?" Jo'sha urged, trying to convince himself as much as his friends.

"Did you burn the shoes that we wore to the park Sunday night like I asked you to?" Matthew asked Jo'sha.

"Yes I did. No evidence left," Jo'sha responded, avoiding eye contact.

"Chance, I'll pay you back for those sneakers. I promise. Thanks for letting me wear this new pair too," Matthew said.

"Don't worry about the shoes after all I did throw your old ones away. Let's just figure out what we do next."

"I agree with Jo'sha. If we alter our schedules too much, then we'll appear suspect," Wade said.

"This is a big campus. No one is even thinking about us. We should just go about our business as usual. Just do us. You're being way too dramatic," Jo'sha interjected.

"Exactly," said Wade.

"You guys are forgetting the most important thing here—we haven't done anything wrong," Chance said.

"Are *you* forgetting that we broke into that office at the university library? Or that at least five people know that Wade and Jo'sha were there the night Victor Greene was run over? *And* that all four of us were at the junkyard the night the tenth body was dumped? It looks very suspicious," Matthew said.

"You don't know if that was the body that we heard," Chance challenged.

"And you don't know that it wasn't," Matthew responded. "We can't afford to have authorities questioning us."

"It's obvious the football players don't want to be implicated in Victor's death either. Otherwise they would have said something by now," Wade added.

"You don't know that they haven't," Chance responded.

"So what do you recommend we do, Matthew?" Wade asked.

"The sooner the authorities find the Atlanta Male Murderer then the less likely it is that clues may accidentally lead them back to us," Matthew said.

"I know you aren't suggesting that we play superheroes and go find the killer," Chance said. "I didn't sign up for that."

"And we do have lives. I don't know if you remember, but I have a baby on the way, and a family in Baltimore who doesn't know anything about it. Not to mention my classes," Wade said.

"And I have the homecoming talent show coming up," Jo'sha added.

"*Real* important," Wade said.

"The prize is $1500 and a chance to go to meet Agonize. Not a big deal to you brothers with money, but a lot to me," Jo'sha said, defensively.

"Yeah, homecoming is right around the corner. We already backed out of the oratory contest. This is our first college homecoming. Are we supposed to miss everything?" Chance asked.

"These aren't just trinkets around our necks. With them on we have the ability to control nature, but we know very little about them. Who knows what they could do to us next. And just in case you don't remember, we can't take them off—or have we forgotten what happened to Wade?"

Wade was trying hard to control the headache that was escalating as a result of the argument. Though he wasn't able to completely relieve it, he was at least getting better at managing the effect that other people's emotions had on him.

Matthew went over to his desk and pulled out a binder containing newspaper clippings and notes.

"I haven't had any female attention in over a week," Jo'sha complained.

"Hmmph! We all know what happened the last time you were with a female," Wade said.

"It's Friday and you mean to tell me that you think I'm going to spend the night in here looking at you three?" Jo'sha asked, looking around the room.

"It is not like we can trust you by yourself. You damn near killed Robert Black! It's a good thing that Chance was there. Who knows? That same thing could happen to any of us," Matthew said.

"Well we can't act like hermits for four years, Matthew" Chance reasoned.

"My family is coming for homecoming," Wade added.

"I know all of this. I do," Matthew said quickly. "It's just that we can't afford to be too careless. We can't control the ankhs yet, and if we aren't careful we could hurt ourselves or someone else. If anyone found out about these powers, then our lives would cease to be normal. I haven't seen Tessa in a while either."

"You call being stuck in this room all the time normal? Even when I go to the gym, I have to go out of my way to avoid other people," Chance griped.

Matthew sighed. He could feel their frustration, but knew how important it was to keep the situation under wraps as best as possible. There was still so much to learn about the ankhs and the power they now possessed. He only hoped he could convince them to remain low-key.

"By the way, you have eight messages," Jo'sha said. "Tessa and Olivia have been calling the room like crazy. If you don't start returning phone calls, then they may begin to worry and you know your little sister will just show up."

"Thanks," Matthew said, becoming overwhelmed.

"When are you going to tell your family about Quay?" Jo'sha asked, changing the subject.

"I was thinking about doing it at homecoming. Maybe even have her come to Atlanta so they can meet her face-to-face and see how great she is."

"Are you sure that you can deal with all the emotions that will generate from that situation?" Matthew asked.

Wade didn't say anything. He hadn't thought of that aspect. There was no doubt that bringing his family and Quay together would cause quite a stir, and now with his heightened emotional awareness, he would definitely have to consider how he would handle it.

"Foster says he may come to Atlanta for homecoming. I've told him all about you guys," Jo'sha said.

"What if we all invited our families?" Chance asked. "We could have a big tailgate party before the game."

That seemed like a good idea to everyone except Matthew who didn't find the proposition too inviting.

"Everyone could come see me in the talent show," Jo'sha added.

Matthew sighed again. He could see that he was decidedly out voted.

"Matt, don't worry. We know how serious this is," Chance said, placing his hand on Matthew's shoulder.

"I can't tell," he said sullenly. Matthew couldn't understand why it seemed as though he was the only one who thought the history of the ankhs and the events that had occurred since they found them was important. But despite their lack of interest, he refused to let the subject go.

Matthew opened his notebook and pulled out an 11x17 inch piece of paper. "Here are profiles of all the victims of the Atlanta Male Murderer. The authorities have mistakenly assumed that Victor was also killed by the murderer, but even without Victor's death most of the other murders seem to have very little in common," Matthew said, revealing his extensive research.

"Where did you get that chart from and what are you doing with it?" Chance asked.

"I drew it up. Some of the information comes from the security guard at the library. Some of it came from the web. You'd be surprised at how many serial killer fan sites there are. Most of it came from the newspaper and television though."

"You *are* playing superhero," Chance accused.

"No. I'm just looking for clues that may help us find this guy," Matthew said.

"Us?" Chance asked.

"What if Jo'sha is right?" Matthew asked.

"About what?" Chance shot back.

"What if that was James' cross? What if Dr. Smith did have something to do with his murder?" Matthew speculated.

Jo'sha listened to their exchange, and made a mental note to get rid of the cross from Dr. Smith's office along with Victor Greene's watch, wallet, and ring.

"He's a college professor!" Chance defended.

"You were the one who said that the cross might have belonged to James Lynch. And he did have a pair of muddy shoes in his office, and it has been raining a lot lately," Matthew added.

"That proves nothing. So what if he had a cross in his office. Lots of people carry crosses, and the mud could have come from anywhere."

"Matthew, all of this is really going to your head isn't it?" Jo'sha said, laughing.

Matthew sighed again, his frustration returning.

"What's with all the sighing?" Jo'sha asked.

"I just wish you guys would start taking things more seriously," Matthew said, half defeated, having been bombarded with the same argument for days.

"What else should we be doing besides staying locked up in our rooms until they find the Atlanta Male Murderer?" Wade asked.

"Getting mistakenly fingered by the police isn't our only problem. Each of us is a ticking time bomb, capable of passing out or nearly killing someone else. For one thing, I suggest that we start some type of daily meditation ritual. I started it myself as a test based on some sketchy entries from the journal. I've found that it helps me to keep my mind from racing. I think it can help all of us keep our powers under control," Matthew said.

"You may have a point. Meditation is powerful stuff," Jo'sha said, finally agreeing with something Matthew said.

"Chance has already got us on a daily workout schedule and we are in the library every evening. I think you have control issues, and we don't have any more spare time," Wade whined.

"We need to make time!" Matthew snapped.

"I have a surprise for you guys," Jo'sha said.

"Now what?" Matthew asked, sounding exasperated.

Wade and Chance welcomed the diversion.

"I think you all have noticed that I've been working on a little project of my own," Jo'sha said, going to his closet to retrieve a large, covered canvas board.

"Yes. We just assumed it was schoolwork," Wade said.

"Well it isn't. Matthew isn't the only genius in this suite. Gentlemen, I present to you the newest and best Black Greek letter organization—Omega Tau!" Jo'sha ceremoniously unveiled a beautifully illustrated green, silver, and gold Omega Tau fraternity crest.

"What the—" Matthew stopped, unable to comment on what Jo'sha had just revealed.

"We need an identity for Omega Tau—something dynamic and strong. The existing fraternities have taken most of the more obvious color combinations, so it was no easy task. I experimented with several colors and finally came up with the perfect match—platinum, gold and green. The four stars at the top represent our four founders, Cyrus Wilkes, Nathaniel Charles, Oleander Vaughn, and Winston Wright. The year 1904 represents the year of the organization's inception, again paying homage to the founders. The Greek letters Omega and Tau are organized vertically in the center creating an outline of an ankh. *And*," Jo'sha said, pausing for effect. "If that weren't enough, I have also taken the liberty of capturing the history of Cyrus, Nathaniel, Oleander and Winston without telling too many of our secrets."

"Are you serious?" Matthew asked.

"Absolutely," Jo'sha said.

"I like it," Chance said immediately.

"It *does* look like a real fraternity shield," Wade said, surprising Jo'sha with his supportive tone.

"Is this all you guys can think of?" Matthew snapped.

"What's wrong with it?" Chance asked.

"Don't you think we have other things to deal with right now?"

"You were the one who said that we should lay low 'til homecoming and then reconsider the idea. I just gave us a head start," Jo'sha defended.

"What's going to make this fraternity any different than the others?" Matthew challenged.

"It really will be an organization that is designed to help its members and the community. First of all, there won't be any hazing in the initiation process. Ain't no need for brothers to be disrespecting other brothers," Jo'sha said.

"Still sounds like every other fraternity to me," Matthew replied.

"We'll also be hitting 'em hard with the academics. You know we are all going to be carrying 4.0 grade point averages. We won't just be some society of knuckleheads. We'll come correct."

"Hmmph," Matthew frowned.

Even though Jo'sha's ideas for the fraternity were good, Matthew couldn't help wishing that his friends were as enthusiastic about learning about the new powers they'd attained as they were about starting another boring fraternity.

"And when it comes to community service we won't be all over the place," Jo'sha continued. "We're going to focus on one thing and get that right. I kinda like Wade's ideas about brothers like us helping younger brothers who are not as fortunate."

"Sounds nice," Chance agreed.

"How do you keep people out?" Wade asked.

Jo'sha shot him a look. "What do you sound like? It doesn't surprise me that *you* would say that. That's part of the problem with fraternities today. They screen people out, when they should be screening them in. There's power in numbers," he said emphatically.

"That's the truth," Chance said, nodding his head.

Seeing that he had their attention, Jo'sha continued, "We have a unique opportunity to create the perfect fraternity."

"Can we talk about this over dinner?" Matthew asked, growing frustrated with his friends and their lack of focus.

"Yes. It'll be a chance to get out of the room," Wade said.

"I have a surprise too. We're going off campus for dinner this evening," Matthew said.

"Where are we going?" Chance asked.

"To see Miss Vaughn."

"Why do you keep going to see Miss Vaughn? I thought she told you everything that she knew."

"Miss Vaughn is old and she has forgotten a lot. She tells me something new every time we get together. We should get ready to go. You all need to bring overnight bags and a change of old clothes," Matthew said quickly.

"What is this? Are we having a sleep over with Miss Vaughn?" Chance asked incredulously.

"Old clothes?" Wade asked, raising his eyebrows.

"Don't worry. You can borrow some of mine," Chance volunteered, jokingly.

"That's not what I meant? I'm just wondering *why* we need old clothes. I have old clothes," Wade responded.

"That isn't the kind of female company I was referring to," Jo'sha complained.

"Just trust me," Matthew begged.

Reluctantly they nodded, and went to gather their overnight bags. They left the dorm minutes later.

"I like the fraternity shield," Wade said, walking to the van.

"Me too," Chance added.

"Really?" Jo'sha asked proudly.

The conversation on the way to Miss Vaughn's house was primarily about Quay's pregnancy—adolescent minds attempting to solve adult problems.

"How did you and Quay meet?" Chance asked.

"I was tutoring her cousin Tony at the recreation center. She was up from D.C. and we met and just started talking. She came back to Baltimore a few more times and we realized that we liked each other," Wade explained.

"Was she your first?" Jo'sha asked.

"Huh?"

"Yeah. She was your first," Jo'sha said, knowingly.

"What's the big deal with introducing her to your family?" Matthew asked, finally becoming a part of the conversation.

"My family has got this thing about background and pedigree," Wade said.

"Well then what about us?" Jo'sha asked.

"I am not dating any of you," Wade said sharply.

"Is that okay with you that your family decides who you date?" Matthew continued.

"That's just the way it is," Wade answered.

"You're practically a grown man. What can they do to you?" Jo'sha asked.

"It's complicated," Wade responded.

"Well, I don't think springing her on them at homecoming is such a good idea," Matthew said.

"Why not?" Chance asked. "I think it's the perfect time. They'll be in a good mood and in public so they won't show off," Chance said.

"You don't know my aunts," Wade replied.

"I say the sooner the better," Jo'sha interjected.

"Yeah. We should all invite our families to homecoming. We could have one big ole tailgate party before the game," Chance said.

"Or a dinner party," Wade said.

"We only have a few weeks to figure it out if we're going to do it," Jo'sha said.

They were within a few blocks of Miss Vaughn's house when Chance asked Wade to stop at the corner store. "Miss Vaughn likes tea and pound cake. We should get some for her," Chance said, hopping out of the car.

"He is *so* southern," Jo'sha said.

"But in a good way," Wade said, impressed by Chance's thoughtfulness.

They knocked on the door for several minutes before Miss Vaughn answered. "Hello, Matthew. Hello, Chance," Miss Vaughn said, elated to have company.

"Hello, Miss Vaughn. We brought you some tea and pound cake," Chance offered.

"This will be perfect after dinner," Miss Vaughn announced. She smiled and gave Chance a big bear hug. "Are these the other friends that you told me about?" she asked.

"Yes," Matthew answered.

"Well come on in."

"This is Jo'sha Imarah, and Wade Graham IV," Matthew said.

"Any relation to the Grahams that sponsored that new wing on the library," she asked.

"Yes," Wade answered, pleased that she recognized his family's contribution.

Wade studied Miss Vaughn. She was dressed in a conservative blue dress that he figured she had sewn herself, and her hair was styled in the same way that it had been for the last twenty years. When she rushed off to the kitchen with the tea and pound cake he looked around at all of the porcelain baubles and plastic covers in her house. While she was gone the four of them made themselves comfortable in the living room.

"This is a picture of Cyrus, Nathaniel, Oleander, and Winston," Matthew said, pointing out each in a picture on the mantel.

The smell of pork chops, kale greens, and sweet potatoes wafted gently from the kitchen. It was just then that Matthew realized that he had forgotten to tell Miss Vaughn that Jo'sha didn't eat meat.

"Dinner is almost ready," Miss Vaughn announced when she came back into the living room.

"Great," Chance responded enthusiastically.

Miss Vaughn took her seat and crossed her legs at the ankles. "I want to thank you boys for agreeing to help me out with my old property in Fayetteville. It has been a while since I spent time down there. Up until six weeks ago I had renters and they left the property in a mess. Since I am still suspended from my job at the library, I might as well busy myself with other things. There are a lot of old family heirlooms there. I was so pleased when Matthew told me that you young men were willing to help me tidy things up at the old Vaughn house," she said.

"What?" Wade exclaimed.

Matthew poked him in the back. "Yes, Miss Vaughn. It's the least we can do for this great home cooked meal," Matthew interjected.

"We can head to Fayetteville just as soon as we finish eating. We want to get there before it gets too dark. Then we can get up bright and early tomorrow morning and begin working," she said, heading back toward the kitchen to check on dinner.

"You mean to tell me we *are* going to have a sleep over with an old librarian? I can't take any more of this," Jo'sha said, shaking his head in disbelief.

"C'mon, now just relax. She *is* feeding us. She's lonely and obviously enjoys our company. Most importantly, she tells me that a lot of Oleander's personal items are stored in an old shed behind the house," Matthew explained.

"Great," Wade said, echoing Jo'sha's frustration.

"More importantly, it might be a place for us to practice using these ankhs. It's out in the country and completely isolated," Matthew said.

"Okay, but what's this about working? What exactly does she expect us to do?" Wade asked.

"She just has a few things that she needs help with," Matthew answered.

"You should really check with us before you volunteer us for something else like this," Wade snapped.

"Dinner is ready," Miss Vaughn announced from the kitchen.

They all ambled into the dining room where Miss Vaughn had proudly laid out her finest china. The aroma of the food was intoxicating. They took their places and began fixing plates. Jo'sha politely refused the pork chops and ate only vegetables.

"This is very good," Wade said, shoveling food in his mouth. Every bite seemed to come alive in Wade's mouth. Surprisingly, he had finished two full pork chops before Chance could finish one.

"I am glad you like it," Miss Vaughn said smiling. "Don't you like my pork chops?" she asked, looking at Jo'sha.

"He doesn't eat meat," the others chimed in before Jo'sha could answer.

The young men listened politely as Miss Vaughn spent the rest of dinner talking about her long association with Georgia Central. When they finished their meal Jo'sha and Chance volunteered to wash the dishes. Matthew and Wade helped Miss Vaughn serve the tea and pound cake.

After dessert Miss Vaughn excused herself, and went to get her old floral train case. It was already packed with the items that she would need for the trip to the country. "I have to go get one more thing and then I will be ready to go," Miss Vaughn said, heading to the kitchen for a box of pans and groceries.

"That dinner was excellent," Wade said again.

Jo'sha and Chance exchanged curious looks, still perplexed by Wade's new appetite for southern cuisine.

Dusk followed them on the half hour ride to Fayetteville, Georgia. The expansive landscape and greenery reminded Chance of his family's land back home in North Carolina. The rural darkness seemed deeper than any Wade or Jo'sha had seen before.

The Vaughn estate was a full twelve acres. The house sat an acre back off of a secondary highway. Directly behind it stood a matching utility shed and an old oak tree with a tire swing that looked like it had come right out of a Henry O. Tanner painting.

"The original house was made of wood, but Pa had a stone mason finish it before he died. He had the stone imported all the way from Europe," Miss Vaughn said proudly, smiling up at the old structure.

"Oh how nice," Wade said under his breath.

"It's wonderful," said Chance.

Matthew looked at the house and realized that Miss Vaughn had more means than he'd thought, and that her suspension from the university wasn't about to present a financial hardship.

"We had better get in and get settled. There are four bedrooms in the house, so two of you will have to room together. We have a long day tomorrow." She turned towards the house, delicately searching for the cobblestone walk that lead to the front porch.

Wade glared at Matthew. He was still not happy with the prospect of having to perform manual labor.

They all picked up their overnight bags and were on their way to the house when Jo'sha suddenly stopped. "Did you see that?" he asked.

"What?" Chance asked.

"Down there near the trees. It looks like a big dog."

"You mean way down there at that tree line? That's at least two acres away. I doubt that you can see that far this late in the evening. Even if you could, it's probably just a deer."

"Oh," Jo'sha said, rubbing his eyes and looking into the darkness again. He had never seen a live deer before in his life.

"Come on, boys," Miss Vaughn called out to them from the porch.

"Ugh," Wade sighed.

CHAPTER 20

Miss Vaughn retired to the master suite shortly after they arrived. Since none of them were tired, the young men were left to amuse themselves. Without the modern conveniences of video games and televisions, they found an old deck of cards in the kitchen drawer and after giving Wade a quick lesson, they played Spades.

"If these walls could talk I bet they would have stories to tell. It seems like there are so many memories here," Chance said.

"And smells too," Matthew added.

"Just smells like an old house to me," Chance said.

"Don't you smell the rotting wood, or the old paint?" Matthew responded.

"I guess," Chance said. He threw down an ace of spades on Jo'sha's king.

"That is it. You guys won. I'm about to go to bed," Jo'sha said, yawning and stretching.

"Me too," Wade echoed.

"I'm not that sleepy," said Chance. "I'm feeling kind of jumpy for some reason. Too bad there isn't a television here."

"I'll stay up with you. I brought my folder. You can help me go through the Atlanta Male Murder files," Matthew offered.

Jo'sha and Wade looked at each other and smirked. They gave Chance a glad-it's-you-and-not-me-look, and then headed upstairs toward the first two available bedrooms.

With nothing better to do, Chance helped Matthew finish a color-coded map of the locations where male murder victims had been found and where they lived. They worked well past 1:00 a.m.

Meanwhile, Jo'sha was tossing and turning inside a purple haze of nothingness until the world seemed to abandon him, leaving him floating in space. Floating and then flying amongst a small group of birds more beautiful than any he had ever seen. And then, as suddenly as he had risen, he began to fall past emotions and feelings as old as time. As he fell he saw one of the glorious birds break formation and fly off into the lavender sunset. After minutes of falling, he finally hit the ground in a clearing of woods. He sensed the presence of death and the wake of a great fire. He steadied himself to stand. A familiar dark figure appeared before him and presented him with five small stones. But before he could grab them, the ominous figure closed his hand leaving Jo'sha anxious and wanting. The figure opened his hand again and only four stones remained. Jo'sha blinked, and suddenly the figure was gone. Jo'sha turned to search for him, but he was nowhere to be found. And then off in the distance he heard a cry.

"Nathaniel! Oleander! Winston!"

Then Jo'sha heard a great commotion in the distance. Blood curdling screams and cries—and he cried out too.

"That's Jo'sha!" Matthew yelled, throwing down his pen and heading for the stairs. Chance was right behind him.   They arrived in the first bedroom at the top of the stairs and found Jo'sha sitting straight up in bed, covered in sweat.

"Nightmare?" Matthew asked.

"Vision," Jo'sha answered.

"What's the difference?" Chance asked.

"A nightmare isn't real. This was *very* real," Jo'sha said emphatically.

"So what do we do?" Chance asked, after Jo'sha finished recounting his vision to them.

"Go back to sleep. There's nothing that you guys can do. I just have to figure out what these visions are all about and why I'm the only one having them."

The two of them left Jo'sha and retired to the fourth bedroom. Both of them were asleep within minutes. Jo'sha's sleep after that was not a peaceful one, but it was free of visions. They were all awakened by the sounds of a cowbell hours later.

"Is she serious? It's Saturday morning," Wade grumbled, looking at his cell phone and seeing that it was only 6:00 a.m.

By the time they all trudged downstairs Miss Vaughn had prepared bacon, eggs, pancakes, and a vegetarian omelet for Jo'sha. She handed out chores over breakfast, instructing them that they needed to make a quick trip to the hardware store and gas station.

"Late September is the best time for cleaning," Miss Vaughn said, digging into her bra for a roll of money. She gave them directions, handed Wade two twenties and a list, and told them to hurry back. Wade grabbed the bills with the tips of his fingers and headed out the door behind the others.

By nine-thirty Matthew was mowing the lawn, Jo'sha was painting the outside of the house, and Chance and Wade were planting flowers.

"You've never done this before have you?" Chance said, stating the obvious.

"How can you tell?" Wade answered, rolling his eyes.

"Well, you have yet to get your hands really dirty, you seem to be afraid of worms, and you look like you've never seen a shovel before in your life. Here, let me show you," Chance offered.

With a nice new row of weeded and clipped shrubs, Chance continued to instruct Wade on the finer points of gardening and lawn care.

"Now all we need to do is water them. I'll go get the hose."

Chance darted off to the storage shed at the end of the large backyard in nothing but running shorts and Timberland boots. The ankh beat against his chest as he galloped around the house. In just a few minutes, he darted back around the house without the hose, barely breathing from the sprint.

"This is great! I used to have terrible coughing and sneezing fits every time I did yard work. I nearly always had to use my inhaler."

"Yeah, I know how it is to be free too," Wade responded, remembering how cumbersome his old glasses had been.

"The bad news is that we don't have a water hose. With as much time as we have spent at the hardware store, you would think that we would have remembered. And that old shed is a mess! It's cluttered with a bunch of rusty old fire extinguishers, chests, and trunks. We should take some time to clean it out and go through all of that stuff."

"Hmmph," Wade muttered, having done more manual labor in that day than he had done most of his life.

"I guess we have to go back to the hardware store," Chance concluded.

"Maybe not," Wade said.

He crouched down to the ground and placed his palms into the earth. He motioned for Chance to do the same. The two of them sat for a moment in complete silence.

"Can you feel it?" Wade asked, barely above a whisper.

"Feel what?"

"Water. It's deep, but it's there. *You* should be able to feel it coursing through the earth."

Just then Matthew and Jo'sha came into the front yard. Both of them were taking a break from their assigned chores.

"What are you doing?" Jo'sha asked.

"Sssshhhhh!" Wade warned. "Chance, can you feel it now?" he asked again still slightly above a whisper.

"Uhhhmmmm, I guess so," Chance responded skeptically. Jo'sha and Matthew continued to look on in amazement.

"Now help me bring it up!" Wade commanded.

Chance looked at him, his expression a mixture of shock and confusion.

"Help me bring it up!" he said more firmly.

"What do you mean?" Chance asked.

"Separate the soil. Loosen the earth, and I'll bring up the water." Wade said, further clarifying his direction.

Chance looked up at Jo'sha and Matthew, both of whom seemed to be as puzzled as he was. Then he looked back at Wade who now had his eyes closed, and was inhaling slowly and deeply. Chance replanted his fingers in the earth past the grass and into the soil. He wasn't sure if he could follow Wade's instructions, but he concentrated anyway. In seconds, the earth became damp and began to shift. Suddenly a funnel of water shot up from the ground just two feet in front of Wade. Before they knew it, a spring had emerged right before them. Jo'sha and Matthew stood in complete amazement as every blade of grass and every flower seemed to give them a standing ovation. Chance still wasn't sure if he had helped.

"What are you boys doing out here?" Miss Vaughn asked, stepping out on the porch.

"Nothing. Just finishing up," Matthew explained.

"Where did all this water come from?" she asked.

"Looks like a natural spring," Jo'sha said smiling.

Miss Vaughn looked on skeptically for a few moments before taking a seat on the porch swing. "That was never there before," she said.

"I think it'll work just fine for these shrubs," Chance answered.

"You boys did good work here today. There's no shame in hard work," Miss Vaughn said, nodding slowly.

Wade was sure that she was looking directly at him.

Chance, no stranger to yard work, asked, "Is there anything else that you need done, Miss Vaughn?"

Jo'sha and Wade shot him dirty looks.

Chance saw the looks his friends gave him and quickly tried to change the subject. "Miss Vaughn, our families are coming for homecoming in a few weeks. You're more than welcome to come to our tailgate party."

Jo'sha smiled, agreeing with the invitation. Wade and Matthew both cringed at the thought of a cookout. Neither of them was particularly enthused by the idea of their families attending the event.

"I would love that," Miss Vaughn said with a smile. "It would be just like old times. I haven't been to a football game in years."

"Miss Vaughn, you said that you thought some of Oleander's old things were here. May we see them? We're all fascinated with the history of the university," Matthew interjected, ready to change the conversation again.

"Why sure. There's a box of his things upstairs in the attic," she answered.

"Great!" Matthew said, hurrying toward the porch so they could head to the attic.

They spent the rest of the afternoon going through the attic. What began as a search for Oleander's personal items resulted in Chance forcing them to clean out the attic. It was early evening by the time they finished. Matthew was glad that they finally found the chest of Oleander's belongings. Jo'sha and Wade were simply glad to be finished. Chance was happy knowing that he'd found a way to help Miss Vaughn.

"We found Oleander's things," Matthew said when they came downstairs.

"And we cleaned out that da—"

"Dark. We cleaned out that dark attic," Matthew finished, shooting Jo'sha a disapproving look.

"Do you mind if we take these things back to campus and look at them? I promise we'll return them when we're done," Matthew said politely.

"Well, I guess it's alright. I don't need them, and really don't have anyone to leave them to. Go ahead and take them," she agreed.

"Shouldn't we be getting back now?" Wade hinted. He wanted to get out the door before Chance could volunteer to do anymore work.

"I guess we should," Matthew relented.

"I noticed that the old shed out back could use some cleaning. Maybe we can do it next weekend," Chance offered.

"Yippee," Wade said sarcastically.

CHAPTER 21

The next few weeks were uneventful. Despite their continued arguments, Jo'sha, Wade, and Chance understood and adhered to Matthew's stipulations about staying out of the public eye. They slipped into a comfortable routine of morning meditations and workout sessions, classes, and study meetings. While most of their freshman peers were getting lost in parties, alcohol and sexual encounters, they were finding themselves through improved mental, spiritual, emotional, and physical states of being.

The prospect of starting their own fraternity was also becoming more real for each of them. They became students of Black Greek letter organizations, memorizing histories and studying fraternity social traditions, norms and rituals. Jo'sha took the lead on creating the fraternity materials and paraphernalia with significant input from Wade, while Matthew continued his research on Cyrus and the Atlanta Male Murder case. With the exception of Chance, they were also becoming more comfortable with wielding the powers of the ankh. They made routine trips to Miss Vaughn's house in Fayetteville to make minor property repairs and practice controlling the elements. They went so frequently that she gave them their own set of keys to keep as long as the property was without tenants.

Quiet times found them back in the 400 suite of Winfrey-Combs freshman dormitory complaining less and contemplating more about who and what they were becoming.

"Matthew, I just finished Wade. Come and get your haircut. Hurry up!" Chance yelled from the bathroom.

"Nice haircut considering what you had to work with," Jo'sha said, sitting on the bathroom windowsill tuning Oleander's banjo.

"Yeah. That was the most relaxing haircut I ever had. And *you* need to shut up with your dreadlocks," Wade said, admiring his new longer hairstyle in the mirror. Chance had convinced him to keep his hair a little longer, edging it up in the front and back, and using the scissors to trim it down some.

"Thanks," Chance said proudly. "I used to cut in my uncle's barber shop."

"You and your uncle must be close," Jo'sha said.

Chance didn't respond.

"Why did you bother to grow dreadlocks anyway? They seem to be an awful lot of trouble," Wade asked as he watched Jo'sha pull his locks back and retie them with a strip of string.

"I think they look good," Chance defended. "I've thought about growing some myself."

"First, there is nothing dreadful about them, so I prefer to call them locks. Second, its not about the look," Jo'sha replied in a thick Chicago accent.

"What do you mean?" Chance asked.

"Well," Jo'sha sighed as he continued, "my decision to grow my hair was a spiritual one. It had very little to do with my physical appearance. When you grow your hair or lock your hair, you have to exercise patience. It requires discipline to maintain it and care for it. And anything that you care for you will eventually grow to love. My hair takes its own shape from day to day and I have to accept that, understand it, and love it. The same way that I have to accept and love myself or people that I don't understand," Jo'sha remarked, glancing pointedly at Wade. "It's been a learning process for me. I also believe that there is power and strength in our hair. That's why our hair has been at the center of controversy for so much of our history," Jo'sha ended.

"What controversy?" Chance asked.

"Here we go with the black and white thing again," Wade sighed.

"Foster says that the simple man fights the flesh, the smart man fights the mind, but the victor conquers the spirit. Nappy, kinky, and knotty are the words that are used to describe our hair—all of which are meant to be spiritual arrows. Silky, smooth, and straight are the adjectives that they use to describe their own. We have been systematically taught to hate, hide, and reconstruct our hair for centuries," Jo'sha finished.

"I never really thought about hair as something more than a part of our physical appearance," Chance admitted.

"And that really is all there is to it," Wade added.

183

"Not really," Jo'sha said, shaking his head. "African-American hair insulated the head from the intensity of the African sun. We are the original sun people. The creator was doing some of his best work when he made us. From the tight curls of the Mandingos to the loosely curled locks of the Ashanti. Each tribe or village wore a particular hairstyle and even within each tribe, the hairstyles communicated something about the individual's status or condition. You have got to know your history, son."

Jo'sha tapped his head and looked at his friends. Their blank expressions spurned him on in his educative lecture.

"When we got over here, we didn't have the time or tools to care for our hair, and like anything else that is uncared for, it deteriorated and became tangled and matted. The only things available were the tools that were used for livestock. Those tools caused lice infestations, scalp diseases, and ringworms. Our ancestors also had to protect their hair from the sun and flies while they were out in the fields so they wore head rags. Again, something that wasn't good for the hair. So we learned to be ashamed of something that had once been a source of great pride. For me, it is about reclaiming my heritage, and getting in touch with me," Jo'sha finished.

"I thought you said that their hair was supposed to protect them from the sun. If that's true, how come they needed rags to protect them? Doesn't make sense," Wade said, looking puzzled.

"It did protect them from the sun," Jo'sha stressed. "But when they came here, they were forced to be in the field all day. We weren't meant for that much exposure."

"Seems like an awful lot of trouble to me just to get in touch with oneself," Wade said finally.

"You gotta do what works for you. We all have different journeys and methods of expression. Be it bald, like my man Chance here, or an Afro and braids like Matthew. But we all need to understand the power we carry. Personally, I wonder if you are really in touch with *any* aspects of the black experience." Jo'sha answered.

"What does that mean?" Wade shot back.

"Have you ever even been to a real barbershop, or did you go to a salon? Or did the barber come to your house?" Jo'sha challenged.

"Well, of course I've been to a barbershop" Wade said defensively.

"And I can look at you and tell that you were uncomfortable being around a bunch of brothers,"

"No, I wasn't uncomfortable. I just found it to be a little unorganized."

"Unorganized to the unfamiliar, but perfectly orchestrated to the properly initiated. The barbershop is a place for us to commune, share, and experience us."

"You never know who is waiting for which barber, and it takes for*ever*." Wade challenged.

"You see. That's a part of the process. It's about establishing a relationship with a barber—about understanding his flow, and in some cases even challenging another brother when he is trying to take your place in line. And the time spent waiting for the barber— that's valuable talk time," Jo'sha concluded.

"Why does it have to be about all of that?" Wade asked, sounding exasperated.

"It's a part of the African-American male initiation and maturation process. Our people have so few traditions. We should embrace the few that we do have," Jo'sha answered.

Wade shook his head but didn't say anything further. Jo'sha's answers didn't satisfy him, but he didn't care to entertain the topic any further.

"He's right," Chance chimed in. He had been listening intently, and Jo'sha's words sparked a memory for him. "I can remember my father taking me to my uncle's barbershop when I was growing up, and I have to say that I heard more conversation from older men on real issues in the barbershop than I ever heard in my uncle's church."

"Our hair defines us," Jo'sha continued. "If we don't accept it, then we can't accept ourselves." Jo'sha got up and brushed past Wade to look at himself in the mirror.

"Is that marijuana I smell on you?" Wade asked.

"Re-lax. It's not a big deal," Jo'sha responded.

"Not a big deal?" Wade asked incredulously. "Do you know what would happen to us if Ronnie found marijuana in our suite?"

"He does have a point," Chance agreed.

"And who knows what else it could lead to. I worked with inner-city kids and that's exactly how it starts—with casual use," Wade added.

"See, that's just it! You *worked* with inner-city kids and I *was* one. And for the record, *it* started when the first slave ship arrived in America. And *it* started with your United States government." Jo'sha challenged.

"Not this shit again," Wade groaned.

"What are they arguing about now?" Matthew asked Chance as he came into the bathroom with his Atlanta Male Murder fact book.

"Jo'sha's hair, marijuana, the government, you name it," Chance answered.

Matthew laughed and shook his head. "I think I am on to something here," he said.

"What is it?" Chance asked.

"With the exception of Victor Greene, who we know was killed by an anonymous hit and run driver and not the murderer, all of the other victims were small in stature, like James."

"So what?" Wade said, still looking at his new short, curly Afro.

"Maybe that means that the murderer has an odd affinity for small men—small black men," Matthew explained. He took off his shirt and sat down at Chance's makeshift barber station. Chance draped a barber's cape around Matthew and began to edge up the hairline around his large Afro.

"What is that you have there? More research?" Wade asked.

"I did an Internet search on Dr. Smith, but I'm having a hard time finding information. It's like he just sprang up from out of nowhere. There are only articles about his recent academic past. The only thing that dates back beyond the last decade is an article by an African geologist of the same name," Matthew said.

"He looks just like him," Wade said peering over Matthew's shoulder at the printed article.

"Probably a relative," Chance offered.

"Yes, probably," Matthew said contemplatively.

Jo'sha began strumming the banjo riff from the movie *Deliverance*. Chance and Matthew laughed. Wade missed the joke. They took the next five minutes explaining the movie to Wade, who had never seen it.

Matthew relaxed and Chance continued to edge his hairline, turning Matthew's head to get the perfect angles. "You're very good at this. Feels really relaxing," Matthew commented.

"Don't get freaky on me," Chance said.

"Shut up," Matthew retorted.

"I noticed it too," Wade said.

"I just have big hands is all that is. It runs in the family," Chance responded.

"I'm hungry. Let's go get something to eat when you finish," Wade said, heading back toward his room.

"Where is his damn appetite coming from?" Chance asked.

"I don't know. I can barely stand to keep anything down. I've been nauseous for a few days now, but he's been the exact opposite. It's like he just discovered food. That's not a bad thing though. He can stand to add a few pounds. Maybe it's all the working out that we've been doing," Matthew added.

"*He* can stand to gain a few pounds? Look who is talking," Chance laughed.

Jo'sha was plucking out a banjo tune to one of Agonize's newest songs. Chance and Matthew smiled in recognition.

"You still haven't told us what song you're planning to perform for the homecoming talent show. Are you going to play or sing or both?" Chance asked.

"It's a surprise. Just know that I am going to lay it down," Jo'sha said.

"Don't embarrass us. You have got to represent for the W.C.," Matthew said.

"I got you," Jo'sha said confidently.

Chance finished edging up Matthew's hair and started sweeping up. Jo'sha finished cleaning the banjo and gently placed it back into its Turner & Hall Conti case.

"Let's go get something to eat," Wade yelled from the other room.

Jo'sha glanced out of the window. "Look! It's a pledge line. Another fraternity must be crossing over tonight."

Matthew walked over to the bathroom windowsill and looked out onto the courtyard.

"What are you looking at?" Wade asked, walking back into the bathroom to see what was taking them so long.

"Are you looking at those tiny little figures over on central campus?" Matthew asked, pointing to a spot across campus.

"Yeah. Don't you see it?" Jo'sha asked.

Chance ran over to the window.

"Look over at the bell tower," Matthew instructed quickly.

Chance and Wade could only see the outline of the campus clock bell tower.

"What time is it?" Matthew asked.

"5:14 p.m.," Jo'sha answered.

"How many people are in line?" Matthew asked pointing back at the fraternity pledge line, growing more excited.

"Seven."

"What fraternity is it?" Matthew asked again.

"Can't tell. They have on gold shirts. It could be the Alphas, Iotas, or Omegas," Jo'sha said.

Matthew stepped back from the window and scratched his head while Chance and Wade exchanged puzzled looks. Jo'sha continued to look out of the bathroom window, announcing all of the other things that he could see in the distance.

Matthew began laughing uncontrollably.

"What is it?" Wade asked.

"The senses," Matthew answered.

"What?" Wade asked.

"I was wondering what was happening. It's our senses. We each have a heightened sense. Chance has been so anxious lately because he has a heightened sense of touch. Wade and I noticed it when he was cutting our hair. And somehow it's not just limited to what Chance can feel, but what he can make other's feel," Matthew explained.

Chance looked down at his massive hands.

"And I must have a heightened sense of taste," Wade added, thinking of his increased appreciation for food.

"You got it," Matthew agreed.

"That's why everything tastes so good to me now."

"Jo'sha obviously has improved vision, and I, unfortunately, only have a heightened sense of smell. That's why I've been so nauseous lately. Every new scent turns my stomach," Matthew said.

"Deep," Chance said, rubbing his ankh.

"Hey, why don't we go party tonight, Matthew?" Jo'sha said excitedly. "A line is going over tonight so you know there'll be a free party on campus. We've been practicing using our powers. We haven't had any flare ups lately, and we'll all be together in case something goes weird."

"I guess it can't hurt to go out for just a little bit," Matthew said tentatively.

"Let's get dressed," Chance said, already thinking about what he was going to wear.

"We've got to eat first," Wade reiterated.

"We can do all of that before the party, but I have to stop by a phone booth and make an anonymous call to the Atlanta police. I need to tell them what I found out about the similarities in size of the victims," Matthew said.

Jo'sha and Chance sighed.

"How many phone calls have you made to the police already with anonymous tips?" Jo'sha asked.

"Only four," Matthew said apologetically.

The four of them got dressed, drove to *Lucille's* restaurant for some home cooking, stopped by a phone booth, and waited while Matthew made his phone call. Then they returned back to campus for the party.

It seemed as if the entire Atlanta University Center community had turned out for the fraternity celebration. The heavy bass was punctuated with fraternity calls and chants. Even with all of the excitement surrounding the new fraternity members, Wade, Jo'sha, Chance, and Matthew turned heads. They hadn't been at the party long before Jo'sha hit the dance floor with a female friend. Matthew began conversation with a few of his former high school classmates, while Chance and Wade found comfortable spots against the wall.

"We meet again?"

Chance heard a delicate soprano pierce through the wall of dance music. He smiled and then gained his composure before turning to face Aspen Walker. She had on a tight sorority t-shirt, a faded denim skirt and designer boots.

"Are you following me?" he asked, surprising himself with such a flawless delivery.

"Should I be?" she asked, smiling at him.

"Only if you're prepared to catch me," Chance replied, extending his right hand. "Chance Walker," he said with a smile. "It's nice to meet you."

"Aspen Walker, nice to meet you too. Any relation I wonder?" she asked.

"I hope not."

Aspen was immediately taken by Chance's dazzling white smile, which was visible even under the muted party lights. When she placed her small hand in Chance's large palm she felt the power that Wade and Matthew had been talking about earlier. The difference was that this time it was charged with sexual energy and pure attraction. It sent shivers through her body and raised the hair on the back of her neck.

"Umm, yeah, w-w-where is your family from?" she stuttered.

"North Carolina. Where are your people from?" Chance asked, trying not to sound too southern.

"New York."

Aspen was still holding onto Chance's hand. With each passing second his attraction to her grew with the intensity in his touch.

"Any relatives from down south?" Chance asked.

"Not that I know of," she answered, her voice breathy.

Chance moved in close enough for her to smell his cologne pretending as if he were trying to hear more clearly. He brushed his bicep against her shoulder, a move that he had seen Jo'sha use. She pretended not to notice.

"Maybe we can get together some time. My friends and I are having a tailgate party before the homecoming football game," he said, finally releasing Aspen's hand and his control.

"I'll be pretty busy for the next few weeks. I'm running for homecoming queen, and my sorority sisters always have a cookout for returning alumni. I doubt that I'll be able to make it, but we'll have to see," Aspen said.

Since Georgia Central was one of Atlanta's all male schools, co-eds from surrounding schools were allowed to run for homecoming queen. The title of Ms. Georgia Central University was one of the most coveted queen titles.

"I didn't realize that you were running for homecoming queen. Good luck. Just in case your busy schedule opens up, you can reach me in 400 Winfrey-Combs Hall for details and directions."

"The new freshman dorm, huh?" she smiled and gave Chance a once over. "Again, I doubt it, but we'll see."

Chance shrugged, hoping to appear nonchalant. "It isn't a big deal. I'll still vote for you even if you don't come."

"I would appreciate that," Aspen said, removing an *Aspen for Homecoming Queen* pin from her pocket and placing it on Chance's jersey.

"No problem," Chance said, tightening his pectoral muscles while she placed the pin.

"You're a confident little country freshman aren't you?"

"Freshman, yes. Country, maybe, but there is nothing *little* about me." His response caused her to blush. He was just about to comment on how pretty her smile was, when Matthew came over and interrupted them.

"Uh, excuse me, Chance," he said, tapping him on the shoulder. "I think we have a problem—well, two problems."

Chance turned around and saw the entire football team, led by Robert Black, coming in the door. It was obvious that they had been drinking, which made a fight almost inevitable because even sober they were known for fighting.

"It gets better," Matthew said, pointing across the room to the dance floor.

"What? You mean Jo'sha? That's just the way he dances," Chance said.

"No. Look up on the speaker," Matthew said.

Chance followed Matthew's finger, and saw Wade on top of the speaker dancing wildly and spinning his shirt above his head like a helicopter. As the crowd's energy and excitement increased, Wade's movements became more animated.

"Oh God!" Chance whispered.

"We should probably leave. I think Wade is channeling all of the emotion from this party. I knew something like this might happen," Matthew said.

"You get Jo'sha and I'll pull Wade off the speaker. It's probably best if we leave out the back," Chance said. He turned to apologize to Aspen, but she was already gone. She obviously was not used to being ignored. "Damn!" he yelled.

Getting Wade off the speaker proved to be more of a challenge than Chance anticipated. If not for brute strength, he probably would have had to wrestle him to the ground. With the exception of Chance snatching Wade off of the speaker, they managed to make a discreet exit through the back door and out into the cool night.

None of them were tired and they had been spending a lot of time in their suite so it was no wonder that they all quickly agreed when Chance suggested they take a walk across campus.

"Are you alright," Jo'sha asked, still laughing at Wade.

"Shut up," Wade snapped.

"What happened? What did it feel like?" Matthew asked.

"It was gradual. One minute I was standing on the wall listening to the music, watching the neophyte fraternity brothers celebrate, and everyone congratulating them. Then the next thing I knew my pulse was racing and my heart was pounding, and I was just—happy. I could feel what the crowd was feeling and I just wanted to dance," Wade explained.

"I guess we should count this as a lesson not to take any situation for granted now," Matthew said, attempting to make a point.

"What's the big deal? He was dancing on a speaker! Worst case people will think he was just drunk," Jo'sha said.

"Who knows? It could have been much worse," Matthew lectured.

"Well it wasn't, so quit worrying," Jo'sha said. He was still angry that he had to leave the party. "And so what if Robert and the football team were there?"

"They'd been drinking. It could have gotten ugly," Matthew said.

"Even without these powers I ain't no punk! You know we could have handled them."

"Yeah, and we could have been suspended, expelled, or arrested," Matthew said.

"Seriously, we need to find a way to diffuse the Robert Black situation. We can't expect to get in a fight every time we see him," Wade said.

"I was thinking the same thing," Matthew said.

"I say we just whip his ass and be done with it," Jo'sha said.

"Not a good solution."

"Have you noticed how much better it feels to be outside?" Chance asked, changing the subject.

"You know you're right," Matthew said, looking around.

"I guess it makes sense. We're closer to nature and the elements," Wade added.

They had been aimlessly meandering toward the east side of campus while they were talking and were approaching Bonder's cemetery. Bonder's Cemetery was a small cemetery that was several years older than the university. The university had been forced to build around it due to covenants in the purchase of the land. It was surrounded by a black wrought iron gate and sat at the foot of a small hill called Bonder's Pointe. It was no secret that some fraternity pledges had been forced to spend the night in the cemetery as a part of their initiation. There was a cobblestone path from the cemetery to the top of Bonder's Pointe. Bonder's Pointe gave an excellent view of the Atlanta skyline. The campus had begun major construction at the foot of the hill on the other side of Bonder's Pointe. Chance, Jo'sha, Wade, and Matthew walked around the cemetery and up the cobblestone path to the top of the hill.

"I wonder what they're building down there," Matthew commented.

"Never mind that. Look at the view," Chance said, sitting down and digging his hands into the dirt.

They all sat down and quietly enjoyed the scenic skyline. Matthew leaned his head back, closed his eyes, raised his arms, and created a wind that surrounded them all like a huge blanket. Jo'sha inhaled and concentrated, and warmed the air blanket that Matthew had created.

"Nice work," Chance said, enjoying the warmth.

And they communed under the cover of night.

"I've never seen brothers so happy. I don't care what anyone says, they must have been through something," Jo'sha said, referring to the new fraternity initiates at the party.

"I could feel what they were all feeling. The new initiates were hopeful and elated, but I could sense that some of the older fraternity members were just a little bit jealous," Wade said.

"Well they all looked happy. Can you imagine if that was us? I can't wait until we start our own fraternity. First, we'll take over Georgia Central's campus and then we'll go national," Jo'sha said.

"What you don't realize is that no one respects a new fraternity. There's no history. Anyone can go get some Greek letters and start a fraternity," Wade said.

"But not everyone can do this," Chance said, referring to the warm wall of wind that Jo'sha and Matthew had created.

"And you know that this is something that the world can never ever know about. I'm as excited as you all are about possibly starting a fraternity, one without the needless incidents of hazing. One that is dedicated to helping its members so that they can help other people, but we also can't afford to get found out," Matthew said, only half serious about the fraternity.

"What if people knew?" Jo'sha speculated.

"We could become lab rats," Matthew said.

"Or famous," Jo'sha countered.

"The ankhs could be taken off of us," Matthew responded.

"And that wouldn't be good," Wade answered.

"It probably is best if we keep this to ourselves," Chance agreed.

"Watch this," Wade said, forming small pellets of water just in front of them."

"Impressive," Matthew said.

"I've been working on this for a while. I can feel the moisture in the air and condense it."

Wade formed the pellets into a solid sheet of water. Matthew saw Chance focusing on a mound of earth surrounding a small grove of trees just on the other side of the hill. Nothing happened.

"Don't worry. You'll figure it out," Matthew assured him.

"I just can't get the hang of it like you guys have. Jo'sha can actually create fire now, you can command wind, and Wade can pull water from the air and form just about any shape that he can imagine. All I can do is uproot an occasional tree," Chance complained.

"The ankh is working for you. You've gotten much stronger and your sense of touch is damn near intoxicating," Wade added.

"I guess you're right," Chance said. He was still not happy with his lack of progression.

"We'll keep practicing until you get it," Matthew said.

"Jo'sha, what are you looking at?" Chance asked.

Jo'sha didn't respond.

"Jo'sha? What's wrong?" Matthew repeated.

"I don't know what it is. It just feels like we're being watched." Jo'sha said, looking back down the hill at the silent shadows in Bonder's Cemetery.

CHAPTER 22

Chance's father, grandfather, Uncle Carl, and two younger brothers, Jacoby and Cobyn, drove up early from North Carolina to attend the talent show and help with the preparation for the tailgate party. With more than five hours before the game, the Walkers staked out prime territory and set up a tent that promised to be one of the biggest and best outside the Georgia Central University football stadium.

Jacoby and Cobyn were putting the finishing touches on the tent. Olivia and Miss Vaughn were organizing the side dishes. Matthew, Chance, and Chance's father and uncle were preparing the meat for the grill. Jo'sha was hooking a microphone up to the Walker stereo system. Grandfather T.C. Walker sat back in an old rocker and enjoyed the autumn breeze.

"That was some mighty fine singing you did last night at the talent show, Joshua," T.C. said.

"Thank you, sir. I'm just glad I won. The competition was pretty tough," Jo'sha replied, amused that Chance's grandfather still hadn't gotten his name right after two days.

"What you gon' do with all that money, son?"

"I may just put it away for a rainy day," Jo'sha replied.

"Your mother and father taught you well," T.C. replied, standing up and walking toward Jo'sha at the microphone.

"My mother and father died when I was a little boy," Jo'sha shared.

"I am sorry to hear that. Seems like you turned out fine anyway," T.C. responded.

"Thank you, sir."

"Do you know any Sam Cooke?" T.C. asked.

Jo'sha smiled and began a medley of Sam Cooke tunes. Before long they were both singing in the microphone.

"You're in an awfully good mood. What's up?" Matthew asked.

"I have a surprise guest coming," Chance said, smiling.

"Who is it?" Matthew asked, raising an eyebrow and leaning in closer.

"Aspen. She was still a little angry that we had to run out of that party the other night. A girl like her isn't used to being ignored. I saw her on campus the other day and convinced her to come out. Just call it my magic touch," Chance whispered.

Matthew smiled, "Do the others know she is coming?"

"No. I figured I would surprise them. Jo'sha is going to flip. Who said an upperclassman wouldn't be interested in me?" Chance bragged.

"And a sorority girl," Matthew said.

"*And* a member of the homecoming court—maybe even the homecoming queen," Chance added.

"That's right! How does she have time to come to our cookout? Doesn't she have to get ready for the crowning at half time this evening?" Matthew asked.

"She can't stay long. She's coming through just long enough to meet the family. I hear she stands a good chance of winning."

"Good job," Matthew said, as he finished seasoning the hamburgers.

"Look at them," Chance said pointing to Jo'sha and his grandfather still singing on the microphone.

"I don't think he's come off his high since he won last night," Matthew said, referring to Jo'sha and his win at the homecoming talent show.

"He deserves it. He practiced hard and he did a good job. He got to meet Thursday Brownleigh, the CEO of U.S. Telesource, backstage last night too," Chance said.

"He says he may be able to get all of us backstage to meet Agonize tonight at the homecoming concert," Matthew added.

"You know we could have won that oratorical contest last night don't you? We had much more information than most of the groups, and with Wade's personal knowledge, your voice and research, and Jo'sha's charisma we could have taken it home easy," Chance said.

"Yeah, but it's best that we don't expose all of our knowledge about the university's beginnings," Matthew responded.

"What are you boys whispering about over here?" Chance's father asked, setting a pan of hotdogs down next to a grill.

"Nothing," Chance said.

"Matthew, I met your sister earlier, but are your parents coming?" he asked.

"Yes. They should be here within the hour," Matthew answered.

"Good. I understand your father was an Army man," he replied.

"Yes," Matthew replied.

"Who else is coming?"

"Wade's family has directions. They're staying in a hotel in downtown Atlanta but should be here soon. Wade spoke to them this morning. His father, mother and aunts will all be coming to homecoming. Chancellor Weatherspoon may even stop by to see his parents. They're old friends," Chance said proudly.

"Now which one is Wade?" he asked.

"Wade went to the airport to pick up his girlfriend and Jo'sha's dad," Chance said.

"Legal guardian," Matthew corrected.

"Same thing," Chance said.

"Where is Wade's girlfriend from?" Mr. Walker asked.

"Washington, D.C.," answered Chance.

"Why didn't she just fly down with his family from Baltimore?" he asked.

"Long story," Matthew interjected.

"I see," Mr. Walker responded.

"My girlfriend Tessa is coming too and she's bringing a friend," Matthew said quickly, hoping to prevent any further questions.

"We should have more than enough food," Uncle Carl said, joining the conversation.

"When are momma and 'em getting here?" Chance asked.

Matthew chuckled to himself. He noticed that Chance's accent was much more pronounced now that he was with his family. Their voices were all filled with solid base. They sounded alike and most certainly looked like family. It was obvious that all of the Walker men were molded from the same dark clay. Jacoby and Cobyn looked like perfectly crafted replicas of Chance only a little smaller.

"They left early. I spoke to them this morning. You know how your mother is. She's leading the caravan. Your grandmother, uncles, aunts, and older brother should all be here soon. Your mother has a special surprise for you, too." he said.

Chance smiled, assuming that his mother was bringing him another of her homemade banana puddings.

When Jo'sha and Grandfather T.C. finished singing they turned the radio on over the loud speaker. Other families, fraternities and organizations were beginning to set up their tailgate parties nearby as well. The radio announcer was congratulating Georgia Central University on its homecoming and 100th anniversary.

Atlanta! We will have Georgia Central's hottest alumni, Agonize, here with us in the studio this evening before the homecoming concert. So stay tuned—be the seventh caller when you hear Agonize's latest hit, Lick Lick, Juicy Juicy, and win free tickets to tonight's concert. And now breaking news—local police have been reevaluating each of the recent deaths attributed to the Atlanta Male Murderer, and are now saying that at least one of the deaths may be the result of a copycat killer. Additionally, there is speculation that the killer is profiling young, urban, homeless, small-framed African-American males. A large majority of the victims are under five foot seven, and less than one hundred fifty pounds. There have been no new reported deaths in recent weeks.

Matthew, Jo'sha, and Chance exchanged glances from across the yard. Jacoby shot off across the stadium parking lot, his arms upraised, ready to receive a spiral pass from Cobyn.

"Finish with that damn tent before ya'll start playing!" T.C. yelled from across the yard.

The boys laughed loudly, and trotted back over to the tent. They were amused by their grandfather—knowing that if their grandmother had been around she would have had something to say about his cursing.

Olivia and Miss Vaughn were at a table nearby preparing skewers of vegetables for the grill. As Olivia moved about the table, both Cobyn and Jacoby stole glances in her direction.

Just then Wade arrived with Quay. Quay was a chocolate-toned sister with natural hair pulled back tight into an Afro puff. Large gold hoop earrings complemented her beauty. Her high cheekbones and large dark eyes gave her an exotic look that could have placed her anywhere from Compton to the Caribbean. She wore a loose fitting red dress that drew an interesting contrast to her rich skin, and comfortable black shoes.

"Everyone, this is Quay," Wade said from the center of the backyard. He quickly scanned the area and was relieved to see that his parents had not yet arrived.

"Hello," Quay responded in a sweet B-more girl accent, switching her large red leather purse to her other shoulder.

Chance, Matthew and Jo'sha went over for more personal greetings. Wade was proud that his friends made such a big deal out of meeting her, and he could tell that she appreciated the attention.

"Are you alright? You aren't getting any emotional feedback from the crowd are you?" Matthew whispered to Wade.

"Don't worry! I'll be fine. We're surrounded by friends and family," Wade hissed back, annoyed that Matthew had even brought up the subject.

Uncle Carl began putting food on the grill as everyone began to mix and mingle.

"Where's Foster?" Jo'sha asked, looking around for his surrogate father.

"He stopped at the stadium entrance to use the restroom. He should be over in a minute. And don't worry, I didn't tell him anything about the talent show," Wade responded.

A few minutes later Jo'sha saw Foster walking across the parking lot. As Jo'sha watched him, he couldn't help but notice that Foster appeared much less composed and put together than he remembered.

"I am so sorry that I couldn't get here for the talent show last night," Foster said, walking toward Jo'sha with open arms.

Jo'sha hugged Foster and noticed that he seemed thinner.

"I see you, young brother," Foster said.

"And I you," Jo'sha returned.

"How did you do?" Foster asked.

"I won!" Jo'sha exclaimed, pulling a check from his back pocket. They both laughed and embraced again. Jo'sha recounted his performance note by note for Foster.

"Hey everyone, this is Jo'sha's father, Mr. David Foster," Chance announced.

Jo'sha smiled and led Foster around, introducing him to each of the other guests.

A short time later Tessa and Chandler came tipping up to the tent as if on eggshells, not wanting to get the soles of their designer heels dirty. Matthew rose reluctantly to meet them.

"This is quite some tent, Matthew," Tessa said.

"Yeah," Matthew said.

"I wasn't aware that you knew how to throw this type of party."

"Hey, T," Olivia yelled from across the yard.

Tessa managed a phony smile, and gave Olivia a delicate wave in response.

"Matthew, this is my roommate, Chandler Young. She's from Baltimore," Tessa announced.

"Hi. Maybe you know my friend Wade. He's from Baltimore too," Matthew said.

"Wade Graham IV? Is that the Wade you were talking about Tessa?" Chandler asked, clutching her Mikimoto pearl necklace.

"Yeah," Matthew said, already sensing the drama that Tessa and Chandler were capable of creating.

"Oh yes, I know him. Where *is* the elusive Mr. Graham? He hasn't called me since we got to Atlanta, and I've left him several messages. Our families are very close you know," Chandler boasted.

Matthew was barely listening as he carelessly led Tessa and Chandler towards Wade and Quay.

Almost as if on cue, Aspen Walker glided around the corner dressed in a black turtleneck, jeans, and black boots. Chance saw her and brightened up immediately. His father and uncle exchanged an uneasy glance and watched as Chance ran to greet Aspen.

"Glad you could make it," Chance said, smiling from ear to ear.

"Glad you invited me," Aspen said, giving Chance a firm hug.

Chance managed to brush her hand as they ended the embrace, causing Aspen to smile. "Come meet everyone," he said. "My father and grandfather are here already, and my mother will be here soon." Chance was too excited to notice that his father seemed just a little bit hesitant about meeting Aspen.

Wade looked up and saw Matthew, Tessa, and Chandler coming directly toward him. "Oh no," he whispered.

"What is it, Wade?" Quay asked, instantly noticing the change in his demeanor.

"Just an old friend," Wade said. Before he could explain any further, the trio was upon them.

"Wade! How have you been?" Chandler sang. "I hear you know my girl Tessa. It's a small, small world."

"Hi, Chandler," Wade responded dryly.

Chandler moved in to kiss Wade on his left cheek, but he stopped her just before she made contact and directed her attention toward Quay. "Chandler, this is my girlfriend, Quay."

Chandler stepped back and studied Quay from head to toe for a half second, doing a double take when she saw her rounded belly.

"Quay. What an interesting name," she said, continuing to give Quay the once over. "Did you meet Wade here at school?"

"No," Quay responded sarcastically.

"I have to go help with the food. I'll be right back," Matthew said, leaving hurriedly. He felt bad leaving Wade in the midst of what he was sure was an uncomfortable situation, but was thankful to be rid of Tessa.

Chandler continued to interrogate Quay. "So where are you from?"

"D.C.," Quay said icily. She was already growing irritated with Chandler's questions.

"Are you in school in D.C.?" Chandler pressed.

"I go to community college."

"Oh." Chandler looked over at Wade, clearly puzzled. Her look of disbelief vanished quickly, and was replaced by a knowing smirk. "I see you've been busy, Wade. Who knew? Look at you—you're filling out nicely, and your hair is longer. And I see you must have traded your glasses in for contact lenses."

"Yes," Wade answered edgily. He could tell that Quay was growing both angry and insecure, and he knew he needed to separate the two of them for his sake and theirs.

"I didn't realize that Wade was dating anyone," Chandler stated, returning her attention to Quay. "Have you met Mr. and Mrs. Graham yet?"

"No. I'll be meeting them today," Quay said defensively.

"Oh. I am sure they're looking forward to it," Chandler said, shooting a glance in Wade's direction.

Wade exhaled quietly. He was growing weary of Chandler's condescending banter and desperately wanted it to stop. Isadora and Roland Meredith's arrival was just the diversion Wade was praying for.

"Why did we have to park so damn far away? My feet are already sore," Isadora snapped.

"Issy, do you have to be so loud all of the time?" Roland asked.

He was struggling to carry the two apple pies that his wife had made, along with his guitar and two lawn chairs. He looked good, and was surprisingly still sober. Isadora walked slightly ahead of him, her short Afro complimenting her caramel features. She seemed to have lost a little weight, and looked nice in the floral sundress that she was wearing.

Matthew cringed as soon as he heard his mother's shrill voice. He was relieved when he saw Olivia go over to quiet them.

"Everyone, these are Matthew and my parents, Isadora and Roland Meredith," Olivia yelled.

Tessa exchanged quick pleasantries with Matthew's parents, who had always made her nervous, and then turned to watch Chandler continue to interrogate Quay.

Isadora immediately began to meet and mingle, but seemed to gravitate toward Miss Vaughn. The two women ended up discussing recipes, Matthew, his friends, the university, and local Atlanta gossip.

As the guests continued to arrive, the energy level started to escalate. Everyone was interacting, caught up in their own conversations. Tessa and Chandler were trying to determine if Quay was pregnant by Wade without actually coming out and asking. Roland and Uncle Carl were talking about the military, while T.C. and David Foster were trading philosophies. Jo'sha, Jacoby, and Cobyn were vying for Olivia's attention under the guise of talking about the Agonize concert. Matthew was watching Tessa and Chandler from a distance, keeping a watchful eye on Wade. Chance and Aspen were off to themselves, flirting and giggling. It seemed that the drama had tapered off until Mr. Walker stepped up cautiously to Chance and Aspen.

"Excuse me you two. Son, I need your help for a quick moment. Can you leave this pretty young lady and join me over here at the grill?" he asked.

"Dad, can't you get one of the twins? They're finished with the tent," Chance responded, still smiling at Aspen.

"Son, I need your help now," his father said more assertively, looking towards a group approaching from the distance.

Chance reluctantly excused himself and followed his father back toward the grill.

"Chance, about that surprise that I was telling you about earlier—"

Before he could continue the remainder of the Walker family arrived and swarmed into the tent greeting friends and strangers alike. The sudden increase in psychic energy gave Wade a small jolt.

Chance took off before his father could finish his sentence and ran over to hug his mother and grandmother. As he was expecting, his mother was holding a banana pudding in one hand and her purse in the other. Chance kissed her on the cheek and took the banana pudding from her.

"Dad told me that you had a surprise. I knew it was one of your banana puddings."

"This isn't the surprise," his mother responded with a smile. She stepped aside, revealing Sharon Battle, Chance's high school girlfriend. "Sharon said that you hadn't been calling her regularly, and I knew it had to be because you were so busy with school work— so I decided to bring her up to surprise you," she said, happily.

Chance's heart stopped and Wade felt his anxiety. Chandler and Quay were still snipping at each other and didn't know that trouble was brewing.

Aspen walked up to meet Chance's mother. Chance was speechless, and couldn't stop the train wreck that was about to happen.

"Hello, Mrs. Walker. My name is Aspen."

Mrs. Walker shook Aspen's hand slowly, immediately realizing what she had done.

"Hello, Chance. Who is this?" Sharon asked, tears forming in her eyes.

Aspen looked at Sharon and then glared at Chance in disbelief. "You have a *girlfriend*?" she asked angrily.

Chance was speechless. He didn't hear his grandmother's greeting. He didn't see his older brother smiling in triumph. He was simply at a loss for words.

Wade was doing his best to manage the surge of emotion that resulted from Quay and Chandler's tension, and Chance's growing anxiety. He thought he had things pretty much under control when he was hit with the hardest jolt yet. His mother and aunts paraded into the backyard followed closely by his father who was smoking an expensive cigar.

"Wade!" Victoria squealed, heading straight for her son.

Wade stood, hoping to meet her and his aunts before she reached his table, but he was too late.

"Oh, I see you invited Chandler," Josephine cackled, reaching for his cheek.

"Where are your glasses, Wade? And why is your hair so long?" Victoria asked, stepping back to take a look at her son. Though she couldn't put her finger on it, she sensed that something wasn't right.

Wade finished greeting his aunts and his father, and then stepped aside, revealing Quay. Chandler and Tessa looked on attentively.

"Mother, this is my girlfriend, Quay," Wade said, trying to appear confident.

"Hello," Quay said, extending her hand.

Victoria Graham looked at Quay in much the same way that Chandler had. "What did you say?" she whispered, ignoring Quay's gesture.

"This is my girlfriend, Quay," Wade repeated boldly.

"Is this young lady pregnant, Wade?" Josephine asked quickly, taking secret pleasure in stating the obvious.

Wade's head began to pound.

"Wade! Answer me!" Victoria screeched.

From a distance the Walker tent looked like the place to be, but in a matter of minutes things had spiraled out of control. Aspen had stormed off not bothering to listen to anything Chance had to say. Sharon had run off screaming toward the bathroom. Victoria fainted right there in the center of the tent, and Quay was weeping uncontrollably. In short, their first gathering had been a disaster.

Olivia leaned over and whispered in Matthew's ear. "And you were worried about Isadora!"

CHAPTER 23

Jo'sha and Foster sat at a small round table near the window in *Lucille's* restaurant over humus and grape leaves, in a world of their own, oblivious to the lunch hour gatherings and gossip.

"Quite an event," Foster said, aware that Jo'sha seemed troubled.

"Are you talking about the homecoming centennial celebration or that damned tailgate party?"

"Both," Foster answered.

"Yeah, I guess you're right."

"Care to recap it all for me. Maybe talking about it will help lighten your mood. I think there are some things that I missed."

Jo'sha took a deep breath. "The tailgate party was a chance for all of our friends and families to meet. It was supposed to be a good thing, but things seem to have blown up in our faces. Wade's mother wasn't ready to find out that she's going to be a grandmother. They didn't even know about his girlfriend, let alone the pregnancy. Chandler and Tessa terrorized the poor girl to tears even before his parents got there. Chance's mother brought his old girlfriend and that blew it for Chance with Aspen. All of that fainting and crying—it couldn't have been worse," Jo'sha said, picking over his grape leaves.

"Well you forgot to mention that you won the talent show and the prize money. You and your friends had an opportunity to meet Agonize and Thursday Brownleigh. And despite the pain that they went through, Chance and Wade had an opportunity to come clean with their loved ones—to cleanse themselves. The cookout ended with a pretty powerful prayer by Chance's uncle, and hopefully it will bring about some restoration for everybody. You met your objective. All of your families did meet. It was a great idea. And quite frankly,

I'm glad to see that you are caring about someone besides yourself," Foster stated.

"What do you mean?" Jo'sha asked.

"You care. You actually have friends. You're starting to connect with other people. I don't know how it happened so quickly, but I'm glad. You're no longer hiding from life behind sex and drugs. Your life is beginning to have texture and meaning. You're growing up," Foster answered.

"Yeah, I guess," Jo'sha smiled, suddenly reminded of how much he had missed Foster.

"Foster, have you ever found yourself liking someone that you weren't supposed to?" Jo'sha asked suddenly.

"What do you mean?"

"Someone that is kinda off limits."

"Are you referring to Matthew's sister, Olivia?"

"How did you know?"

"You would be surprised at what we old soldiers can see. T.C. and I had quite the view of the goings-on at the little tailgate party. We saw you all vying for her attention. She's a fine young woman too. Strong spirit." Foster said.

"And a great body," Jo'sha added. "But she's Matthew's sister and he's kind of protective. It's almost as if he thinks I'm not good enough for her," Jo'sha said.

"Well you probably haven't shown yourself to be a real gentleman with the ladies, but if your friendship with Matthew is real and your motives with his sister are pure then go for it," Foster advised.

A beautiful young Asian waitress, with a nametag that read Gretchen, came up and asked them if they needed more ginger root juice. Foster smiled politely, told her that they were just about ready to leave, and asked for the check. She smiled seductively and gave Foster a lingering look before sauntering away.

Foster politely acknowledged her glare with a glance and returned his attention to Jo'sha. "Jo'sha, if you remember nothing else that I have ever told you, remember to make your life matter," Foster continued.

"What are you talking about? You sound like you're giving your last will and testament. You ain't going nowhere," Jo'sha teased, hoping the levity in his tone would lighten the growing gravity of Foster's mood.

"I'm planning to take a little vacation," Foster said.

"Where?" Jo'sha asked hesitantly.

"I've always wanted to see the Ivory Coast of Africa. Maybe we can go back together this summer," Foster said, sounding more solemn than the words allowed.

"That would be nice," Jo'sha said, looking at Foster skeptically.

"There's something that I need to tell you."

"What is it?"

"I have prostate cancer and it's pretty serious," Foster said.

"What do you mean?" Jo'sha asked incredulously.

"Jo'sha, I'm not well, but I am okay with it," Foster said.

Jo'sha suddenly found himself fighting back tears. "This ain't right. You eat right. You work out. You're a good person. Is it—terminal?"

"Jo'sha, relax. Don't try to process it too quickly. Just deal with the here and now."

Jo'sha sat back and took a deep breath, suddenly realizing that the restaurant was filled with other people and their issues.

"Look, Jo'sha I need to go get some rest. I'm going back to the hotel to take a nap. I'd like for us to go to dinner tonight before I head back to Chicago tomorrow. We can talk more about it then. Here's an extra room key. I'm at the Swissotel in room 1017. Take the rental car and spend some time out with your friends—maybe even go see that pretty little girl you like." Foster reached into his wallet. "As a matter of fact, here's some spending change. Come back by the hotel at six and we can go out to dinner. Just drop me back off at the hotel and the car is yours for a few hours. It's an SUV," Foster winked.

Jo'sha realized that he had not seen Foster splurge on anything like a hotel or a rental car since he had known him. For him to be staying at the Swissotel and driving an SUV, spoke volumes about the seriousness of his condition. Jo'sha looked into Foster's eyes and for the first time Foster looked his age.

Foster paid the bill and gave the attractive young waitress a healthy tip. She gave him his receipt and her phone number. Jo'sha spent the ride back to the hotel, avoiding the real issue, choosing instead to ask Foster father-son questions about friendships and females. They exchanged uncomfortable goodbyes as Jo'sha dropped Foster off at the Swissotel. Jo'sha watched Foster enter the hotel hoping to see that familiar swagger, but he only saw a middle-aged man that he barely recognized walk away. Once Foster disappeared inside Jo'sha sat there for a moment. He really didn't have anywhere to go. Wade and Chance were spending time with their families and Matthew was working at the library. With nothing better to do, he decided to go to the mall, which happened to be adjacent to the hotel.

After passing several clothing shops adorned with flashy window dressing, Jo'sha opted to go to the music store. He hoped he'd find something to catch his interest. Jo'sha meandered into the record store and moved aimlessly from section to section. He was half way through the store when he heard a familiar voice.

"Is there anything that I can help you find, sir?"

Jo'sha turned and smiled when he saw Olivia standing in front of him. "I never knew that you worked in a record store. I used to work in a record store back home in Chicago," he said.

"Is there anything that I can help you find," Olivia repeated, discreetly motioning that her manager was just two aisles over.

"Oh yes. I'm looking for a gift for my roommate's sister," Jo'sha said, smiling.

Olivia guided him through the store, section by section, with her sugar and vanilla scented body oil creating a trail that he couldn't help but follow.

She licked her lips and moved in dangerously close while they perused the popular section. She brushed against him; he felt the full softness of her young womanhood while flipping through fusion. He smelled her lust, and heard the desire in her voice when they came upon the classics. Olivia recommended the collected works of Etta James, one of her personal favorites, but Jo'sha told her that it brought back a few bad memories. They finally decided on Sade's *Lover's Rock* compact disc. Olivia escorted him to the cash register and outside earshot of her boss.

"You seem bothered. Not your normal happy self. What's wrong? Is everything alright with you and Matthew?" Olivia asked.

"I just have a lot going on right now. The last few days have been pretty intense."

"Tell me about it," Olivia sighed heavily. "Why don't we go back to your room and listen to this new CD? I love Sade," she purred.

"What about your brother?" Jo'sha asked.

"He doesn't really care for her music," Olivia joked.

Jo'sha laughed. "What time do you get off work?"

"In about twenty minutes. We can take the train back to campus, okay?"

"No need. I have transportation," Jo'sha said proudly.

"Alright," Olivia said.

"I'll just hang out in the mall and then swing back by to pick you up in twenty minutes."

Jo'sha raced off to the florist and then the candy store, where he bought some lilies and candy. He was waiting at the door of the record store for Olivia when she got off work.

"The flowers are beautiful," Olivia said.

"I'm glad you like them," he responded, trying to hide his deep satisfaction.

"Lilies are my favorite. How did you know?"

"Just lucky I guess. I hope you like chocolate."

"I love it," Olivia said, taking the chocolates.

The ride back to campus was awkward for Jo'sha. As happy as he was to be with Olivia, he couldn't stop wondering what Matthew would think if he saw them together.

"Quite a bit of activity at the cookout, huh?" Olivia asked, finally breaking the silence.

"Didn't think you noticed, what with Chance's twin brothers all in your face," Jo'sha blurted. The words spilled out before he had a chance to realize what he was saying.

Olivia didn't respond. She simply smiled and continued looking out of the window.

When they reached the dorm Jo'sha rushed in, quickly picking up Matthew's dirty clothes and straightening the sheets on his bed.

"He is my brother, remember? I know how messy he is," Olivia chuckled.

"Oh, yeah," Jo'sha replied, wondering why he felt so nervous.

"Where did you get the compact disc player?" Olivia asked, setting the candy and flowers down on Jo'sha's desk.

"It belongs to Chance. I borrow it sometimes to record my sessions," Jo'sha answered.

"That's right. You are a musician aren't you," she said, admiringly.

"Something like that."

Olivia took the Sade CD from Jo'sha and popped it into the player. Jo'sha's nervousness and Olivia's last few inhibitions seemed to melt away from the heat of Sade's voice. Jo'sha turned off the lights, closed the blinds, and lit a small half burned candle on his desk. The seductive scent of patchouli filled the air. Olivia began to dance sensually and slowly in the center of the room, her moves putting the flickering flame to shame. Jo'sha removed his shoes and shirt and sat back on the bed, allowing her passion to warm him. She motioned for him to join her. The two of them danced intimately, and something inside of Jo'sha clicked, causing him to realize that he had never ever felt that way before.

"It's getting hot in here. We should stop," Olivia said breathlessly.

In all of his excitement, Jo'sha had literally turned up the heat in the room. Olivia lay down on Jo'sha's bed like a kitten, and Jo'sha curled up beside her as Sade and the flame continued to burn. She went to sleep in his arms, and for the first time in his life, Jo'sha felt necessary. And also for the first time it wasn't just about sex. He wanted Olivia, but more than just as a sexual partner. It was different with her. With previous relationships he had used sex as a means to define the relationship. No girl that he slept with on the first date could possibly be considered an ideal mate. For Jo'sha sex was a weapon—a weapon to protect his heart, but with Olivia he felt as though the pain might just be worth the risk.

With Olivia wrapped comfortably in his arms, Jo'sha fell into a deep and happy sleep. He dreamt of flowers that grew from seedlings to sprouts in a matter of seconds and then into full-grown flowers. He sat among them and admired their beauty until they shriveled and died as quickly as they had grown. He began to cry.

"What's wrong?" Olivia asked, wiping his tears.

Jo'sha remained quiet. He was embarrassed that she had seen his tears, and didn't know what to say. Olivia sensed his apprehension. She curled up beneath him and hugged him gently. They lay there motionless for a moment until Jo'sha realized that it was getting late.

"What time is it?"

"It's five o'clock."

"We have to go. Your brother gets off work at five, and I have to meet Foster at the Swissotel at six."

"Matthew is my brother, not my father," Olivia said, folding her arms.

"No matter, we still have to go," Jo'sha responded.

Olivia reluctantly gathered her flowers and candy before slipping on her shoes.

"I'll make it up to you. I promise," Jo'sha said, pausing long enough to catch her by her trim waist and kiss her softly on the neck before leaving the room. Before he closed the door Jo'sha checked the room to make sure there was no trace of Olivia's presence.

"My brother was right. You are quite the ladies' man," Olivia said once they got back in the car.

"Your brother doesn't know everything," Jo'sha answered curtly. Olivia's statement seemed to confirm his fear that Matthew didn't think he was good enough for her, and that bothered him.

"Don't get mad. He didn't mean anything by it. You're an attractive brother. I can see why the sisters are digging you," she said.

Jo'sha smiled, relieved that she wasn't judging him.

"Being with you makes things seem so simple. You have a gift for giving life new meaning. Everything is so much clearer when I'm with you," she explained.

"That's it!" Jo'sha exclaimed.

"What?" Olivia asked.

"Nothing. Can I call you later tonight?"

"Sure," she said, reaching into her purse for a pen.

"I already have the number. I got it off of the caller ID," Jo'sha admitted.

This time Olivia smiled.

"Listen, not a word of this to your brother, alright?" Jo'sha cautioned.

"He's not nearly as bad as you think. Sure he's a little protective, but he's my big brother, he's supposed to be."

"Have you ever had a boyfriend that he liked?" Jo'sha asked.

Olivia thought for a few minutes and then shook her head.

"I didn't think so," he confirmed. "So, not a word about this to Matthew, okay? Which way to your street?" he asked, continuing down toward Olivia's house.

"The second one on the right. Glad you found me today. Without you, I would have been on the train."

"Glad I could be of service."

Jo'sha pulled up in Olivia's driveway and waited for her to get out. Instead she sat there, looking at him, and then at the car door.

"Oh, right," Jo'sha said, jumping out quickly.

Olivia smiled and waited for him to come around and open her door. When she got out she gave him a kiss on his cheek and walked up to the house.

Jo'sha stared at her round hips as she sashayed away. From the corner of his eye he saw the living room curtain move. He looked and noticed Isadora peeking out of the window. Olivia's words rang in his head as he backed out of her driveway and drove down the street.

You have a gift to give life new meaning.

He clutched the red ankh around his neck and sped toward Foster's hotel. He knocked on the door several times before using the electronic key card that Foster had given him. The room was unusually cool, and completely dark. Nancy Wilson was playing on the radio. Jo'sha closed the door gently and turned on the light in the bathroom so he could see. Rows of pill bottles lined the bathroom counter like little wooden soldiers. Foster lay motionless in the oversized bed amongst a mound of pillows. Jo'sha took a deep breath and entered slowly.

"Foster," he said softly.

There was no answer. Jo'sha went to the edge of the bed and knelt close enough to hear Foster's shallow breathing, and in the cool, dark, melancholy room, he began to pray. Foster was oblivious to his presence. After several minutes of praying, Jo'sha slowly removed the ankh from his neck and slipped it over Foster's head and let it rest on his chest.

Instantly blood rushed to Jo'sha's head and his temples began to pound. He tried to scream but his breaths were shallow and raspy. His left forearm felt like it was on fire, and his skin began to sizzle and wrinkle in the place where his burn mark had been. He fell to the floor, grasping desperately for something to hold onto, but instead knocked the bed lamp to the floor. Foster woke to see Jo'sha writhing helplessly.

CHAPTER 24

Matthew rushed back to his dorm with all of the information that he had collected on Dr. Smith. He hoped that Jo'sha wasn't there so that he could spread out his materials and concentrate. He had spent most of his afternoon at work researching Dr. Smith, only to find contradictory fact after fact. His gut told him that something just wasn't right about their mysterious professor. Sade serenaded Matthew when he entered the dark dorm room, the compact disc player still on repeat play. Matthew turned the disc player off and turned on all of the lights. He could tell from the warm candle that Jo'sha hadn't been gone too long.

Matthew was spreading all of his information out on the floor, when he felt a sharp and sudden pain at the base of his skull. He sat up to clear his head and after several minutes, the pain subsided to a low dull ache. He assumed that the pain stemmed from a headache, and figured he would get an aspirin from Wade or Chance's well-stocked medicine kit when they returned.

Disregarding the nagging ache, Matthew began to study the information he'd gathered. He had found several biographies of Dr. Smith with detailed endings, but no clear beginnings. Generations of his forefathers were similarly chronicled in academic journals and research studies. Each seemed to be closely tied to academia and the study of history. Matthew rifled through article after article, picture after picture until he found one photograph that stopped him cold. It was a picture of a man that looked surprisingly like a young Dr. Smith, probably his grandfather, standing beside the corpse of a black man who had been burned at a stake.

Matthew rushed to the suite phone to call Chance and Wade on their cell phones. Before he could begin dialing, the phone rang.

"Matthew?"

"Yes, this is Matthew," he responded.

"This is Foster. Something terrible has happened. I'm at the hospital near campus with Jo'sha. He passed out and we don't know what's wrong with him. He's unconscious, his skin is charred in several places, and he has a terrible fever. The doctor wants to know if you've noticed anything like this before. They think it might be an allergic reaction to something. Can you get down to the hospital and meet me in the main lobby? Do you—"

"We'll be there in a minute," Matthew said, slamming the phone down before Foster could finish his next sentence. Matthew picked the phone back up and frantically dialed his friends' phone numbers.

∞

There was tension amongst the Walker clan. Chance was still angry with his mother, who had taken it upon herself to bring his ex-girlfriend to the tailgate party. His father had hoped that a family dinner at the local buffet would smooth things over, but Chance was still furious. His father had already warned him about being so rude to his mother, after he'd snapped at her several times over dinner.

"Why are you so quiet?" she asked.

"I have a headache all of a sudden," Chance barked, his tone nearly bringing his mother to tears.

Chance's entire family and poor Sharon sat at the table in awkward silence until Chance's cell phone rang and Matthew gave him a good reason to leave.

"Jo'sha is in the hospital. I have to go," Chance said.

"Wait, honey, we'll go with you. We can take you," his mother suggested.

"I think I've had enough help," he said sarcastically. He excused himself and headed out of the restaurant toward the train to the hospital.

On the other side of town Wade found himself in a similar situation with his family. Wade, his mother, his aunts, his father, and Quay sat in a corner table of Atlanta's upscale *Blue Pointe* restaurant bathed in the same awkward silence of adolescent assertion that had washed over Chance's family.

"You seem so different. Your hair is so long and you don't wear your glasses anymore. All of these new friends from *everywhere* and then this situation, it's almost like we don't even know you," his Aunt Josephine said, piercing the silence with her shrill, stabbing soprano and acting as if Quay wasn't even sitting at the other end of the table. His mother remained quiet, trying hard to fight back the tears of betrayal, anger, embarrassment, and hurt.

"Josephine. You're not helping," Grace admonished.

Wade's father smiled politely at Quay. Her eyes reminded him of a young lady that he had known once in his own youth. Together at the far end of the table, Judge Graham and Quay began to exchange pleasantries, which eventually turned into a more meaningful conversation about politics. Judge Graham was pleasantly surprised by her depth.

"All I would like to know is why didn't you tell us?" Victoria finally blurted out.

"Because I knew you would act just like this!" Wade shot back.

"Well it's obviously too late to do anything about it now," Josephine said snidely.

"Anything like what? Abortion? Is that what you're suggesting, Aunt Josie?" Wade said hotly, suddenly feeling a sharp pain at the base of his skull.

"I was just giving you the same counsel that I would give my own William if he found himself in this same unfortunate situation. I think parent and child communication is key in situations like this," Josephine said with feigned sympathy.

"Well you don't have to worry about something like this happening to William because he likes boys. All that drama with girls was just a cover. You see I'm not the only one that wants you all out of his business or didn't he *communicate* that to you?" Wade snapped, feeling the sharp pain at the base of his neck reduce to a dull ache.

Josephine gasped. Victoria began to weep again and Grace looked around the restaurant to make sure that there was no one there who could report the spectacle. At the other end of the table Quay and his father who had actually been enjoying each other's company became quiet. In the sudden silence Wade's phone rang. He answered it and after a few seconds hung up quickly.

"That was Matthew. Jo'sha's been hurt and he's at the hospital. We'll have to talk about this later. Have a safe trip back to Maryland," he said dismissively. "Father, excuse us. Quay let's go."

Quay gathered her things, and made a point of saying goodbye to each of them. She mouthed a heart felt, *thank you* to Judge Graham and tipped quickly after Wade who was halfway out of the door by the time she had finished saying her goodbyes.

∞

Wade was the last one to arrive at the hospital.

"What took you so long?" Chance asked.

"I took Quay back to our room to rest. Dinner with my family wore her out."

"Let's go find Foster," Matthew said, already striding toward the main reception desk.

"We're here to see a Jo'sha Imarah," Matthew informed the inattentive receptionist.

"How do you spell that?" she asked.

"I-M-A-R-A-H. Imarah," Matthew said.

"Do you know when he arrived?" she asked.

"Maybe two or three hours ago," Matthew said.

"Well he isn't showing up in our system," she responded, clicking computer keys with one hand and holding her mobile phone in the other.

"Well find him," Wade snapped.

She rolled her eyes and looked from Matthew to Wade and then back to Matthew again. "Are you related to Mr. Imarah?" she asked.

"Well, no," Matthew said.

"Then you'll have to wait until visiting hours anyway," she challenged.

Just then Foster came barreling out of the elevator with a doctor following closely behind him. "This is Dr. Baptiste. He's in charge here," Foster said.

"I normally don't get involved with walk-in patients, but this case seems so rare. Do you boys know if Jo'sha has had any episodes like this before?"

"No," Matthew said, taking the lead.

"Do you know if he's allergic to anything?" Dr. Baptiste asked.

"Umm, no," Matthew answered again.

"Are any of you aware of any type of substance abuse?"

They all paused for a moment before Wade finally answered, "He does smoke marijuana."

The rest of them remained silent; slightly embarrassed to reveal that detail about their friend.

"Not good, but still not capable of causing this type of reaction," Dr. Baptiste answered.

"Does he do any other types of street drugs?" Dr. Baptiste asked turning to Wade.

"Not to my knowledge," Wade answered.

Foster was becoming more nervous and obviously more concerned. It was when he began pacing and rubbing his head that Matthew noticed the red ankh around his neck.

"What is that?" Matthew asked, pulling Foster over to a corner.

"What? This thing?" Foster asked, pulling at the ankh. "Just a trinket that Jo'sha must have given me. It was around my neck when I woke up this afternoon. Why?" Foster asked, sensing the concern in Matthew's face.

Matthew motioned for Foster to follow him up the hallway out of earshot of the others. "That is not just a trinket."

"What is it?" Foster whispered.

"We should get out of here," Matthew instructed.

"What about Jo'sha?" Foster asked.

"You won't be able to help until I can explain this to you and this is not the place. Trust me. The sooner you let me—let us, explain, the sooner we can help Jo'sha."

Wade could feel the emotional pall over the hospital. Worry, anxiety, fear, and anger blended with occasional blotches of joy and hope. His head started to swim and Dr. Baptiste noticed that he seemed to be getting paler and lighter on his feet. Matthew rushed back toward Wade, grabbed his arm and motioned for Chance to follow.

"The boys are pretty upset. I should go talk to them," Foster said to Dr. Baptiste.

Foster rushed off after them. They walked toward the hospital parking lot and kept going until they reached a small grove of trees at the end of the lot.

"Now what is this all about, Matthew?" Foster asked anxiously.

"That ankh around your neck is not just some trinket that Jo'sha gave you," Matthew said.

Wade and Chance noticed the red ankh around Foster's neck and began to shake their heads.

"What is it?" Foster asked.

"It's the gift of life," Matthew said.

"And maybe death," Wade added.

"These ankhs have the ability to heal, but when we take them off they cause advanced degeneration of whatever ailed us before we put them on. I was diagnosed with cancer, Wade had poor vision, Chance used to have asthma, and Jo'sha used to have that burn mark on his arm. We put on these ankhs and we were all healed of things that we knew about and probably things that we didn't. But it comes with a price. Removing them causes a greater and opposite reaction," Matthew explained.

"Is this real? How did you get them?" Foster asked, realizing that he no longer felt tired or drained and was experiencing a level of vigor that he hadn't noticed since his teens.

Matthew looked at Chance and then Wade for approval.

"We have to tell him. Jo'sha's life hangs in the balance," Chance said.

Matthew explained how they got the ankhs and why they had chosen not to share the news with anyone. He shared explicit details of the library office break in, the death of Victor Greene, and the link to the Atlanta Male Murders. He even explained his suspicions about Dr. Smith. Foster asked question after question until he was absolutely clear, without the disapproving and condescending tone offered by most adults.

"What I can't figure out is why Jo'sha would have taken it off and given it to you. He was there when I took my ankh off and lost my sight," Wade wondered aloud.

"I have cancer. I just told him earlier today that I have cancer," Foster said.

"Terminal?" Matthew asked, surprising Chance and Wade with his candidness.

"Yes."

"So now what do we do?" Chance asked.

"We only have one choice. Come on. We don't have much time," Foster said.

CHAPTER 25

By the time Jo'sha finally woke up Foster had died, and his remains had been cremated. For nearly three and a half weeks Jo'sha's status remained touch and go. The mysterious illness had the doctors baffled and his friends gravely concerned. Each of them took turns sitting by Jo'sha's bedside and praying for him. Olivia cared for his locks while the others read excerpts from Octavia Butler books. From time to time Quay would sing old Donnie Hathaway songs softening the mood and entertaining the hosts of angels that were watching over Jo'sha. Though Olivia and Quay had no idea what had caused his strange illness their prayers were no less fervent. Matthew insisted that they not know. The only other person that they had told about the ankhs was Foster and he had taken their secret with him to his grave.

As soon as they discovered the cause of Jo'sha's sudden decline, Foster, Matthew, Chance and Wade secretly placed the ruby ankh back around Jo'sha's neck. They had expected it to immediately restore him and reverse the condition that had developed, but the weeks began to pass, and it had taken longer than any of them had hoped for the ankh to regenerate his body. In contrast, Foster's cancer returned with a vengeance shortly after he removed the ankh. His death was quick but painful. He died in the hospital in Atlanta, insisting that he be near Jo'sha for as long as possible. When the time came, Chance's family assisted him in making the arrangements for his body to be cremated and flown back to Chicago for his memorial service.

Foster spent his last days on earth reviewing his will, calling dear friends to say his final goodbyes, listening to Nancy Wilson, hoping all the while that Jo'sha would awake before his demise.

The doctors had started to see steady improvements, save consciousness, from the moment that Matthew had placed the ankh back around Jo'sha's neck, but none of the medical staff had any idea what caused the miraculous turnaround. He went from low blood pressure, burn marks, convulsions and fevers, to stable vital signs overnight. One nurse noticed the ankh and attempted to remove the necklace, but Chance's begging and pleading convinced her to leave it even though it was against hospital policy.

It was early Saturday morning and Jo'sha was still caught in a state of unconsciousness. Matthew and Chance sat watching over him.

"I thought Quay was staying with us a little longer," Matthew said.

"She already stayed longer than she planned. She said she had some business back home that she had to get back to. She had an early morning flight back to Washington. Wade should be back from the airport any minute. Maybe now we can stop trying to hide her from Ronnie and I can quit sleeping in Jo'sha's bed," Chance chuckled.

"She's a nice girl," Matthew said. "It's a shame Wade's mother and aunts stopped speaking to him."

"Yeah. At least his dad is still paying for his education," Chance sighed.

"I guess money doesn't solve all of your problems," Matthew thought out loud.

Chance looked back down at his calculus book while Matthew continued to pour over his facts on Dr. Smith. He was now obsessed with what he saw as the doctor's increasingly incomplete history.

About half an hour later the door creaked open slowly and Wade walked in. He looked a mess, obviously sad that Quay had decided to return to Baltimore, and equally overwhelmed by the steady state of depression that rested over the hospital.

"How is he?" he asked.

"All of the physical marks are completely gone and his vital signs are all stable," Matthew answered, having spoken to Dr. Baptiste several times about Jo'sha's condition.

"It's like he's asleep and just won't wake up," Chance added.

Wade sat down in the chair by the window where he always sat and began meditating, a practice that had become essential for his own peace of mind. Matthew and Chance knew that he needed silence, so they returned their attention to their work.

Jo'sha's claim to consciousness was controlled and slow. They felt his return and sensed his awakening thanks to Matthew's exercises and drills.

"I see you," Chance said softly.

"And I you," Jo'sha responded in a feeble voice. "Come closer," he requested.

All three of them quietly moved closer to the bed as they had many times before. Jo'sha responded to their presence with an increase in energy and a smile. He looked at them, closed his eyes, and then blinked open quickly.

"Foster," he finally whispered.

None of them spoke right away. Both Wade and Chance instinctively looked to Matthew.

"Foster! Foster!" Jo'sha called, struggling to sit up. This time his voice was much louder.

"Jo'sha, calm down," Matthew said assertively.

"Where is Foster?" he asked again. He searched the eyes of each of his friends, and after several seconds of silence he knew.

He started to weep, then cry, and then sob uncontrollably. Wade went to him and hugged him, and in his empathy he siphoned off some of the pain. They mourned together in the early morning light. Chance fought back tears, and Matthew stood looking out of the window searching for an intellectual solution to an emotional situation.

An hour later, the nurse came in for her morning check and found Jo'sha sitting up in the bed. The entire nursing staff had grown fond of Jo'sha's friends and they were as invested in his case as strangers could be. The nurse shrieked and rushed out of the room. She came back in minutes with the attending physician and two more nurses. They gave Jo'sha a complete physical, took blood samples for testing, and checked and rechecked his temperature and blood pressure.

"Do you think he's well enough to leave?" Chance asked.

"No. We should keep him here for observation. I'm sure that Dr. Baptiste will want to check him also. He should be in later today," the young doctor advised.

After forty more minutes of poking and prodding, the medical staff left, promising to return with an extra special lunch.

"He's a vegetarian," Wade informed them as they left the room still speculating about Jo'sha's case.

"I only wanted to help him. I loved him. I never thought it would come to this," Jo'sha whispered.

"We know that. And he knew that," Matthew said.

"Did he—"

"Yes," Matthew interjected. "He knew about the ankhs. We had to tell him. He also knew that by giving it back to you he was probably ending his own life."

"What I did was stupid," Jo'sha said.

"He was dying anyway," Matthew said, sounding more callous than he had intended.

"Foster was a good man. He was everything that you said he was. We learned a lot from him in the short time that we spent with him. He made the very best of the situation," Wade said quietly, shooting Matthew a hostile look.

"Here's a copy of his will, and the lawyer's name in Chicago. Wade's father recommended him. He left just about everything to you. Seems he didn't have a large family either. The money from the sale of his house in Chicago will be put in a trust fund for you when you graduate. He settled all of his bills, liquidated his other assets, and left a few gifts for you too. It is all here in this videotape," Matthew said, pulling a VHS from his old tattered book bag.

Another tear streaked down Jo'sha's cheek.

"What about all of his things?"

"Some he sold. Some he had sent to people who needed them. Most of the more valuable things he had shipped here for you. My dad made sure that all of the legal stuff was in order," Wade answered.

"His body?" Jo'sha whispered.

"Cremated and shipped back to Chicago for a memorial service," Chance answered.

"Where are the ashes now?"

"Foster wanted you to have them. They were shipped back here after the memorial service in Chicago. He said that you would know what to do with them. It's all in his will and this videotape. He mentioned something about going to Africa," Matthew answered.

Jo'sha wept quietly, each answer to his questions stabbing deeper and deeper into his soul.

Chance shook his head at Matthew's seeming insensitivity.

"Jo'sha, you need to get some rest. Give me the videotape. You can look at it later." He stared pointedly at Matthew, demanding with his gaze that the subject be dropped.

"I don't want to be alone," Jo'sha whispered, running his hand through his locks. "Who's been in my hair?" he asked, feeling the moisturizing effects of the oil.

"Olivia. She massaged your scalp, oiled your locks, and left a silk pillow case," Matthew said.

Jo'sha smiled genuinely. The thought of Olivia's presence and care touched him deeply. "What about my classes?" he asked.

"I met with all of your instructors, explained that your father had passed and got your assignments. I've been doing most of your homework and turning it in for you," Matthew said.

"What about my tests? How will I take my exams if I don't know the material?"

"I tried to tell him," Wade said. He had already suggested that it wasn't a good idea when Matthew first started turning in the assignments.

"Don't worry. I'll tutor you in all of your classes. You haven't really missed that much," Matthew defended.

Jo'sha shrugged it off. He was too spent to think, and just hoped that Matthew had thought of all of the consequences.

"Look at you," Jo'sha said, taking notice of Wade's new appearance.

"You like?"

"Do your thing, Bruh! I'm feeling it," Jo'sha responded, sounding much happier than he was.

"Thanks. Quay likes it too. Wasn't a big hit with my family though," Wade said remorsefully.

"And you're growing muscles. I can tell that you're working out. You brothers still been hitting the gym, huh?" he noted.

"We've been at it. When we weren't in here or in class, we were at the gym. Helped us relieve some stress," Chance said.

"You all came by to check on me?" Jo'sha asked.

"Of course we did, every available moment. Quay, Olivia, all of us were here," Wade said.

"Thanks."

Jo'sha was quiet for a moment, contemplating his friends' dedication to him. He suddenly realized that they were the closest thing that he had to family now.

"We had to," Matthew said.

"You really didn't. I know you all have things going on too," Jo'sha responded.

"No. We really had to. You see we're all connected now. The day you took the ankh off we all felt it. We sensed your pain. That's how we knew you were getting better. Late at night before visiting hours were over, we would stand by your bed and just meditate. We could tell it was making a difference," Matthew said.

"What about Foster?" Jo'sha asked.

"Even though he only had the ankh on for a short time, we felt it when he took it off too. The headaches and nausea got pretty bad. It was rough for all of us until he finally died," Matthew said.

"Does anyone else know?" Jo'sha asked.

"Not a soul. Foster was the first and last person besides us to know," Matthew said.

"And your ankhs?" Jo'sha continued.

"I've been charting our powers. Wade seems to be making the most progress in handling other people's emotions. He can feel what other people are feeling and he is even learning to manage and manipulate those emotions. Chance continues to get stronger and stronger physically. We just have to get him to quit showing off in the gym. As for his power to manipulate earth—it's still not as reliable as the rest of ours. Nothing a bit more practice shouldn't be able to fix," Matthew said, starring at Chance, who seemed to be ignoring him.

"Did he get better before he—died?" Jo'sha swallowed hard, fighting back his emotions. He was tired of crying.

"As long as he wore the ankh he was fine—"

He made the most of it," Wade interjected before Matthew could say something insensitive.

"How is Quay?" Jo'sha asked, changing the subject.

"Fine," Wade said smiling. "My mother and aunts aren't too happy, but it's my life. My dad, who I never really had much of a relationship with before now, has been the coolest of all. I always thought he didn't really care much for me, but I think we are actually getting closer as a result of all of this."

"Glad to hear it. She seems like a cool sister," Jo'sha said, repositioning in the bed.

"Any luck with Ms. Georgia Central?" Jo'sha asked, looking at Chance.

Chance shook his head and frowned.

"I think I know who is responsible for the Atlanta Male Murders," Matthew blurted out. He was looking for an opportunity to discuss his latest obsession, Dr. Smith.

Chance and Wade sighed, having heard the story several times before.

"Who?" Jo'sha asked.

"I think it's Dr. Smith."

The nurse knocked on the door and entered before waiting for a response. She had an extra large plate of vegetables and fruit. "We had to get permission, but we had them special ordered from Lucille's for you," she whispered.

Jo'sha smiled, sat up, and began eating. Matthew continued where he had left off as soon as the nurse left.

"I've found all of these pictures of his ancestors. I even found a picture of one of Dr. Smith's relatives at a lynching in 1895."

"That isn't how serial killing works. It isn't something that's passed down from generation to generation," Wade challenged.

"Maybe, but I still think it's pretty odd. Not to mention the fact that the murders didn't start until he came to Atlanta to teach. And he has all of these books about African-American hangings and church burnings in his office."

"Still pretty unlikely," Wade said skeptically.

"Well someone is doing it," Matthew responded, unwilling to rule Dr. Smith out.

"How long was I out?" Jo'sha asked thoughtfully.

"Damn near a month," Chance answered.

"Oh."

"The good news is that there haven't been anymore murders," Matthew continued.

"Whatever," Chance said, rolling his eyes.

"Do you think he knows you're on to him?" Jo'sha asked.

"I think he thinks Matthew is crazy," said Wade. "He sits there in Dr. Smith's class and just stares at him."

"But haven't you noticed how he acts when he's around us?" Matthew asked.

"Yeah. Like he thinks we're all crazy, and that's probably because we all hang around you," Chance commented.

"Why else would he be so weird around us?" Matthew asked.

"So what are you going to do now? Tell the authorities?" Jo'sha asked, humoring his roommate, as well as keeping himself distracted.

"No. They wouldn't believe us and we don't want to draw any more attention. This whole thing with you and Foster was a close enough call as it is."

"You just don't know when the hell to shut up, do you?" Wade snapped. He was about at the end of his rope with Matthew's continued lack of empathy for Jo'sha's feelings.

"What about the fraternity idea?" Jo'sha asked, changing the subject yet again.

"What about it?" Matthew asked, irritated that Wade had put him on blast, and that no one wanted to discuss his theory.

"Are we still going to do it?"

"We haven't really thought about it with everything that's been going on," Chance said.

"Well I think we still should."

"I still like the idea. Maybe Aspen will notice me then."

"Sounds good to me," Wade said. "No more trying to please my family. I was kind of interested before. Now I want to do it—"

"To spite your family?" Matthew finished.

"No. I want to do it for me. As long as it doesn't interfere with me, Quay and the baby, then I'm in," Wade responded.

"So how about you, Meredith? This is really important to me now. I wanna leave a mark. I want to do things that matter. This could be it, but I need your help. I need all of you to help," Jo'sha stressed.

"I tell you what. If you three help me prove that Dr. Smith has something to do with the Atlanta Male Murders, then I'll help with the fraternity," Matthew agreed.

CHAPTER 26

Jo'sha sat in his dorm room still not quite used to all of the things, old and new, that Foster had left to him. Jo'sha and Matthew's room now rivaled Chance and Wade's for the number of new electronic gadgets. Matthew and Jo'sha's room differed, however, in that it also had quite a few antique items as well. A beautiful antique oil painting of a young, dark-skinned woman by a river and several old musical instruments covered the once bare walls, creating an interesting juxtaposition to the platinum and black entertainment equipment. Jo'sha also bought several new items for him and Matthew with his new inheritance. Matthew refused to wear many of the new clothes that Jo'sha bought, but he carried the new book bag everywhere he went.

Jo'sha sat on his crisp, new amber comforter with a brand new diary and pen in hand. He had spent the last three weeks catching up on his course work and submitting the necessary paperwork to have Omega Tau recognized as an official campus organization. His schedule and head had cleared enough for him to begin to document his recurring dreams and visions. His most recent episode with Foster had taught him not to take his new powers or life for granted. He lit two cinnamon and myrrh incenses, lay back and relaxed and remembered. When he was satisfied that he had recounted every detail of every dream or vision, he began to write, documenting the stories of the stones and then the flowers. He wrote feverishly for twenty minutes before stopping. When he finished, he read and reread each line, searching between each of them for the hidden meaning.

Jo'sha was interrupted by a succession of soft raps at the door. He looked at the shiny new alarm clock on his desk and saw that it was 7:21 p.m. Matthew wasn't scheduled off work until nine, and would have probably used his key. Jo'sha looked through the peephole and didn't see anyone so he opened the door slowly.

"Sup, baby," Olivia exclaimed, jumping from the hallway and into his arms. She had her hair pulled back into a curly black ponytail with large hoop earrings. She wore a light blue baby doll sweat suit that showed all of her curves, and new white sneakers with light blue accenting stripes.

"Heeyyyyy!" Jo'sha responded, holding her at a distance while looking up and down the hallway to see if anyone had seen them.

"Is that how you're greeting me now?" Olivia asked, putting her hand on her hip.

"You know we have to keep this on the low. At least until I figure out a way to tell your brother," Jo'sha said, slightly irritated by Olivia's lack of discretion.

Olivia gently pushed Jo'sha into the room and locked the door behind her.

"Quit worrying. Matthew doesn't get off of work until nine. We have a little bit of time," she said, walking over to Jo'sha's new stereo system and putting in the Sade CD.

"I *was* busy you know," Jo'sha said, only half serious.

"Too busy for this?" Olivia asked, unzipping her top revealing round ample breasts.

"The doctor says that I should still take it easy," he grinned.

Olivia pressed her body against his and kissed him. Their passion ignited, as does only the ardor of young lovers. Before Sade finished her second song, they were both completely naked atop Jo'sha's new comforter. Their foreplay was fierce and intense.

"Wait," Jo'sha whispered, as he rushed to his dresser to get two large condoms.

Olivia lay back on the bed admiring every inch of his hard male form. By the time he got back to the bed she was hard and soft in all of the right places.

Jo'sha had just begun kissing her when he heard three knocks on the door.

"Dammit! That's Wade," Jo'sha whispered.

"How do you know?" Olivia asked.

"Umm, I can tell by his knock," Jo'sha lied, having recently learned to sense Wade, Matthew, and Chance's individual signatures.

"Are you going to answer it?"

"Hell no! Be quiet," Jo'sha whispered, holding his hand over her mouth.

Olivia giggled and seductively licked his palms.

"Jo'sha. I know you're in the room 'cause I can smell the incense burning and I can hear your stereo. I guess you're *busy*. Remember what Ronnie said about burning incense in the dorm room and don't forget that we have to go to Ms. Vaughn's tonight,"

Jo'sha remained quiet. After several more seconds of silence, he could hear Wade walking away.

Olivia bit his hand.

"Ouch," he whispered.

Olivia laughed and began kissing his neck.

"What is this?" she asked.

"What?" Jo'sha asked, still distracted by Olivia's incredibly soft body.

"This charm. It looks like the one I saw on Matthew. Is it his?" Olivia continued, grabbing the ruby ankh in her small hand. Jo'sha grabbed her hand and gently released her grip on the ankh.

"No. Foster gave them to us," Jo'sha lied.

"Oh," Olivia said, trying to remember when she had seen Matthew's necklace.

Jo'sha held her tight and close.

"Can I wear it?" she asked.

"Umm, it has sentimental value," Jo'sha stuttered, still exploring her body.

"Oh," Olivia said, rising to get her clothes.

"Olivia, please," Jo'sha begged, clutching her naked body as she attempted to get up from the bed.

"I thought I was important to you. I can't believe that I was actually going to sleep with you," Olivia said, pouting, but willingly remaining bound by Jo'sha's arms.

"Liv, I've been through a lot lately. You know that. Just be patient with me," Jo'sha said, looking into her eyes.

"You know what? Maybe you're right. Maybe it's too soon for us to sleep together," Olivia sighed.

"Maybe so," Jo'sha responded, rubbing her back while his breath touched her neck and his locks tickled her shoulders.

"You keeping a diary now?" Olivia asked, reaching for Jo'sha's diary.

"Yeah," Jo'sha said, snatching it just before she could put her hand on it.

"Is there anything it in about me?"

"Not yet," Jo'sha answered.

Olivia seemed disappointed and jumped up from the bed before Jo'sha could grab her this time.

"How did you get in the dorm anyway?" Jo'sha asked, standing up and putting on his clothes.

"I know the security guard. His sister is on the cheer squad with me," Olivia said with a smile.

Jo'sha blew out the incense and lay back on his bed. He looked over at Olivia. She smiled back at him and lay down on Matthew's bed in an identical pose, her naked body forming a beautiful composition of curves and lines unlike any Jo'sha had ever seen.

"Jo'sha, it feels like there's something you're not telling me."

"What do you mean?"

"Seems like you're holding back from me. Like you and Matthew are up to something. What's going on with you guys? And why do you spend so much time at Miss Vaughn's house in Fayetteville? What's that about?" Olivia asked, sounding more like a prosecuting attorney than a potential girlfriend.

"You're just imagining things. Miss Vaughn has been really good to your brother. Having us help her fix up the old house is his way of repaying her?" Jo'sha lied.

"Great for Matthew and Miss Vaughn, but what do the rest of you get out of it? I know Wade isn't rushing to do yard work," she said, looking at him doubtfully.

"You ask way too many questions."

Jo'sha stood up and walked over to her. When he got to the bed he knelt down and kissed her softly, caressing her back and bottom.

"I am not crazy, Jo'sha," Olivia said, rejecting his touch and gathering her clothes.

"If I tell you, then you have to promise not to tell anyone that I told you. Especially your brother," Jo'sha said.

Olivia stopped in her tracks. "I promise," she said.

"We're going to start a fraternity, and it's going to be hot!" Jo'sha exclaimed, excited to tell someone about the fraternity, and glad that he was diverting Olivia's attention.

"Really? That sounds exciting. Who's going to be in it?"

"Me, Matthew, Wade, and Chance. Wanna see the fraternity letters and colors," Jo'sha asked proudly.

"Sure," Olivia said, glad that Jo'sha was opening up to her.

Jo'sha showed her everything that he had been doing for Omega Tau and she loved it. He shared select portions of the fraternity's history, pictures of the founders and their letters and colors. He was careful not to tell her anything about the ankhs' connection or how they had acquired them. When he was finished, he decided that it was time for her to leave.

"Now you can't tell anyone 'cause we want to surprise the entire campus."

"I know, I know."

Jo'sha looked at the alarm clock. As much as he enjoyed her company, he knew he needed to hurry her along. He also knew she wouldn't be happy about him rushing her off. "It is getting late, Liv," he said tentatively.

"Arrgh! Not that again. I know the drill. 'Olivia, you have to go before Matthew gets here,'" she mocked.

Jo'sha grabbed Olivia and pulled her to him. They kissed and caressed for ten more minutes before he finally walked her to the door.

"You aren't going to walk me downstairs?" she asked, frowning at him.

"It's bad enough that you're in here. We don't need to have someone in the dorm tell Matthew that we were together." Jo'sha explained.

"You are way too paranoid," she said, snatching the doorknob and yanking the door open.

Wade was propped in the doorway of his room across the hall with his arms crossed. Olivia laughed out loud and then quickly put her hand over her mouth. Jo'sha nervously adjusted his clothing.

"Hey, Wade," Olivia giggled.

"Hey, Olivia," Wade responded, shooting a disapproving glare in Jo'sha's direction.

"This isn't what you think," Jo'sha said quickly.

"Oh it isn't?" Olivia asked, rolling her neck.

"No. I mean we haven't done anything—" Jo'sha stammered.

"Way too much information for me," Wade interrupted. "I'm not the one you have to worry about. It's Matthew."

"How's Quay?" Olivia interjected.

"Fine," Wade responded, giving Olivia a hug and a smile.

"Tell her that I asked about her."

"I sure will."

"How far along is she now?"

"She's into her second trimester," Wade said proudly.

"I know you miss her," Olivia said sympathetically.

"I do, but we both know that school is important."

Jo'sha was too busy looking up the hallway for Matthew to pay much attention to the conversation.

"Well I have to go. You boys be good," Olivia said, waving to Wade and then kissing Jo'sha on the lips.

When Olivia was down the hall and around the corner, Wade followed Jo'sha into his room.

"Looks so different in here now," Wade said.

"Are you going to tell Matthew?" Jo'sha asked, ignoring Wade's comment about the room.

"It is not my place to tell it."

"Thanks. I am going to tell him when the time is right," Jo'sha said, sighing relief.

"Far be it from me to tell anyone whom they should fall in love with. I know first hand that love doesn't follow any rules. If you really care about her like I sense that you do, then it doesn't matter what Matthew says," Wade added.

"You don't room with him. I know how protective he is over his sister, and I know what he thinks of the way I've treated females in the past."

"Matthew just broke up with Tessa. He has his own female problems."

"He didn't really care for her that much anyway. That was long overdue."

"Well breaking up with her in the student center was not a good idea. All of that yelling and screaming was embarrassing," Wade said, shaking his head as he recalled the incident.

Jo'sha laughed and began straightening up the room, placing his diary in his drawer, putting away the fraternity letters, and clearing away the incense.

"Were you showing her the Omega Tau stuff?" Wade asked.

"Yeah," Jo'sha said hesitantly.

"Don't worry. I told Quay too," Wade admitted.

"You didn't tell her anything about the ankhs, did you?"

"Of course not. I never would. I didn't see any harm in telling her about the fraternity though."

"That's unless you ask Matthew," Jo'sha joked.

"I think our secret is safe. Neither Quay, nor Olivia has a reason to tell. And besides why would it matter. Quay is in Maryland and Olivia doesn't even go to school here. She's still in high school," Wade reasoned.

"True."

"Have you looked at the tape that Foster left for you yet?" Wade asked cautiously.

"No," Jo'sha answered flatly.

"You need to," Wade insisted.

"Why is it so important to you?" Jo'sha asked, struggling to harness his feelings.

"Because you need closure. I can sense all of your unresolved feelings. You're mad at yourself for what happened—sad about losing Foster—angry at Foster for dying—happy about all the new things that you have, and guilty because you're enjoying them. It's okay. But you have to deal with it. You can't just shut down your emotions. It's not good for you or us. Trust me."

Jo'sha sucked in a breath, fiercely fighting back a flood of emotions.

"See that's what I mean," Wade said, referring to Jo'sha's tears and sadness.

Jo'sha plopped down on the bed, buried his face in his hands and began to cry. He couldn't tell if Wade had somehow forced him to tears, but it felt good to let go.

"Alright. I'll look at the tape tonight when we get back from Miss Vaughn's place if it isn't too late," he said finally.

"Promise?"

"Promise."

"Good. It's almost nine. Chance and Matthew should be here any minute," Wade said.

"Where's Chance? At the gym again?"

"No. He's the dorm representative for the Campus Council. They're planning the Spring Festival," Wade answered.

"That's right. He was looking forward to the meeting. Aspen is a part of the planning committee. He was excited about seeing her again," Jo'sha remembered. "Anyway, enough on that. How are you doing?" Jo'sha asked.

"Fine, it's hard being away from Quay right now. I feel guilty being here while she's there. And my family is so stubborn. Things are either their way or no way. It's frustrating," Wade sighed.

They heard heavy footsteps in the suite hallway, and knew immediately that it was Chance.

"Wade!" he yelled.

"I'm in here," Wade called.

Chance burst through the door, not bothering to knock. "I see you," he exclaimed.

"And I you, my brother," Jo'sha responded with a smile. Though the greeting was a painful reminder of Foster's absence, it felt good to be able to carry on his legacy even in such a small way.

"Why are you so happy?" Wade asked.

"I think Aspen is warming up to me again," Chance said, grinning.

"How do you know?" Jo'sha asked.

"She couldn't keep her eyes off of me. She tried not to let me catch her looking, but I know that she was."

"Any big plans for the Spring Festival?" Wade asked.

"Huge plans. The University Building and Grounds Department came to the meeting and announced that they are building an outdoor amphitheater on the other side of Bonder's Cemetery," Chance announced.

"So that's what they're building," Wade said, remembering all the construction material they'd seen when they were out there.

"They still don't know what they are going to name it or who they are going to dedicate it to, but from the looks of it, it should be real nice," Chance said.

"I wouldn't be surprised if they named it after old Dr. Weatherspoon. It would be great publicity for him," Jo'sha scoffed.

"He has done some amazing things with this school," Wade defended.

"That isn't even the best news," Chance continued. "The Campus Council decided to have an all campus step show for the Spring Festival this year. All of the Black Greek, dorm, and organizational fraternities are going to participate."

"Are you thinking what I'm thinking?" Jo'sha asked excitedly.

"Hell yeah!" Chance exclaimed.

"And what exactly is that?" Wade asked hesitantly.

"That's when we introduce Omega Tau! We step at the Spring Festival," Chance enthused.

"I thought we were going to be more than just another social organization," Wade objected.

"We are, but have to get on the map, and this is the perfect way to do it," Chance explained.

"I agree," Jo'sha said, nodding his head.

"You're forgetting that none of us have ever been in a step show," Wade said.

"Just a technicality. We have time to go to a couple of step shows at some neighboring schools and pick up the basics. Then we'll create our own steps," Jo'sha said assuredly.

"And who's going to convince Matthew to go along with this?" Wade asked.

"Leave that to me, I'll handle Matthew." Chance said confidently.

"Alright," Wade agreed.

A cell phone rang. Wade and Chance instinctively looked at their phones.

"Not me," Chance said.

"Me either," Wade said.

"Oh," Jo'sha said, reaching for his sleek, new cell phone. "It's me. I'm still not used to having one of these things. " Jo'sha said, sheepishly. "Hello." After a few seconds he hung up the phone. "Matthew is downstairs. He wants us to come down and meet him so that we can get to Miss Vaughn's house before it gets too late."

They collected their things and rushed downstairs to meet Matthew.

CHAPTER 27

"Are you sure Miss Vaughn isn't getting suspicious? We've been here an awful lot lately, and we really haven't fixed anything," Chance questioned.

"First, I don't really tell her every time that we come out here. Second, she probably won't ever come out here alone, and if she did it wouldn't be at night," Matthew answered.

"It's kind of cloudy out tonight," Wade announced, looking up at the sky. He was growing a steady appreciation for nature.

"What are you so excited about, Matthew. I can tell something's up," Jo'sha said, as they made their way to the backyard, where they normally practiced Matthew's drills.

"It has either got something to do with Dr. Smith or our powers," Wade said sarcastically.

"This is your lucky day. It's both," Matthew responded, ignoring Wade's tone.

"Oh goody!" Wade mocked.

"Let's start with our powers. I am really proud of you guys. We have come a long way in a short period of time. Wade, you have learned to not only sense other people's emotions, but curb them as well. You've even learned to shield yourself from the emotional outbursts of large crowds. And your mastery of water is phenomenal!"

Matthew gave Wade an approving nod before turning to Chance. "Chance, we still have to figure out your ability to control the earth, but it is coming along. So far you're only able to uproot trees, but you are uprooting larger trees so there is progress. Your sense of touch has evolved to a point of being able to cause pleasure, we just need to experiment with that a little more," he said.   "Jo'sha, you've only been back with us for a short time, but you wield fire like you've been doing it all of your life. I'm convinced that your dreams and visions are also a part of your gift. Keep working on figuring them out. I know that there's something great there. *And,* we all have gotten pretty good at sensing each other," Matthew said, concluding his pep talk.

"And let's not forget about that small hurricane that you whipped up last week. Very impressive," Chance added.

"Thanks," Matthew said modestly. "Now I know each of you are wondering what could be next, right? Here's a hint. Take a look up at the sky. What do you see there in the distance?" he asked.

"Stars?" Chance guessed.

"No."

"The moon?" Jo'sha followed.

"No."

"Clouds," Wade said finally.

"One of the most underestimated things in the sky," Matthew responded.

"And?" Jo'sha asked.

"Powerful and beautiful visible masses of condensed watery vapor floating in the air," Matthew said, staring up at them. "Wade, just think about that for a minute. All of you think about clouds. And not just clouds, but thunderclouds! They develop in areas where an intense upward movement of air exists, such as the tropics and middle latitudes. Or where I am," Matthew said confidently, as he forced a column of air up toward the heavens creating a large swishing sound.

"In the middle latitudes thunderstorms commonly form from a cold front break-in. The dense cold air goes under the warm air masses originally sitting in the area, making the warm air rise rapidly. The warm air rises and cools, condensing water vapor and forming clouds. Thunderclouds have a large vertical extension. The base can be 1-2 kilometers in altitude; the top can reach 12 kilometers. This causes large differences in temperature, with the bottom above freezing and the top commonly at -60 degrees Celsius. Now we don't have to rely on Mother Nature to control the temperature."

Matthew looked at the blank stares of each of his friends and sighed. "Jo'sha, you can create pockets of heat. And if you can create pockets of heat, then it stands to reason that you can create areas of variant temperature," Matthew explained.

His friends were still unclear about where Matthew was headed with his detailed explanation, so he continued. "Due to complex mechanisms, electric charges separate in thunderclouds—the upper part becomes positive, and the lower part becomes negative. The lower negative charges induce a positive charge in the ground just under the thundercloud. As more charges separate, the electric field gets stronger. Chance, I am hoping that with some concentration you can somehow sense and maybe even manage the charge in the ground."

"Wait! Are you trying to tell us that you think you can create lightning?" Chance asked incredulously.

"Not just me, us. Now listen, when the electric field between the lower part of the cloud and the ground reaches a certain voltage, the air molecules ionize along a narrow path and air becomes a conductor. This allows a free flow of charge between the cloud and the ground. Lightning starts with a leading stroke as electrons flow from the cloud to the ground, leaving the cloud with a positive net charge. Right after the leading stroke along the built-up ionized path comes the main stroke from the ground to the cloud, neutralizing the positive charges. Gas ions move fast along a narrow ionized path, colliding with each other frequently. Their kinetic energy lost in the collisions is transformed to visible light and heat. *That* is lightning," Matthew said with a satisfied smile.

Jo'sha, Wade, and Chance continued to stare at him blankly.

"And what exactly in hell do you think we're going to do again?" Chance asked.

"Take it to the next level," Matthew said confidently.

"Lightning *kills*, Matthew. You're letting another one of your little obsessions get in the way of practicality," Wade warned.

"But just think about it," Jo'sha began.

Matthew smiled. He knew that Jo'sha would be up for the excitement and the challenge.

"We have learned to localize our powers. We wouldn't create lightning near us. We could do it off in the distance. Just beyond the storage shed there," Matthew said pointing.

After several minutes of convincing and an hour of failed attempts, Wade managed to move a pregnant rain cloud from the horizon, drenching them in rain. Jo'sha dried them off with a blast of heat, but was still struggling to create variant temperature zones. Chance couldn't understand what Matthew was saying about electrical fields, let alone determine positive and negative charges.

"You're not concentrating!" Matthew yelled after another hour of air blasts, heat zone generation, cloud movement, and electrical field determination. He was beginning to get discouraged, when Wade yelled out.

"Do you feel it?"

"I think I do," Chance said, digging his dark, huge hands into the earth.

"What does it feel like?" Wade asked, holding a mid-sized cloud miles above them in the sky.

"It feels like tiny pins pricking my palms."

"Matthew, I think we're close," Wade yelled.

Matthew forced up several columns of air, and directed Jo'sha to change the temperature at various horizontal levels up to a thousand feet. The fine wavy black hairs on Wade's neck began to stand on end. Jo'sha's locks seem to come to life and the air began to snap and crackle. Then an extraordinary flash of light touched down just twenty feet in front of them, temporarily blinding them and knocking them back on the ground.

"We did it!" Matthew yelled.

Jo'sha, Wade, and Chance laughed and cheered. Having finally achieved success, they did it several times more before the morning light forced them to retreat back to campus. With the exception of Chance, they were all tired on the ride back to campus. Wade surrendered his car keys to Chance who was speeding back toward campus.

"Hurry up, Chance. I have to get back. I have a class at 7:50 a.m.," Jo'sha said.

"I don't want to get a ticket," Chance said, speeding up anyway.

"Hey, what was that other thing that you were going to tell us?" Wade asked Matthew.

"Can't believe I nearly forgot. I have Dr. Smith's complete weekly itinerary. I've been following him for weeks, but it didn't take me long to realize that he is definitely a creature of habit. The only strange thing about his schedule is that he spends a lot of time in this bookstore on Auburn Avenue, The Shrine of the Black Madonna."

"He *is* a teacher. The bookstore sells books. What's the big deal?" Chance challenged.

"No. He goes every Tuesday and Wednesday afternoon when he doesn't have office hours. He spends time with this old man who sits right outside the bookstore. Then he just walks up and down Auburn Avenue for hours," Matthew said.

"You need to get a life," Wade said.

"So this is what we're going to do," Matthew continued.

"We?" Wade asked.

"Yes, 'we'," Chance echoed, remembering that the only way to get Matthew to agree to start the fraternity was to help him nail Dr. Smith.

Matthew reached into his new book bag, which was in the floor of the automobile, and pulled out four pieces of paper. Here is Dr. Smith's weekly schedule, and his home address. I know he's up to something sneaky. I can feel it," Matthew said.

"And what do we do with this?" Wade asked.

"Jo'sha and Wade, you two head to his house next Monday after class. He has office hours on campus and his neighbors on both sides are gone by nine. He lives in Buckhead. You should drive by the house this weekend so that you know exactly how to get there on Monday. And make sure that he doesn't see you. I recommend Saturday morning between seven and eight. He normally walks his little dog to the park during that time," Matthew said.

"So you want us to break into his house?" Wade asked, not believing what Matthew was asking them to do.

"Well, yeah," Matthew stammered.

"And look for what?" Wade snapped.

"Anything that connects him to the Atlanta Male Murders," Matthew said.

"Why are we doing this again?" Wade asked, sighing heavily.

"The sooner the authorities find out that he's the killer, the less worried we'll have to be about them accidentally stumbling up on us. We've been in some pretty compromising situations that we can't explain to anyone. More importantly, we all want the Atlanta Male Murders to stop now, don't we?" Matthew asked, looking around at his friends.

"What do I do?" Chance asked, feeling a little left out.

"Chance, you need to go really search his office," Matthew instructed.

"What am I looking for in his office?" Chance asked.

"Same thing, anything that connects him to the Atlanta Male Murders. You should plan to hit his office on Saturday morning too. The building is usually open until 6:00 p.m. You're the only one of us that is strong enough to break the lock. Just wear gloves and don't leave any fingerprints. There are no cameras in the building so all you have to do is make sure that no one sees you going in or out," Matthew said.

"And what are you going to do while we're all breaking and entering?" Wade asked.

"I already checked his Saab. I didn't find anything there, except that he's a neat freak," Matthew said.

"That is certainly a reason to alert the authorities," Wade said mockingly.

Matthew ignored Wade's tone and continued. "I'm also going to go talk to that old man and see if he can tell me why he and Dr. Smith are such good friends."

"Don't give yourself away in the process," Chance warned.

"I know. I know. I'll think of way to find out what we need to know without letting on that I'm curious about Dr. Smith. I'll do it this Saturday morning too," Matthew said.

"I guess this makes sense," Wade said reluctantly.

"We have to protect our secret. No one will take care of us but us," Matthew stressed.

"Speaking of taking care of us, Wade, have you thought about maybe using your powers of emotional persuasion to take the edge off of your mother's attitude?" Jo'sha asked.

"Yes, but there are a couple of issues. It only seems to work when I am in close proximity. I can assuage fear, and even anger, but it tends to wear off. And so far I've only been able to do it on one person at a time. Not to mention the fact that I want them to genuinely accept me and Quay," Wade explained.

"And how do you know so much about your powers now? Who've you been practicing on?" Jo'sha teased.

"You and Chance. It's a little exercise that Matthew and I came up with," Wade said.

Both Jo'sha and Chance, who had been laughing, suddenly grew quiet. They felt violated and embarrassed that they had been manipulated without their knowledge. Wade and Matthew spent the next fifteen minutes explaining instances of when Wade had managed their emotions for them, helping Jo'sha deal with the pain of Foster's death, and Chance the anger of losing Aspen. After he'd heard everything, Jo'sha found it fascinating. Chance, however, wasn't as excited.

"What's wrong with you?" Wade asked, sensing Chance's anger.

"You manipulated us!" Chance argued.

"I didn't hurt you. I wouldn't do anything to hurt either one of you. You know that. We have to trust each other," Wade explained.

"Trust? Well the next time you do something like that you should tell me. I don't appreciate being used. It's manipulative and it's wrong," Chance said, feeling powerless.

"That would have defeated the whole purpose of the exercise," Matthew explained, still approaching the entire activity from a very clinical perspective.

"You're probably right, but it isn't any different from what you do when you touch someone—like Aspen." Wade challenged.

"Alright already. We're all just a little tired and there is some truth on both sides. Perhaps we shouldn't use these powers on the unsuspecting. Least of all each other," Matthew said.

"Maybe you are right," Wade mumbled.

"Maybe so," Chance chimed.

"And now with that out of the way, let's talk about Omega Tau," said Jo'sha.

CHAPTER 28

It was 4:00 a.m. on Monday morning when Wade's cell phone buzzed.

"Hello," he mumbled groggily. "Huh?" he asked, sitting up and rubbing his eyes. He listened a few more seconds. "Are you sure?" he asked, throwing the covers off of him. "I'll get a flight home first thing," he said, now fully awakened by the news. "Are you sure?" he asked again. After several more minutes of listening, he hung up.

"You alright, roommate?" Chance asked sleepily.

"Sorry if I woke you," Wade said rubbing his hand through his finger length, wavy black hair.

"What's up?" Chance asked again.

"That was Quay. She said she's spotting. The doctor said that it was nothing serious, but that she should take it easy. I don't know how she's supposed to do that she's on her feet all day," Wade explained.

"She's still working?" Chance asked?

Wade nodded. "She won't take money from me, says she doesn't want me to think that's why she's with me."

"Wow. What are you going to do?"

"I don't know. I'm really torn. I want to go to her, but I have school to consider. I've been thinking about dropping out all together," Wade said.

"Well that wouldn't solve anything," Chance reasoned.

"It would give me a chance to be a good father." Wade countered.

"A father without a college degree and parents that don't support his new baby," Chance responded. He hoped that Wade didn't take his remarks too personally but he wanted to get his point across.

"Have you ever thought about what all this means to our future?" Wade asked.

"All of what?" Chance asked.

"You know what I'm talking about. It seems like we've been avoiding the issue, but we have to talk about it sooner or later," Wade answered.

Chance sighed and flopped back into his pillow.

"You remember what it felt like when Jo'sha was close to death. We all got just a little bit weaker. The longer he was out the more we all felt it. Truth is we weren't there just to make him feel better. It made us all feel more whole. And you know how good it feels when we're all together and using these powers. These things have made us dependent on one another. What happens to us if one of us decides to leave school? What happens to us next year if we're not in the same dorm?" Wade said, becoming more troubled with each of his personal revelations.

"I guess I have noticed, but haven't thought about it as much as you have," Chance said.

The light tap on the door startled them both.

"Jo'sha," they said in unison.

"Yeah, it's me."

"Come in," Wade said.

Jo'sha opened the door slowly and entered in nothing but alligator print boxers.

"You sleep in *that*?" Wade asked.

"You sleep in *that*?" Jo'sha countered, referring to Wade's designer pajamas.

"C'mon now, it's too early for that," Chance said, rising up just enough to turn on his desk lamp. Jo'sha plopped down on the foot of Chance's bed. Matthew trailed Jo'sha by just a few seconds.

"Couldn't sleep either?" Wade asked.

"Couldn't get you out of my head," Matthew said, pulling his fingers through his sleep worn Afro.

"What do you mean?" Wade said.

"You were worried about something— shocked about it, and woke us both," Matthew explained.

"Was it a bad dream?" Jo'sha asked sympathetically.

"No, a bad phone call," Wade said, explaining Quay's phone call.

"I thought I just woke up," Chance said.

"It isn't that simple," Matthew said, shaking his head. "We're more connected now— better able to sense each other's presence and emotions, especially Wade's feelings. It's like he's broadcasting," Matthew said.

"I've been learning to control it. I guess I wasn't concentrating when I got the call," Wade said apologetically.

"The good news is that we're getting used to these things," Matthew said, pointing to the ankh around his neck.

"And they're becoming a part of us," Chance echoed.

"And *controlling* us," Jo'sha sighed, remembering his ankh, and how his ambition had been responsible for Foster's death.

"Matthew, do you think we are becoming more dependent on each other?" Wade asked.

"In some ways," he said thoughtfully. "We are definitely stronger when we're together. Kind of like a fraternity."

"But what if one of us decides to leave the dorm or school? Do you think that will have long term affects on the rest of us?" Wade asked anxiously.

"I don't know. But you've seen what we can do together. Our powers are extraordinary," Matthew said.

"Yeah, but what good is it if we can't share it with anyone," Jo'sha complained.

"The more time that passes, the more these ankhs and powers become ours. I'm starting to feel comfortable that no one knew that these ankhs were in the chest," Matthew said.

"I don't agree. I'm starting to get a little bit more skeptical of Dr. Smith after being in his office. The university chest, the time capsule, was in his office when I looked on Saturday. And the cross that we thought belonged to James Lynch was gone," Chance reminded them.

Jo'sha was silent for a moment at the mention of the cross. "He must have been on the planning committee, and he's a history professor. As a matter of fact, he's head of the history department. It makes sense that he would be interested in an artifact like the chest," Jo'sha challenged.

"I guess so, but that doesn't explain all of the articles and papers in his office on lynchings and Negro murders," Chance said.

"See. I knew there was something there. Chance is starting to see it too," said Matthew. He was glad that finally someone else was suspicious of Dr. Smith.

"I don't like Dr. Smith anymore than the rest of you, but I think you're grasping at straws. It's just coincidence. You said yourself that the old man at the bookstore couldn't tell you anything unusual about his conversations with Dr. Smith. He was just interested in the local history of Auburn Avenue for a book he's writing about the history of Atlanta. I think the guy is blameless," Jo'sha said.

"You and Wade should still plan to check out his house in the morning just to see what you might find. There's something strange about all of this," Matthew instructed.

"Fair enough, but you're going to help us with the fraternity," Jo'sha said, reminding Matthew of his promise.

"Fair enough," Matthew agreed.

"Can we get back to sleep now? We have to hit the gym before Dr. Smith's class and the Spring Festival planning committee has a lunch meeting. I have a long day ahead of me," Chance reminded them.

"And we have to break into his house," Wade interjected, only half kidding.

"*Investigate*," Matthew corrected.

CHAPTER 29

Monday morning started the same way it had every week since they started Dr. Smith's class. The boys took their seats and greeted classmates, preparing themselves for Dr. Smith's punctual arrival, and his pomposity and arrogance.

Jo'sha and Robert "Blaze" Black still hadn't settled their differences, but time, Jo'sha's recent stint out of school, and the reasonable voices of their peers had cooled their interaction to a point of civility. The sobering reality of James Lynch's empty seat also helped to put things in perspective.

Dr. Smith entered the classroom several minutes before it was scheduled to begin as usual, and methodically prepared for his lecture.

"Do you feel that?" Jo'sha whispered to Matthew.

"Sshh!"

Jo'sha looked over at Matthew, who seemed to be just as puzzled by the strange feeling in the air. Jo'sha pulled out a slip of paper and wrote Matthew a note asking him if he noticed or felt anything unusual. Matthew balled up the note and threw it to Wade while the instructor wasn't looking. Wade read the note and then nodded. He felt something strange, but didn't know exactly what it was. Robert Black, who had been watching them, cleared his throat in an attempt to alert Dr. Smith to Matthew's note passing. Jo'sha rolled his eyes and shook his head.

Dr. Smith's lecture about African-Americans and the benefits of the community college experience put most of the class to sleep, except for Jo'sha and Wade. They listened intently, and seemed mesmerized by Dr. Smith. When class ended exactly at nine the students filed out, and headed toward their other classes and destinations.

"Did you feel anything in class?" Jo'sha asked Chance, as the four waited in the hallway just outside Dr. Smith's class.

"Yeah, sleepy," Chance responded, stretching to wake himself.

"Do you two know what you have to do?" Matthew asked quietly.

"We got it," Jo'sha said. He was getting a little irritated by Matthew constantly talking to them as if he were the only one capable of comprehending their plan.

"Let's just go and get it over with," Wade said.

"And make sure that none of his neighbors are home," Matthew continued.

"Do you want to do this or do you want us to do this?" Wade snapped.

"Come on. I'll drive," Jo'sha said, proudly. Now that he had the new convertible that Foster had left him he no longer had to hitch a ride with Wade.

"Do you remember how to get there?" Matthew asked.

"We just drove by there on Saturday," Wade said, growing irritated with Matthew's continued instruction.

"Let's meet at lunch today to hear what you find," Matthew suggested.

"Can't. I have to go to a Spring Festival planning meeting today at lunch," Chance said.

"Then let's meet at the library tonight at seven. We can catch up, go study, and then go get something to eat."

"Works for me," Chance agreed.

Both Wade and Jo'sha nodded as well. Having settled that, they turned to walk out of the building, and came face to face with a glaring Dr. Smith.

"Gentleman," Dr. Smith said, seeming to have come from nowhere.

"Dr. Smith," they responded in unison.

"I trust that you are congregating in our hallways discussing school work," he said.

"Of course," Matthew answered, hurrying toward the exit with the others trailing behind.

Dr. Smith watched them until they rounded the corner toward the elevator.

On the drive to Dr. Smith's house, Jo'sha couldn't help but recall the weird feeling he had gotten during class. "What do you think it was?" he asked Wade.

"I don't know. Maybe we're just more in tune with each other. Dr. Smith's class is one of the few occasions where we're all together and quiet and concentrating. In some ways it's like meditating. Maybe that's what we felt," Wade surmised.

"Maybe so," Jo'sha said doubtfully.

Just then Jo'sha's cell phone rang. He didn't recognize the New York area code and answered the phone quickly. "Hello?" He listened for several minutes and offered a few "uh huh's" before hanging up the phone.

"Who was that?" Wade asked.

"You will never believe it," Jo'sha said excitedly. "It was Anthony Goins—Agonize. He's going to be in Atlanta recording in a few months and needs a backup singer. He remembered me from the talent show and asked if I wanted to sit in with him," Jo'sha said, beaming.

"I thought you said you would never sing backup for anyone. That you were a star," Wade mocked.

"This is different. Me and Agonize are like friends," Jo'sha said.

"Whatever. How did he get your number anyway?"

"He must have called university information and gotten the room number. I left my cell phone number on the dorm voicemail."

"Are you going to do it?"

"Hell, yeah!"

"Will they pay you?" Wade asked.

"I don't know. I didn't ask."

Wade sighed at Jo'sha's lack of attention to what he believed to be an important detail.

The next few minutes of the drive to Dr. Smith's house were completely quiet.

"Are you alright?" Jo'sha asked.

"You know I'm not. I couldn't hide it from you if I tried," Wade said.

"Then you might as well tell me what it is," Jo'sha said, sounding genuinely concerned.

"Same old stuff, my family, Quay, the baby. This is supposed to be the happiest time of my life. I have good friends. I have great grades thanks to Matthew's tutoring. I'm in better shape than I have ever been thanks to Chance."

"What about me?" Jo'sha complained.

"You know what I mean. This whole baby thing is heavy. Maybe my aunt was right," Wade said.

"You'll get through this. Brothers deal with this kind of situation everyday. Who are you that you shouldn't have a little rain in your life? You'll manage. *We'll* manage," Jo'sha said supportively.

Wade sighed again and stared out the window at the passing buildings. Sensing that his friend didn't want to talk anymore, Jo'sha turned on the radio and sang.

They were at Dr. Smith's house by 9:42 a.m. They drove by slowly to make sure that his neighbors on either side were gone.

"It looks like everything is all clear," Jo'sha said.

"We should park on Pomegranate Street and come back over behind the house," Wade suggested.

"Good idea," Jo'sha said, impressed by Wade's forethought.

Pomegranate Street faced a local park and was completely empty at this time of day. Jo'sha parked at the corner and they made their way toward the back of Dr. Smith's house.

"Nice house," Jo'sha commented.

"I guess," Wade responded, looking unimpressed.

"Here you go, put these on," Jo'sha said, handing Wade a pair of gloves.

They put the gloves on quickly as they searched for a window or door at the back of the house that might be loose or open.

"How in the hell are we supposed to get in here? This was a dumb idea," Wade said, looking through the kitchen window.

"Here," Jo'sha called. He walked toward the cellar door, pulled off his gloves, and put his hand on the metal lock. He held it until the metal became white hot and malleable. Then he popped the lock, and pulled the cellar door up and open with little effort.

"What about the latch?" Wade asked.

"He'll never know what happened. I can bend the metal back while it's still hot. When it cools, it'll look just like it did before. He'll never know what happened."

"Alright, put your gloves back on and let's get this over with," Wade said, checking to make sure no one had seen them.

They entered Dr. Smith's cellar, careful to close the door behind them. The sunlight disappeared as the door closed, and they stood still for a few minutes waiting for their eyes to adjust. When they could see again, they walked down into Dr. Smith's expertly organized wine cellar. Wade stopped at the first rack and looked at the label on the bottle.

"1965 Chateau LeFont. Nice," he said, approvingly.

"We didn't come here for a wine tasting," Jo'sha mocked.

"Shut up!"

The rest of Dr. Smith's basement cellar was as organized as the wine racks—alphabetized rows of books, expertly labeled boxes, and various types of camera equipment.

"Everything here seems in order," Jo'sha said, noticing how different this basement looked from Foster's basement back in Chicago.

"Let's go upstairs," Wade suggested. "Maybe he has an office."

The two of them ascended the stairs to the first floor. The first floor dining room, den, kitchen, library, and sitting room were replete with the mahogany charm of traditional furnishing and fixtures.

"That is a Blackshear piece," Wade said, referring to a statuette of a black angel sitting atop an end table.

"This is *not* a museum," Jo'sha said sarcastically.

"That angel looks a lot like Chance, doesn't it?" Wade said, referring to the dark, bald sculpture.

"It does," Jo'sha said, stopping to admire the piece.

"Weird that Dr. Smith would have African-American art in his home," Wade commented.

"There's nothing here on the first floor, but old white man shit. Let's go upstairs and look around and then get out of here," Jo'sha said.

They went upstairs and looked into the first three rooms, which happened to be bedrooms. A fourth and final room sat at the end of the long hallway.

"Let's do this," Wade said, moving toward the door.

Wade opened the door to Dr. Smith's bedroom slowly. The room was expansive, with a large king-sized bed at one end, and a stone fireplace at the other. A chaise lounge sat in front of the fireplace with Dr. Smith's robe draped across it as if were a prop for a photo shoot.

The two boys searched the dresser and the bureau, but didn't find anything except pairs of Dr. Smith's ironed and folded socks and undergarments. They searched both end tables and only found books, reading glasses, and a checkbook. The room was filled with clocks—alarm clocks, both old and new, all of them ticking in time.

"I wonder why he has so many clocks," Wade commented.

"The sound alone would drive me crazy. I've never seen so many alarm clocks," Jo'sha responded.

"*The Prophet* by Kahlil Gibraun," Wade said admiringly. "You should really read this."

"I have already," Jo'sha said, thumbing through Dr. Smith's checkbook.

"Put that back! We're not here for that. It's bad enough that we broke in here," Wade admonished.

"I was just looking," Jo'sha said.

"You're lucky that no one was looking for Victor Greene's things. And you're really lucky that I didn't say anything to Chance or Matthew," Wade snapped.

Jo'sha put the checkbook back, closed the drawer, and looked under the bed, where he found a cardboard box filled with old papers.

"What do you have there?" Wade asked. He was across the room looking through Dr. Smith's closet. He noticed that whatever Jo'sha had found seemed to have him pre-occupied.

"It's a box filled with old papers and pictures. Pictures of lynchings, and hangings, and article after article about the murders of young black men," Jo'sha said, flipping through the contents.

Wade walked over and knelt beside Jo'sha. "Look at this. There are articles about the Atlanta Male Murders," he said, reaching around Jo'sha and into the box.

"This is a picture of a Nightrider—a masked racist who used to hunt young black men for sport," Jo'sha said solemnly.

"Look at the handwriting on the bottom. It says his name is Alfred Cranford," Wade said, studying the photograph.

"Did you hear that?" Jo'sha asked suddenly.

"What?"

They heard the clicking sound of the front door being unlocked downstairs.

"That!" Jo'sha whispered.

"Shit! Shit! Shit! Do you think it's him?" Wade whispered.

"Who else could it be?"

"Damn!"

"Stay here and put everything back like we found out. I'll go see what's up," Jo'sha instructed.

Ten minutes seemed to have gone by before Jo'sha returned.

"Who was it?" Wade whispered when Jo'sha tipped back into the bedroom.

"It looks like a cleaning lady. Seems that Matthew didn't have *her* schedule," Jo'sha said.

"So what do we do now?" Wade asked.

"Did you put everything back?" Jo'sha asked.

"Yes," Wade answered.

"Follow me," Jo'sha said, crawling against the wall toward the staircase. Wade followed him until they reached the catwalk leading to the staircase overlooking the living room.

"She's dusting in the living room. Can you see her?"

"Yeah," Wade said looking over Jo'sha's shoulder, not quite sure what Jo'sha was thinking.

"We need to get her out of the living room and then we can go out the front door," Jo'sha instructed.

"How do we do that without drawing any attention to ourselves?"

"Just watch," Jo'sha said.

Jo'sha concentrated on the elderly cleaning lady in the same way that he had focused on Robert Black. Only a few seconds passed before she began to sweat profusely. Instinctively, she opened her blouse and began fanning herself.

"Ugh," Wade whispered.

"Shhh," Jo'sha replied, "She'll be heading to the kitchen for a drink of water any second now, but before she goes, make sure that she can't see or hear clearly."

"Huh?" Wade asked.

"She has sweat all over her face right? Sweat is water right? Fill her ears and eyes with it," Jo'sha said.

Wade began to concentrate. In seconds the sweat was stinging her eyes and filling her ears. She stumbled into the kitchen screaming and crying.

"Let's go!"

Jo'sha shot down the stairs. Wade took off behind him and they managed to get out the front door without being noticed by the cleaning lady or any neighbors. They ran down the street and around the block toward Pomegranate Street.

∞

"Then that solves it. Dr. Smith is our man," Matthew commented after hearing Jo'sha and Wade's account of Dr. Smith's house.

"So are we going to tell the police?" Chance asked, leaning up against the library bookshelf.

"While I'll admit it all seems pretty compelling, what makes us think that we're any smarter than the police?" Wade questioned.

"We've just been in the right places at the right times. His sketchy background, his interest in lynchings, the picture of Alfred Cranford—" Matthew started.

"—Is circumstantial at best," Wade finished.

"So how about this as a solution? We give the police an anonymous tip and we continue to watch him until we can get hardcore evidence," Chance offered.

"That works for me. Now let's go get something to eat," Wade suggested.

CHAPTER 30

Wade stood, almost posing, in front of the Butler Student Affairs building. More than a few young women had noticed him in passing and he was enjoying the attention. Despite their efforts to stay out of the public eye, they were fast becoming four of the more popular freshmen on campus. The attention came from a combination of their good looks and camaraderie.

Thanks to Jo'sha, Wade's dress was becoming less conservative. He wore faded jeans, a white Calvin Klein dress shirt, Varvatos suit jacket, and Aldo loafers. His physique was more defined than it had been in his whole life, and he was enjoying his new body. Without his glasses, his light brown eyes were more pronounced, and his hair had grown into a stylish, short curly Afro. He had managed to live through the confrontation with his family, he had good friends, and with the ankh he had power. Where he would have normally avoided direct eye contact with other young men, every interaction was now more like a confrontation.

"What are you selling?" Jo'sha asked, bouncing down the stairs of the student affairs building?"

"Whatever they need," Wade said, flattered that Jo'sha noticed his more casual look.

"Haha, okay. Well, I got it," Jo'sha exclaimed, changing the subject.

"Let me see," Wade asked, snatching the paper from Jo'sha's hand.

"There it is. Omega Tau is now officially recognized by the university as a service and social organization. You, Matthew, Chance and I, are the founders and only members. All we have to do is keep $5000 in our organizational student account," Jo'sha said.

"That shouldn't be a problem."

"You're right," Jo'sha said, realizing that he now had access to money too.

"Are there any other stipulations?" Wade asked.

"We only needed four people to start the organization, but we have a year to get the membership above ten to maintain our position on the university roster. We also have to keep a 2.5 grade point average," Jo'sha answered.

"That shouldn't be a problem either. You're back on track with your classes now thanks to Matthew. We should all finish our first semester with 4.0 grade point averages," Wade said proudly.

"Thank God for Matthew! It's hard to believe that our first semester in college will be over soon. It has flown by," Jo'sha said, pulling his locks back over his shoulder.

"What are you doing during the holiday break?" Wade asked.

"Matthew said that I could go home with him," Jo'sha answered, trying hard not to feel sorry for himself. Now that Foster was gone and he didn't have a home to go to.

"Well you're welcome to go home with me," Wade offered.

"Thanks," Jo'sha said.

"But I guess you'll get to see Olivia for the holidays if you stay with Matthew," Wade said slyly.

Jo'sha smiled.

"Thanks for not saying anything to Matthew."

"It is not my place to say anything," Wade responded still remembering his confrontation with his family over Quay.

"What do you think about me and Olivia?" Jo'sha asked.

"I don't think, I know. You really like her," Wade answered.

"That's right. I forgot you could tell about emotional stuff. Do you think Matthew suspects anything?"

"I don't think so, but you need to figure out if you're serious about her or not. We already have enough going on and we don't need to have your relationship with Olivia causing problems if it is just another one of your flings."

"Yeah, you're right. I guess I also need to figure out if she's serious about me, too."

They walked through campus enjoying Atlanta's fall weather. Being from Baltimore and Chicago, they didn't often see the majestic colors of autumn.

"How does it feel?" Jo'sha asked.

"How does what feel?"

"Emotion—how does it feel to feel someone else's emotions?" Jo'sha continued.

"It depends on the person and the emotion, and the depth of the emotion," Wade answered.

"Oh. How about the way I feel for Olivia? What can you tell?" Jo'sha asked.

"It's kind of complicated. It's like I can see a light about two to four inches away from people. It's normally around their head. They're like rainbow colored clouds. Positive feelings generally create bright colors, and negative feelings generally create dark colors."

"Like auras?" Jo'sha asked enthusiastically.

"I guess. I'm getting to the point where I can differentiate basic emotions. Like love, joy, and surprise, which are normally brighter, and anger, sadness, and fear which are darker," Wade explained.

"What do you see when I'm around Olivia?" Jo'sha asked.

"It is hard to tell. The whole love emotion has so many facets like affection, lust, and longing," Wade said.

"It isn't lust is it?"

"Don't you know how you feel about the girl?"

"I know that I really like her and this isn't like all of the other girls, but it can't hurt to have a second opinion. I never felt like this before," Jo'sha explained.

"Have you—"

"No we haven't," Jo'sha finished.

"Just asking," Wade said defensively.

"How is Quay?" Jo'sha asked, ready to change the subject.

"Fine."

"When's her due date?"

"May 26th."

"Are you ready?"

"I don't know. Everything is moving so quickly."

"Yeah I know."

"Do you think I am doing the right thing?"

"About what?"

"About staying in school while Quay is back at home," Wade asked anxiously.

"We've talked about this before. You have to do what you have to do. You are not going to do Quay or the baby any good if you don't have an education," Jo'sha stressed.

"I know. I know. But I could go back home and go to a college there," Wade answered.

"Or you could move her here. It's not like you would leave before the semester ended anyway," Jo'sha said.

"I guess," Wade said.

Besides, what would big old Chance do without you?" Jo'sha asked.

"He would be fine," Wade said smiling.

"How are he and Aspen?" Jo'sha asked.

"Not too well, but he's not one to give up. He gets to see her at the Spring Festival planning meetings," Wade said.

"Which reminds me, I think we should make Spring Festival our big introduction to the Georgia Central University community," Jo'sha said.

"We should have a public relations campaign too." Wade said, suddenly flooded with ideas.

"What are you thinking?" Jo'sha asked getting excited as well.

"Like teasers. Right now no one knows that Omega Tau even exists. We should start to put out little hints. Get the campus excited, you know?"

"I like it," Jo'sha said, envisioning the realization of their dream. "We can spend some time talking about it later this evening. I have to go to the music room now. I have to keep my voice in shape for the Agonize recording."

"When is your session with him anyway?"

"He hasn't told me yet, but his agent sent me a copy of the agreement. Will you have your dad take a look at it for me before I sign it?"

"No problem. It's funny, since this whole Quay thing happened, it seems like my father and I are closer."

"Are you headed back to the room for your daily nap?" Jo'sha asked.

"No. I think I'll stay out on campus. Maybe meet Chance after his math class or something," Wade answered. "I don't know yet, although I'm sure Matthew would have a fit if he knew I was hanging out unnecessarily."

"Matthew needs to relax. Maybe he would be a little bit less uptight if he started seeing Tessa again," Jo'sha said.

"Or just *someone*," Wade agreed.

"He doesn't seem really interested in seeing anyone," Jo'sha said, shaking his head. "That's my roommate though, always in the books. Between the books, classes, and Dr. Smith, he doesn't have time to think about anything else." Jo'sha said.

"I guess," Wade said skeptically. "I'll see you later this afternoon," he added.

"Aight," Jo'sha said, turning in the direction of the music room.

Wade was never one to just hang out. Without Jo'sha or Chance around he really didn't know where to go or what to do, so he walked aimlessly around campus enjoying the second glances that he received from other students. Although he had always been noticed for who he was, he welcomed the new attention of being noticed because of how he looked. Before he realized it, he was on the academic side of campus just a few yards away from The Fountain.

The Fountain was in the center of the academic area of campus. Students often gathered there in between classes, so Wade took a seat hoping to see and be seen. Unfortunately, classes had already begun and there was no one at The Fountain but Wade and two ducks. Wade sat and looked at the water. He checked to make sure that no one was around before creating several small whirlpools in the water around Hines and Coppedge, the two ducks that frequented The Fountain. The students had lovingly named the two webbed creatures after two of the University founders. Hines and Coppedge quickly tired of Wade's water games and stepped out of The Fountain.

With no one to talk to, or amuse him, Wade decided to walk over to the library to see if Matthew was still at work. He glanced at his watch and made a note that Chance would be in class for another thirty minutes. As he got up to head toward the library, he looked across campus toward Hughes Hall and saw Dr. Smith and his classmate, Sundiata, engaged in what appeared to be a very intense conversation by the faculty parking deck. Wade found a place just behind a growth of bushes so that he could watch them without being seen. After a few more minutes of conversation, Dr. Smith and Sundiata shook hands and parted quickly. Wade watched until Dr. Smith entered the garage, got in his Saab, and drove away. Sundiata made a direct line back to the residential side of campus.

Confused by the clandestine meeting that he had witnessed, Wade continued on to the library. He knew that Matthew would be really interested in hearing about the meeting he had just witnessed. As he got closer, he remembered his walk toward the library on the day that Victor Green had gotten killed. The smells, the sounds, and the sights brought back every instant in vibrant color. He felt himself being pulled back into the moment until he was startled by a familiar voice.

"Wade!" It was Nia Baptiste.

"How are you?" Wade asked, walking up to the front desk.

"Fine, and you?" Nia returned. "You guys sure do spend a lot of time here. You must be trying to win that Freshman GPA contest," Nia said.

"We're just doing us," he responded. "You know a brother's got to study," Wade said, sounding like Jo'sha.

"Didn't you used to wear glasses?"

"Yeah, but I got rid of them,"

"Did you have surgery?"

"Uh, yeah, nice to see that you're back at the library," Wade said, changing the subject.

"Yeah, my father had to pull a few strings," she answered, still staring at Wade. "You know you look different," she said finally.

"Like you said, maybe it was the glasses," Wade offered.

"No,"

"My hair is longer now," Wade said, rubbing his fingers through his hair.

"I noticed that and I like it, but it seems like something else. Almost like this is my first time seeing you," Nia probed.

"Thanks for the compliment," Wade said, growing nervous over her head to toe examination.

"Are you getting taller?" she asked.

"O-o-of course not," Wade stuttered. "Is Matthew here?"

"No, the bookworm, just left," Nia pouted. She had already made several unreturned advances toward Matthew as well.

"Alright," Wade responded, turning to leave.

"You sure you don't want to stay and keep me company," she asked hopefully.

Wade studied Nia and thought about it for a second, but then he remembered Quay.

"No, I really do need to study. Can I get a rain check?"

"Sure," Nia said, not bothering to mask the rejection in her voice.

Wade turned to exit. Maybe it was time for a nap after all.

The walk back toward the dorms remained as uneventful as his trek to the library. His mind bounced back and forth from thoughts about Dr. Smith and Sundiata, to Nia's continued references about his appearance. Before he knew it he was back at his dorm, in his picture perfect room. Chance was the ideal roommate for Wade. Despite their different taste in clothes and music, Chance was just as neat.

Wade took off his clothes and hung them back in their exact location in his closet. He stood in front of the mirror and looked at himself in his wife beater t-shirt, designer boxers, and socks. The blue ankh hung around his neck like a small weight and seemed to glow. He examined himself in the mirror and concluded that somehow he did look different. And not different in the way that one looks different after a haircut, but rather more pronounced. For the life of him, he could not put his finger on it. Muscles were starting to develop in his arms, thighs, and calves, and the outline of a six-pack was forming where his stomach had previously been soft and flat. His hair was longer, but none of those things quite explained the difference that he saw staring back at him. After several more seconds of running his hands through his hair and examining his physique, he decided that it must not be that important if he couldn't figure it out.

He knew that Jo'sha was in the music room and Chance was still in class. Wade closed his eyes, concentrated, and waited to be moved in the way that a calm water is moved by a breeze. He felt nothing, so he knew that Matthew was nowhere around either. His afternoon naps started with meditation, which was essential for maintaining his peace of mind and clarity of thought. He closed the blinds, stretched out on his bed in nothing but his underwear and socks, and let his mind, body, spirit, and soul reach out into the universe. His being began to soar into otherworldly places, past the emotions of everyone and the essence of everything around him. Eventually he fell into deep and restful slumber.

Some time later Wade was awakened by a loud banging noise. It took him several seconds before he realized that it was someone knocking on the door. From the urgency of the knock, it seemed as though whoever it was had been knocking for quite some time. Wade knew immediately that it wasn't Chance, Jo'sha, or Matthew. Without thinking, he rushed to the door in his boxers, turned the lock, and snatched the door open.

"What in the hell do you think you're doing?" yelled a tall, slim, light-complexioned young man who looked remarkably like Wade.

"William?" Wade asked,

Wade looked at his cousin William, confused about both his obvious hostility, and his reason for being there.

"Don't 'William' me," his cousin said angrily.

"What's wrong?" Wade asked timidly.

When they were kids, William, who was his older cousin, had picked on him a lot, and Wade remembered those times vividly. He had temporarily forgotten about the power he now possessed.

"Where do you get off telling my mom about my personal life?" William charged.

"Oh," Wade said, immediately recalling his outburst during his argument with his family.

"*Oh*, is that all you have to say, dammit?" William demanded.

"William, I'm sorry. It just came out. I didn't mean anything by it. It was just that they were all so upset with me about Quay and—"

"Whatever you do is your business," William interrupted. "It has nothing to do with me. You had no right to tell my mom that!" he yelled.

"It's not like she wouldn't have found out sooner or later anyway," Wade reasoned. "We all knew it. I know you didn't think that everything you were running around and doing your first two years in college wouldn't get back to the family. You know how people talk. We were the first ones people came back and told," Wade said.

"That's beside the point. It wasn't your place to tell her," William said angrily. "I should have had the opportunity to tell her when the time was right. Do you know that she had a private investigator follow me around for two weeks? She has pictures, Wade! Pictures!" William exclaimed painfully. Tears began welling up in his eyes.

"I'm sorry. I didn't know," Wade apologized.

"You're right. You *don't* know. You have no idea what I've been through with them."

"You came all the way to Georgia to yell at me?" Wade asked. He sensed that William was finally starting to calm down now that he had spoken his peace.

"I don't know why I came here. I really didn't have any place else to go. The private investigator was snooping around Bartram's law firm asking questions, and now he isn't even speaking to me," William said.

"Bartram Landler, the attorney?" Wade asked.

"Yes," William said, realizing that he had shared more than he had intended.

"I am so sorry. What can I do to help?" Wade asked.

Just then another series of heavy knocks crashed against the door.

"Wade, are you alright in there?" Matthew asked from the other side of the door.

In all of the commotion, Wade hadn't noticed that Matthew had entered the suite, but Matthew had noticed that Wade was disturbed, and had heard the yelling.

"I'm fine," Wade yelled, stepping past William to open the door. "I just—"

"Meet my cousin, William," Wade interjected before Matthew could continue.

"Oh," Matthew said, extending his hand to greet William.

William smiled politely and offered his hand in return. The seconds of silence that followed the introduction were uncomfortable until Matthew finally spoke.

"What brings you here to visit?" Matthew asked, still holding William's hand.

"Family business," William offered, awkwardly snatching his hand from Matthew's grasp.

Matthew also felt awkward, not realizing that he hadn't let go of William's hand.

"Nice to meet you, William—" Matthew began, ready to back out of the room.

"You don't have to go. You want to go get something to eat?" Wade asked. Somehow he felt that Matthew's presence had taken the edge off of William's anger. William cut a glance at Wade from the corner of his eye as if to tell him that they still had unfinished business.

"Yeah, why not?" Matthew said, accepting the offer.

"William, would you like to get something to eat? I'm sure that you're hungry after your long trip," Wade said.

"Uh, yeah," William said reluctantly.

"Where are you staying while you are here?" Matthew asked.

"Not sure yet."

"Well you know you can kick it here with us if you don't mind rooming with four other people. We have a small couch in the common room," Matthew offered.

"I'll think about it," William said, much to Wade's surprise.

"Are you still in school?" Matthew asked.

"Yes. I'm in medical school in Maryland," William said proudly.

"Where are you in school?"

"I did my undergrad here, now I'm at Johns Hopkins," William answered patiently. He was still angry that he hadn't yet had an opportunity to finish his conversation with Wade. His upbringing, however, wouldn't allow him to be impolite to a stranger or share family business, no matter how angry he was.

"Great, well glad you came to visit us here at GCU," Matthew said again.

"Where should we go eat?" Wade asked, glad for the diversion.

"How about Lucille's?"

"Great choice," Wade echoed as he rushed to his closet to put on clothes.

"What's that you have there?" William asked Matthew, referring to the giant book that Matthew was carrying.

"Lynchings in the 20ᵗʰ Century by Sanford DuVall," Matthew answered.

"Is that for a class?" William continued.

"Uhm, yeah," Matthew said, glancing at Wade.

"Matthew is a history buff just like you William," Wade added.

"Are you familiar with the book?" Matthew asked.

"Professor DuVall taught me history in my sophomore year," William bragged.

"So you know Sanford DuVall?" Matthew asked excitedly.

"Sure," William said smiling for the first time.

Matthew looked into William's eyes and noticed William and Wade's strong family resemblance.

"He has some pretty interesting theories about what was behind lynchings in the early 20ᵗʰ century. Do you know much about his work?" Matthew asked intently.

"You must be referring to DuVall's famous conspiracy theory, that masked riders and slave owners were hunting black men, not just for sport, but for clues to a great treasure that came over from Africa," William answered.

"That's exactly it. Did he ever lecture on it?"

"Did he *ever*! We had to write a paper on whether or not we thought his theory was true or not. He said our position wouldn't affect our grade, but none of us who dared to disagree got above a B-," William said.

Matthew was completely engrossed in the conversation. They continued talking while Wade finished dressing.

"I'm ready," Wade said finally.

He followed William and Matthew, who walked ahead of him, still deeply engaged in conversation about Dr. DuVall's work. Wade pulled out his cell phone and dialed Chance, who had been out of class for over an hour.

"Where have you been?"

"I stopped by the Butler building to drop off paperwork for the Spring Festival entertainment committee," Chance answered.

"Well, my cousin is in town and Matthew and I are taking him to Lucille's. Call Jo'sha and meet us there."

"Ok. I'll call Jo'sha now."

Wade hung up his cell phone and noticed that William and Matthew were still engaged in conversation. As he watched them he couldn't help but feel hopeful—perhaps he and William would be able to make amends.

CHAPTER 31

Jo'sha and Chance arrived at Lucille's shortly after Wade, Matthew, and William. Lucille's was crowded so they were forced to get a table in the back corner of the restaurant near the kitchen. Wade could tell that William was still very angry with him, but he seemed to appreciate the company of Wade's friends, especially Matthew.

"How are you fine young men doing today?" Lucille asked.

Lucille and her restaurant were a part of the Georgia Central University experience. Her food was much better than the student cafeteria, and students often rewarded themselves with a trip to Lucille's after a long night of studying. And even though she was getting older and rarely came out of the kitchen to wait on customers these days, she still seemed to know everyone's name.

"We're fine, Auntie," Chance responded.

The others smiled and nodded in agreement. Lucille insisted that all of her regulars call her Auntie, especially Georgia Central men, who she seemed to favor. They each ordered their usual. Chance got salmon and broccoli. Matthew got a grilled chicken salad. Jo'sha ordered hummus and falafel, and Wade ordered a fried three-piece chicken dinner, with side orders of potatoes, squash, green beans and an extra serving of country-fried steak.

"I don't remember you eating that much," William commented.

Jo'sha, Matthew and Chance exchanged glances, wondering what other new things William would notice about Wade.

"Just a growing boy I guess," Wade answered, handing the menu back to Lucille without even having looked at it.

"What's good here?" William asked turning to Matthew.

"All of the salads are good. I like the grilled chicken salad, but the shrimp salad is pretty good, too" Matthew answered.

"I'll have a shrimp salad," William said, handing his menu back to Lucille.

Once the orders were taken, William and Matthew continued their conversation about lynchings in the 20th century, turning to specific passages in the text for reference. Wade leaned in close to Jo'sha and Chance and began to tell them about his afternoon without appearing too obvious. It didn't matter though, because William didn't seem to be paying them any attention anyway.

"Guess who I saw talking to Dr. Smith today?" Wade asked.

"Who?" Jo'sha asked.

"Sundiata Bazemore," Wade said.

"So what? They were probably just talking about class work or something," Chance said.

"It just seemed strange. They were talking over by the faculty parking deck. It just seemed strange," Wade repeated.

"Well if Dr. Smith is our man, then Sundiata could be in big trouble," Jo'sha said.

"Exactly," Wade answered.

"Any new leads on the murder?" Chance asked.

"Do you mean from the authorities or from Detective Matthew Meredith?" Jo'sha joked just above a whisper.

"Either," Chance answered.

"Maybe all of this attention has got him laying low," Wade offered.

"You never really mentioned your cousin before. What brings him here for a visit now?" Jo'sha asked, changing the subject.

"Family business, " Wade answered, not bothering to offer any further information.

CHAPTER 32

William had not completely forgiven Wade, but he appreciated the fact that Wade and his friends had offered him a place to stay until he figured out how to sort out his life. He was not in the right frame of mind to finish out the semester, and going home to Baltimore definitely was not an option. He slept on the small couch in the common area at night, and spent his days conducting research for Matthew on lynchings and characters named Alfred Canford and Cornelius Smith. William wasn't sure what exactly he was searching for, but the research kept his mind off of his problems and gave him something to do during the day until Wade and Matthew returned.

With William in the suite, it was much more difficult to get away with using their powers. They hadn't realized how comfortable they had become using their powers within the confines of their suite. They often made excuses to leave individually before meeting up to drive to Fayetteville. When they weren't practicing their powers in the evening, Matthew and William spent hours pouring over research. William slipped into the groove and eventually became a part of their routine, establishing relationships with Chance, Jo'sha and Matthew, and reestablishing his relationship with Wade.

It was a Wednesday afternoon and Wade and William were alone in the suite as they often were on Wednesdays.

"You have some really good friends," William said.

"I know," Wade said proudly.

"I can tell that they really care about you."

"We are pretty close."

"I see you all get up and meditate in the morning. You're not in some kind of cult are you?"

"Of course not!" Wade exclaimed, insulted that William would even suggest something like that.

"That's what all cult members say," William said skeptically.

"We are *not* in a cult," Wade stressed. "We have just fallen into a pretty solid routine that seems to be working for us. We get up in the morning and meditate. Then we go work out and head to class. Most of our evenings are spent studying. We have better bodies and great grades to show for it."

"I can tell that you're working out. I haven't seen you look better."

"Thanks," Wade said, enjoying the positive attention.

"You all wear those cross things around your necks. Are you sure you're not in a cult?" William questioned.

"It's just a piece of jewelry that Jo'sha found for us," Wade said, not realizing that William had been so observant.

"Oh," William said. He wasn't sure if he believed Wade, but figured he should give him the benefit of the doubt.

"But that's enough about me," Wade said, taking control of the conversation before William could probe further. "What about you? You can't hide forever. What about school? What about the family? They've got to be worried sick about you."

"I called Aunt Grace. I didn't tell her where I was, but I told her that I'm all right. And the last time I checked, you and the family weren't on such great speaking terms either," William said, sounding a little miffed by Wade's chastising.

"Yeah, you're right, but seeing you hiding out here, putting your life on hold has made me realize that we can't run away from our problems. I plan to confront them when I go home for Christmas break, and I think you should, too. I have to tell them that I am a young man now, and that although I appreciate and need their help and support, I have to be free to make my own decisions."

"Maybe you're right."

"I know I'm right," Wade said, sounding more like the older cousin.

"Thanks for letting me crash here with you and your friends. I'd thought about confronting the family before you suggested it, but I didn't know if I could. Being here has definitely given me some time to clear my mind."

"So you'll go home to Baltimore with me when I go for holiday break? We can face them together," Wade said reassuringly.

"Sure," William agreed with more conviction than he really felt. He exhaled loudly, apprehensive about what he'd just agreed to do.

The next few weeks before the Christmas break were uneventful. The boys continued to hold their morning meditations without any interruptions from William. In fact, some mornings he joined them, unknowingly leaving his emotional activity an open book for Wade to peruse. Although William often started out the meditation sessions with good intentions, he always ended up fast asleep. By the time he woke up, the others were always already gone to the gym. Matthew wasn't able to explain why the meditation sessions had that effect on William, but he was sure that it had something to do with him somehow getting caught up in their flow.

Wade had been careful not to share William's real reason for coming with Jo'sha, Chance or Matthew, but he wondered what they all would say if they knew why he chose to stay so long.

Jo'sha was working overtime in the music room getting ready for his big recording session with Agonize after the holidays. Chance had become a committee chairperson for the Spring Festival event, and was doing everything he could to make sure that Omega Tau had a place in the step show. Wade was working on the Omega Tau introduction to the university community. Matthew and William were spending even more time together as the holidays drew near.

They continued to watch Dr. Smith's comings and goings, but nothing seemed out of the ordinary with the exception of the fact that Dr. Smith was paying Sundiata more attention in the classroom. The male murders seemed to have stopped completely, and Matthew began to wonder if Dr. Smith knew they were watching him.

As the semester drew to a close, they attacked their final exams with the intent of maintaining their perfect grade point averages. As they prepared to part ways, Wade insisted that they all come back to campus a day early after the holidays to prepare for Omega Tau's public relations campaign. Matthew had arranged for them to spend the last night at Miss Vaughn's home in Fayetteville, and for reasons that he still had yet to explain, he suggested that they spend half the night in meditation. William felt a little miffed that he was being left alone in the suite until Wade confided in him they were attempting to start a new fraternity. William seemed satisfied with the explanation and was glad that his cousin thought enough of him to share his secret.

"You know the family will frown on this don't you?" William advised.

"I know, but this is what I want to do," Wade responded on his way out the door.

This time the drive to Fayetteville was different. Matthew, normally excited about their trips to the country, was somber. The others had become accustomed to Matthew's bouts of silence. They knew that he would eventually share his thoughts, but his revelations were more oft times than not, life altering for them all.

Once in the country, they sat under the cool moonlight in the backyard of Miss Vaughn's Fayetteville estate. Just a few months ago they would have all thought sitting out in the country night air as strange behavior, but now things of this nature were considered common amongst the four of them.

"This'll be the first time that we've been separated since—everything happened," Matthew said solemnly.

"Are you concerned?" Wade asked, having often wondered if a separation would do them any harm.

"I don't know, but it's better to be safe than sorry. When Jo'sha was out we all felt the effects. We know that the daily meditations have helped all of us and we won't be able to meditate together for the next two weeks," Matthew explained.

The icy fingers of December seemed to taunt them. Matthew drew up a cushion of air, which Jo'sha warmed to form a blanket against the cool night air. They meditated and the ankhs seemed to glow with a supernatural light. Chance's was less bright than the others, and in the December night it was obvious.

"Why can't I do as much as the rest of you can?" Chance wondered aloud.

"Not again," Matthew said sounding exasperated.

"Shhhh," Jo'sha added.

"I'm serious? Why did I get the short end of the stick?" Chance asked.

"We handed the ankhs out at random. And you *are* able to do wonderful things just like the rest of us," Wade offered.

"But not as *much* as the rest of you," Chance persisted.

"I didn't give you that one on purpose," Jo'sha said, feeling a little defensive.

"I know, I know, but it would be nice to do more things like the rest of you," Chance sighed.

"Since it doesn't seem that we're going to be able to finish meditation, we might as well fellowship," Matthew suggested.

"Fellowship?" asked Wade.

"I got the word from one of Cyrus' letters. That is what he called it when the four of them got together," Matthew explained.

"I like it," said Jo'sha, recognizing the spirituality of the term. "You know, this whole Omega Tau thing is coming along nicely," he said.

"Are we going to be able to step in the Spring Festival?" Wade asked.

"Yes," said Chance. "Because there are so many fraternities, social organizations, and dorms that want to step, they're going to limit it to the six organizations with the highest grade point averages. By the spring semester we will most certainly be in that number."

"And how exactly are we going to learn how to step?" Wade asked.

"I've got that covered," said Jo'sha confidently. "I was talking to Anthony about our recording session here in Atlanta and I just ran the concept by him—in confidence. And wouldn't you know it, his choreographer graduated from Tuskegee, and he's a Greek. Anthony said he was sure that he could get him to help us out," Jo'sha said proudly.

"Maybe you shouldn't have done that," Chance said skeptically.

"No, actually, that was probably a good idea," Matthew said.

"Huh?" the rest said in unison.

"I mean it. I know I've been somewhat of a stick in the mud when it comes to this whole fraternity thing, but it does have merit," Matthew admitted.

"I can't believe this is you," Jo'sha teased.

"I've been thinking about it. The shroud of secrecy that covers fraternities will provide the perfect cover for us. It'll explain why we're always together, why we all wear ankhs, and why we always need to meet," Matthew reasoned.

"Good thinking," Chance said.

"But it's more than that. We have to actually act like a fraternity," Jo'sha admonished.

"That won't be so bad either. Just having William spend time with us has shown me how important it is to have people around you that you can trust," Matthew said.

"Glad to see that someone got through to you," Jo'sha said.

"So when we get back from holiday break we'll plaster the entire campus with huge green, gold, and silver posters that say, 'watch it come together.' It'll have an Omega at the top of the poster, and a Tau at the bottom. Each week we'll put up new posters, and each week the Omega and the Tau will be closer and closer together until finally they will form a huge green, gold and silver ankh," Wade said excitedly.

"That is hot!" Jo'sha exclaimed.

"And that isn't all. As it gets closer to the Spring Festival, we'll put up posters with a silhouette of Chance—we don't want anyone to be able to recognize him so it'll just be an outline. I can already see it. We can get a photograph of Chance standing on Bonder's point with a bolt of lightening behind him and the caption will read, 'From Here Tau Fraternity,'" Wade said.

"I'm digging that!" Chance said with a smile.

"I think that last part is a little corny," Jo'sha interjected.

Wade smirked at him, but kept quiet.

"What about outfits? You know that's always an important part of a good show," Chance said. "Black Greeks usually dress alike in step shows as a sign of unity."

"I've got that, too. I already asked Agonize if he could lend us some help from his personal stylist. There are only four of us, so it shouldn't be a big deal," Jo'sha said, happy to step up to the plate again.

"I have another idea," said Wade. "In addition to pooling our resources and making a sizable donation to the amphitheater project in the name of Omega Tau and our founders, I think we should submit a ghost written letter to the school paper detailing Cyrus' great idea of starting a fraternity back in 1904, but were unable to since they all went missing," he added.

"As long as we don't tip our hands about the ankhs," Matthew warned.

"Jo'sha wrote the history and I've reread it a thousand times. It's a great story and sure to get people talking," Wade continued.

"Nice touch," Chance echoed.

"Then we come back and hit them with our service project when the semester starts. And not a hundred different service projects either, we'll concentrate on service with a laser-like focus. Helping young black boys become men," Wade said proudly.

"Foster would have liked that," Jo'sha said thoughtfully.

"What about being anonymous?" Chance asked.

"We'll be off campus with our service projects at first and by the time anyone realizes all that we're doing, the Spring Festival will be here," Wade said.

"We'll pick the high school in greatest need and every elementary and middle school that feeds into it. It'll be our mission to make sure that every young black male makes better grades this year than they did last year. Our reach will be small, but our impact will be great," Wade said, becoming more passionate each time he spoke.

"And are you ready for the icing on the cake?" Jo'sha asked.

"My recording session with Agonize is just a few weeks before Spring Festival. I've already reserved the Cultural Complex for what will be the biggest party of the year," Jo'sha said.

"And how do you expect to fill up the Cultural Complex? It's huge!" Chance said.

"This is my biggest surprise. Anthony is thinking about shooting his next video on the campus of Georgia Central. His people have already started talking to University officials. He said that we could bill it as an Omega Tau party as long as we handle getting the word out. He wants the video to feel like a frat party. He said he's been trying to get some of the other fraternities to work with him, but none of them will return his call. For Omega Tau we are the only approval that he needs. He's even planning to have DJ Fantom do the party," Jo'sha added.

"*The* DJ Fantom?" Chance asked, sounding impressed.

"The one and only."

"Again, what about us staying on the low until the step show?" Chance asked.

"I've already thought about that. That's what will make it so hot. The record label's public relations department will handle the radio spots with the local media. We'll put up the posters late at night when no one can see us. We'll even have the Cultural Complex decorated for the party, but the big hype will be about the whole campus trying to figure out who is really in the organization," Jo'sha exclaimed.

"Well what is your contribution to all of this?" Wade asked Matthew.

Matthew smiled and said, "You'll see, but much later. I have to check some things out first."

They gave him a puzzled look, but he didn't bother to explain any further.

"It is getting late," he said. "Time for one quick experiment."

They all stood instinctively and listened as Matthew began to lecture on optical effects related to the weather—things like rainbows, coronas, iridescence, haloes, and auroras. Much to his surprise they all seemed to have numerous questions. Eventually they got on the topic of dust devils and tornados.

"Now dust devils or small tornados normally begin when winds create a rotating air mass in the low levels of the troposphere. When this rotation combines with strong updrafts produced by surface heating of the ground, then it creates a funnel," Matthew explained. He moved toward Jo'sha and motioned for him to heat a large area of the earth in front of them. Then Matthew raised his hands, threw his head back, and called down the wind until the air began to rotate above them. Before they knew it a small tornado whirled before them.

"Now that's a dust devil," said Chance. "We have those at home."

"Are you sure you can control it?" Wade asked cautiously.

Matthew seemed to grow in pride and stature as he motioned toward the whirling mass of wind. It danced for him and bowed to him before he sent it off toward the trees, where it snapped pine trees like twigs and sucked up brush and grass, feeding it's frenzy.

"I think you should stop," Wade yelled.

But Matthew didn't hear him. The wind puppet he'd created grew and twisted and tore up the trees behind Miss Vaughn's house. Birds flew from their homes in fear of the unnatural occurrence. Chance grabbed his chest. The stronger the wind got, the less he was able to control his breathing. Each time a tree was torn from the earth, he felt it, but Matthew didn't notice. Chance pushed passed Jo'sha and Wade and tackled Matthew, knocking him to the ground. Proximity to the earth ankh put a damper on Matthew's power, as did the tackle.

Just like that, the cyclonic activity stopped as suddenly as it had started. Chance lay on the ground breathing heavily.

"Wasn't that great?" Matthew asked breathlessly. He was still oblivious to the effect his display had on Chance.

It was after 3:00 a.m. when they got back to the dorm, but the energy in the building seemed different. They did not sense the peacefulness that normally greeted them when they returned in the wee hours of the morning.

Chance was still winded and a little upset with Matthew for the episode back at Miss Vaughn's property so he didn't have much to say, but the difference was unsettling to Wade.

"Do you feel that?" he asked anxiously.

"What?" Matthew asked.

"Something doesn't feel right here," Jo'sha agreed.

"It isn't broad, but it runs deep," Wade commented.

Instinctively they rushed toward the elevator to their suite. When they arrived, William was sitting in the common room glued to the television that Wade had put in the common room to keep him company.

"What is it?" Wade asked, with the others directly behind. William waited a few seconds before responding.

"It's a special news report. They've found an eleventh murder victim. This time the body was left right downtown in the city just off of Peachtree Street."

CHAPTER 33

Wade's heart raced as he entered the recreation center on the south side of Baltimore. The letters between him and the boys had kept him up with the goings-on in their lives, but letters weren't a substitute for the real thing. He knew that Kenny's brother was back in jail for armed robbery, that Raphi had learned to ride his big sister's bike even though the handlebars weren't straight and one of the pedals was missing, and that Tony had made a new friend who knew how to sign too.

Wade hadn't thought about it until now, but he was saddened by the fact that the boys were moving on without him. And that he was moving on without them. Practically everything about him had changed.

With the encouragement of his friends he returned home a little more relaxed, with baggy jeans, an Atlanta Falcon's football jersey, and a pair of Chance's Timberland boots. He stopped just outside the recreation center great room, ran his hands through his hair, and adjusted his clothes the way he had seen Chance do it. All of a sudden he felt uncomfortable. He grabbed the ankh around his neck for reassurance.

When he entered the room, the young boys looked up. And like he had so many times before, Tony ran up to hug him. The difference was that Wade's physique was more solid than it had been the last time they saw him, and Tony could tell the difference. After hugging Wade, Tony stood back.

"You have muscles," he signed.

"I've been lifting weights," Wade responded. "You have fewer teeth," he commented.

Tony smiled and hugged Wade again.

After that they bombarded him with question after question. "Where are your glasses?"

"What happened to your hair?"

"What is college like?"

Wade laughed. He settled down in the floor and answered each question one by one, and it felt just like old times.

"Did you bring us anything?" Kenny asked.

"Did you want to see me or did you want to see what I brought you?" Wade asked.

"Well—" Kenny hesitated.

Wade walked over to the window and motioned for William to bring the huge bags of toys into the center.

"Are they for us?" Raphi asked.

"If you're nice to me," Wade teased.

William's family wasn't known for producing strong men and William was no exception. He struggled to get the huge bags out of the car, up the stairs, and down the long hallway to the recreation room. The boys were practically in a frenzy by the time William finally made it.

"You could have come and helped me," William wheezed.

"The exercise is good for you," Wade responded.

"You sound like Chance," William said.

"These are your Christmas gifts so you can't open them until Christmas morning," Wade instructed.

William pulled off his leather coat and looked around for a safe place to put it before deciding to put it back on. That's when he noticed that Wade wasn't wearing a coat. "Why aren't you wearing a coat?" he asked.

"Just not cold," Wade answered before he realized that it was odd not to be wearing a coat in December in Baltimore.

"Can we at least open one?" Raphi begged.

Wade pretended to think about it for a moment, keeping them in suspense. "All right, just one," he said. The rest you have to take home and open on Christmas morning."

"But my cousins will steal them if I take them home," Kenny whined.

"I'll tell you what. Leave them with me and I'll bring them to you Christmas morning," Wade said.

The boys began sorting their presents, trying to decide which one to open now.

"You know they'll all be at your house when we get there," William said while the boys were occupied with their gifts.

"I know, but avoiding them won't make it go away. We're going to get Quay and go to my house just like we all planned. It'll be all right. It has to be," he said confidently.

"I'm glad that you're so sure about that," William said doubtfully.

"Our family has always used money to make problems go away. It is about time we started talking and resolving some of our issues," Wade said.

Wade gave Quay a phone call and told her that they were on their way to pick her up for dinner. Quay was as excited about going to dinner as Victoria and her sisters were about having her, but they all knew that there was no avoiding the fact that they were going to be family.

"I'll be ready when you get here," she said.

"I love you," Wade said more confidently than he ever had before. The new insight that the ankh gave him had revealed to him that Quay genuinely loved him too—more than he had imagined.

William envied Wade's ability to show public affection, even if his family didn't approve.

They spent another hour at the center talking to the boys and making arrangements to see them again before he left. Wade exchanged conversation with a few of the new recreation center volunteers and gave them his contact information at college. They were glad to finally meet the man that the boys called the best volunteer ever.

The ride to D.C. from Baltimore was filled with honest conversation. Wade imagined that William was gearing up for the conversation with the family.

"That was good work that you did back there. I knew you volunteered at the recreation center, but I didn't realize that you had such an impact," William acknowledged.

"I didn't realize how much I missed them," Wade said.

"Wade, I'm tired of hiding who I am. Maybe all of this was for the best. You know—the family finding out this way. At least that part is over," William said.

"That's one way to look at it," Wade responded.

Quay saw Wade from her second story window. Her belly was much larger than it was the last time she had seen Wade. She didn't know what he would think of her. She had spent all of her last paycheck on a black, crushed velvet maternity dress, and gifts for Wade and his parents. She had never been to Wade's house before, and she was more than a little anxious. She knew his family wasn't fond of her, but she was determined to make a good impression.

Quay was downstairs with her bag of gifts before Wade and William could find a parking space. She wobbled down the stoop, her arms filled with bags. Wade ran up the block towards her. It had been too long since he had seen her. He grabbed her in his arms, lifted her up, and hugged her.

"Careful, you might hurt the baby," Quay giggled.

Wade put her down gently, kissed her cheek, and then her belly.

"You look awesome," Wade said.

"You look good too. What are you doing down there at college? The hair and the clothes are all different," Quay said.

"Your tummy has gotten bigger," Wade remarked.

"I know," Quay mumbled, disappointed that he noticed that before he noticed the new dress.

"No, I love it. I think it is beautiful. There's a little Graham growing in there!"

They both laughed.

"Um-hmph," William cleared his throat as he walked up behind them.

"Oh, Quay, this is my cousin William," Wade announced proudly.

"Nice to meet you," Quay said in her most proper tone.

"You're more beautiful than Wade described you," William said, surprising both Wade and Quay by giving her a big hug.

Wade smiled. The hug seemed to break the tension of the introduction. William grabbed the bags from her.

"Let a gentleman take these. I don't know what my cousin is thinking," William teased.

The Graham men were nothing if not charming.

They got to Baltimore much quicker than William or Quay had hoped. The conversation was flowing and the ride was a buffer from Josephine, Victoria, and Grace. Much to Wade's surprise, William told Quay all about his situation with his family on the long ride. It made for interesting conversation and seemed to create a bond between William and Quay, who was surprisingly insightful and understanding. After the discussion about William's situation, the conversation turned to the Atlanta Male Murders and the eleventh victim. By the time that conversation was over, Quay felt comfortable enough to pick William for information on the Graham family and what made them tick. Much to her dismay, they seemed as pretentious as she'd thought.

When they were twenty miles from the house, Wade stopped at a gas station and asked William to drive.

"I just need to take a quick nap before we get to the house," Wade said.

"But we are almost home," William said.

"I know, but I just need to rest my eyes," Wade said.

"Are you alright," Quay asked, running her fingers through his wavy hair. She liked Wade's longer hair, but was unsettled by the fact that he seemed to be growing and changing without her.

"I'm fine. I just need to get some rest before we get to the house," Wade demanded.

Quay and William obliged him. William took the driver's seat, and Quay took the front passenger's seat.

Wade stretched out in the back seat and allowed his breathing to level off. He hadn't tried to calm a room full of people before, but he knew that if there were ever a need this would be it. That made his need for meditation essential. Wade closed his eyes, took a deep breath, and hummed while he searched for higher energies.

Quay looked back at him, puzzled by his behavior.

"He and his friends meditate," William explained.

"You know Chance and 'em?" she asked.

"Oh yes," William said proudly.

"Has he been doing it long?" Quay asked, referring to Wade.

"For a while now, it's actually very relaxing," William answered.

Wade's mind drifted beyond their conversation and the physical confines of the truck. When he found harmony he knew it. He hesitated in it and let it consume him.

It was dusk by the time William pulled up to the house. William and Quay gave each other knowing looks and then smiles of reassurance before getting out of the truck.

"I have to get my bags," Quay said nervously.

"I'll get the bags," William said.

"I'd like to carry them in if it's okay," she said.

"No problem," William said as he unlocked the back door.

"Wade, we're here. I can't believe that you went to sleep that quickly," William said.

Quay was at the back of the truck checking her bags and making sure that the bows and wrapping were straight, as well as checking her hair and make-up.

"Wade!" William snapped.

"I'm awake."

Wade rose slowly and deliberately. When he opened his eyes they seemed to glow against the dusky canvas of evening.

"Are you alright?" William asked, looking at him curiously.

"Perfect," Wade answered.

"Is everything alright?" Quay asked from the back of the truck.

"Just fine," William said, not completely convinced. He didn't know what it was, but Wade's presence and confidence comforted him, and he would need all of that to face his family.

Wade was becoming more adept in the use of the ankh. After meditating he could feel things and his interpretation of people and their feelings was visible to him in colors and auras. He could sense harmony or discord in the colors that surrounded people. As they made their way up the long walk to the door, he sensed the nervousness and discomfort from Quay and William. Sharp, electric colors that pulsed brighter and brighter the closer they got to the house. William was starting to perspire, and Quay was practicing what seemed to be a fake smile. Wade breathed deeply and concentrated. Soon the burgundy and black colors that he sensed around them both calmed to lighter shades of red. Not ideal he thought, but better.

"Are we ready?" Wade asked.

"Yes, I feel—ready," Quay said, surprising herself.

"Me too," William echoed.

"Good. Just remember they can kill you but they can't eat you," Wade joked, borrowing a line from Chance.

"Huh?" Quay asked, giving him a puzzled look.

"Never mind," Wade smiled.

Neither Quay nor William laughed.

Although it was his house, Wade felt enough like an outsider now to have to knock on the door. It was almost a minute before anyone answered. Both William and Wade were relieved to see that it was Aunt Grace who answered the door.

"My babies," she said, opening her arms to give both of them a hug. Her aura was a warm and inviting shade of blue, and although Wade had never been able to see or sense it before, he imagined that it had always been that way, which was why Aunt Grace was his favorite.

"Auntie Grace, you remember Quay don't you?" he asked, stepping aside so that she could see Quay.

"Of course I do," Grace sang.

Quay's arms were filled with the packages that she was holding just above her belly, but Aunt Grace managed to give her a hug anyway.

"Hello, Miss Grace," Quay stuttered. She didn't want to sound too familiar by calling her Aunt.

"It'll be alright, and you can call me Aunt Grace," Grace whispered in Quay's ear.

Wade felt Quay's tension ease slightly.

The lights in the foyer were stark and exposing. From the balance of the lights, muffled voices, and smell of the food, Wade guessed that the entire family was in the dining room at the table—a setting he had come to despise for its superficial conversation and constant judgment. As they walked down the corridor he let his mind reach out to Quay and William. He tried his best to tune their auras to Aunt Grace's, but it was harder now that they were actually in the house.

They could hear the dinner conversation more clearly as they got closer to the dining area. When they arrived, the conversation stopped, they stopped, and everyone stared. Although there were only five people at the table, it seemed as though they were before an audience of thousands. Wade's father sat at the head of the table smoking his old gnawed pipe. His mother sat directly to his father's left as she always had, but tonight she seemed so very out of place.

Josephine Wallington Smalls, Wade's aunt and William's mother, was probably the most uptight person in the room. She sat straight up in her chair with an expression that was something just short of a scowl. Directly beside her sat Jocelyn Smalls, her daughter, no less pretentious or beautiful than her mother. Beside them sat Josephine's brow beaten and henpecked husband, Herman Smalls. Uncle Herman's family was long on money, but he was short on backbone.

The emotions mixed like noxious fumes, rolled through the room like smog and Wade could find no cover from them. He took a deeper breath and tried to find a common place to harmonize everyone's feelings. He found a plum tinted emotion that must have been akin to resolution—something that they all wanted. Everyone in the room with the exception of his Aunt Grace was fighting him on a subconscious level, but he managed to maintain his composure.

"Well say, 'hello' to the children," Grace announced.

They all exchanged the obligatory greetings and looked for places at the table.

"Where is Uncle Lambert?" Wade leaned in and asked Aunt Grace.

"He was busy tonight," she answered.

Wade could tell that the question saddened her. Wade had always thought that Uncle Lambert didn't come around the family because they didn't make him feel welcome. He didn't come from money like the rest of Aunt Grace's sister's husbands.

"College seems to have changed you. What an *interesting* look," Victoria said, noticing her son's changed appearance.

"I like it. It's hip," Judge Graham said, attempting to be supportive.

"I, uh, have Christmas gifts for you," Quay stuttered. She walked over to Victoria with two packages and a big round belly.

"Oh, thank you, dear," Victoria spat, placing the gifts on the corner of the table.

Wade thought the gesture nice, but noticed that it didn't seem to change Victoria's mood.

"I hope you like them," Quay continued, handing Judge Graham a smaller, delicately wrapped package.

"Why thank you," he bellowed, opening it immediately.

"I remembered that you were smoking a pipe at dinner," Quay said, as he pulled a beautiful rosewood pipe from its case.

"Why this is wonderful," he said, rising to give Quay a hug.

She was pleased that he liked it. Victoria and Josephine exchanged skeptical glances.

Shrimp and oysters were served as appetizers. Quay, who didn't have much of an appetite for seafood in her current condition, picked around it, eating the crackers and garnishes so as not to offend Victoria.

They ate without significant conversation, until the forced peace was shattered. Wade could tell it was coming. He sensed a surge in Aunt Josephine's aura and tried to brace himself, William and Quay for it.

"So the prodigal son has returned. We were worried sick about you," Josephine mumbled, stabbing her shrimp.

"Here we go," William huffed.

"I would just like to know what we did wrong," she snapped.

Everyone looked up from their plates, but no one answered. The colors in the room were turning to a sharp shade of red.

"I mean it. Tell me! Where did we go wrong?" she said, louder than before.

Again silence.

"William, I know you hear me," she said, glaring at William. Jocelyn looked at her brother smugly, as if she had been waiting for this moment all of her life. William had long been Josephine's favorite, and Jocelyn was relishing his discomfort.

"Mother, what do you mean?" William asked defiantly.

"You know very well what I mean," Josephine said

"Do you mean my sexuality? Is that what you mean? Or do you mean the fact that you had me followed and practically ruined my life?" William snapped.

"I *mean* homosexuality, fornication, lying. When did we decide that any of that was okay behavior for our family," Josephine asked, from her moral high chair.

"I had heard the rumors from friends, but didn't want to believe it was true," Jocelyn inserted.

William and Wade both shot her nasty looks. Quay continued picking through her food, glad to be out of the line of fire.

"You stay out of this," William shot.

"This is family business," Jocelyn snapped back.

"Was it family business when you got an abortion last summer?" William snapped.

Victoria and Grace gasped.

"Whoa," Wade exclaimed, unaware of that family secret.

Quay looked up sheepishly to gauge Jocelyn's reaction. Jocelyn rolled her eyes at Quay.

"Leave her out of this!" Josephine yelled, trying not to glance at her sisters.

Wade's head started to ache.

"All I am saying is that we are no different than anyone else, and all of your antiquated ideas about being better than everyone else because of breeding is stupid. We spend more time trying to cover up who we are than we do understanding each other," William challenged.

Jocelyn was still flushed from William's earlier comment.

"It's just that we had such high hopes for you all," Josephine whimpered, with tears forming in her eyes.

"You still can and should have high hopes for us, but you have to understand that we have to live our own lives," Wade interjected.

"Who are her people?" Victoria whimpered, filled with her own set of questions.

"She's sitting right here, Mother," Wade defended.

"Well, who are your people?" Victoria asked, looking directly at Quay.

Quay looked up slowly with a puzzled expression.

"Why is that important?" Wade asked.

William sat quietly, glad that he was no longer the topic of conversation.

"You wanted me to get to know her. I'm trying!" Victoria screeched.

Wade could tell that even though she was anxious, she was sincere, so he nodded to Quay that it was all right to respond.

"My people are Quinton and Elizabeth Harold, Ma'am," Quay responded, not sure if she had properly answered the question.

"What do they do?" Victoria continued.

"My father owns his own cleaning business, and my mother is a law clerk," Quay said.

"And what do they think of your condition?" Victoria continued, while the rest of the room regrouped.

"They would just like to make sure that we have a healthy baby," Quay answered.

"Oh, so they have met our Wade have they?" Victoria snapped.

"Mother, perhaps this isn't the time for all these questions. We don't want to upset the baby," Wade said.

"Oh, so now you want to be responsible," Victoria snapped.

"Victoria!" Judge Graham warned.

The dull ache in Wade's head came back.

"How do you even know that this is your baby?" Victoria questioned.

"Victoria!" Judge Graham yelled again.

Victoria sighed, sat back in her chair, and looked up at the ceiling.

"And I guess all of those stories about those girls you were dating were just more lies," Josephine resumed. "What do we do now?" she asked.

"What do you mean?" William asked.

"How will we hold our heads up in church now? Bastard children, fornication, and God only knows what else," she answered.

"Who gives a damn?" William snapped.

"Now that kind of talk isn't going to solve anything," Aunt Grace added.

Quay began to weep.

"Now look at what you did," Wade said, sliding closer to Quay so that he could put his arm around her.

"*I* didn't get her pregnant," Josephine snapped.

"You're impossible!" William shot.

"Maybe if your father had been more of a man, then you wouldn't haven't turned out the way that you did," Victoria hissed.

William's father sat back in his chair and threw his napkin in his plate.

"You are such a bitch!" William yelled, pushing himself back from the table.

"Herman, are you going to let him talk to me like that?" Victoria screeched.

Victoria started to cry too. Wade tried hard to hold it all together, but the emotions were becoming too intense. Before he knew it, he had wrapped everyone in the room up in an emotional catatonic web.

∞

When Wade came to, everyone else in the room was still unconscious and barely breathing. He stumbled over to Quay who had fallen forward onto the table leaving her stomach in an awkward position. Everyone else, with the exception of his father, who had also fallen forward onto the table, had passed out onto the floor.

Wade moved over to Quay and pressed his finger against the vein in her neck to check her pulse. Then he placed his cheek near her face to see if she was breathing. He couldn't tell.

"Quay!" he cried, holding her and rocking.

There was no response.

"The baby, the baby," he whimpered rubbing her swollen belly.

Wade lost focus for a moment and began screaming and crying.

"William get up! I need you!" he yelled.

Suddenly from behind the walls the water began surging through the pipes in response to his anger and confusion. His heartbeat and blood raced. The water pulsed in the pipes inside the wall until neither Wade nor the metal pipes could stand the pressure any longer.

CHAPTER 34

Chance was just returning to his room after saying goodbye to Matthew and Jo'sha. Matthew had tried to encourage him to come with them and wait for his brothers, Jacoby and Cobyn, at his house, instead of alone on campus because of the recent news about the eleventh Male Murder victim. Chance declined because he wasn't one to worry about such things. He was capable of taking care of himself. As usual, Jo'sha made a joke out of the whole thing by conjuring up images of old horror movies, but Chance dismissed them and assured them that he would call when his brothers arrived. Besides, he stood a better chance of seeing Aspen before the Christmas holidays if he stayed on campus.

Jo'sha was spending the Christmas holidays with Matthew's family, since he really didn't have anywhere else to go. Chance had offered to let Jo'sha come home with him for the holidays, but he declined saying that Matthew had asked him first. Chance guessed that Jo'sha just didn't want to make the seven-hour drive back to North Carolina. Chance had never imagined that going back home for the Christmas holidays would be so tough. He and his mother hadn't completely patched things up from the fight at homecoming, and he still owed Sharon an explanation as to why he had just stopped calling her. His grandfather, T.C., had warned him about being so serious about one young lady. He told Chance that college offered a world of new possibilities, and he owed it to himself to try and explore them all. Breaking up with Sharon had been easy to postpone with the emotional and physical distance of college. Chance had never agreed that he would come back to marry Sharon after four years of college, but because they had never discussed it, both Sharon and Chance's mother felt comfortable assuming that was the plan.

The suite was lifeless without the energy of Jo'sha's music, Matthew's musings and contemplations, and Wade's complaining. Chance turned on the television and switched to ESPN. Jacoby and Cobyn wouldn't be there to pick him up for another hour, and he had finished packing earlier that morning. He pulled out his Spring Festival committee folder and went down the list. The home phone numbers and addresses for all of the committee members was listed in the back, since most of them would be working on committee projects through the holiday and would need to be in contact. Chance circled Aspen's address and telephone number, planning to get in contact with her over the holidays. She had all but stopped speaking to him shortly after the ordeal at homecoming but had started to come around recently by at least acknowledging him with a glance in Spring Festival meetings.

Chance wasn't one to give up and Aspen was everything that Sharon was not. T.C. had told him that you could tell the measure of a man by the house he lived in, the shoes he wore, and the woman that he kept on his arm—Chance intended to have Aspen on his arm.

He picked up the phone and called Cobyn's cell phone but there was no answer. He called Wade to see how things were in Baltimore with Quay, but he didn't get an answer from him either. He guessed that they both must have been in areas with bad reception.

ESPN was showing reruns so Chance pulled his dumbbells from the corner of the room and began doing bicep curls. His strength had multiplied considerably because of the ankh, so the fifty-pound weights were no longer a challenge for him.

Chance grabbed the ankh around his neck and began thinking about how it had changed his life. What would T.C., Jacoby, and Cobyn say if he told them how powerful he had become? Would they even believe him if he told them? If he showed them, could he trust them with his secret?

Chance was accustomed to keeping secrets. Dark secrets that he couldn't tell anyone—not even T.C. But with all of the recent events in his life he wondered if this was the right time to exorcise his demons.

Perhaps he would tell Sharon that he didn't love her and that they would never get married. Maybe he would tell his family that he had no intention of returning home after college, and just maybe he would confront his Uncle Earl about the things that he had done to him when he was just a boy.

Chance turned off the television, checked to make sure that all of the appliances were unplugged, tidied up the room, and gathered the last few bits of trash to be taken out. He left his door unlocked, sure that he was only one of a few people still left in the dorm. Ronnie had signed him out for holiday break earlier that morning so there was nothing else for Chance to do.

He walked leisurely down the hallway toward the trash chute. After dropping it down the chute, Chance glided back into the room humming the Anthony Goins song that Jo'sha had been rehearsing for the last few weeks. Jo'sha sounded great singing it and Chance couldn't get the song out of his head. He walked into the suite and entered his dorm room the way he had since his first day of college, but as he opened the door and stepped into his room he sensed something unusual.

For one thing, the ceiling light was off and he was sure that he had left it on before going to the trash chute. Chance instinctively reached toward the light switch by the door, but felt someone grab his wrist. Then he felt a choke hold around his neck. Chance struggled for a few seconds before he gathered his composure. With his increased strength, protecting himself against two men wasn't a problem. Before they knew it, Chance had thrown one of his attackers across the room and pinned the other against the wall with his right hand.

"Ugh," Jacoby moaned, standing up, rubbing his neck and shoulder from the impact of hitting the wall.

Cobyn was still struggling to free himself from his big brother's hold. Jacoby charged at Chance to resume the fight, but before he knew it, Cobyn came hurling at him like a rag doll. The twins lay huddled in the floor—a pile of arms, legs, groaning and cussing.

"Damn, Torrin. We was just playing!" Jacoby yelled.

"Ouch," Cobyn echoed, checking the back of his head for bleeding.

Chance laughed uncontrollably. They had all wrestled since they were young boys. It was always Chance against Jacoby and Cobyn. Despite him being older and slightly larger, they had started to get the best of him in the last two years.

"That ain't funny. You could have really hurt us," Jacoby whined.

"What are they feeding you down here?" Cobyn asked.

"I've been working out," Chance said, as he switched on the light.

"Wow!" Jacoby and Cobyn said when they saw Chance's expanded frame.

"You have muscles all over the place!" Jacoby exclaimed.

Chance flexed, "You two want some more?"

"We just wasn't ready that time," Cobyn said defensively.

"You pounce on me in the dark, and you weren't ready that time?" Chance mocked, noticing the pronounced accents of his brothers, and how much they actually did look like miniature versions of him.

They had competed with and emulated him since the moment they could walk, and although they had followed in his footsteps all of his life, he always found their adoration of him humbling.

"I thought that Chauncey was coming with you," Chance said.

"He changed his mind at the last minute," Jacoby started.

"Said something about having more important things to do," Cobyn finished.

"Oh," Chance responded.

"Don't worry about it, Torrin. Chauncey is just a little bit jealous. You were always better at everything than him. He couldn't even make it through community college," Jacoby began.

"And here you are with great grades at Georgia Central University. Not to mention the fact that you are everybody's favorite," Cobyn ended.

"What do you mean?" Chance asked.

"You know Grandpa likes you best. You're all he talks about. 'When Torrin was here', 'Torrin always did this', 'Torrin always did that', 'Torrin, Torrin, Torrin'," Cobyn mocked.

"I guess Chauncey never really got the attention that he deserved being the oldest. You were always in the spotlight with your grades and sports. And we always got attention just because we were twins. Seems like no matter how hard Chauncey tries he always comes up last," Jacoby said.

"Whatever," Chance said modestly.

"What's that necklace you're wearing? Where did you get it?" Jacoby asked, reaching for Chance's ankh.

Chance moved away instinctively.

"We'll wrestle you for it," Cobyn challenged.

"I don't think you want anymore of that," Jacoby warned.

"He just got lucky," Cobyn responded.

"Where did you get it?" Jacoby continued probing.

"It's just an old necklace. Jo'sha gave it to me," Chance said.

"Looks like something he would wear," Cobyn responded.

"Tell him to get us one," Jacoby said.

"I'll see what I can do," Chance said.

"How are your boys anyway?" Jacoby asked.

"All good. Jo'sha went home with Matthew, and Wade and his cousin left for Baltimore last night," Chance answered.

"Too bad about that latest murder victim," Cobyn said, changing the subject.

Chance had forgotten what it was like communicating with the twins. Their minds raced, conversations flipped constantly, and they finished each other's thoughts and sentences. It was unnerving to most people, but Chance had learned to speak their language.

"Do they know anything about him?" Jacoby asked.

"The latest victim he means," Cobyn explained.

"Yeah, well he was the eleventh. Some have been homeless and some have been college students. This last one was a homeless dude. Not much family to speak of. Near as they can tell, he migrated here from Chicago," Chance explained.

"How is Matthew's ol' fine ass sister, Olivia?" Jacoby asked.

"She's fine," Chance said, piling his luggage in the center of the room.

"You're just coming home for this holiday. It ain't permanent," Jacoby said.

"Shut up," Chance shot.

"Why are you taking all of this stuff home?" Cobyn asked.

"I never know what I might need. How is Ma?"

"You should ask her yourself," Jacoby said.

"She misses you," Cobyn answered.

"It was an honest mistake that she made," Jacoby offered.

"It was none of her business," Chance snapped.

"Well, I guess she knows that now," Cobyn responded.

"And another thing, Torrin," Jacoby said hesitantly.

"About Sharon," Cobyn finished.

"Well, she and Chauncey sorted kinda started dating," said Jacoby.

"What?" Chance asked, not sure he'd heard his brother right.

"Well she was at the house all the time. I guess she missed you, and Chauncey was by the house all the time, and they just kind of started talking," Cobyn explained.

"How long has this been going on?" Chance asked.

"Not long," Jacoby answered.

"Since we got back from homecoming," Cobyn answered.

Chance grew silent. Although he knew that he didn't want Sharon, he felt betrayed that his own brother would start dating her. The idea also saddened him, and confirmed one suspicion he'd had about Sharon. One way or another, Sharon was going to make it into the Walker family.

"It is getting late. We need to get on the road," Chance said, looking at his watch. Dusk had settled in and the ride back to Carolina promised to be a long one. Jacoby and Cobyn looked at each other, not sure if they needed to say anything more about Sharon and Chauncey or if they should have said anything at all.

They walked out into the hallway, each with his hands and arms filled with luggage. Chance checked the room one last time to make sure that he hadn't forgotten anything. As he bent over to pick up his last suitcase he felt the wind being knocked out of him.

"Ugggnnhhh," he moaned and fell to the floor.

CHAPTER 35

"Are you sure you are alright?" Jacoby asked from the passenger's seat as Cobyn drove up highway 85 North toward North Carolina.

"I'm fine," Chance responded from the back seat of the twins' sport utility vehicle.

"You like our new ride?" Cobyn asked.

"Yeah, it is nice. I never got a new car," Chance said.

"No, you just got a '79 Mustang convertible," Jacoby answered.

"It isn't doing me any good sitting at home in North Carolina while I'm in Atlanta," Chance said, fighting through the nagging pain in his gut.

"Just keep getting good grades and Dad will probably let you take it back to campus next year," Cobyn encouraged.

"Are you sure you are alright?" Jacoby said, growing more concerned with Chance's lack of explanation over what had caused him to double over in pain before leaving campus. The truth was that Chance didn't know what had caused the pain either.

"We are thinking about going to Georgia Central next year. Coach says that there is a good chance that we could both get recruited on full scholarship. Especially since the GCU recruiters were so hyped about you playing ball there last year," Jacoby continued talking.

Somehow the fact that they were considering following him to Central didn't surprise him. Perhaps their love of football would keep them out of his way if they did decide on Central. Chance had been a great cornerback with college potential but didn't love the game nearly as much as his younger brothers. There wasn't a doubt in his mind that they could both go professional if they wanted it.

Jacoby and Cobyn were in the front seat arguing about who had the most females while Chance continued to try to reach Wade, Matthew, or Jo'sha.

He tried Wade's mobile phone first—no answer. He tried Matthew's home number next—no answer.

Ring. Ring. Ring.

"Hello,"

"Jo'sha?"

"Chance?"

"Did you—?" Chance asked, making sure to whisper even though Jacoby and Cobyn were engulfed in their own conversation.

"—feel something earlier? Definitely, man. I don't know what it was either. I was sitting in the living room with Matthew's old man watching ESPN and it just hit me like a punch in the gut. It literally knocked the air out of me," Jo'sha explained.

"The same thing here. Did anyone see it?"

"No. Mr. Meredith and I are the only ones here, and he is asleep on the couch. Matthew took my car and went to the city library to do more research. I've had enough of books and studying for a while. It seems like the discovery of an eleventh victim has got him even more consumed with this whole murder mystery. I tried to call the city library to ask them if they have seen anyone that looks like him, but there is no answer and you know Matthew doesn't have a cell phone," Jo'sha explained.

"Well, if you're alright and I'm alright, then it must mean that something happened to Wade or Matthew. Call me just as soon as you find something out," Chance instructed.

"Olivia and Mrs. Meredith are out Christmas shopping so when they get back I'll see if Olivia would mind taking me over to the library just to check on Matthew."

"Don't tell Olivia what's up."

"I won't."

"Are you talking to Matthew? Is Olivia around? I want to talk to her," Jacoby said from the front seat. Chance had forgotten how nosey younger brothers could be.

"No she isn't around," Chance responded.

"Tell the young bloods I got this," Jo'sha responded, having heard Jacoby through the phone.

"What?" Chance asked.

"Nothing, just call me if you hear anything," Jo'sha answered.

"You, too," Chance said.

Jo'sha hung up the phone and lay down across Matthew's small bed. The room reminded him of his room back in Foster's house in Chicago. He couldn't practice his banjo because he didn't want to disturb Mr. Meredith. If Olivia and her mother didn't show up soon, he would just have to take the bus downtown to the public library to check on Matthew. Jo'sha looked around Matthew's room at his academic awards and track trophies. Matthew was a lot more modest than Chance when it came to his physical accomplishments. Jo'sha was reading one of Matthew's plaques when the phone rang.

"Hello."

"Are you alright?" Matthew asked.

"Yes, are you?" Jo'sha responded.

"With the exception of this pain in my stomach I'm fine. It felt just like—"

"Someone punched you in the stomach?" Jo'sha finished.

"Exactly. Did you feel it too?"

"Me and Chance both. I just got off of the phone with him," Jo'sha explained.

"Well if the three of us are fine, then it must be Wade. Have either of you tried to call him?"

"What a great idea!" Jo'sha said sarcastically.

"So I guess that means that you have tried to call him," Matthew responded dryly.

"Of course, brainiac!" Jo'sha shot.

"Oh."

"So what now?"

"I guess we just have to wait. He will call eventually and if it was anything major, then—well, we would know it," Matthew answered.

"Are you sure?" Jo'sha asked dubiously.

"Yes, I'm sure. When you were out we could sense you. We could tell when you were close to the edge and when you were getting better," Matthew explained.

"How much longer are you going to be?" Jo'sha asked.

"Not much longer. If you're hungry, my Mom should be home with groceries soon. She mentioned that she was going to be getting a lot of vegetables since you're staying with us," Matthew answered.

"I know and I appreciate it. I'll probably just put on my headphones and practice with my electric piano while I wait," Jo'sha responded.

"Alright. I'll see you later and thanks again for letting me use your car."

"No problem."

Jo'sha plugged his headphones into his new electric keyboard and began to play and hum. He had been playing for twenty minutes when he felt a hand on his shoulder that caused him to nearly jump out of his skin.

"Sorry to startle you, son," Mr. Meredith said.

"I hope I didn't disturb you," Jo'sha apologized.

"Oh no. I wish I could stay and listen to you play, but I have to go work. This is a real busy time for us at the airport and I can pick up some overtime. Christmas around here is going to be a lot different this year," Mr. Meredith bragged.

"Thank you again for having me," Jo'sha said humbly.

"You're like family," Mr. Meredith said, patting Jo'sha on the back. "Issy and Olivia went shopping. They should be back soon to cook dinner. Tell Issy that I went to work and I'll be back at 3:00 a.m.," he instructed.

"Yes, sir," Jo'sha responded, missing Foster in that instant.

Once Mr. Meredith was gone Jo'sha picked up his cell phone and tried to call Wade but there was no answer. Since the house was now empty Jo'sha pulled the headphones out of his keyboard—able to play as loudly as he wanted. He lit a candle, and then filled the air with keys, then chords, and then complete compositions. He had been playing for an hour, finding new arrangements when he felt another hand on his shoulder.

"Mr. Meredith?" he startled.

"No, not Mr. Meredith. Are my hands that rough?" Olivia asked jokingly.

They both laughed.

"I'm sorry. I thought your father came back. You must have just missed him. He went to work and he'll be back at 3:00 a.m."

"Cool. When we didn't see your car, we assumed that you and Matthew were gone. Mom dropped me off to start dinner for you guys. She went to the fresh market to get some vegetables for you."

"Well, I do appreciate it," Jo'sha said smiling.

He completely removed his headphones and turned to face Olivia.

"I don't know why their generation thinks that women should cook for men. If a man is hungry, then he should cook for his damn self. But you're company so I'll make an exception this time," Olivia teased.

"Girl, what do you know about cooking?"

"Brother, I can burn. I didn't say I couldn't cook. I just said I don't feel obligated to cook for a man," Olivia retorted.

"Is that right?" Jo'sha asked.

"That's right," Olivia smiled.

Jo'sha looked her over. He couldn't help but notice how even an oversized sweat suit couldn't hide the fact that Olivia had a killer body.

"So what's for dinner?" Jo'sha asked, licking his lips.

"That depends on how big your appetite is," Olivia said with a devilish smile.

"I have a very big appetite," Jo'sha answered, staring directly into her eyes.

Olivia pulled the sweatshirt over her head revealing full round breasts that were barely contained by a baby tank top.

"So where did Matthew go with your car anyway?" she asked.

"He went to the library."

"Awfully nice of you to lend him your car."

"It was awfully nice of your family to let me spend the Christmas holidays here."

Olivia considered that for a minute. She had never thought of her family as nice before.

"We're glad to have you."

"Matthew is like family to me," Jo'sha answered.

"Have you noticed anything strange about him lately?" she asked.

"What do you mean?"

Olivia looked at him skeptically. "He always seems preoccupied. It's like he always has something on his mind. He acts like he isn't even paying attention to me when I am talking to him, and sometimes I swear he knows what I am going to say even before I say it," Olivia said.

"I think it's just your imagination," Jo'sha said, trying to sound reassuring.

"And he's always at the library or in some book," Olivia continued.

"Well he does *work* at the library," Jo'sha answered.

"I can't put my finger on it, but there's something going on with him and I'm going to find out what it is," Olivia stated.

"It's probably just the break up with Tessa. If I had to put my money on it, then I would say that's probably what it is," Jo'sha offered.

"Maybe," Olivia said, not completely convinced.

Jo'sha knew full well that Matthew could care less about Tessa, and that the reason that he was acting different had nothing to do with any female, but everything in the world to do with the ankhs.

Olivia's sweatpants hung low around her hips revealing the arch of her back and curve of her ass. Jo'sha tried not to stare, but the growing bulge in his pants made it clear what was on his mind. He turned back to his piano and began to play the latest Anthony Goins piece.

"I like that." Olivia said.

"Do you?" Jo'sha asked, glad that the conversation had changed.

"Yes. What is that?" she asked.

"I haven't told a lot of people. And I probably won't until it's over, but Agonize is coming to Atlanta to record a few songs for his next album and he asked me if I would mind singing back-up," Jo'sha said, hoping to impress Olivia.

"Wow! Are you serious?" Olivia shouted.

Jo'sha laughed.

"I knew you were good, but I didn't realize that you had it like that," Olivia said, as she gave Jo'sha a celebratory hug.

The gesture took Jo'sha by surprise, but when she pulled back, he didn't let her go. His locks brushed against her face and the smell of his body oil made her tingle. Jo'sha felt her nipples harden as he brushed her neck. Olivia responded by gently kissing his ear and before they knew it they were enthralled in a passionate kiss on Matthew's bed. They were both so engrossed that they didn't notice someone had come in.

"What the hell is this?" Matthew screamed.

"Shit!" Jo'sha screamed, buttoning his shirt. Olivia grabbed her sweatshirt and covered herself.

"Matthew, wait a minute. I can explain," Jo'sha stuttered.

"What in the hell is this shit?" he yelled again.

"Now just wait a minute," Olivia said, trying to calm her brother down.

"Olivia, you stay out of this! This is between Jo'sha and me," he exclaimed.

The air in the room began to stir and then whirl. Matthew charged toward Jo'sha and Olivia jumped between them. Matthew meant to push her back out of the way so that he could get to Jo'sha, but instead he knocked her back into an old wooden bookcase that collapsed as soon as she hit it. One of Matthew's track trophies fell from the top shelf knocking Olivia unconscious. The wind in the room was whipping papers and small objects around the room in a whirlpool.

"Dammit, Matthew, stop it!" Jo'sha exclaimed. He was trying to get to Olivia, but Matthew hadn't realized what he had done and continued to charge toward Jo'sha.

Matthew's fury had created a full-fledged windstorm in the room and the walls started to shake. The candle that Jo'sha lit had been knocked to the floor and the flame caught several of the loose papers. Before Jo'sha could get to Olivia, Matthew had struck him across the face with a solid right hook. That was when everything in Jo'sha that had taught him how to survive on the streets came up and out.

Although Jo'sha was more muscular than Matthew, Matthew was much faster than Jo'sha. The two were evenly matched and the more they fought, the less control they had over their powers. The flame grew in intensity within a matter of seconds and wind got stronger still.

∞

"Auuuuuurrrrrgggggghhhhh!" Chance screamed from the back seat of the sport utility vehicle.

"What the hell is wrong with you?" Jacoby yelled, swerving off the highway and onto the grassy median.

"Pull over, pull over," Cobyn instructed.

"What's wrong?" Jacoby yelled again.

Chance doubled over and grabbed his skull. Jacoby managed to pull over on the side of the highway under an overpass.

"Are you alright?" Cobyn asked.

"I'm fine," Chance whispered, laying his head back on the seat.

"You're sweating," Cobyn said, turning on the interior light.

"I'm going to get off at the next exit and get him some water," Jacoby said, starting the car up and moving slowly.

"Maybe we should call Dad," suggested Cobyn.

"No, I'm fine," Chance managed.

"You don't sound fine," Jacoby said.

"You don't look fine either," Cobyn added.

"I think we should call Dad," Jacoby agreed.

"Just shut the hell up!" Chance yelled. "I need to concentrate."

"You need to quit yelling before we pull over again and whip your ass! That's what *you* need to do," Jacoby yelled.

"Leave him alone," Cobyn said.

Jacoby remained quiet, his face a mixture of irritation and concern for his brother. He got off at the next exit and pulled into the first gas station he saw.

Chance was still lying back in the seat.

"I'll go get him some water. You be quiet and leave him alone until I get back," Cobyn instructed.

Chance closed his eyes and tried to focus—tried to see if he could tell if something was wrong with Jo'sha, Matthew or Wade. But he couldn't feel anything. He wished that he had been more attentive during their morning meditations. The truth was he didn't seem to feel as connected as the rest of them and he wondered if it was because he wasn't trying hard enough.

No matter, he thought. *I know something is wrong. I just don't know what it is.*

"Here you go, Torrin," Cobyn said, handing his big brother a bottle of water. He had always been the more dutiful of the twins.

"Thanks."

"Now what's wrong with you?" Cobyn asked again.

"I think it was just a migraine," he answered.

"Since when did you start having migraine headaches?" Jacoby asked skeptically.

"Since you two picked me up," Chance responded, trying to lighten the mood.

Cobyn laughed.

"Well you seem fine now," Jacoby said.

"It's cool. I'm fine. Now let's just go," Chance instructed.

The rest of the ride home was much more pleasant and although Chance was preoccupied he managed to keep Jacoby and Cobyn engaged with stories about college life.

CHAPTER 36

Torrin Chance Walker was sitting in a wooden swing chair held between two huge oak trees. His grandfather had built it the year Chance was born and it had always been one of his favorite places. The two oaks were on the property line between his parent's house and his grandparent's house. His uncles had similarly sized homes on either side. Although no one would ever say it, several people thought that the Walker family owned more than their fair share of the county. The family took up the entire country road from the main highway up to Old Church Road.

This was an area that Chance knew all too well, but now it all seemed so unfamiliar. It had been two days since he left college and his friends, and despite several attempts, he still had not been able to reach them by phone. He had even tried to call Aspen, but a male voice answered the phone and began cursing when he didn't immediately state his name. This was not at all how he had imagined his Christmas break. And if all that weren't enough, he couldn't shake the lethargic feeling that had been growing since he got home. Chance rocked back and forth in the old swing letting his large boots dig deeper grooves into the earth. He picked at the detail in the sleeve of Nathaniel Charles' dark gray sweater.

"That is a mighty fine sweater you got there. It looks like one that my own grandmother mighta knitted for me. I can tell fine craftsmanship from a mile away," T.C. sang as he hobbled up the small path toward the swing.

"You like this old school joint?" Chance asked.

T.C. wasn't exactly sure what his grandson had said, but it sounded like it made sense for him to agree. "Sho' nuff," he answered.

"Paw-paw, I didn't even hear you coming."

"All this noise I am making trying to get up this path to see you and you ain't hear me? You must have something awful potent on yo' mind," he responded.

Chance laughed, "I guess you could say that." He hadn't realized how much he'd missed his grandfather.

T.C. backed up to the swing, waited for Chance to steady it and then slowly and carefully sat down.

"Are you alright, Paw-paw?"

"I came out here to ask you the same thing."

"I'm fine. I guess I just have a few things on my mind."

"Well I can tell that you're taking care of yourself. You got muscles on you now that you didn't have when you left. Look like I did when I was your age," T.C. boasted.

"Thanks, I've been working at it."

"You still having female troubles?"

"I guess I really don't have a female to have troubles with, Paw-paw. I'm not really interested in Sharon, and the girl that I really like barely gives me the time of day," Chance said.

"At least you know what you want. That's half the battle. Keep at her, son. Them gals love the chase 'bout much as we love chasin' them. Sounds like you done found yourself a feisty one. Your grandma was one of them back in her day," T.C. reminisced.

Chance laughed again. "But what if she just doesn't like me?" he asked.

"She likes you or she wouldn't be mad at you. She's just trying to establish her territory, and that's fine. But there is going to come a time when you are going to have to show her what you made of too."

"What do you mean?"

"A woman likes to be chased, but she don't want to be chased by no weak ass man. Make your intentions known and then leave it at that. You is a good man—from good stock. She would be lucky to have you. Don't forget who you is. Don't be running 'hind her like no puppy now. Pursuing her is one thing, pining after her is another," T.C. said sternly.

Chance nodded slowly, letting the weight of his grandfather's words sink in. They sat there quietly for a few moments, rocking in the swing, until Chance thought he saw T.C. wince.

"Paw-paw, how are you feeling?" Chance asked.

"Torrin, I ain't gonna even try to lie to you. And I ain't told this to no one. I ain't feeling so well these days. The arthritis is in my joints bad," he said, extending his hand for Chance to see.

Not confined by parent and child rules, and of the same ilk, T.C. had often shared secrets with Chance.

Chance instinctively grabbed his grandfather's crooked hand and held it between his two large palms. T.C.'s hands were once as large as Chance's, but time had wrinkled and gnarled them considerably. T.C.'s rich dark skin blended into Chance's, and Chance remembered when his small hand fit neatly in his grandfather's palm. Now T.C.'s twisted fingers bent like shadows across Chance's contrasting palms. The reaction had been a natural one—to comfort someone that he loved. And although he was aware that the ankh had given him a comforting touch, he had no idea of the extent of his gift.

"What you doing?" T.C. asked.

The moment Chance wrapped his hands around his grandfather a supernatural warmth salved the old man's arthritic hands. Chance felt the pain pass through him, and he gritted his teeth so that his grandfather wouldn't notice. He wondered how his grandfather endured the pain.

"Something I learned in college," Chance lied.

"What is it called?" T.C. asked amazed at the relief he felt in his joints.

"Uh, reflexology. I've actually been thinking about sports medicine," Chance lied.

T.C. held up his hand and looked at it in disbelief. He painlessly balled it into a fist. "I don't know what they teaching up at that school, but it sho' is something," T.C. said excitedly.

Chance smiled, glad that he could help his grandfather. "Paw-paw," he said.

"Yeah?" T.C. asked.

"Let this be our secret. I don't want to let Mom and Dad know that I'm thinking about changing my major until I'm absolutely sure about it," Chance said.

"Now you knows we tight," T.C. smiled.

"Cool," Chance smiled back.

"I won't tell it on one condition," T.C. said in a serious voice.

"What's that?"

"That you just do something to this here knee," T.C. grinned.

Chance grabbed the old man's knee and once again felt the pain course through his body, but it didn't matter, this was his grandfather.

This was someone he loved more than anyone in the world, and he was more than willing to deal with a little bit of pain if it meant relief for his Paw-paw.

Chance released his grandfather's knee and sat back and exhaled. He wondered what his grandfather would say if he knew what he had just done, but he knew he couldn't tell him the truth—or could he? While he was contemplating this, his cell phone rang. Chance looked at his phone. It was Wade. He looked at his grandfather.

"Oh, I guess you needs your privacy. You children and these cellular phones," T.C. said, rising much more quickly than he had sat down.

"Thanks, Paw-paw," Chance said.

"Willie Jenkins is being buried this evening. You wanna come down and help me prepare?" he asked.

"Yeah, Paw-paw. I'll go," Chance said, trying not to rush his grandfather.

"Well I'll come back ova' and—"

"Okay, Paw-paw." Chance said, cutting him off.

T.C. took the cue, and walked away mumbling.

Chance caught the phone on the last ring. "Hello."

"Chance, it's me."

"Wade!"

Chance looked around to see if his grandfather was still within earshot, but T.C. had already made it halfway back down the path.

"How are you?" Wade asked.

"Other than the fact that I think I just healed my grandfather, I'm fine. I'm tired as hell though." Chance said.

"Huh?"

"Never mind that for now. We can talk about that later. What's going on with you?"

"I guess a better question is what isn't going on. First William, Quay, and I were at a family dinner when all hell broke loose. I was trying to keep everyone calm—trying to keep their emotions in check, and I guess I lost control. I was fine for a while, but everything just escalated." Wade explained.

"Then what happened?" Chance asked.

"It just became too much. I lashed out, and the next thing I knew everyone was passed out." Wade said.

"Are they alright?" Chance asked.

"They are now. It was a scary night in the hospital. I called 911 and told them that I was William. When the ambulance got here I faked like I was knocked out too. Luckily everyone else was regaining consciousness at about the same time. Of course William doesn't remember making the phone call and no one knows what happened. The medics tested us for everything from food poisoning to carbon monoxide poisoning, but didn't find anything. The whole family is still on pins and needles." Wade ended.

"Is the baby okay?" Chance asked.

"He's fine," Wade announced.

"He?"

"They took Quay in for tests and gave her an ultrasound. They were afraid that the baby might have lost oxygen. But he seems to be doing fine," Wade explained.

"Good," Chance said.

"Everyone seems to be just a little bit more empathetic now too. I can't explain it, but it's like everyone was emotionally knitted together for a moment. The flood of emotions was just too much for any of them to handle," Wade said.

"Have you talked to the others?"

"I just got off of the phone with Jo'sha. He'll be calling you soon."

"Are they alright?" Chance asked.

"Not exactly. Matthew found out about Jo'sha and Olivia," Wade said.

"What do you mean?" Chance asked.

"That they like each other," Wade said.

"Did you know?" Chance asked.

Wade was silent.

"Why am I always the last one to know shit?"

"I found out by accident. Nobody told me either. And I am the last person that needs to be telling other people's business given the secrets I was keeping."

"Well, what happened?"

"Matthew flew off the handle and let's just say that fire and air isn't necessarily a good combination in an old house," Wade said.

"Damn! Is everyone alright?"

"There was fire damage in Matthew's room, but the rest of the house was fine. Jo'sha said that there is an awful burnt odor in the house. It will certainly put a damper on the holidays. And another thing—Olivia got knocked out in the scuffle. Now Jo'sha and Matthew aren't speaking. Jo'sha just got a room in a hotel in downtown Atlanta."

"We can't let him spend the holiday alone," Chance said.

"You're in North Carolina and I'm in Maryland. What are we going to do?" Wade asked.

"I don't know. I don't know about any of this," Chance sighed.

"Jo'sha will be calling you in a minute. You can talk to him about it yourself." Wade said.

"I knew something was wrong. I could feel it."

"I think we all felt it all."

"Are you feeling okay?" Chance asked.

"Now that you mention it, I *have* been feeling awfully tired lately," Wade said.

"Me too," Chance responded.

"What do you think it means?" Wade asked.

Before Chance could answer his phone beeped with another call.

"Wade, I have another call coming in. It's an Atlanta number. It must be Jo'sha."

"Or Matthew," Wade said.

"Either way—I need to take it. I want to hear the story first hand from one of them."

When Wade hung up, Chance clicked over. "Hello."

"Chance, what's up?" Jo'sha asked.

"You tell me."

"Man, I don't know. One minute I was chillin' in Matthew's crib with Olivia, and the next minute he was swinging on me," Jo'sha answered.

"Chillin' how?" Chance asked.

"It was nothing heavy. I ain't disrespect his sister. We're just cool, and we have been for a minute," Jo'sha answered.

"Evidently Matthew didn't see it that way," Chance said.

"I just think he misunderstood," Jo'sha said.

"You were running game on his sister," Chance defended.

"That's just it. I wasn't running game. It's real with me and Olivia," Jo'sha said.

"If it's so real, then why were you hiding it from him?" Chance asked.

"I, uhh—we were waiting for the right time to tell him," Jo'sha said.

"Sounds shaky to me," Chance admitted.

"Look, I wouldn't do anything to hurt Matthew or his sister. You guys are like my family now—like brothers," Jo'sha said.

"And even brothers have boundaries and require respect," Chance said, thinking of his own relationship with his brother Chauncey. "I guess Matthew saw what you did as a sign of disrespect."

"So you're on his side, too, I see," Jo'sha said defensively.

"I'm not on anyone's side. Neither is Wade for that matter. I just spoke to him, and he's got his own problems. One thing that my grandfather always taught us is that brothers will have arguments and disagree. The real test is how the disagreements are resolved," Chance said.

"So what do I do?" Jo'sha asked.

"Well under normal circumstances I would tell you that you have to determine what is more important to you - this relationship with Olivia or your friendship with Matthew, but, this situation isn't normal, man. I felt it when Wade damn near cleared out his whole family, and I felt it when you and Matthew were fighting. I didn't know what it was, but it felt like someone was pulling my spine out at the base of my skull. And I'm getting more and more tired no matter what I eat, how much I rest I get, or how much I exercise. I don't think you have a choice. I don't think either one of you has a choice. You, have got to resolve this," Chance said.

"Well, he is pretty mad at me," Jo'sha said doubtfully. We damn near burned down his house, his sister got knocked out, I busted his lip and he dotted my eye," Jo'sha said.

"So where are you now?"

"I just left and got a hotel room. It was too much."

"You can't run away from this forever."

"I just needed to put some space in between me and all this shit," Jo'sha remarked.

"I can see that," Chance responded. He thought for a moment. "Well, we are supposed to meet back at campus before everyone gets back. That'll give us some time to talk. In the meantime, I'll try to talk to Matthew," Chance advised. "Where exactly are you now?"

"I got a room at the Swissotel," Jo'sha answered.

"The Merediths are good people. They'll be worried about you. You owe it to them to let them know where you are," said Chance.

"Yeah, you're right. I'll call Olivia or Mrs. Meredith," he said.

"Look, man, don't let this get you down. It'll be all right. These things happen."

"Yeah, I hope so," Jo'sha responded.

"Trust me, and stay in touch," Chance said.

"I will," Jo'sha said, hanging up the phone.

Jo'sha lay back on the bed in room 1017 of the Swissotel. He had specifically requested this room. It was the room that Foster had stayed in. Jo'sha lay on the bed and cried until he drifted off to sleep—and there he dreamed. This time, every vision that he had repeated itself as if it demanded to be understood, while he floated in a place between consciousness and unconsciousness. First the fire, then the stones, then the birds, and then the flowers—each vignette repeating and moving more rapidly each time. Until finally, he was whisked out of the fire, but this time it wasn't by Samuel Wilkes, but by a small and delicate hand—the hand of an angel with skin like brass, hair like wool, and large beautiful black wings. She flew high into the sky up past the clouds, going faster and faster until they stopped atop a huge mountain, where she dug her hand into the earth and pulled up five small stones. She held them to her bosom until they glowed, and when she opened her hand to reveal them, they were five perfectly shaped ankhs. Then she looked to the sky and a bird like the ones that he had seen in his vision circled high above them. She closed her eyes, called to him, and he drifted gently down to earth, where he lifted the stone ankhs from her hand with his beak, and then flew away. Jo'sha looked at his dream angel and wondered why she had come to him. When she looked back at Jo'sha a large tear fell from her eye. Without notice she grabbed his hand and flew up over the mountain and then down into a valley of flowers like the ones in his dreams, only much taller. She fell to her knees and began weeping before a figure in front of her. Jo'sha looked over her shoulder and saw the dead lifeless body of the beautiful bird that had taken the stones. And for reasons that he could not explain—Jo'sha wept too.

CHAPTER 37

It was the day before Georgia Central students were scheduled to arrive back on campus. Despite the fact that Jo'sha and Matthew were still not speaking, the four worked together and covered the entire campus with Omega Tau posters just as planned. When they finished Wade was pretty pleased with the first phase of his public relations campaign. It was 9:30 in the evening when they finally sat down. The world seemed void of life from the top of Bonder's Pointe.

"Stop it, Wade," Matthew snapped.

"Stop what?"

"I can tell what you're doing. Stop trying to manage our emotions," Matthew complained.

"I didn't know I was doing it. I just want you two to get over this," Wade shot.

"You guys have got to talk about this," Chance interjected.

"I'm ready to talk about it," Jo'sha said.

"There isn't anything to talk about," Matthew hissed.

"She's your sister, not your daughter. She's practically a grown woman," Chance said.

"You have nothing to do with this," said Matthew sharply.

"I have everything to do with this," Chance yelled.

Wade stood, walked over and sat between Jo'sha and Matthew. He grabbed each of their hands and focused.

"I said stop it," Matthew yelled, attempting to free his hand. Wade held on firmly until Matthew could feel what Jo'sha felt, and Jo'sha could feel what Matthew felt.

Chance had no idea what just happened, but he knew that it made a difference. They all sat quietly for fifteen more minutes before anyone else spoke.

"I'm sorry," Matthew said.

"Me, too," Jo'sha responded.

They sat there quietly under the cold January moon. Matthew called up a curtain of air and Jo'sha warmed it. Wade smiled because it felt like old times.

"How did you know how to do that?" Jo'sha asked.

"I damn near killed my whole family trying to figure it out," Wade said.

"What happened?" Chance asked.

"I just allowed them to see how the other was feeling," Wade said.

"Isn't that dangerous?" Chance asked.

"Not when the emotions are pure. I could tell that Jo'sha's feelings for Olivia were real, and I knew if Matthew could see that then he would know that Jo'sha had no intention of hurting his sister. Jo'sha was concerned that Matthew thought that he wasn't good enough for his sister. That wasn't the case either, and I knew if Jo'sha could really see how much Matthew loved him, then there was no way that they could stay angry with one another," Wade said.

"Wow, that's pretty deep," Chance said. "Watch this, you're not the only one who has figured some things out." Chance picked up a large sharp rock and dashed it across Wade's forearm. Wade's creamy tan skin opened up and began to bleed immediately.

"Ouch! What the hell did you do that for?" Wade screamed.

"What's wrong with you?" Matthew echoed.

"Wait! Watch this." Chance grabbed Wade's bleeding forearm in his large palms. Wade felt a warm sensation surge up his forearm and into his shoulder and when Chance removed his hand the scar was gone.

"Damn! Now, that's amazing," said Jo'sha.

"Great demonstration, but you didn't have to rip my damn arm open. We would have believed you," Wade said.

"No you wouldn't," Chance responded.

"Nice to see that your powers are growing," Matthew said. "Maybe now you'll stop whining," he joked.

Chance dove onto Matthew and they began wrestling. Jo'sha joined in.

"Nobody beats up my roommate, but me," he laughed.

"Wade, are you going to just sit there or are you going to help me?" Chance joked, tossing Jo'sha and Matthew to and fro.

"It doesn't look like you need any help to me," Wade laughed.

Matthew whirled around and whipped up a windstorm that knocked Chance off balance. To Matthew's surprise, Chance braced himself and focused on Matthew until his windstorm fizzled into a breeze.

"Impressive! Earth opposes air. You *have* been paying attention," Matthew said excitedly.

"But it does nothing to fire," Jo'sha replied, creating a swirling cage of fire around Chance. Wade stepped up behind Jo'sha and concentrated. A few moments later Jo'sha's cage of fire sputtered and sparked until nothing but a hot, steamy mist surrounded Chance.

"And water opposes fire," Wade mocked.

They all laughed and wrestled for almost another twenty minutes before deciding to rest.

"I missed you guys," Chance said.

"Me, too," Matthew echoed.

"Why are you so quiet, Wade?" Jo'sha asked, noticing the change in Wade's demeanor.

"I missed you guys, too, but I'm not sure that I don't need to go home and take care of Quay and the baby," said he answered.

"It isn't that simple anymore," Jo'sha said.

"I know. I felt it, too. It seems like I had to get fifteen hours of sleep just to function," Wade said.

"Me, too," Jo'sha added.

"It's true. We seem to be connected to these ankhs and each other. The distance took a toll on all of us," Matthew concluded.

"So where does that leave us? We can't live together for the rest of our lives. Can we?" Chance asked.

Everyone looked to Matthew for answers, but this time he didn't have any.

"I don't know, but we'll figure something out. Let's just take it one problem at a time," he said.

"Well, I have a son coming, and I wouldn't refer to him as the problem. The problem is the fact that I am torn between being here and being with Quay," Wade clarified.

"You're having a son? Congratulations," Jo'sha said.

Wade smiled despite his dilemma.

"Why don't you move Quay here?" Matthew suggested.

"She doesn't want to leave her family," Wade answered.

"If you marry her, then she'll have to come here," Chance said.

Wade didn't respond.

"How long do you have before you have to decide?" Matthew asked.

"Her due date is May 26th," Wade answered.

"We'll figure this out. I promise," Matthew said.

"Makes my situation with Aspen seem so unimportant," Chance said.

"Just stay on her. You're wearing her down," Jo'sha advised.

"And then there's the serial killer. He's killed eleven young brothers," Matthew interjected.

"Have they identified the last one?" Chance asked.

"Willis Baker was his name. He moved to Atlanta from Alabama and never could get on his feet. He ended up on the streets begging for money, turning tricks, and eating out of garbage cans."

"Do you still think it's Dr. Smith?" Jo'sha asked.

"The police have profiled the killer and they say that it's probably an older white male with an agenda driven by some type of racial hatred," Matthew answered.

"Could be him," Chance reasoned.

"Could be not," Jo'sha retorted.

"But there are just as many things that don't make sense. They also say he is probably a recluse, and since he knows the area so well he is probably also a local. Dr. Smith is none of those," Matthew said.

"So back to square one," Wade sighed.

"I guess," Matthew resigned.

"Matthew, what is it that you aren't telling us? I can tell that you're holding back," Chance said.

"I've been doing some studying and it seems that the distance wasn't the only thing that affected us," Matthew began.

"What do you mean?" Wade asked.

"Well I think the things that we crave, the things that we gravitate toward, are actually feeding us," Matthew explained.

"And what in the hell does that mean?" Jo'sha asked.

"You know how Chance is always working out? It isn't just that he likes to do it—he needs to do it to thrive. We all need it because we're connected, but not nearly as much as Chance. And you know how Wade taps into people's emotions? Well he actually needs that. These aren't just mere obsessions with us. These things nourish us on some supernatural level. My thirst for knowledge and Jo'sha's dream visions feed us all. So it isn't as simple as us needing to be in close proximity to each other. It's more complicated than that," Matthew said.

"That doesn't sound so bad," Jo'sha said.

"No, not really, but it is interesting," said Chance.

"How do you know this?" Wade asked.

"I find that my mind is always racing. The only time that I slow down is when I sleep, and I'm finding that I need less and less sleep as time progresses. If I'm not thinking or researching or studying, then I start to get headaches. There's no such thing as quiet time for me," Matthew explained.

"So how do you know all this about our cravings feeding us?" Wade asked again.

"I've been charting our behavior and our highs and our lows. I didn't want to tell you before we left for Christmas vacation because I didn't want it to change your behaviors. I had to let things progress naturally. I was pretty sure that being apart was going to affect us, but I didn't know how much. Based on all of the stories that we've shared, each of us was trying to fill the void caused by being separated through our powers. Chance, you kept working out and healing. Those were the manifestations of your powers that sustained you. Wade, you were literally feeding on your family's emotions. I kept my head buried in books all break long. Jo'sha, you probably stayed in a dream state the entire time, didn't you?"

Jo'sha nodded in agreement.

"Hmmm," said Wade.

"And that's another thing," Matthew said. "I don't think Jo'sha's dreams are random. I think they're trying to tell us something."

"Yeah, but what?" Jo'sha asked.

"That's for you to figure out and tell us. We need to know. There's no way that those dreams could just be random. It's a part of your gift and you have to learn how to use it," Matthew directed.

"Just more questions and still no answers," Wade mocked.

"No answers *yet*," Matthew said.

"Well there is something that we can figure out—the Spring Festival and Omega Tau step show," Chance interjected.

"Now that we have all of the posters up, people will start to talk. We'll definitely be able to make our grand debut at the Spring Festival step show as planned," Wade said.

"What about step practice?" Matthew asked.

"Agonize said his choreographer will be in town next week working on a couple of videos. He said we can start as early as Sunday evening if we like," Jo'sha answered.

"Do we need that much time? It's just a step show," Chance said.

"He said that we shouldn't underestimate the amount of preparation required to pull off a good step show."

"William said the same thing," Matthew chimed in.

"You talked to William?" asked Wade, sounding surprised.

"Yeah, he was helping me out with some research. He said he would come down and help us out, too, as long as we didn't tell any of his chapter brothers," Matthew answered.

"Oh," Wade said quietly.

"This is going to be so hot!" Chance exclaimed.

"Yeah," Matthew said, suddenly sounding unenthused.

"We know you are not a big fan of this whole fraternity thing, but we only live once. We need to have a little fun. It'll help take the edge off of everything that we are dealing with," Chance said.

"I know. I know," Matthew agreed.

"Besides, it's not our job to catch that killer. That's for the police to do. In the unlikely event that it is Dr Smith, they'll catch him. They always do. Any notion that you had of us getting linked to the killings based on circumstances is less valid each day. Wade and Quay are going to have a healthy baby boy and they—*we* are going to figure out how to take care of him. And I am going to get Aspen Walker to be my girl," Chance stated.

"Fat chance on that last one country boy," Jo'sha teased.

"Shut up," Chance retorted good-naturedly.

Wade smiled. He lay back and reveled in the new sense of hope that was beginning to fill the air.

"Are you sure this is a good idea?" Chance asked.

"Why wouldn't it be?" Matthew asked.

"Well, it's just that this choreographer guy is from New York and we're going to stick him in an old house in the country the entire time he's here," Chance answered.

"He doesn't have to pay an expensive hotel bill, and he said he likes the great outdoors," Jo'sha responded.

"Besides, we can practice our stepping in the great room in the old house. And we won't have to worry about anyone breaking in on us," Matthew continued.

"Are you sure that Miss Vaughn is cool with this?" Chance asked.

"Yes, I'm sure. Especially after I told her that we were going to be putting locks on those windows in the back of the house," Matthew said.

"There you go," Wade said sarcastically.

"I'm with Wade on this one," said Jo'sha. "I'm not fixing a damn thing. That's between you, Chance, and Miss Vaughn."

"What does this guy look like anyway?" Wade asked circling the passenger pick-up lane of the Hartsfield-Jackson Airport for the third time.

"Here's the picture that I pulled off the Internet from some awards show. He said that he would have two big Louis Vutton bags," Jo'sha answered.

"His plane landed twenty minutes ago. He should be out by now," Chance said, scanning the sea of passengers.

"Is that him?" Matthew pointed from the backseat.

"Could be," Jo'sha said, looking at the man coming out of door #2 and then back again at the picture in his hand.

"He does have Louis luggage," Chance answered.

"Status!" Jo'sha yelled out the window.

The gentleman looked over toward the SUV and raised his hand. Even under a leather jacket and baggy jeans it was obvious that he was fit. He carried himself comfortably and moved the heavy bags effortlessly. Wade pulled over to the curb right in front of him. Chance hopped out to help him with his bags, lifting one bag and tossing it in the trunk of Wade's SUV with his left hand. Status did a double take.

"Wow, you're a strong brother," he said.

"He works out a lot," Matthew explained quickly, glaring at Chance behind Status' back. Matthew grabbed the other bag and struggled to tip it up and over into the back of the truck.

"I can't tell you guys how much I appreciate you letting me stay at your place for free," he said.

"No problem," said Jo'sha. "It's twenty minutes from the city, but I'll let you borrow my car when you need it," he added.

"I really do appreciate that, too."

Status' real name was Stanley Titus Brawn. He was one of hip-hop's most sought after choreographers. One only had to glance at Stanley to see that he was well put together—almost too well put together. His nails were professionally manicured, each and every hair was in place, and his skin glowed as if he had regular facials.

"I normally don't help out with projects like step shows and certainly not for free, but Agonize asked me as a personal favor. Plus you guys were cool enough to let me stay at your house—it was hard for me to decline. Not to mention the fact that I used to be a pretty good stepper back in my day. I think hip-hop could use a little bit of a step infusion right about now. Working with you guys may give me some ideas," said Status.

Before going to Miss Vaughn's estate, they stopped off at Lucille's and got some food. When they pulled up, Chance looked over at Status to see if he appeared put off by the accommodations. As best as Chance could tell, Status didn't seem to mind at all, even though the old house greeted them with leftover emotions and dank odors.

"I hope this is fine for you," Jo'sha said. "We made a bed for you upstairs, and the kitchen is already stocked with food and plenty of beer."

"I'm not much of a beer person, but I appreciate it."

"My car is around the house and here are the keys so that you can get back and forth to town," said Jo'sha, producing a ring of keys and passing them to Status.

Status took the keys and nodded. "Now tell me again why you young brothers want to start your own fraternity. Why not just join one of the ones that already exists?" he asked.

"We want a fresh blueprint. We want to create a new standard of academic excellence and meaningful community service," Wade said.

"Fair enough, but you know that stepping is just a part of the social aspect of fraternity life," he said.

"We know that, but a good step show is a way to get instant credibility and recognition," Jo'sha answered.

"How are your grades?" Status asked.

"All 4.0's," Matthew bragged.

"Impressive. What about community service?"

"We're setting up the David Foster Program for Young Boys, which is going to be a nationwide program that will tutor and mentor young black boys," Jo'sha said.

"Sounds like you've thought of everything."

"We just don't know how to step," said Matthew.

"That's easy—if you all have some type of rhythm."

"What do you mean?" Chance asked.

"Stepping isn't quite like dancing, but it requires rhythm. Stepping is syncopated stomping and clapping. The shows today have evolved into productions that are damn near as elaborate as some videos that I do. You'll need outfits, a theme, a strong entrance, and a strong exit," Status explained.

"Agonize's wardrobe stylist is going to help us with our outfits. I told her that our colors are green, gold, and silver," Jo'sha explained.

"And we already have some ideas for a big entrance," Matthew interjected.

"Well it sounds like all you need to know from me is how to step." He moved through the house looking at each room and tapping his foot on the floor as if he were thumping melons. "This is perfect," he said when he got to the dining room. "It's large enough, and the hardwood floors will work nicely. Now let's move this furniture out so we have some room to work with."

They moved the table, chairs, and china cabinet into the living room. When they came back they found Status stripped of his clothes, wearing a tight tank top and shorts cut a little too close for their comfort. He had also put on a pair of tap shoes.

"Come on, we don't have all night. Go ahead and stretch," he advised.

The boys stretched as if they were about to work out. Their method of loosening up was a stiff comparison to Status' dance moves with full splits, deep knee bends, first position and second position.

"Now line up behind me," he said.

"Like this?" Matthew asked.

"Yes, in a row just like that," he said, suddenly sounding more like Leroy from *Fame* than the seemingly masculine dude they had picked up from the airport.

"But we don't have on tap shoes," Wade protested.

"You don't need them now. You'll want to bring hard bottom shoes when we meet again so that you hear the beats you're making, but tonight we need to learn basics. The hard part for you guys is that the other organizations have pretty much cornered most of the good step styles. One organization uses canes or sticks to create an extra beat. Another organization already accents its stepping with clapping, and another is known for stepping really hard and rough. We'll have to find your particular style and hone it,"

"Okay, this is starting to seem complicated," Wade admitted.

Status ignored Wade's comment and kept on instructing, "Now stepping isn't just about creating beat, and it isn't just about creating great beats. It's about creating great beats together," he explained.

"How do we know what beats to make?" asked Chance.

"Some step teams use songs as inspiration. A lot of fraternities have steps that have been handed down from generation to generation, but the better step teams create their own fresh new beats," Status said with a smile.

He began to move back and forward slowly, tapping out a beat punctuated by hand claps and gestures. When he was finished they all smiled and laughed.

"Do you think we can do that?" Wade asked.

"Of course you can with me teaching. Now do as I do," he said.

They mimicked him as best they could, staring down at their feet and then at each other in an attempt to get it right. It sounded like a team of horses galloping through the house, but Status didn't seem to mind. He made them repeat the basic step over and over again until they could do it in unison.

"I think we got it!" Chance said excitedly.

"Stop!" Status yelled.

"What's wrong?" Matthew asked.

"Anyone can step. But not everybody can give you a show. Any four brothers from campus can get together and step in unison. Most of them can even create complicated steps with original beats, but not everyone is a showman. Now you will not be looking down at your feet and you will not be looking at each other. You will be performing for your audience. More than likely you will be chanting, talking, or singing while you are stepping and your audience has to feel it as much as you do. If this Omega Tau fraternity thing that you all have created is real and is about brotherhood, then let them feel it. Give it to them. Keep the eye contact and pull them under your spell. Use whatever works. I can see that you young brothers have been working out, especially you Chance. Share glimpses of your gift with your audience without being vulgar. You have to remember that less is more, but you have to give them something!"

"Wow!" said Jo'sha.

"Now, let's start over. We're going to do it until we get it right," he barked, his voice changing again, this time sounding more like a drill sergeant.

They stepped well into the night and into the early morning. It was 3:00 a.m. before they finished, but none of them was tired. They were all excited about what they had learned and anxious to learn more.

"Let's plan to get together every night this week. By Thursday you will have learned your very own Omega Tau step. I promise you there won't be another step around as bad as yours," Status said.

They all laughed and gave each other handshakes and high fives before bidding Status goodnight. Omega Tau was beginning to take form.

CHAPTER 38

Jo'sha, Matthew, Olivia, and Wade arrived at the Black Rabbit recording studios a full thirty minutes before the session was scheduled to start. Jo'sha was sitting in the passenger seat of Wade's truck with his neck wrapped in a wool scarf, sipping chamomile tea and sucking on a lemon.

"Thanks for coming with me you guys," he said.

"I've never been to one of these things before. It'll be interesting to see how things work," Matthew answered.

"I didn't really have anything else to do today. It's no big deal," Wade said.

"It's a big deal to me," Jo'sha said.

"I've never seen you this nervous," Wade responded.

"I don't think that I've ever been this nervous."

"You don't have anything to worry about. You'll be just fine," Olivia said, rubbing Jo'sha's locks from the backseat.

It was a quarter past the hour when Agonize's limousine pulled up in front of the recording studio. Three large bodyguards, two attractive young women, two equally attractive heavyset women who must have been background singers, Status, and Agonize's manager exited the limousine and waited dutifully for Agonize to glide out.

"Now *that* is an entourage," Jo'sha said.

"*That* is a circus," Wade said, shaking his head.

"There's Status," Matthew said, identifying the only person that he knew in the group.

"We'd better get going. We don't want to be late," Jo'sha said.

"*He* was late," Matthew pointed out.

"It's his recording session. He can do that," Jo'sha said.

"Are you sure they are going to let us watch?" Wade asked.

"You're with me. He has an entourage, and sad as it is, you guys are my entourage," Jo'sha joked.

"It's *his* recording session. He can have an entourage," Matthew teased.

Olivia gave Jo'sha a kiss on the check when they got out of the truck. "That's for good luck," she purred.

"My God," Matthew moaned, rolling his eyes.

"Shut up," Olivia shot.

"I don't need that right now," Jo'sha whispered before they could start arguing.

One of the large bodyguards stopped them at the door. "Who are you?" he asked.

"My name is Jo'sha. I'm one of the background singers."

"Well who in the hell are all the rest of these motherfu—"

"Shadow, it's cool. You can let them all come in," Status yelled from the other end of the hallway.

"Fellas," he greeted them. "How's step practice coming?"

"Good. We're getting better everyday. Thanks again for all of your help. You know Wade and Matthew. This is Matt's sister and my girl, Olivia. I told you about her."

"And she's just as beautiful as you said she would be," Status said.

"Thank you," Olivia responded with a smile.

"Have you ever thought about doing any video work?" Status asked.

"No!" Jo'sha and Matthew answered in unison.

"Oh, I get the point," Status said, leading them into the recording area.

"By the way, I have a new step for you guys. It was something that I was going to use for a video, but I decided that it would be better for you guys," Status said, patting Matthew on the back.

"Really?" Wade asked.

"No doubt. You know I've got to have my boys looking good. As a matter of fact, Shayla should be finished with the outfits in a couple of weeks," Status said.

"Outfits?" Olivia asked.

"Never mind," Matthew said quickly.

Everyone was settling into place when they got into the recording area. The technicians, producers, and musicians had been in the studio all morning preparing. The two healthy female background singers slid quickly into place.

"Which one of you is the newbie?" asked the light complexioned sister.

"You didn't tell us that the Weather Girls were going to be here," Wade whispered.

Jo'sha chuckled. "That would be me," he announced raising his hand.

"Well come on over here between us. Can you handle two full grown women, boy?" she teased.

Olivia shot her a look and cleared her throat loudly enough for everyone to hear.

"Hmmph!" exclaimed the large, dark-skinned singer, catching Olivia's hint.

Jo'sha unwrapped the scarf from around his neck and took his place quickly.

"Does everyone know the music," the engineer asked from outside the booth.

The two large women looked at Jo'sha.

"Uh, yeah, I know it," he said.

"Good, 'cause I ain't trying to be in here all day. Anthony said you were good, but we ain't heard you yet," the dark-skinned woman teased.

The energy in the room was generally positive, and where it wasn't Wade made sure that it came nowhere near Jo'sha.

"Would you like to get a tour of the studio?" Status whispered to Matthew.

"Sure," Matthew said, motioning to Olivia and Wade that he would be right back.

"Now this is going to be the first cut that is released from my new album so it's got to be hot. New blood, I need for you to bring it. I picked you for this because I like your range and passion, so don't be afraid to let go toward the end of the song. Follow Fontella and Brassy if you get lost in the song. They're some of the best and they'll take good care of you."

Fontella adjusted her cleavage and glanced at Jo'sha. Olivia cleared her throat again.

"Does she need a throat lozenge?" Brassy asked.

Jo'sha chuckled. "No, she's fine."

Olivia rolled her eyes.

"Now the song is about 90% complete. We're going to have to work out the ad-libs at the end. Fontella that's your thing so do what you do," Anthony said.

"I got you, Ant," she said with a wink.

"Jo'sha, I want you to echo me through the first two verses and help me lay down a strong chorus. We'll move into a call and response kind of deal in the last verse and then into ad-libs. Just let it flow naturally," Anthony advised.

When they got ready to start Status and Matthew were still off touring the studio. Olivia blew Jo'sha another kiss for luck.

Anthony motioned for the engineer to start. The song was mid-tempo and very catchy. Jo'sha had been practicing it for several weeks and was very anxious to show Agonize and everyone else how prepared he was.

"Let's do a dry run with me and Jo'sha first," Agonize suggested.

The name of the song was Spring Love Child, and Anthony delivered the song as if it were the last love song on earth. Jo'sha came in halfway through the first verse just as he was supposed to, echoing Agonize with perfect pitch and right on key. Anthony and his two background singers smiled at each other. Anthony motioned for the recording engineer to begin taping and the group went through the song nearly flawlessly the first time.

"I'd like to try it a few different ways. Jo'sha, this time you sing lead and I'll follow," Anthony said.

"But I haven't practiced that part," Jo'sha protested.

"You've heard it enough and you can read. I just want to see what you do with it. There's still something missing and maybe I'm just too close to it to see it," Anthony said.

Fontella and Brassy glanced at each other. Jo'sha looked at Olivia and then at Wade. Wade sensed that the vibe was still positive and gave Jo'sha a slight nod.

Jo'sha closed his eyes and began singing. His voice covered each of the notes like warm honey. When he got to the second verse he relaxed the tempo slightly and went down a half octave to reveal the pain that is always a part of true love. He opened his eyes and sang directly to Olivia, who by that point was in complete tears. Fontella and Brassy joined in and the three of them railed and ad libbed beautifully through the end of the track. Anthony and his manager and the engineers were huddled over in a corner when Jo'sha finished.

"That was great, Jo'sha. Everyone take a break, we want to remix the track. We have a few ideas now based on that last run through. Jo'sha, great job," Anthony praised him again.

"Yeah, new breeze, that was hot," Brassy added.

"Thanks," Jo'sha responded.

Status and Matthew returned from their tour just when Wade, Olivia, and Jo'sha were gathering their things to leave.

"That was incredible," Wade said.

"It felt good too," Jo'sha said.

"It felt like you were singing right to me," said Olivia.

"I was."

"Oh boy," Matthew sighed.

"Where were you anyway," Olivia asked.

When Matthew hesitated Wade looked at him to see how he would respond.

"Just went to tour the recording studio. I've never seen one before, and you know how curious I am," Matthew explained. "Status said he'll meet us at the house later," he added.

"Thanks everyone for the awesome opportunity," Jo'sha said.

They all chimed in about how great he had been and how much promise he had in the business.

"Jo'sha, the record label will cut a check and mail it to you tomorrow. I'll be calling you. Let me know if you need anything else for your step show," Agonize called after them.

"Thanks, Anthony," Jo'sha answered as he exited the studio. He wrapped his arm around Olivia's shoulder and kissed her forehead. Wade and Matthew looked on, feeling jealous that they didn't have anyone to hold onto at that moment.

"We have got to get you home, baby girl," Jo'sha teased.

"Why can't I hang out with you some more today?" Olivia asked.

"We—uh—I have to study tonight. I have an exam tomorrow," he stuttered.

"It's that damned fraternity isn't it?"

"No," Matthew interjected, shooting Jo'sha a look.

"Don't lie for him."

"Liv, we are in school you know," Matthew snapped in a tone that seemed to convince Olivia.

"Call me later," she said, kissing Jo'sha on the lips and climbing out of the truck when they reached her house.

Wade waited until she was inside, and then pulled off. Though Jo'sha hated to lie to Olivia, the truth was that the boys had step practice at Miss Vaughn's house with Status and none of them wanted to miss it. Their show had been coming together nicely over the last few weeks and they each had ideas about how to make it just a little bit better.

∞

Chance looked at his watch. It was 8:00 p.m. and he was supposed to meet Status, Matthew, Jo'sha, and Wade on the south side of campus to drive down to Miss Vaughn's house for step practice. With Status staying at the Vaughn estate, they were getting more than enough step practice, but not nearly enough time to practice or release their powers. That was something that Jo'sha hadn't thought through before he had Matthew ask Miss Vaughn if she minded having a celebrity guest stay at the old house.

Chance could feel the power surging up inside of him. Working out just wasn't enough anymore. To wear the ankh required discipline, morning meditations, extreme physical activity, an exertion of his earth-moving powers, and proximity to the others in order for him to feel balanced. He felt the need to exhale on a supernatural level, but couldn't. He would most certainly have to talk to Matthew and the others about the way he was feeling.

Chance hadn't gone with the others to Jo'sha's recording session. As much as he would have enjoyed the experience, he had a calculus test the next day and he wasn't about to be the one who didn't have all A's at the end of the semester. His pride wouldn't let that happen. He checked his watch again. It was 8:04 p.m. and he figured he'd better get going soon if he was going to meet the others on time. He looked over his notes and decided to do just one more problem to make sure that he completely understood all of the material for the exam.

The calculus problem blurred in front of Chance's eyes and he shook his head to try to clear things up. Suddenly he felt nauseous and then cold. He imagined that the lack of an outlet was having more of an effect on him than he had imagined.

"Ahemm—"

Chance looked up and around but didn't see anyone. He stood up quickly and came face to face with Dr. Smith.

"Uh, Dr. Smith, you startled me. I didn't see you come up," Chance said.

"I see that you were heavily involved in your school work, Mr. Walker. I haven't seen you or your friends since my class last semester.

I trust that they are still in the pursuit of academic excellence," Dr. Smith cooed.

"Yes sir, I have a calculus test tomorrow and I want to make sure that I get a good grade," Chance explained.

"Very well then, please give them my best, will you?" Dr. Smith said. He was so close to Chance's personal space that Chance could smell his breath.

"Uh, I sure will. Well, I'd better be going now. I have to meet my friends. It was very nice seeing you, Dr. Smith," Chance stuttered.

Dr. Smith continued to glare at Chance as if he were looking for something. Chance backed away politely, gathered his books and quickly dismissed himself. When Chance reached the library he looked back. Dr. Smith smiled and waved.

Chance could see Status, Matthew, Jo'sha, and Wade standing beside Jo'sha's sports car over a city block away. He began jogging toward them. His jog turned into a run, and before he knew it he was sprinting toward the four of them.

"Wow, you're fast!" Status exclaimed.

Chance wasn't even sweating or breathing heavy. He hadn't realized how quickly he was running, but the exertion felt good. Matthew glared at him.

"Are you all ready to go?" Jo'sha asked.

Jo'sha and Status jumped into Jo'sha's car, while the rest got into Wade's truck. Instead of step practice that night, Status had arranged for them to watch videos from several recent national step competitions.

"I thought we were going to practice tonight," Wade whined.

"This is practice. You're training your mind," Status said, plopping down on the couch next to Matthew. "Now look at this step show. This is the last national step competition from my fraternity. These guys are awesome! They're synchronized and intense. Not to mention the fact that there are ten of them. If one of them makes a mistake they won't be nearly as obvious as if any of you do," Status explained.

"Good point," Matthew said.

"Thanks. I'll be leaving Atlanta in a few days, but I have work here two weeks before your show. I've given you five steps so you have a good foundation. Keep practicing, practicing, practicing! I recommend that you create two to three more steps for a great show. I haven't seen this great entrance that you keep talking about, but if it's half as good as you say it is, then you'll have an awesome show.

Your outfits should be here soon from the stylist. Start practicing in them during the last two to three weeks before the show," he advised.

"We got you," Jo'sha said.

They watched several more tapes with Status pointing out high points and low points from each step. After another hour of videotape, Status decided to turn in.

"That's it for tonight guys. I have an early day tomorrow. We start the first day of the new video shoot and I have to be fresh."

"Cool, we can see ourselves out," Wade said.

Status gave them all handshakes and hugs, and then turned in upstairs. The four made their way to the door.

"Guys, I've been feeling kind of pent up lately," Chance said, inhaling the cold night air from the porch.

"Me too, to be honest," Jo'sha said.

"Well you know we can't use the backyard. Stanley might see us," Wade said.

"The bedroom that he's in is on the side of the house. There isn't a window facing the back. Besides, he has to get to bed tonight, remember?" Chance said.

Matthew didn't say a word, but nodded his head. Chance couldn't tell if he agreed or disagreed, but he seemed to be following the rest of them.

"Let's at least go back toward the woods," Matthew urged.

They walked across the large backyard toward the tree line. Chance pulled off his shirt, threw it on the ground and dug his big black hands into the dark earth and grunted. The ground shook for several minutes while Chance melded with the earth. When he finished he sighed and fell back on the ground.

"Better now?" Matthew asked.

"Much better," Chance sighed.

"Anybody else?" he asked.

Wade was looking into the woods almost as if in a trance. Suddenly, without a word, he started walking.

"What's wrong with him? Jo'sha asked, following Wade into the thick wooded mesh.

They followed Wade a tenth of a mile into the woods. "There's water here," Wade explained. He walked a few feet further and discovered a small brook. He immediately stepped in.

"Now what?" Jo'sha asked.

Wade opened his arms and the water raced and surged, moving rocks, small fish and stones in its way. The small brook began to swell and Matthew imagined that this is what it must have looked like when Moses parted the Red Sea. The brook became deeper and thicker until Wade was waist deep in water. Jo'sha, Chance and Matthew backed up and were standing on what had become an embankment. After several minutes, Wade sighed and the water stopped moving. He reveled in the release.

CHAPTER 39

It was the middle of February and the young men's lives had reached some semblance of normalcy. They had planned each of their class schedules around a daily routine of mediation and exercise. Three times a week they managed to make it out to the Vaughn estate for an exertion of their various powers, and even Chance was becoming more adept.

There had been no more murder victims since the eleventh, which was several weeks ago. Everyone, except Matthew, was starting to believe that they would never find any leads on the real killer.

The campus was buzzing about Omega Tau's posters, charitable contributions, and mysterious school paper editorials. Several athletes were boasting that they were starting the new fraternity. Quite a few people assumed that Omega Tau was an honor organization seeking social credibility, but the truth was that the organization was a complete mystery. Only a select few school administrators and the men of Omega Tau knew about the organization's beginnings. The ladies in the administrative office responsible for handling the institution of new campus organizations were delighted to keep the secret until the Spring Festival event. The old guard fraternities had become arrogant and haughty, and the word that there was a new fraternity starting on campus with members boasting a perfect 4.0 grade point average had put them all on notice.

Chance, Jo'sha, Wade, and Matthew sat in the floor of the suite meditating and communing. Their meditation had advanced so much that it caused Jo'sha to chant in unfamiliar tongues. Wade often joined in by humming in perfect harmony. The result was a song that sounded like a beautiful lost language. In this session Jo'sha was replaying each and every dream vision for them in vivid detail, and because of the bond that they shared they all experienced each vision with him. It had taken them a long time to get to this point and it hadn't been easy, but they all agreed it was worth it.

During their meditations, they could see the world through each other's eyes, sharing thoughts and feeling and emotions in ways that no humans had in quite some time. Their mental capacities were heightened, and while they were linked in meditation they had access to thought processes and patterns that they never before realized. Despite all of this, none of them could figure out Jo'sha's dream visions. Still he replayed them over and over again, stopping at particular points of interest.

Look here at the stones, Jo'sha thought.

What does it mean? Wade wondered.

In the midst of their meditation they heard a scratch at the door.

What was that? Chance looked toward the door.

There's someone at the door—someone listening to us. I can't tell who it is, but they are—familiar, Matthew relayed.

Slowly, they disengaged from Jo'sha's dream journey, took deep breaths, and released themselves from meditation. Chance motioned for each of them to be still while he crept quietly toward the door. Even though they were out of meditation, they could still sense the presence on the other side of the door. Matthew was amazed at what they could do when they were all focused on the same subject.

Chance stood at the door in complete silence for several seconds. Then in one swift and flowing move he unlocked the door, snatched it open, and grabbed the person on the other side before he could realize what happened.

"Heeyyyyy!" Sundiata screamed.

"Can we help you?" Chance asked, holding Sundiata several inches off the floor with one hand. Matthew motioned for Chance to let him down slowly.

"Nawww," he stuttered.

"Seems like you were trying to eavesdrop," Chance accused.

"No, not all," Sundiata said.

"He's lying," said Wade.

"I'm going to ask you one more time—can we help you?" Chance asked, lifting Sundiata back up off the floor.

"Let him go, Chance," Matthew urged when he noticed the blood rushing to Sundiata's face, deepening his already ruddy complexion.

Chance hesitated and then tossed him to the floor.

"Is there something you wanted?" Matthew asked.

"I was just in the building and thought I would stop by to say what's up," Sundiata stated, trying to regain his composure.

"At six in the morning?" Wade asked incredulously. "He's lying again."

"Well, we just got up and were about to get ready for class, so this probably isn't a good time," Matthew advised.

"Alright, I'll catch you all later," Sundiata said, tugging the wrinkles out of his shirt. He tipped quickly past Chance and out the door.

"There's something going on with him," Matthew said once he was sure Sundiata was gone.

"At first, I thought it was just that he was trying to get at Olivia, but it seems like something more," Jo'sha said.

"A hell of a lot more," Wade said.

"Why would he be outside our door at six in the morning?" Chance asked.

"More importantly, do you think he heard anything?" Wade asked.

"Well, the most he could have heard is Jo'sha chanting and you humming. No one can hear us when we're thought-sharing," Matthew reminded them.

"I wonder if his meeting with Dr. Smith last semester has anything to do with him snooping on us now," Wade commented.

"I don't know, but I don't like the way it feels," said Matthew.

"Do you think he knows about Omega Tau?" asked Chance.

"Could be," Matthew answered.

"Maybe we shouldn't have let him go so quickly," said Jo'sha.

"What good would keeping him here have done?" Matthew asked.

"We could have made him tell us why he was really here. We know and he knows that he didn't just stop by to say hello," Jo'sha stated.

"Yeah, but we probably would have had to torture him to get the truth, and that could have gotten us in trouble," Matthew reasoned.

"This isn't the first time that I've felt like we were being watched. I felt it one night when we were on Bonder's Pointe, and once while we were walking back from class one evening. This is just the first time we've been able to prove it," said Jo'sha.

"Well no matter what he couldn't have heard much."

"Do you think he knows about the ankhs?" Wade asked.

They all paused for several seconds.

"Of course he doesn't know about the ankhs. There's no way that he could."

"Well we aren't going to figure it out now, and we need to get to the gym," Chance stated.

The others agreed and silently began collecting their things for the trip to the gym. Matthew couldn't help but think that maybe they were outgrowing the confines of the campus and putting themselves at risk by staying there.

"Why are you in such a rush?" Wade asked Chance.

"I've got a Spring Festival committee meeting this morning. I'll get to see Aspen," Chance smiled.

"I should have known."

"Before we get off the subject, we need to keep an eye out for anyone that might be following us," Matthew cautioned.

"So what does that mean?" asked Jo'sha.

"It means we need to change up our routes a little bit, instead of just walking home from class we need to be mindful of everyone that is around us. We need to begin sensing anyone that is focused on us. I know that it's more difficult when we're alone, but when there are two or three of us gathered together it should be pretty easy to tell if we're being followed. We just need to focus. Less talk about girls and more concentration," Matthew warned.

"*Okay*," Wade said, not in the mood for another of Matthew's lectures, especially not this morning. "I'm going to Baltimore this weekend," he blurted out.

"Where did that come from?" Chance asked.

"I knew you guys would try to stop me, but I have to go check on Quay."

"No, we're not going to try to stop you," Chance assured him.

"But we will have to do a few things before you go. You'll have to make sure to do a few things while you're there too. You'll have to meditate everyday, find some release for your power, and exercise. It isn't hard. You just have to stay disciplined. You'll probably be weak when you get back, but we'll be here for you," said Matthew.

Wade smiled.

"And whatever you miss from step practice, we'll catch you up when you return," Jo'sha added.

"When are you leaving?" Chance asked.

"Thursday morning. I'll be back Sunday night."

"We need to go if we're going to get a good workout," said Chance.

The gym was practically empty when they got there with the exception of a few student athletes. Chance was throwing up more weight than anyone in the gym and people were starting to notice. Matthew's constant attempts at getting him to tone it down were pointless. Chance, more than any of the others, needed the daily release, and because his strength was steadily increasing he couldn't tell when he was overdoing it. That was just one more reason for Matthew to think that perhaps they couldn't stay on campus without eventually drawing too much attention. Jo'sha encouraged Chance to display feats of strength, often boasting that his boy could take anyone in the gym. His argument to Matthew was that someone had to be the strongest person in the gym, so why couldn't it be Chance. They finished their morning workout, showered and headed to class. As always, Wade was the last to get dressed.

The twelve students who had comprised Dr Smith's university orientation class were still required to stay together for another class in the second semester. During the second semester the class was monitored by an honored upperclassman, responsible for scheduling university professors as guest speakers. Students referred to these class monitors as Pinnacles. Ronnie was the Pinnacle for Jo'sha, Wade, Chance, and Matthew's class. This time was often used by professors of underrepresented majors to sell freshmen on their programs before they declared their majors.

"Come on, Wade. We can't be late for orientation. You know we don't want to hear Ronnie's mouth. It's bad enough that we have to listen to Matthew," Chance said.

"What does that mean?" asked Matthew, slightly offended.

"I'm coming," said Wade, rushing out of the gym locker room, pulling his wavy hair back into a ponytail.

They made it to class five minutes later, but Ronnie gave them slack anyway. When they entered the room Sundiata slid down in his seat. Everyone else greeted them with salutations and handshakes, except for Robert Black, who had grown to despise the four of them. He especially hated Jo'sha, who he connected to the sudden feverish outbreaks, heat rashes, and blisters that he only experienced during the orientation class.

Jo'sha had gotten good enough with his powers to focus and localize the concentration of heat. On the first day of class in the second semester, Jo'sha had managed to set Robert's groin area on fire leaving him with first-degree burns on his scrotum. The doctors couldn't explain what had caused it, but a rumor quickly spread that Robert had a sexually transmitted disease.

"Now that everyone is here, we can get started," Ronnie said in a country drawl that was as pronounced as any relative of Chance's. "Our special guest today is Dr. Zachary. He teaches several classes in religion and philosophy."

Dr. Zachary was a small, slim man with sharp features and dreadlocks that fell to his waist. He was the head of the religion department, a chair in the English department, and acclaimed for having written several best-selling science fiction novels. Dr. Zachary was witty, spontaneous, and fun. He quickly had the entire class roaring with laughter.

While discussing one of his religion classes, Dr. Zachary talked about prophecies and dreams, which caused Jo'sha's eyes to light up. Finally, he'd found someone who could help him with his dream visions. When class ended several students stayed over to speak to Dr. Zachary. He spent time with all of them and answered all of their questions. Jo'sha waited in the back of the line on purpose.

"Are you going to talk to him about your dreams?" Matthew asked.

"Yes," Jo'sha replied.

"Well just make sure that you don't tell him too much. We already have people following us," Matthew whispered.

"Would you please go away before I set you on fire!" Jo'sha snapped.

"I am just saying—"

Jo'sha shot a sharp spark at Matthew, causing him to flinch at the public display of power. Matthew rushed off in frustration. Once Matthew was gone Jo'sha was the last student in the classroom.

"I see you," Dr. Zachary said.

"And I you," Jo'sha smiled.

"Most don't understand that greeting or the meaning behind it," Dr. Zachary admitted.

"My—father used it often," Jo'sha replied.

"How can I help you?" he asked.

"I wanted to tell you how much I enjoyed your lecture—"

"Thank you."

"And to get your help with something," Jo'sha continued.

"Well what is it?"

"During your lecture you spoke about dreams and their meanings. I've been having recurring dreams. I need to know if they mean something," Jo'sha said.

"All dreams mean something. There are eleven levels of consciousness. Life isn't just about what we can see. We sense on so many different levels, and dreams or visions are just another way of tapping into what is happening in the time and space all around us. More often times than not, however, dreams are a way of working something out that has happened to us in the past. Tell me, what dreams are you having?" Dr. Zachary sat on top of the wooden table and folded his legs.

"It's personal."

"I see," Dr. Zachary said, looking off in the distance.

"I'm sorry, but I just can't share the details. I probably shouldn't have bothered you."

"No, I think I can still help you. Remember this. When your dreams are not obvious or are not easily understood, then it is very likely that the things that you see in your dreams are symbols, that they represent something that is very real in your life. Dreams are messages from your past, present or future. It is a gift to dream. Don't fight it. Lose yourself in it."

Jo'sha smiled, thanked Dr. Zachary, and ran back to his room. Jo'sha's next class wasn't until 2:00 p.m. Normally he went to the music room, but based on Dr. Zachary's feedback, he was going to review his dream journal. When Jo'sha got back to his room, there was a special delivery post taped to the door with his name on it.

He ripped it off immediately and tore it open. Inside was a check, a compact disc entitled, *Deliberate Verses*, and a handwritten note from Agonize that read:

You were a great addition to this album. I'm glad that I got my career started before you got to the game. You are going to be the next big thing and I'd like to help you. I've spoken to my record label and my manager and we want you to come on the road with us to promote the album. It's only thirty-four cities. You can put school on hold for a semester and have the time of your life.

Jo'sha looked at the check, and then at the note, and then at the compact disc. He flipped the disc open and fingered through the credits until he found his name. He smiled. The moment was bittersweet as he thought that Foster would have been so proud of him.

CHAPTER 40

The four friends stayed in close contact while Wade was away in Baltimore. They wanted to make sure that he was all right, and just as they imagined, he was weakening by the day. However, the regimen of exercise, meditation, and power releases, allowed him to keep up a decent façade. Just the same, they all were anxiously awaiting his return so they could regain the normalcy of their lives together. Matthew was already at the airport waiting when Wade's flight arrived. Wade was one of the last people to come up the escalator and through the concourse. Even though he looked worn, he sensed Matthew immediately through the crowd.

"Very good," Matthew said.

"I figured you'd be hiding somewhere just to see if I could find you."

"You look more tired than I thought you would," Matthew said, taking Wade's bag from him as they headed toward the parking garage.

"I'm exhausted. I thought I'd be able to get some rest on the plane. What I didn't figure on was that I'd be placed between two people who were deathly afraid of flying. I asked to be moved, but there were no more seats available, and no one wanted to trade seats."

"You couldn't shield yourself?"

"It was coming from two different directions, and what I've figured out is that the purer emotions, happiness, anger, and fear, are more difficult for me to combat. Especially if I am not at my best."

"Yeah, I remember you dancing on the speaker at that party," Matthew said.

"Don't remind me," Wade snapped.

"How are Quay and the baby?"

"They're doing fine."

Matthew glanced over at the relaxed expression on Wade's face, and could tell that Wade was drawing energy from him. "How's your family?" he asked.

"They're getting more comfortable with the idea of becoming grandparents and great aunties," Wade said.

"With a little help from you I bet," Matthew grinned.

"William said to tell you hello, and that he'll be here next week to show us a few steps."

Matthew smiled before he realized it. "Great," he said, trying not to sound too excited.

Wade glanced at him out of the corner of his eye, and took note of his friend's noticeable change.

"We have a surprise for you," Matthew said quickly.

"What kind of surprise?"

"You'll see. It's out at the Vaughn place."

Wade drifted off, and slept the entire way out to the country. When Matthew pulled into the driveway Jo'sha and Chance were already in the backyard waiting. Wade woke up as soon as the car stopped.

"This way," Matthew said, directing Wade toward the backyard.

"How are you, roomie?" Chance asked, grabbing Wade by the shoulder and lifting him up off the floor.

"Put me down!" Wade yelled.

Chance set Wade down gently. "I see you haven't changed much," he teased.

"We have a surprise for you," Jo'sha said, motioning for Wade to follow them.

They led Wade out back and into the woods near the brook they had found. Chance had carved a chair out of a large rock that sat alongside the water. Sitting there in the pallid moonlight, it exuded a majestic aura. When Wade saw it he smiled appreciatively. "You shouldn't have," Wade said.

"We thought you might need it," Chance answered.

"It gave him something to do without showing off in the gym," Matthew added referring to Chance.

Wade made his way through the woods and over to the stone chair. He removed his shoes while he rubbed the smooth finish of the chair.

"The edges are smooth," Wade said.

"I did the heat polishing," Jo'sha said proudly.

"Thanks guys." Wade sat back in the chair, and let his feet dangle in the cool water. First he let the water rush up to his ankles, and then he called it up to his knees, and then to his waist.

They all caught a rush from Wade's charge.

"It's funny you know," Matthew said.

"What's that?" Jo'sha asked as they watched Wade in the water.

"No matter what we do for each other, it always ends up benefiting us all in the end," Matthew said.

"Somehow I think that's the way it's supposed to be," Chance answered quietly.

The boys spent the rest of the night exercising their powers until Wade was completely rejuvenated.

∞

Time leading up to Spring Festival passed quickly. As promised, William came down to show them a few steps that his fraternity chapter hadn't used in its last step show, and the boys held step practice religiously every night. Their costumes were delivered three weeks before the show, and they were nicer than anything that they could have imagined. At Chance's suggestion, the boys had traveled to every step show at every nearby university to see the best and the baddest step teams in the southeast. Chance videotaped every show and they watched them all, dissecting each and every step, song, and routine. Also as promised, Status returned just a couple of weeks before the step show.

"Do you see him?" Matthew asked Wade.

"Relax, he'll be out soon," Wade said, as he pulled through the passenger pick-up lane of the airport. He glanced quickly at his friend. "Matthew, there's something that I've been meaning to ask you—" he began.

"There he is!" Matthew yelled.

Status was coming out of the airport with a large rolling Louis Vutton trunk and overnight bag. Wade pulled up to the curb and Matthew immediately jumped out of the truck.

"Matthew!" Status yelled, scooping Matthew into his muscular arms and hugging him.

"How are you?" Matthew responded.

"Things have been great! I just got back from a concert tour in Europe."

"Were you doing choreography there?" Matthew asked.

"No, back-up dancing."

Matthew took Status' shoulder bag, and the two of them walked over to Wade's truck, which was parked at the curb. They lifted the large chest into the back of the truck and then jumped in.

"Wade, how are you?"

"Fine, Status, how are you?"

"I've been good, but the real question is has my favorite step team been practicing?" Status asked.

"Almost every night," Matthew said.

"Did the costumes arrive?"

"They came about a week ago," Matthew answered.

"And have you been practicing in them?"

"Yeah, so much that we have to get them dry cleaned."

"My cousin William, came down with one of his fraternity brothers and showed us a couple of steps too," Wade said, interrupting Matthew.

"I can't wait to see how the show is coming," Status remarked.

"And we can't wait to show you," Matthew answered enthusiastically.

"I guess the step show will be your last hoorah as a group for a while."

"What do you mean?" asked Wade.

"Well, with Anthony asking Jo'sha to tour with him, I figured he would be gone for a while," Status said.

"What?" Matthew and Wade asked in unison.

"You didn't know?" asked Status, sensing he may have said too much.

"I'm sure that he was planning to tell us soon," Matthew said quickly.

"How long are you going to be staying here with us this time?" Wade asked, ready to change the subject.

"I'll be here for three weeks working on a few videos."

"Well we've made a few improvements out at the house, so your stay should be more enjoyable this time," said Matthew.

"Didn't Jo'sha tell you that either? I'll be staying at the Four Seasons hotel downtown. The record label has got me covered this time."

"How are we going to practice?" Wade asked.

"I've already called and reserved one of the smaller ballrooms for practice, and I thought it would be a good idea if we actually snuck out to the amphitheater tonight and took a look at the layout," Status explained.

"Great idea," said Wade.

The rest of the ride to the hotel was void of verbal conversation. Status drifted in and out of sleep while Matthew and Wade sat wondering about why Jo'sha hadn't told either of them about the tour. Matthew was worried and Wade could feel it.

Matthew? Wade thought.

Huh? Matthew responded.

Matthew? Wade projected again. *I can feel your thoughts.*

We've never done this outside meditation, and with only two of us before, Matthew thought.

Truth is, I've been able to hear your thoughts for quite some time now. This is just my first time letting you hear mine, Wade projected.

What? Matthew couldn't contain his surprise, but he quickly recovered. *Is it just me or can you hear Jo'sha and Chance's thoughts too?*

Occasionally, I can pick up a few of Chance's random thoughts, but never Jo'sha's.

"So that means you know—"

Yes, it does. Wade interrupted before he could finish.

"Have you told—"

"No."

Status woke abruptly from his sleep. "Can we stop by Lucille's and get something to eat?" he asked.

We'll finish this later, Wade concluded.

As requested, Wade stopped by Lucille's for takeout, and then dropped Status off at his hotel.

"We'll be back with the other guys at 7:00 p.m.," Matthew said.

"Bring your outfits," Status called out as they pulled away from the curb of the hotel.

"Is Jo'sha thinking about trying to leave us?" Matthew asked once they were alone.

"I can't hear his thoughts, but I could tell that he's been worried about something lately," Wade answered.

"Do you think he's worried about leaving us?"

"It's not unusual for any one of us to be worried, so I didn't really pay it any attention."

"I think we should ask him about it as soon as we see him," Matthew said, feeling slightly betrayed.

"And I think he's a grown man, needs time to sort this out by himself. We're connected, but we're not one person. We are four distinct individuals and we can't forget that. You know how much he loves his music, but he also understands the obligation that he has to us. Not to mention the possibility of leaving Olivia. This can't be easy for him."

"So what are you saying?"

"I mean exactly what I said, Jo'sha needs some time to sort some things out—just like you obviously do. We should respect that. He'll come to us when he's ready to talk about it."

The weight of Wade's words gave Matthew a lot to think about, and he was quiet for the rest of the ride home.

CHAPTER 41

The Spring Festival was a tremendous success. The entire campus had been enthusiastically engrossed in all the scheduled activity, and was buzzing about the impending step show. Aspen Walker's sorority was the first group to step and the ladies did a phenomenal job. The next four groups included three fraternities and one sorority, with each as good as the next.

It was the end of the evening and Omega Tau's turn to step. With all the build up in the weeks before the event, the crowd was anxious to see just who had been making large university donations, plastering the campus with posters, and creating such a buzz. They couldn't wait for the mystery of Omega Tau to be revealed.

Chance, Jo'sha, Matthew and Wade stood off in the wings of the amphitheater and waited for Dr. Weatherspoon to finish introducing them. The entire amphitheater sat in anxious anticipation.

Neither Jo'sha nor Chance was the least bit nervous. Jo'sha was a natural performer and loved the spotlight. Chance had been a star athlete in high school and was used to being in the limelight. Wade siphoned off any nervousness that he and Matthew were feeling, and replaced it with the confidence that Jo'sha exuded. William, Judge Graham, Status, Miss Vaughn, Olivia, Matthew's parents, Jacoby and Cobyn were in the second row. Even though Foster wasn't there for Jo'sha, he didn't really feel alone.

Dr. Weatherspoon exited the stage after a lengthy introduction. It was a beautiful 78 degrees and there wasn't a cloud in the sky—until Matthew raised his hand from behind the stage. The sky filled with lightning and the crowd screamed in surprise. The impromptu volt disappeared as quickly as it came, and when the lightening no longer lit up the sky, all that the crowd could see on the stage was the silhouette of the brothers of Omega Tau. Chance stood in the middle with Matthew on his left, and Wade and Jo'sha on his right. Their frames created a silhouette that made several young women in the audience shout out in approval.

In the next instant, Jo'sha began singing Spring Love Child to a track that Anthony Goins had allowed him to borrow for the step show. Several of the students from the campus recognized Jo'sha's voice immediately and began to applaud after a few notes. Jo'sha sang two verses before the house lights came up and the speakers began to pour out a driving house beat. Chance, Jo'sha, Wade and Matthew began to step in unison and the crowd went wild. Their outfits, which had been designed by Anthony's stylist, urban clothing designer Eric Grace, were amazing. The four wore green-tinted designer denim pants from Eric Grace's Platinum Collection, Eric Grace dark green, suede combat boots, and hand stitched jerseys with the Omega Tau ankh embroidered into the chest. The performers went through each step flawlessly and their excitement was infectious—Wade made sure of it. The show ended with pyrotechnic fireworks courtesy of Jo'sha, Wade, Chance and Matthew. When they were finished, the four ran off the stage leaving behind a thunderous standing ovation.

"Can you believe it?" Wade shouted.

"It was great!" Jo'sha yelled.

Chance had managed to rip off his shirt during the last part of the show, and the women in the crowd loved it.

"What happened to your shirt?" Matthew asked.

"It accidentally came off," Chance joked.

"Did Aspen see?" Jo'sha asked.

"I made sure of it," Chance winked.

It wasn't long before their friends and family met them back stage.

"That was great, Wade. It reminded me of my old step days," said Judge Graham.

Olivia kissed Matthew on the cheek and then wrapped her arms around Jo'sha's neck.

"I ain't never seen nothing like that," Isadora said admiringly.

"How did you all do all of those fireworks?" Miss Vaughn asked.

"We can't give away all of our fraternity secrets," answered Matthew.

"Well, however you did it, it was wonderful! We are definitely going to have to have a celebratory dinner out at the old house tomorrow," Miss Vaughn announced.

"Quiet everybody," said Matthew's father. "They're about to announce the winners."

Dr. Weatherspoon came back onto the stage with a large envelope in his hand. He thanked the judges for their time, and the accounting department for auditing the results.

"This has been a wonderful Spring Festival. Can we get a round of applause for our reigning Homecoming Queen and her planning committee? Will Aspen Walker please come up on stage and help me announce the winners?"

Aspen came back up on stage; still in her step show outfit, to the cheers of the crowd and the calls of her sorority sisters. She was carrying a large three-foot trophy.

Dr. Smith opened the envelope slowly and announced, "The winners of this year's Spring Festival step show, the trophy, and $2000 prize money, are fairly new to the campus, but have already begun to set a standard on the Georgia Central campus—Omega Tau!"

Jo'sha, Chance, Wade, and Matthew ran out onto the stage amidst the cheers and applause of the crowd.

"Do you have any comments?" asked Dr. Weatherspoon.

Matthew took the microphone, "On behalf of the Brothers of Omega Tau, we would like to accept this trophy and donate $1000 of the prize money to the amphitheater building fund, and the other $1000 to the Omega Tau Rites of Passage Program, benefiting local area high school males."

When he finished, the crowd cheered. Chance snatched Aspen up in his arms and hugged her tight. She felt his touch and he knew he had won her over.

CHAPTER 42

The day after the Spring Festival the four members of Omega Tau and their guests went to Miss Vaughn's estate for a celebratory dinner. The table was set with all of their favorite foods and more than enough for all of the guests.

"I can't remember when the great room was filled with so many people. This is how we used to celebrate when I was a girl. Good food and lots of good people," Miss Vaughn reminisced.

"This is a mighty fine spread, Miss Vaughn, and an excellent way to spend the evening before we go back to our respective homes. We should do this more often," Judge Graham said.

"Thank you," Miss Vaughn responded.

Wade smiled. He was glad that his father had come to see his first step show. His mother and aunties decided not to attend since Wade had decided not to honor his family's legacy by joining the same fraternity that his father and grandfathers had joined.

"I would like to make a toast to the best fraternity on campus," Roland said, raising his glass.

They all raised their glasses in response, and then ate and answered question after question about how they got the idea for the fraternity and managed to pull it off without anyone on campus finding out.

"What's next for your fraternity, son?" Judge Graham asked.

"Well our programmatic thrust focuses on extending the rite of passage to qualifying high school males. We intend for it to be the cultural equivalent of a Bah Mitzvah, where we bring in male elders who are willing to be a part of each young boy's life. We want to have a ceremony to mark his passage into manhood by reflections on their mental, physical, emotional, and spiritual development," Wade answered. He could see that his father was really interested in what they were doing, and proud of him for his efforts.

"Sounds great," Judge Graham said. "Just let me know if you young men need any money."

"Yes, we will, Dad."

Matthew was sitting on the other side of the large table between William and Status. "We have a few people that we would like to thank," he said.

Jo'sha excused himself and ran out to the car. He came back with a box.

"The idea for Omega Tau actually started with Miss Vaughn's great uncle, Oleander Vaughn, and three of his classmates, Winston Wright, Cyrus Wilkes and Nathaniel Charles. Miss Vaughn helped us understand our founders, and thus helped us write the history. We had a great step show last night, and we owe that to the help we got from Wade's cousin, William, and our dear friend and the best choreographer out, Status, a.k.a Stanley Titus. We don't have much, just a small token of our appreciation for all that you all have done for us. It's a small pamphlet with the complete history of Omega Tau. It has pictures of the founders and it's signed by all of us," said Matthew.

Chance opened the box and pulled out small hand-bound copies of the fraternity history. Jo'sha had created antique leather covers for each pamphlet.

"This is great!" Status exclaimed.

William accepted his copy and smiled. Then he gave Matthew a hug.

Miss Vaughn began weeping and everyone hugged everyone until everyone had been hugged at least two or three times. "You boys have become like my family. You came to me at a time when I was feeling mighty low and alone," said Miss Vaughn. "I have a special announcement of my own. I have decided to donate this house and the seven acres of land that it sits on to you boys and Omega Tau," she said proudly.

"Are you sure about that?" Judge Graham asked.

"I'm very sure. I'm an old woman, and I know I can't take it with me. I don't have any family to speak of and I want to make a difference. Besides, I'm sure that my great uncle Oleander would approve," she said.

"We don't know what to say," Chance said, deeply touched by the gesture.

"Say thank you and you'll take it," Jacoby remarked. Cobyn jabbed him in the side.

"As a matter of fact, Judge Graham, I want you to help me draw up the papers," Miss Vaughn continued.

"I most certainly will, Miss Vaughn. Well boys, it looks like Omega Tau just got its corporate headquarters."

They spent the rest of the night eating, laughing, and singing. The walk to campus the next day was an enjoyable one for all of them. They received congratulations, shout outs, and well wishes from several of their classmates as they made their way to orientation. "I knew it was you guys all along," they heard from a few of the young women on campus.

"Good work, new Greeks," they heard from a few of the campus' older established fraternities.

"When are you going to have a line?" asked quite a few underclassmen.

"Did you hear that?" Chance asked. "They want to join us."

"Why shouldn't they?" asked Jo'sha.

"Don't go getting the big head," Matthew warned.

"We're on top of the world. We should enjoy it," Jo'sha responded.

"There's more to life than just enjoying it. We have responsibilities too," Matthew argued.

Matthew, stop it! Wade projected.

"What's eating you?" Jo'sha asked with attitude.

"Nothing," Matthew responded. He remained silent the rest of the way to class.

"Class, let's give a big round of applause to the newest campus fraternity, Omega Tau. Not only did they win the step show, but rumor has it that they may also win this year's group freshman scholarship award," Ronnie said proudly. He had been boasting on Omega Tau's victory since the four arrived at class. With the exception of Robert and Sundiata, the rest of the class echoed Ronnie's sentiments. "Alright, let's settle down," he said. "We have a guest speaker who is no stranger to this class. He is a professor at this university and a noted historian. I had originally planned to have one of the Atlanta City Council members speak today to cover your Social Sciences lecture, but when Dr. Smith called me and told me that he was interested in coming in to speak I couldn't turn him down."

Dr. Smith walked into the class on cue. "Gentlemen," he said, nodding curtly. They responded with half-hearted greetings and salutations. "Since you were my first orientation class here at Georgia Central University, I thought it fitting to share some of my latest work with you," said Dr. Smith. He seemed much more animated than any of them remembered.

Matthew! Matthew! Wade thought.

What?

Can you feel that?

Yes, but what is it?

I started feeling it when Dr. Smith came into the room.

It feels like a power surge. It's the same feeling I get when Chance is using his powers, or when we're meditating. Can you tell what Chance is feeling?

I can't feel anything from him. He looks like he's almost in a trance.

How about Jo'sha?

He's still looking through his dream journal. I don't think he intends to pay attention to Dr. Smith.

Well keep your eyes and ears open because this is weird.

"—and so one of the reasons that I came to Georgia Central was because all of my findings indicated that the Crux Ansata were actually somewhere near this campus—maybe even on this campus. The Crux Ansata were rumored to be stones crafted by angels at the place where the four rivers meet in what was the Garden of Eden. Furthermore, rumor has it that they were brought to America by African slaves, and moved from slave to slave through the centuries, finally resting somewhere here in this area," Dr. Smith lectured. Unlike previous lectures, the class was fascinated by what Dr. Smith had to say.

"That's it! That's it!" Jo'sha screamed, suddenly attentive.

"I see some things never change," Dr. Smith snapped.

"Jo'sha, please contain yourself. Dr. Smith is speaking," Ronnie advised.

"I'm sorry," Jo'sha said, looking at Dr. Smith, then Matthew and Wade.

"What is it?" mouthed Matthew. Jo'sha held up five fingers. "Huh?" Matthew shook his head in frustration.

"—so I have enlisted the aid of one of your classmates, Mr. Sundiata Bazemore, to help me with my research. I must say that we believe we are very close to finding the Crux Ansata," Dr. Smith said, as he paced the length of the room. He stopped in front of Chance's desk. Sundiata, Matthew, Chance, Wade, Jo'sha and Matthew all sat up in their seats. Matthew and Wade weren't the only ones who could feel that something was different. Jo'sha and Chance felt it, too.

"Why is this so important? There must be hundreds of slave relics," asked Amir.

"If found, the Crux Ansata would be the oldest slave relic in history, and if the stories are true, then the Crux Ansata is one of the oldest historical relics in the world," Dr. Smith answered. "It is believed that the Crux Ansata bestows extraordinary power and protection to the wearer, but that, of course, can only be a myth."

Dr. Smith was still standing over Chance. Chance found it hard not to stare into Dr. Smith's eyes, and Dr. Smith found it equally hard not to stare back.

"Uh, I think it is about time for class to be dismissed," Ronnie stuttered growing increasingly uncomfortable with the exchange between the two men.

"Yes, it is about that time," Dr. Smith said, backing away from Chance slowly. Others in the class found the exchange odd and didn't know what to make of it. Neither did Chance for that matter.

"Class dismissed," Ronnie said again.

Slowly, the students began to gather their things and leave. Dr. Smith shook Ronnie's hand, glanced back at Sundiata, and quickly exited the room. Sundiata gathered his things and dashed off behind Dr. Smith.

"What was that all about?" asked Ronnie once they were alone in the room.

"Dr. Smith is eccentric. There's no telling," Matthew said.

"The delivery aside, it was a good lecture," Ronnie admitted.

"I guess so," Wade responded.

"I'll see you guys back at the dorm," said Ronnie.

When Ronnie left the classroom Jo'sha closed the door behind him. He motioned for his friends to join him in the corner. "I figured it out!" he exclaimed.

"Figured what out?" asked Matthew.

"My dreams, I think I've figured them out—the five birds, five flowers, the five stones and the empty bag. I don't know why I didn't figure it out before. There are five ankhs. There's one missing. We only found four of them," he whispered.

"Dammit, he's right!" Matthew echoed.

"How do you know?" Wade asked.

"It makes so much sense. When we first found the ankhs, I did research on several different cultures. Most of them spoke of earth, air, water, and fire, but a few of them identified five elements instead of four. Earth, wood, stone, fire, and water was just one of the combinations. I just dismissed it, but never stopped to think that there was another one," Matthew said.

"And there are five senses, not four," Wade added.

"Exactly."

"That's all well and good, but I think we have more important things to worry about right now. Dr. Smith obviously knows about the ankhs, and based on how he was staring at me in class he thinks I have them," Chance said.

"How in the hell could he know?" Wade asked.

"Maybe it was our lightning and pyrotechnic show from the step show the other night," Matthew said. "I knew I shouldn't have let you all talk me into that."

"It was your idea!" Jo'sha retorted.

"It doesn't matter how he knows. He just knows," Chance interjected.

"It was really strange, too. He sounded as if he thought there was only one," said Matthew. "So it's obvious that he doesn't have all of his facts right."

"He also admitted that Sundiata was working with him, so that explains why you saw them talking on campus, Wade," Jo'sha said.

"Damn, this never seems to stop," Wade said, shaking his head.

"We need to be strong. We need to stick together," Jo'sha said solemnly.

"That's interesting coming from you," Matthew said sarcastically.

"What does that mean? You've been coming at me kind of funny for a while now," Jo'sha said angrily.

"I'm talking about you going on tour with Anthony Goins," Matthew shot.

"How'd you know about that?"

"Is it true?"

"Now is not the time for that," Wade said, attempting to keep the peace.

"I already told him that I wasn't going because I had things to take care of. If that was what was bothering you, then you should have asked," Jo'sha said.

"Dammit, stop it! We don't have time for that right now," Chance boomed.

"Chance is right," Wade agreed. "The real question is what do we do now?"

"Let's meet at the library tonight at 7:00 p.m. Jo'sha, bring your dream journal, and I'll bring all of my notes. We have to figure this out," Matthew said.

CHAPTER 43

Chance and Wade were in the library in their regular study spot by 6:45 p.m. Chance put his head down on the desk and Wade started looking through his computer science text book.

I know you're worried, Wade thought-projected to Chance.

"What?" Chance said, looking over at Wade with surprise.

Wade smiled at him. *Try it*, he thought back.

Like this?

"That's exactly it," Wade said excitedly.

"How long have you been able to do that? We can normally only hear each other's thoughts during meditation," Chance said.

"I've been able to do it for a while. I noticed it first with Matthew. From time to time I can hear your thoughts, like now, but never Jo'sha," Wade answered.

"What about me?" Jo'sha asked, as he walked up to join them.

"I can hear Matthew and Chance's thoughts, and they can hear mine," Wade explained.

"You mean during meditation?"

"No, not just during meditation."

"When did you guys find this out?"

"He just told me, but at least I am not the last one to find out this time," Chance said.

"Show me," Jo'sha said.

"Alright, whisper a number to Chance. Chance you think about that number," Wade said.

Jo'sha whispered a number to Chance, and Chance did as he was instructed.

"Fifteen," Wade said.

"Nice, it seems like we learn something new everyday," Jo'sha said.

"What are you guys talking about?" Matthew asked.

"Wade's new power," Jo'sha said.

"You told them," Matthew said.

"Yeah," Wade answered.

"Good," Matthew responded. "We're going to need every trick at our disposal."

"Why do you say that?" asked Chance.

"First, Dr. Smith knows about the ankh, and there's no telling who else he has told. Second of all, it appears that he thinks Chance has it."

"Which means he thinks that there may be only one," Wade said.

"But if he knows all of that, then how come he doesn't know that there are four of them?" Jo'sha asked.

"Maybe he's lying."

"Or maybe he doesn't know, just like we didn't know that there were five of them," Jo'sha suggested.

"We think there are five of them. We don't know for sure," Matthew said.

"Yes we do. I am sure of it," said Jo'sha.

The elevator bell rang. The elevator was on the other end of the building, but they didn't want to take a chance on someone coming up the stairwell or through the elevator.

"Who would be coming up here?" Jo'sha asked.

"This *is* the library," said Chance.

"That's my point."

They sat quietly for a few minutes and waited to hear footsteps exit the elevator.

"Do you hear anyone?" asked Wade.

"No, hold on. I'll be right back," Chance said, jumping up from his seat.

"I'll go with you," Jo'sha said, following behind him.

Chance and Jo'sha tipped away from their corner of the library. In less than a minute they came back with Sundiata in tow. Chance had Sundiata's right arm twisted behind his back, and had covered Sundiata's mouth with his large palm. Sundiata was struggling, but his efforts were in vain against Chance's strength.

"Do you have to treat him so rough?" asked Wade.

"I think it's time we got some answers," Chance responded.

"Well he can't talk with your big hand all across his face."

Chance released Sundiata's arm and removed his hand from his mouth, then grabbed him by the back of his neck. "Now why is it that you seem to always be following us?" he asked.

"Uhm," Sundiata grunted.

"I can't hear you," Chance yelled in Sundiata's ear.

Sundiata grabbed at Chance's fingers and tried to loosen his grip, but the more he tried, the tighter Chance gripped his neck.

"He can't talk with you choking him to death!" Wade snapped.

Chance let Sundiata go, and pushed him down on the floor. Sundiata got up slowly rubbing his neck and rolling his eyes at Chance.

"Well?" Jo'sha asked.

"I have a message for you from Dr. Smith. He would like to invite you to his house for dinner tomorrow night," Sundiata said.

"For what?" Matthew asked.

"It is just a simple dinner invitation."

"Since when did professors start inviting students to dinner?" Wade asked.

"He just wants to congratulate you on Omega Tau and your academic achievements," Sundiata explained.

"He's lying," Wade said immediately.

Chance grabbed the nape of Sundiata's neck again. "Now we're going to ask you one more time. What does he really want?" Chance asked.

"Ugh! He has a proposition for you," Sundiata groaned.

"What type of proposition?" asked Matthew.

"It's a proposition about the ankh. He knows that you have it and would like to make you an offer for it," Sundiata spat.

"And if we don't?" asked Matthew.

"Then I guess he could go to the authorities and tell them that you stole it from him," Sundiata said.

"And it would be his word against ours," said Jo'sha.

"Do you want to take that chance or deal with that type of publicity now?"

"He would have to prove that we have it," Matthew dared.

"Oh he knows that you have it. He saw Jo'sha wearing it the day he debated in class, and he saw Wade wearing it the day he fainted. Somehow he knew Chance had it the other day in class. One of you always has it," Sundiata said.

"Well now that we know what he wants, we could destroy it or hide it," Wade said.

"You could do that, but it would be foolish. Dr. Smith is prepared to make you a very handsome offer if you work with him," Sundiata said.

"And if we don't," Matthew posed the question again.

"Then, as I said before, he rakes you over the coals," Sundiata responded.

"Why not just meet us on campus or after class? Why a dinner meeting?" Chance asked.

"Things of this nature are better discussed in private"

"Alright, what time?" Matthew asked.

"Seven," Sundiata answered immediately.

"Where?"

"His house."

"No deal!" Matthew responded.

"His house is fine," Jo'sha interjected. Matthew shot Jo'sha a look. Jo'sha simply nodded.

"Alright then, tell Dr Smith that we'll meet him tomorrow night at his house," Matthew said.

"No shady shit either," Sundiata warned. "Don't tell anyone about the meeting, and come alone—just the four of you. Here's the address," Sundiata said, handing Matthew a small slip of paper.

"Just get out of here," Chance said. Sundiata huffed and walked away.

When they were sure that Sundiata had entered the elevator, Matthew turned to Jo'sha. "Why did you want to meet at his house? You know we're stronger outside. It would help to meet at a neutral location. I was thinking Bonder's Pointe."

"Yeah, I know all of that, but you are forgetting that Wade and I have actually been inside Dr. Smith's house. We know the layout. We know where all of the exits and entrances are, and we know what's in there. He isn't expecting us to know that," Jo'sha said.

"Good point I guess," Matthew said reluctantly.

"So what do we say when he offers us money for the ankhs. We can't very well take them off now can we?" Wade interjected.

"No we can't. But remember, he thinks there's only one. We'll make up some story about how Jo'sha found it at a flea market, and that it isn't what he's been searching for. But we have to talk to him because we need to figure out how much he knows," Matthew reasoned.

"And how he's so sure," Chance echoed.

"Well one thing that he's wrong about is that he thinks that there's only one ankh, and that we have been sharing it," Wade said.

"We just need to be ready," Matthew said.

"Meaning?" asked Chance.

"A full hour's worth of meditation before we meet him tomorrow night. Wade we need to work on that telepathy thing that you know how to do," Matthew said.

"Let me guess. You want to start right now and stay up all night until we get it. Is that right?" Wade asked.

"How did you guess?" Matthew said.

CHAPTER 44

Wade parked on Pomegranate Street behind Dr. Smith's house. It was 6:32 p. m.

"Why didn't you just park in front of his house?" asked Matthew.

"He'll be expecting us to do that," Wade answered.

They parked and tiptoed through the yard toward Dr. Smith's house. There didn't appear to be any lights on in the entire house.

"Let's go around to the back door and see if we can see anything from the kitchen window," Jo'sha whispered.

Just as they tipped past the kitchen door, the light came on and it opened.

"Gentleman," Dr. Smith crooned. "Glad to see that you could make it. Although I find it odd that you chose to come around to the back door."

"Southern custom," Chance offered.

"I guess," Dr. Smith responded, holding the door open for them to enter. He directed them to the living room, where they all took seats. Jo'sha, Wade, and Chance sat on the couch. Dr. Smith sat in a large, wing back king's chair, and Matthew sat directly across from him in the queen's chair.

"Can I get you something to drink?" Dr. Smith asked politely.

"No thank you," they all said in unison.

"What a shame. I have some very fine wines here," he said. Just then Sundiata came in from the dining room holding a glass of white wine. "You gentlemen know Mr. Bazemore don't you?" Dr. Smith said sarcastically. None of them responded.

"What is it that you want exactly?" Matthew asked.

"Mr. Meredith—always to the point."

"And the point of this is what?" Matthew asked again.

358

"Here we are. I'm a historian and I have spent my lifetime searching for historical artifacts. It's been a lifetime that has spanned—let's just say several decades. And many, many years ago I stumbled upon a precious and powerful amulet while looking for slave memorabilia in New Orleans, Louisiana. And at that point I thought I knew all that there was to know about this little artifact," Dr. Smith said. He opened his shirt and revealed an ankh that was similar to the ones that Jo'sha, Wade, and Matthew were wearing, and exactly like the one that Chance wore. It, too, was thin and green. "I would have turned it over to a museum or the authorities, and it would have surely made me famous had I not accidentally placed it around my neck and found its power."

Wade! Matthew thought.

Yes.

Can you hear our thoughts? Matthew projected.

Everyone but Jo'sha.

Dr. Smith looked off into the distance as if he had heard a familiar voice.

Dammit! I think he can hear us too, Wade. Stop!"

Dr. Smith smiled and continued talking. "You see I've been around for quite some time."

"Since before 1895?" questioned Matthew.

"Impressive, Mr. Meredith. I see you've been doing some research," Dr. Smith said with a smile.

"Fuck all this! What do you want?" Jo'sha demanded.

"What a temper! What do I want? What I want is what is rightfully mine—something that I've spent over a century researching. I thought I'd found the key when I found this," Dr. Smith said touching the green ankh on his chest.

"But?" Matthew asked, prompting him to continue.

"But I know now that somehow you four have stumbled upon its complement. I know that you've been sharing it. I can feel it. At first, I didn't understand what the attraction was to you young men, but then it dawned on me. This ankh has a mate—a complement carved from the same angelic stone perhaps. You must be sharing it because I've been drawn to each of you at one time or another. I want it. I want its power," he said breathlessly.

"What power?" Matthew hedged.

"See what happens when boys play with things meant for men? You don't even know what you have. Or you are trying to bluff me?

In either event, this is most certainly the end of the game. Mr. Bazemore, come here," Dr. Smith instructed.

Sundiata swaggered over to Dr. Smith's chair with an arrogant gait. Dr. Smith rose and faced Sundiata. He looked into his eyes and spoke gently. He grabbed his face almost lovingly. "You were so loyal. You reminded me of an old consort, Ptolemy. He too, was a dutiful slave."

"Huh?" Sundiata looked confused. Dr. Smith tightened his grasp on Sundiata's face. Suddenly Sundiata screamed and fell to the floor.

"What did you do to him?" Wade exclaimed.

"The same thing that I've done to many others. He outlived his usefulness. I hired him to keep an eye on the four of you. He did that for me. Now that I have you here I don't need him anymore, but I did need him for nourishment." When they gave him a puzzled look he continued. "You see, this ankh has given me immortality, supernatural strength, and extraordinary hearing gifts just to name a few. But my touch can be lethal and I must feed. I must exercise this power."

"It *is* you. You've been responsible for all of the murders here in Atlanta," Matthew accused.

"I've been doing this for over a hundred years. What's one more black life anyway?"

"So that was you that I saw in those pictures," Matthew concluded.

"Unbelievable, huh?" said Dr. Smith almost boastfully. "Slaves hid the ankhs from slave owners for years. I spent several years hunting for them and the slaves that moved them. I know about your Omega Tau founders. I knew Cyrus Wilkes and his young friends. I killed them looking for the ankhs. They led us to believe that they had hidden them in a church—and for several decades I've enlisted the aid of 'special interest' groups to help search churches."

"So you've been responsible for the church burnings all these years!" Jo'sha exclaimed.

"I guess you could give me credit for that. At any rate, shortly after their deaths, clues lead me to New Orleans where I found this one with an old voodoo priestess. Little did I know that there was not one, but two. So now, as you can see, I need that ankh. Maybe it's the key that will free me from this one. I can't take this off, because if I do, I'll most certainly die. Since the four of you have been able to share one, then perhaps that is the key to my freedom. And if not, it is most certainly the key to more power," Dr. Smith said, moving closer toward Chance.

"The authorities will find you," Wade warned.

"No they won't. The world is huge and I've been hiding for too long. All I want is the ankh."

"How do you know that we won't give it to you and then tell the authorities that you've been killing people?" asked Wade.

"You won't," he said confidently.

"Is that what you think?" Jo'sha asked incredulously. He threw a large fire bolt directly at Dr. Smith. Dr. Smith moved with amazing agility, and the fire caught the curtain on the large window. Dr. Smith charged toward Chance and ripped open his shirt.

"I knew that you had the ankh," he said triumphantly. "I could feel it. But how did you throw the fire?" he asked, giving Jo'sha a puzzled look. Jo'sha opened his shirt revealing the fire red ankh. "There are three!" Dr. Smith began laughing wildly as he began tussling with Chance. The two pummeled each other like titans— exchanging shattering blow after shattering blow.

"Wade, put out the fire. Jo'sha, get Sundiata out of here," Matthew instructed as he rushed to help Chance fight Dr. Smith. The battle was epic and Matthew could do little to get between Chance and Dr. Smith. Their ankhs had them equally matched in strength and stamina.

Wade struggled to put out the fire Jo'sha had started. By now it had traveled all the way up the curtain. Jo'sha dragged Sundiata through the kitchen and out into the backyard, then rushed back into the house.

"Help me contain him," Matthew yelled to Wade and Jo'sha.

Wade left the fire, and both he and Jo'sha rushed to help Matthew corner Dr. Smith. Chance and Dr. Smith had stopped fighting for the moment. They stood there, facing each other, panting and heaving. Jo'sha, Wade and Matthew were directly behind Dr. Smith.

"We've got you surrounded old man," Jo'sha called out. The blaze behind him had assumed a life of its own. They could hear it crackling, and feel its heat rise with Jo'sha's tone.

Dr. Smith turned slowly and laughed uncontrollably, "You see that's the difference between youth and wisdom. Young Mr. Walker was focused on the fight, but for me it was never about the fight or subduing young Mr. Walker. It was about this," Dr. Smith said holding up his hand and revealing Chance's green ankh.

Chance grabbed for the ankh that had been around his neck, but it was gone. He fell to the ground, clutching his chest. "I can't breath," he gasped.

Wade and Matthew rushed to help Chance. Dr. Smith charged over Jo'sha and toward the front door. Jo'sha attempted to grab him, but Dr. Smith was much too strong and nimble. Jo'sha jumped up and ran after him.

Wade sat crying with Chance's head in his lap, "You are going to be alright," he whispered. "You are going to be alright."

The fire continued to rage behind them, and had moved from the curtains to the walls.

Jo'sha came rushing back into the house. "I couldn't catch him. He went off toward Pomegranate and then into the woods. I heard sirens in the distance. Someone probably reported the fire."

Matthew, Wade, and Jo'sha grabbed Chance and ran out the back door toward Pomegranate Street and Wade's truck.

"What do we do? What do we do?" Wade yelled while he fumbled for his keys. Jo'sha and Matthew laid Chance down across the second row seat.

"We have to take him to the hospital," Matthew said.

"And what in the hell do we tell them?" Jo'sha exclaimed.

"We tell them that we were just hanging out and he had an asthma attack," Matthew said, trying to sound calm.

"What about Sundiata?" Wade asked.

"He's dead," Jo'sha answered in a solemn voice. Tears streamed from Wade's eyes. "Move over. I'll drive," Jo'sha said, getting into the driver's seat. Wade slid over into the passenger's seat, and Matthew sat in the back holding Chance.

"Hurry up!" Matthew yelled.

As they pulled off and headed toward the hospital, they heard the sirens and saw the bright flashing lights converging on Dr. Smith's house.

"What are they going to do at the hospital?" Wade asked.

"Keep him alive until we find Dr. Smith. Just get there. Dr. Baptiste will know what to do," Matthew said, trying to convince himself as much as the others.

"How long does he have?" asked Jo'sha.

"God only knows."

"We have to call his family," Wade said. Before Wade could pick up his phone to dial Chance's family, it rang. "Hello," he answered.

After several seconds of what was a one-sided conversation, Wade hung up.

"What is it?" Jo'sha asked.

"My dad says I should come home immediately. Quay just went into premature labor!"

ABOUT THE AUTHOR

D. Lee Hatchett is among countless African-Americans who were initiated into one of the nine Black Greek Letter Organizations in the 1980's through a public pledge process called being "on line" or "crossing the burning sands". Inspired by a fascination for the history and evolution of black fraternities and sororities, Lee has served as a college fraternity advisor, lectured on Black Greek Letter Organizations, and written for Black College Today magazine. In addition to his passion for the study of African American service and social organizations, Lee also holds a fascination for science fiction and has been published and applauded for his writing on the Science Fiction & Fantasy web site.

Lee's interest in fraternities & sororities and science fiction collide in an extraordinary work of fiction entitled, The Black Angel Trilogy. Beyond being exceptional reading, the complete trilogy includes interesting and informative historical, cultural, and spiritual references and back stories. With a BS in Engineering and MBA, Lee remains devoted to exploring his world, having lived and worked in Italy, Spain, China, Japan, Germany and several cities in the United States. He now resides in Atlanta, Georgia with his wife, Lillie; twins, Olivia and Zachary; and youngest daughter, Channing.

Printed in the United States
36926LVS00004B/52-69